REVIEWS FOR AL

Harry and the
A gloriously outrageous adv

I wish I'd written Harry and the Wrinklies. It's such a happy book: Anne Fine

A glorious romp of a book... fast and furious fun... Temperley is a talent to watch: *The Independent*

Murdo's War
The narrative is so vigorous, the action so breathless, the atmosphere so powerful... vivid authenticity of the background: Geoffrey Trease, *Times Educational Supplement*

Best novel I've read in weeks... straightforward curl-up-in-front-of-the-fire thriller: *Sunday Post*

Huntress of the Sea
The sea has always been a metaphor for the erotic, but here the imagery is sustained and developed with unforgettable beauty and horror... a powerful and original novel: *New Statesman*

A taut, beautifully-written story: *Mail on Sunday*

The Magician of Samarkand
A true page-turner... packed with beautifully-narrated action... Temperley is a wonderful story-teller: *Guardian*

I defy anyone... not to be caught up in the magic of this robust, thrilling adventure: *Scotsman*

Scar Hill
But this is more than an adventure. More than anything it is a love story – the unconditional love that binds Peter to his dad, his dog, his sister's child and the magnificent landscape of the far north-west of Scotland: *Herald*

Temperley is a consummate storyteller... real edge-of-the-seat stuff: *Daily Telegraph*

ABOUT THE AUTHOR

Alan Temperley was born in Sunderland in the north-east of England and educated at the Bede Grammar School. Aged sixteen he went to sea, served an apprenticeship with Shaw Savill and qualified as deck officer. Wishing to study English, he came ashore and spent two years in the RAF as one of the last national servicemen, then read English at Manchester and Edinburgh Universities.

Thereafter he became a teacher of English, most notably at Bettyhill in the northern Highlands of Scotland. While there he began to write and his life since, with a brief return to sea, has been a combination of teaching and writing. His books have won awards, appear in eighteen languages, and two have been successfully televised. *The Magician of Samarkand* (BBC) won first prize for a children's programme at the World Television Awards. Currently his story *Harry and the Wrinklies* is under development as a feature film.

Alan lives in Galloway, south-west Scotland. He has one son and two granddaughters.

BY THE SAME AUTHOR

Tales of the North Coast
Tales of Galloway
Murdo's War
Harry and the Wrinklies
Ragboy, Rats and the Surging Sea
The Simple Giant
The Brave Whale
Huntress of the Sea
The Magician of Samarkand
Harry and the Treasure of Eddie Carver
Scar Hill
Deck Boy

MARY PEARSON

ALAN TEMPERLEY

Copyright © 2024 Alan Temperley

The moral right of the author has been asserted.

Apart from any fair dealing for the purposes of research or private study, or criticism or review, as permitted under the Copyright, Designs and Patents Act 1988, this publication may only be reproduced, stored or transmitted, in any form or by any means, with the prior permission in writing of the publishers, or in the case of reprographic reproduction in accordance with the terms of licences issued by the Copyright Licensing Agency. Enquiries concerning reproduction outside those terms should be sent to the publishers.

This is a work of fiction. Names, characters, businesses, places, events and incidents are either the products of the author's imagination or used in a fictitious manner. Any resemblance to actual persons, living or dead, or actual events is purely coincidental.

Troubador Publishing Ltd
Unit E2 Airfield Business Park,
Harrison Road, Market Harborough,
Leicestershire LE16 7UL
Tel: 0116 279 2299
Email: books@troubador.co.uk
Web: www.troubador.co.uk

ISBN 978 1805145 448

British Library Cataloguing in Publication Data.
A catalogue record for this book is available from the British Library.

Printed and bound in Great Britain by 4edge Limited
Typeset in 12pt Adobe Jenson Pro by Troubador Publishing Ltd, Leicester, UK

For my brother Howard

Contents

PART 1
1 The Accident   3
2 Girl in the Kitchen   8
3 Wherry Row   14
4 Deck Chairs   20
5 North Sea Trader   29
6 Uncle Dan   35
7 The Man in the Barn   40
8 Vienna   49
9 Sailors   60
10 Party Time   68
11 Remembering Dad   73
12 Into the Fjords   81
13 The Missing Money   91
14 Day at the Beach   97
15 The Soldier's Return   105
16 Uncle Jack   114
17 Flight   122
18 The Road to Wherry Row   130

PART 2
19 An English Jew   139
20 A Wild Streak   147
21 I Like a Windy Day   153
22 Chocolates for Gran   159
23 Gold Watches   166
24 Home with Dad   174
25 A Letter from *The Chronicle*   182

26	Grapes and a Pistol	188
27	Ice Cream, Bread and Trains	194
28	Shaking Hands with the Headmistress	202
29	St Jerome's	207
30	The Unwelcome Boy	213
31	Julius Caesar	221
32	Women Friends	232
33	A Long Bike Ride	239
34	What About My Dad?	246
35	The Man on the Shore	252

PART 3

36	Return to Saltfield Mains	259
37	Human Cargo	264
38	We've Got to Get Out of Here	270
39	The Men in the Farmhouse	275
40	The Pillbox	283
41	Benny	290
42	Death of a Nazi	296
43	Major O'Hare	302
44	On the Run	310
45	Four on a Fishing Boat	318
46	North Quay	326
47	Ebb Tide	335
48	The Hero	340

EPILOGUE

49	Royal Infirmary	349
50	We Talk to the Police	355
51	Uncle Dan	364

1953	374
Acknowledgements	380

Part I

I

The Accident

It was all the fault of that bloody pram. Although I suppose I should blame myself really. I mean that's the reason Mrs Surtees was getting rid of it. "It's dangerous," she told gran. "That bit of metal sticking out the front, I've nearly cut myself a couple of times. I don't suppose our Ingrid will be having any more, and she says if she does she's going to get a new one. But it'll do for the coal, easier than slinging a sack over the crossbar. Mind, Mary," she told me, "if you do use it, you'll have to cover that sharp bit with a cloth or something."

So I did, I wrapped it in an old copy of the Eastport Chronicle and tied it on with string. It was a bit of the frame that had snapped and stuck out through the cloth, but the pram was strong enough and like she said, easier to push than dad's old bike. So easy, in fact, I thought I'd try the pit heaps up past Strawberry Hill. Mrs Surtees' son-in-law told me there were good pickings if you could be bothered to go all that way.

So that afternoon that's where I had been. Back in those days after the war – it was May, 1948 – folk were poor and you often saw people like me, men more than women, black with the dirt, pushing a sack home. Gran didn't like it, "Don't worry about me," she had said often enough, "I'd rather see you sticking in with your school work." Which was OK in the summer, but when it got to autumn she felt the cold and it gave us a few extra fires.

I'd done quite well, half-filled a couple of sacks and carried them down to the track where I'd parked the pram. It wasn't dangerous up there on the pit heap, though people said the smoke came from fires below the surface and men had dropped through and been burned to death. I don't like to think about it. I suppose it might be true but I'd never seen a report in the paper. It was mucky, though, the black seemed to get everywhere, not just my hands and arms but up my legs and dress and onto my face where I'd pushed my hair back.

Anyway, although I could have filled half a dozen sacks I couldn't carry any more, the pram was too heavy. So I got it to the road and somehow, sweating like a pig, pushed it to the top where the lovers' lane branches off up Strawberry Hill. In front of me the road turned downhill again, best part of a mile to some shops and after that it was mostly flat. I wasn't planning to go through the town centre but round the back of the park and down South Street to the dock area which was where gran and I lived.

After all the effort I thought I deserved a break so I sat down on the verge. Gran had made a thermos of tea and I'd brought a book from the school library, Wuthering Heights. Mrs Wardman, who takes us for English, said she thought I'd like it and it's great! After I'd scrubbed my hands on the grass and a raggy tea-towel I always carry, they weren't too bad. So with the tea and a scone, the sunshine, the hawthorn in blossom, a view across the town and a good story, I was well set.

So far the pram had worked perfectly but as I set off again, down the road towards the first houses, it began misbehaving. It was steep, steeper than the road up, and at first I hardly noticed, my head was so full of the story, Heathcliff raging at Cathy and storming off into the night. Then I became aware that the wheels kept turning off the road into the left verge and I had to yank the pram back. It was the weight, I suppose, it was made to carry a baby, not a hundredweight of coal. It got worse, a few steps then tug, and with the weight and the steepness it began to run away with me. I tried to stop it, dug in my heels and gave an almighty heave. The pram couldn't take it. The handle broke loose at one side and with me hanging on for dear life it careered over the grassy bank and down into a ditch half hidden by hawthorns.

It was a spectacular smash but the ditch was dry and I wasn't hurt, just a bit shaken, or so I thought. For a minute I lay there, all tangled up, then pushed the pram from on top of me. That was when I became aware of a stinging pain below my right knee and when I looked down I saw blood, quite a lot of blood. Oh, my God! Clumsily I crawled out and stood in the road. My dress had hitched up round my waist. I pushed it down and examined my leg. It was a nasty cut, blood ran from a flap of skin and made a track through the coal dirt right down to my sock. I knew how it had happened; back at the pit heap the paper had dropped off that bit of metal and I hadn't bothered to put it back. Mrs Surtees had been right, bloody thing! Two miles from home, what was I to do? I had a hanky, though it was pretty filthy by this time. Anyway, I cleaned round the cut with spit and wiped off the blood as best I could, then pressed on top to try and stop the bleeding. It made me feel a bit sick.

There wasn't anyone around nor likely to be; there weren't many cars up that way and it was the middle of the afternoon so people would be at their work. Then I saw this kid outside the top house. I'd spotted him when I was having my tea, trying out his roller skates. Now he was hanging onto a gate post and looking up the road towards me.

I sat down on the grass and examined the cut more closely. Less blood was oozing out, thicker. What could I cover it with? There was nothing. Then I thought of the bag I'd brought the scone in; if I folded it, maybe I could tie it round with the hanky. I rescued the bag from the pram, that shiny brown paper, but the hanky wasn't long enough so I tore it into strips, and I was just in the middle of this when a shadow fell across and this kid stopped right beside me. How I hadn't heard him I don't know because his skates were making a hell of a clatter. I gave a little start and the bag fell on the ground, bloody side down. We looked at each other.

"I cut my leg," I told him, as if he couldn't see for himself.

He nodded and after a bit he said, "Is it sore?"

"Not too bad."

"Are you OK? I mean, do you want a hand?"

Up close I was surprised to see he might be about the same age as me, which was fifteen and a few days. A nice kid with sandy hair wearing a shirt and old school shorts, socks pushed down round his ankles.

I folded the bag the other way and brushed off some bits of grass. "You shouldn't use that," he said. "You've got to keep it clean.".

"That right?"

"It might get infected. Get germs in."

"Golly, I never thought of that," I said. "You a doctor then?"

He blushed. "No, but my dad's a dentist."

"It's my leg not my teeth."

"He has to keep his surgery spotless. And he was in the War, the RAMC in France. Men got infected had to have their legs off."

"Bundle of fun you are. Reckon they might chop my leg off then?"

"No, but you should keep it clean."

"And how do you suggest I do that up here?"

"If you come down the house my mum will put some antiseptic on." You could see he didn't want to say it, him tidy and well-spoken, me this great big dirty girl from the bottom end of town. But it was nice of him.

"Thanks, no, I'll be fine. Gran will patch me up when I get home."

"You should, it's quite deep, it needs a bandage." I was surprised, the way he stood there.

The bag slipped again and a fresh wave of blood spilled out. To be honest, I did feel a bit queer. "I'm so dirty." He looked me over as if I might smell as well. A lot of girls who looked like me did. Boys too.

It crossed my mind that he might be Jewish, nothing I could put my finger on just something about him.

"Come if you want to."

"Sure your mum won't mind?"

"We can put a newspaper down."

That was honest anyway.

"It's up to you."

"OK, then, thanks" I got to my feet. There was nothing I could do about the pram and the blood kept oozing. I had the thermos, my library book and a few things in a bag and collected it from the ditch.

"What's your name, anyway?" I said.

"Teddy." He did a turn on his skates. "Teddy Cohen."

"Mary," I introduced myself. "Mary Pearson."

2

Girl in the Kitchen

This huge girl sat at the table, filthy dirty. She didn't seem to belong in mum's nice clean kitchen. We became good friends later, but that first time it was like having a badger or a bear in the house. When I say she was huge I don't mean fat, just big and strong, twice my size, thick arms and legs, round peasant face and straggly brown hair. It was a while before I spotted those clear, clever eyes.

The air smelled of Dettol. A basin steamed gently and a saucer was filled with bloody wads of cotton wool. "I don't know," mum said. "It's clean, anyway. I'll put on a light dressing but I think it might need a couple of stitches."

"Thanks very much, Mrs Cohen," Mary said for the tenth time. "When I get home gran can decide what to do."

Mum ignored her. "My husband will be back in a few minutes, let him have a look at it." The cut was just below her right knee on the outside. Watery blood ran down as mum cut a square of lint. "Cover it up for the time being." She wiped the blood away and bound it with a bandage. "Come on, Teddy, the kettle's boiled, where's that tea? There's a cake in the blue tin."

She tipped the Dettol down the sink and tidied up. "Do you come up this way often? I know some of the regulars but I haven't seen you before."

"No, it's the first time. Usually I go down the shore for the sea coal – you know, past the South Pier. But I'd just been given the pram and a neighbour – well, her son-in-law – said there were good pickings up this way. It's a lot further but I thought I'd give it a go. He's right, there's enough to keep your fire burning for a year."

I knew what she was talking about because I'd been once myself, scrambling up the pit heap and dragging a sack home on the bogey to give mum and dad a surprise. They'd been grateful but I wasn't allowed to go again. "It's very enterprising of you, Teddy, but it's dangerous and people like us don't do it, we can afford to buy coal. it's the folk who are hard up, poor souls. Put your clothes in the basket and away upstairs for a bath, I think there's enough hot water. And I don't want all my towels black." Mum shook her head and kissed me on the hair. "What a boy!"

Mary sat with her foot on a chair. When mum had finished she stood up and pulled her possessions together. "Thanks very much, Mrs Cohen. There's no need to trouble your husband, I'll be all right now, I'll catch a bus."

Mum looked at her. "Well, if that's what you want, dear, but I think you should wait. It's a long walk to the bus stop, right down the bottom. David will be back in a few minutes. If it needs a stitch he'll take you to the doctor's and give you a run home."

You could see she wanted to go but with me setting her cup on the table she sat down again.

"Rotten luck with the pram," mum said. "All that hard work and there's your coal just lying in the ditch. Maybe Teddy and his dad can go up and collect it for you later."

"No! No!" She was alarmed. "Just leave it, I can go out again. There's plenty more."

"Well, we'll see."

"Unless you'd like it yourselves. And I'll have to get rid of the pram."

"Just forget it, dear, it's doing no harm where it is. Teddy can bring it down to the house, or if you like we can take it to the dump. You drink your tea, you've had a nasty shock."

Mary pulled the cup towards her and tried to straighten her hair. "I feel such a mess."

"Don't think about it, love, it's a dirty job. You look fine. You can have a bath when you get home."

Mum sat opposite. She was Austrian and although she'd lived in England since before I was born she still had an accent. People thought she was German and although she had worked for the Red Cross right through the war, going into bombed houses and collecting for soldiers and prisoners, they still gave her a hard time.

"Where is it you live anyway?"

"Wherry Row," Mary said. "You'll not know it, down the bottom of High Street."

"By the docks?"

"Not that far, just past the Waterman's Arms. Why, do you know that part?"

"Not well. There's a seamen's refuge I go to sometimes. Help sailors who haven't got much English."

"That's just up the road from us. Men from all over end up there."

"Poor souls, they've had a bad time some of them. Up in the arctic convoys, ships gone down, lost their families."

There was a silence then mum said, "And is Wherry Row convenient for your school? I don't know the schools down that way."

"Not really, well it was. I went to the Johnston School in primary, now I have to walk up into town and catch the bus."

"What school's that then?"

What Mary said next gave me such a shock I spilled tea down my chest.

"I go to St Peter's," she said.

St Peter's was the grammar school, the top school for miles around, over by Elm Park. There was terrific competition to get in. Dad had got me special tuition although he wasn't supposed to and I had scraped through somehow. We had to be smart, grey trousers, blue shirt, school tie and a black blazer with a silver phoenix on the pocket: *Post Tenebras Lux*, light after darkness. I was proud for people to know I went there. Now here was this big dirty girl from down by the docks who went there as well.

"Do you, love? Good for you." If mum was surprised she hid it well. "Our Teddy goes to St Peter's, maybe you're in the same year. What class are you in?"

"Lower five one."

Lower five one! That was the top class, the really clever ones.

I'd better explain that St Peter's was split in two, the boys' school and the girls' school, identical buildings surrounded by our own lawns and playing fields. We never met the girls. Because the school was almost on the edge of town most pupils came by bus, so we had different times of starting.

"Yeah?" Mary looked up. "What class you in then?"

"Lower five two."

"Great school isn't it?" she said.

I never thought about it that way. It's what everybody said but now I was there it was just the school I attended. I realised we were lucky because we had laboratories, gyms and for the boys two football pitches and a rugby pitch. Sometimes we saw kids from the other schools trooping down the pavements to play rounders or football on the muddy town pitches with water lying in the goal mouth. Mum and dad were always getting on at me because I was lazy; all these opportunities and I did as little as I could get away with.

Mary's bag lay on the floor. Her library book had slid out. "What's that you're reading?" mum said.

"Wuthering Heights. Do you know it?"

"Years ago," mum said.

"It's great isn't it? Cathy and Heathcliff. The film was on at the Royal a few weeks back but I didn't go, I wanted to read the book first."

"Laurence Olivier," mum said. "It was very good;."

I wasn't out of my depth because of course I'd heard about Wuthering Heights and we listened to grown-up plays on the wireless but I was still reading Biggles and Swallows and Amazons.

Luckily there was the sound of the car and a key in the front door before this was revealed. Dad called from the hall.

"In the kitchen," mum shouted back. "Come through, you're needed."

"I can smell Dettol. Somebody hurt?"

Dad played rugby with a man who owned a fishmonger's and came in carrying a parcel wrapped in newspaper. I take after him more than my mum's side of the family. She has dark hair, dark eyes and a slightly olive skin. Dad has stiff sandy hair, blue eyes and fair skin. You would never know he was Jewish, which might be good for his dental practice although anyone reading his name, *David Cohen, BDS, London*, on the brass plaque outside his surgery must have a good idea. I have sandy hair too but enough of my mum in me for kids to see it in the street and shout out sometimes, "Hey, Jew boy! Dirty Jew!" A couple of times it got me into fights.

"Hello," dad said to Mary.

She scrambled to her feet.

"No, sit down, love," mum said. "Sit down."

Dad put the fish by the sink. "Ooh, cod, lovely!" mum said. "This is Mary, she had an accident up the road. Been picking coal and the pram ran away with her."

"Poor you," Dad looked down at the bandage. "Sore is it?"

"Not really. A bit."

"I'm not sure if it needs a stitch," mum said. "I told her you'd have a look and maybe take her down to Angus."
Dad smiled. "Mind if I have a look?"
Mary nodded. "I just don't want to be a nuisance. Like I told your wife, gran will see to it when I get home."
"Sure, fine. But a look can't hurt can it?" He went to the sink and scrubbed his hands. "Put your foot up on this chair." With careful dentist's fingers he unwound the bandage."

3

Wherry Row

The next day I went to Mass with gran, me with a big sticking plaster on my leg. Afterwards we called on Mrs Surtees to tell her about the pram and stayed for a cup of tea, so it was gone twelve when we got home.

Wherry Row, where we lived, was a cobbled street close to the river, built a century ago for sailors or dock workers and their families. The terraced cottages, fourteen each side, were separated from the pavement by narrow plots and low brick walls with a sandstone coping. There used to be iron railings but they were cut down to make tanks for the war. We lived in number seventeen. The door and windows were freshly painted, gran liked green, and although some of the houses were shabby, she had planted the front of ours with pretty shrubs and a border of daffodils or wallflowers, whatever was in season.

That Sunday we were surprised to see two sacks standing in the path. An envelope was addressed to me:

Dear Mary,

I hope the leg is not too sore. Teddy has gathered up your coal – Rachel wants me to say that she and Dad helped. If you are not there they will leave it by the door. You said you didn't want the pram and I can see it has about had it, so they will take it to the dump on the way.

With every good wish to you and your grandmother,
Anna Cohen

"Well," gran said when I showed it to her, "what very kind people! Come on, take off your good things and I'll get the dinner on then we can carry it through to the back."

The house smelled of cooking. If we had enough coupons, Gran always roasted a small joint of beef or lamb on a Sunday and the potatoes and veg were sitting in pans of cold water. My dress from the day before had been thrown into the dirty clothes basket in the shed where gran did the washing. I rescued it for lugging the coal bags down the yard and went through to the kitchen.

"Give me a minute, Mary, I'll lend you a hand."

"It's all right, I can manage."

"Are you sure? They look heavy. You don't want that cut to open up again."

There wasn't a better, kinder woman in Eastport, in the whole country, than my gran. If she had not been there I don't know what would have become of me. She was a little woman, frail as a bird with thin wrists and white hair but energetic and very determined. Seeing the two of us together, little gran and great big me, you would never have guessed I was her granddaughter.

"I carried them down the pit heap," I said. "I'm sure I can carry them through the house."

"If you say so, love, but I'll be cross if it starts bleeding. And I don't want a mess with the coal."

"I'll be careful. Just keep out the way."

I heaved the sacks through the house and emptied them into the coal shed at the bottom of the yard. The dust flew up so I needed a wash then changed into clean clothes and flopped into my chair by the fire and picked up Wuthering Heights. There was just the one living room with a table at the back window where we ate.

"Really, what very kind people," gran called again through the kitchen door. "And folk go on about the Jews."

My leg had needed stitches. Mr Cohen wanted to consult gran but she had said she was going shopping, so he took me to see Dr McGregor who lived three doors down. Teddy came with us. I was worried how much it would cost because there was no National Health Service in those days, but the Cohens were friends and in the circumstances Dr McGregor said there would be no charge. So he gave me a little jab to take away the pain, put in three stitches and covered it with a neat plaster. Later, after another cup of tea and slice of seed cake, Mr Cohen and Teddy drove me home.

"First the doctor," gran said, "and now they've picked up all your coal. You'll have to go up and thank them." She set two glasses of squash on the table. "I'll give you some money and you can take a bunch of flowers."

"It's Sunday," I said.

"Jackson's will be open."

"There's cherry blossom and you've got tulips. I'll pick my own."

Gran thought about it. "Yes, that will be even nicer." Her eyes fell on my reading. "Wuthering Heights, how your mum loved that book. I remember her sitting right where you are, different chair of course, hair all over her face. Lost in the story, never heard a word when I spoke to her."

I liked to hear things about my mum. She was dead, killed at the beginning of the war when that munitions factory just down the coast blew up. She'd been clever, gone to St Peter's like me, but when she was eighteen she'd got in the family way to my dad. God knows why, he was a waster, good-looking but that's the best you can say about him. Gran never said a bad word but I knew. He worked on the dry dock until he got the sack for thieving, not little stuff, quite big time with a couple of other fellows. Then they started burgling. I was only little but I remember mum going to visit him in jail. He was released early when the war broke out because he was fit and strong and they needed men like him in the army. Army life suited him – action, discipline, companionship – and he got made up to corporal, though he was dead now too, killed by a shell in France some time after D-Day. Gran got a telegram.

Mum was different, good at science and languages, just won a place at Durham University, then I came along and put an end to all her plans. She was only twenty-four when the factory blew up. I was quite little but I can still remember this person who gave me cuddles and smelled of flowers and took me paddling on the beach. There's a picture of her in a silver frame on top of my chest of drawers. I like to think she's watching over me when I'm in bed.

After dinner, while gran shut her eyes for a snooze, I did the washing-up and picked a bunch of tulips from the garden then walked up into town to catch a bus. I had seen a cherry tree covered with blossom in the garden of a bombed-out house, so when the bus dropped me off I climbed in and snipped off a few branches. Wrapped up with the tulips in paper left over from Christmas they made a nice bouquet.

But the Cohens were out, the car gone from the little parking place. I had guessed they might be on such a sunny afternoon and had written a note:

Dear Mr and Mrs Cohen,
  Thank you so much for all your kindness, the way you helped me, and got the stitches, and drove me home. Now you have brought the coal down.
  Dr McGregor was very kind as well and did not want paying. I have found his address in a telephone directory

and I am going to write to say thank you.
Gran also sends her thanks.
Yours sincerely,
Mary Pearson

I left the flowers on the front step with the note tucked in the wrapping paper. You would never notice the place where I had gone into the ditch. Some little bits of coal lay on the bank and the weeds were broken, but apart from that there was no sign. After the crash I had not looked through the hedge but now I saw there was a field of young corn. A straggle of tumbledown barns stood on the crest. This side of the field a drift of bluebells grew in the grass. I walked up the road and climbed a five-bar gate. When I had added bluebells to the tulips and cherry blossom they made a beautiful bouquet and I wished Mrs Cohen had been there so I could hand it to her – or take it home to gran.

*

Gran didn't have much money, just her pension and a few pounds for me, but what was more important to her was that I should do well at school. Mum never got to university but she was keen that I should. Luckily I enjoyed lessons and usually came near the top of my class so she was pleased, but I wanted to help and had taken a couple of little jobs. One of these was looking after deck chairs on the promenade.

Eastport had a terrific golden beach with stretches of shore rocks where children hunted for crabs. It lay north of the river while Wherry Row lay to the south, below the town, so I had to cross by a little rowing ferry. The promenade ran the full length of the beach, from the great North Pier, which protected the river mouth and docks, to far-off dunes dotted with concrete pillboxes. Throughout the war the sand had been mined in case of invasion and protected by tremendous coils of barbed wire. Now these had been removed and people who for six years could only stand and stare, flocked to the seaside to paddle and sunbathe.

There was a charge for the deckchairs but borrowers got half back when they returned them. I had to watch out for boys who stole the chairs while people were in the water and brought them to me demanding money, saying their dads were waiting at the bus stop. You got to know the troublemakers. One boy tried to drag the money satchel from round my neck and it ended in a fight.

Anyway, one Saturday afternoon, two or possibly three weeks after the accident with the pram, I was reading in the shade of an umbrella when amid the chatter of the passers-by I heard someone say my name:

"Look, there's Mary."

4

Deck Chairs

Rachel and I had been swimming. Although it was a hot afternoon the water was freezing. Mum carried the beach bag with the cricket bat and thermos and all the other stuff we took with us. We carried our own sandy towels with our costumes rolled up inside. "Do you think I'm a camel or something?" mum always said. "If you want to go in the water you can carry your own towels." The car was parked on the top road, above the cliffs, but first we were going to Rinaldi's for ice-cream.

It was mum who spotted Mary. She sat in a canvas chair beside a little table with a tattered but cheerful umbrella keeping off the sun and she was reading. Dozens of striped deck chairs, all stencilled EDC, were propped against the back wall. A leather money satchel was hung round her neck.

"Look," mum said. "There's Mary."

I don't know how she heard her name above the chatter and sound of the sea and music from the distant fairground, but at once she looked up, shading her eyes against the glare.

"Oh, hello."

"Mary, how lovely to see you. Is this a Saturday job?"

She jumped to her feet and seemed embarrassed. "When they're playing at home. Gerry, I should say Mr Marshall, he's a keen supporter. He'll come down after he's been to the pub."

"What time's that?"

"About half five."

"Does he leave you in charge? What if there's trouble?"

"There isn't, and there's always people about. It's all right." Mum wasn't convinced. "Anyway," she turned her head to read the title of the book, "I've been wanting to see you. Those beautiful flowers, thank you so much. I put them in the hall and they lasted so well. The scent of the bluebells drifted right up the stairs."

My hair was wet and a drip ran past my ear. I dabbed it off and looked down at Mary's leg. The plaster had gone and the stitches had been removed but there was a dark scab and the skin had a puffy look.

"Has it been sore?" Mum said.

"Not really, not at all." Mary pulled her dress to hide it. "I had to keep it dry for a few days, couldn't go in the showers at school. The doctor says in a couple of months there'll hardly be a mark."

A family brought some chairs back and she returned their deposit.

Rachel introduced herself. She's three years younger than me and while I take after dad with my sandy hair, she takes after mum, dark-haired and dark-eyed, slim and very pretty. Also like mum, she's a chatter-box. "I'm Rachel," she said.

"I thought you must be." Mary held out her hand. "I'm Mary. Hello."

"We're going for ice-cream."

"Lucky you."

"I know about your bad leg and everything. Do you want to come?"

"I can't, I've got to look after the deck chairs."

Rachel thought. "If you like I can bring one over."

Mum said, "Maybe Mary will let us sit down here and we can all have our ice-cream on the promenade."

"Of course," she said.

"Yeah!" I said.

"You go and get them, Teddy." Mum hunted for her purse beneath all the junk in the beach bag.

"No," Mary said. "Let me pay,"

"Not at all," mum said, still rummaging.

"Please," Mary insisted. "You've done so much! Let me get them."

Mum looked her in the face. "Yes, all right, love, if you want to. But there's no need."

"Yes there is." Mary took her wages and handed the satchel to mum. "Could you look after the chairs? When people bring them back you give them—" she told her how much, "but if it's boys wait for me. They'll rob the coat off your back some of them."

Rachel and I went with her and we ran to Rinaldi's on the front. There was a queue but it didn't take long and when we got back mum had pulled out the little table and arranged four canvas chairs around it.

"Seven came back," she said so I did what you told me. She had taken a chair shaded by the umbrella. "I hope you don't mind, dear, but a blink of sun and I turn as brown as an Indian." We knew this at home where a stand was piled with broad-brimmed sun hats.

We sat talking, watching the crowd and catching the melting ice-cream with our tongues.

A ship was idling beyond the breakwater, waiting for tugs. I dug in the beach bag and found the binoculars. There's always something to look at down there, birds or distant ships or people swimming and sunbathing. Now I brought the ship into focus, trying to read the name painted on the bows. She was a tramp ship, well-maintained, black with a tan funnel and white superstructure. "North...North Sea...something."

"North Sea Trader?" Mary said.

I was astonished. "Can you read that from here?"

"Well yes, can't you, even with the binoculars?"

"But it's miles away!"

She laughed. "No, of course I can't, I just know it. My Uncle Dan's the captain."

"Your uncle?"

"My dad's brother. Trades between here and Holland. Well not just Eastport, up and down the coast – you know, Newcastle, Hull, the North Sea ports. He took me with him last year."

"To Holland?"

"In the summer holidays. Rotterdam, then up to Copenhagen."

"I'd love to do that. Was it good?"

"Yeah, great."

"One day," mum said. "Anyway, we're going to Austria this year."

"Austria," Mary said. "Oh, I'd love to see the mountains. Go to Vienna."

"That's where we're going," Rachel said. "To see mum's old house."

"That's right," mum said.

"Is that where you grew up," Mary said, "in Vienna? How marvellous! Have you got family there, your mum and dad? Brothers and sisters?"

I froze.

"I'm afraid not," mum said.

Mary suddenly realised what she had said and went white as a sheet.

"That's all right, love." Mum took her hand. "You weren't to know."

"But I do know," Mary said. "Of course I know. I just wasn't thinking. Oh, I'm so sorry!"

Overcome, she ran to the rails above the beach. I went to

follow but mum said, "No, Teddy, leave her. You too, Rachel." She gave Mary half a minute then crossed to her side. Briefly she spoke and put an arm around Mary's shoulders. When they came back, Mary's eyes were full of tears.

"Oh, I'm so sorry," she said again, to me and Rachel this time.

"Let's not spoil this beautiful afternoon," mum said. "Just tell you a little bit so you're not left wondering."

"No." Mary shook her head.

"Yes," mum said. "What Rachel said is quite right, we lived in Vienna. Daddy owned a small furniture factory, Olswangs, it was quite well known, quality stuff you know. I had two sisters, Esther and Miriam, and a much younger brother called Jakob."

In the weeks that followed Mary heard the whole terrible story but this, as far as I remember, is what we told her that Saturday afternoon, sitting on the promenade with our ice-creams.

"After school," mum said, "I studied piano at the conservatoire and got a job as a repetiteur in the Opera House – that's playing for rehearsals. When the Opera came to London for a season, that was in the early thirties, I came with it and met Teddy's father who was still at dental school at that time."

My daddy too," Rachel said.

"Of course, darling." Mum stroked her wet hair.

"After he qualified we got married and I moved here to England. This was when the Nazis were gaining power in Germany and a lot of Austrians supported them. Daddy knew he should get out but the factory was all he had to provide for his family. He tried to sell it, made himself ill, but no one was interested, not the way things were going with Hitler just across the border. Hitler hated the Jews, blamed us for everything. Then in March, 1938, only ten years ago but ten lifetimes for the Jewish people, there was the Anschluss when German troops just marched into Austria and took over, hardly a shot fired. At that time a lot of Austrians welcomed them. Then Kristallnacht a few months later—"

"That's when they set fire all the synagogues," Rachel said.

"And smashed up Jewish shops and broke all the windows," I said.

"Our factory among them," mum said.

"And papa and grandma and everyone had to wear yellow stars," Rachel said.

"I've read about it," Mary said. "Mrs Goldman told us in history."

"The beginning of the end," mum said. "Then it was too late, they couldn't get out."

"Everyone got taken away in trains," Rachel said.

Mum looked down and turned her wedding ring, she always died that when she was upset. "They were sent to different camps. My family went to Mauthausen, a labour camp, and we're not too sure after that. From what we can make out daddy died in the quarries and the others were sent to…" She looked away.

"It was a death camp too," I said.

"Oh, how terrible!" Mary wiped her eyes with a crumpled hankie. "I've never met anyone who – oh, I'm so—"

Mum took a deep breath. "We're not the only ones, there's families like us all over Europe. Well, you lost your mum and dad, didn't you?" She managed a smile. "So now you know so you won't have to spend your days wondering."

"The factory got bombed," Rachel said.

"Eventually, yes."

"They're building shops," I said, "but it's still our ground. And there's a family living in the house. The Nazis took it but it belongs to mum."

"Papa left it to her." Rachel took her hand.

"So that's why we're going over," mum said, "to try and sort it out. A few days in Vienna then a week walking in the mountains. But now," she found the beach bag under the table and hooked it towards her with a foot, "we must be going. A sunny afternoon at the beach is not the time to be thinking about all that unhappiness, the war's over. Are you ready, you two?"

A tug was busy around the bow of North Sea Trader, another steamed towards her from the river.

"Can I stay for a while?" I said.

"If you want to. Sure you don't want to come in the car?"

"I'll get the bus."

"Done your homework?"

"Everything for Monday."

"Really?"

"Almost."

She gave me that look. "All right, but don't be late or I'll be cross. Have you got money?"

I felt in my pocket. "Two and threepence."

She found her purse and gave me half a crown. "Mind, I want it back if you don't spend it, it's not for the dodgems. Here, give me your towel."

"Can I stay as well?" Rachel said.

"No," mum said shortly. "And if there's any problem, Teddy, phone and dad will come and pick you up."

People returned deck chairs. The last was a rough-looking man who hadn't shaved for several days and looked as if he had downed a few beers. As Mary handed him his deposit I thought how alone she was down there and how brave. She had no mum to take her to the beach and buy her ice cream, no phone, no car, no dad to pick her up if things went wrong, no one but David Copperfield for company. I would have been a bit scared of the man with his tousled hair and crumpled trousers but Mary looked him in the face and he

gave her a nice smile:
"Thanks, pet. All right?"
"Yes, thanks."
"Any idea of the score?"
"Sorry."
"Ah well, nice afternoon for it anyway. Ta-ra." He wandered off.

Mary propped the chairs against the back wall and tied a rope across.

"Well, we'd best be off," mum said. "It's nice to see you again, love. If you're up our way any time look in, you'll be very welcome. And remember what I said, Teddy, don't be late."

They walked off and were lost among the holidaymakers then I saw them climbing the Goat Steps, the long flight that led to the cliff top.

A woman returned two chairs. I gave her the deposit and stacked them with the others. Mary, at the time, was confronting a couple of boys older than she was: "Don't give me that! You were here last week, a couple of chancers. You're not getting a penny out of me, I'll tell you that for nothing. If you want to wait for Mr Marshall, that's up to you."

"Garn!" They saw the game was up. "Stuck-up cow!"

One of them flipped her book to the ground and threw over a chair.

Mary was outraged and flew at him. "Well if that's the way you want it! Bloody oiks!"

Two working girls saw what was happening and came to Mary's aid. The boys ran off shouting threats.

"Cowards!" Mary yelled after them. Her face was scarlet.

"Are you all right, love?" One of the girls, a blonde with Veronica Lake hair, was concerned.

"Yes, fine, thanks." Mary wiped her mouth with the back of a hand. "Tossers! Come this way again I'll give you what for!" She recovered her book and examined it for damage. "Ignorant pigs!"

5

North Sea Trader

Eastport, a seafaring, shipbuilding town, was cut in half by the River Brander which ran into the North Sea. The town centre lay on the south side; here you found most of the shops, the cinemas, the good restaurants, and down by the river the broader, busier quay. This was the side where Teddy and I lived, he almost out in the country, me down by the docks. A single-span bridge, a mile upstream and high above the river, led to the north side with its factories, football ground and long golden beach. Two piers curled about the river mouth like a crab's claws, protecting the docks and shipyards from storms that roared in from the north and broke their fury on the seashore. The North Pier was famous, a mile long with a towering lighthouse painted in broad red and white hoops, the same colours as Eastport United. The South Pier was shorter. Between lay the calmer waters of Monks Bay, so named because in ancient days the brothers from St Peter's Priory fished there in their coracles.

Archie's deckchair stand was situated roughly midway along the promenade. After he had taken over, Teddy and I headed for the river. Beyond the promenade there was a patch of waste ground. I led him across this and through a hole in the fence to reach the North Quay. It was high tide so the water was not racing as it sometimes did but stirred and shifted, raising plumes of silt from the treacherous currents below.

North Sea Trader, still guided by tugs, had passed between the piers by this time, crossed Monks Bay and was approaching a berth on the South Quay. Beyond her the wagons and cranes and warehouses stood beneath a two-hundred foot embankment. Steep streets ran down from the town centre. At the foot of these, amid a welter of small terraced houses, lay Wherry Row where I lived with my gran.

Teddy, who had never seen a ship berthed, was disappointed to find her across the river. "How do we get over?" he said. "Have we got to walk all the way up into town? It'll take ages!"

I smiled. "Come on, I've got a surprise."

Wondering what it could be, he followed me a hundred yards upstream. Although not as broad as the South Quay, the North Quay cobbles were criss-crossed by rail tracks and set with all the usual cranes, rolling stock and warehouses of a busy port. A mountain of coal, ringed by a mesh fence and guarded day and night by a man with dogs and a telephone, stood back from the water's edge.

The brown water rippled beneath us as I approached a shed with a polished ship's bell hanging from a post. A painted board was propped beneath:

RIVER CROSSING
RING BELL FOR ATTENTION

A flight of stone steps, very short at high tide, led to a sixteen-foot rowboat which rocked at its mooring.

I called, "Hey, Barry!" and after a wait a tiny old man appeared at the door.

"Eh, Mary, love. I thought I recognised your voice."

"Hello, Barry." I kissed his whiskery cheek.

"Your gran'll have your tea ready."

"I hope so, I'm starving."

"And who's this?"

"Just a pal, he's coming over with me. Can I row?"

"Course, if you want to."

There were only six steps to the boat, twenty-two at low water. Barry kept them brushed and scattered rough salt and grit so he could never be blamed if one of his customers twisted an ankle, or worse, fell into the river. At the top of the steps a red and white lifebelt hung in a cradle. Barry was the boatman, sixpence to be rowed across and save the walk up into town. People gladly paid although half his customers came just for the pleasure of the crossing. It was hard work in all sorts of weather but he needed the money to supplement the small pension he received for losing a foot at Ypres in the First World War. I'd known him since I was little and he had taught me to row. This year, since I was strong for my age, he sometimes allowed me to take the oars and keep the fares. He always came with me but it was another of my little jobs.

Teddy and I put on life-jackets and soon were out on the lapping tide. It didn't take long, five minutes, and then we were tying up at steps on the South Quay. No sooner had we stepped ashore than the bell rang across the water, Barry had a customer waiting.

"Aye, well. No peace for the wicked." He cast off and took the oars. "See you again, Teddy, son. Ta-ta."

We stood on the quay and watched him go. North Sea Trader was slipping into her berth and we walked to meet her. She was a smart four-thousand ton tramp ship with a black hull, white superstructure and orange funnel, trading between the British North Sea ports and Germany, Holland and Denmark, as I have told you, sometimes through the Keil Canal into the Baltic. She was back in the UK every six weeks or couple of months.

Uncle Dan looked down from the bridge and spotted us. "Hello, sweetheart, coming aboard?"

"If we can."

"Ten minutes we'll have the gangway down."

"OK."

Uncle Dan was my father's younger brother, a stocky man with a wind-burned face and thick brown curls. He was young to be appointed captain but a lot of merchant seamen had been killed in the war. Also he was a hero who had been awarded the George Cross for taking command when the ship on which he was sailing as first mate had been torpedoed, the captain was killed, and he had navigated two lifeboats to safety from far out in the north Atlantic. Frostbite had cost him two fingers from his left hand. He did not look like a naval hero for he rarely shaved, enjoyed a glass or two of whisky or whatever was on offer, and was careless about the state of his uniform. At the same time his crews loved him and he was widely admired for his seamanship. He was great fun and I loved him to bits, which was more than I could say about his wife, my Aunt Winnie, who had divorced him for what she called 'his shenanigans with other women' up and down the coast. I didn't blame him because she was a dry stick with lips that looked as if she sucked lemons for a treat. When I asked him why he had married her he said, "You tell me, sweetheart, not one of my better decisions." I wish Uncle Dan had been my dad rather than my real dad, though that's not fair because he did OK in the army.

Now he said, "Who's that with you, a new boyfriend?"

"One of them. I'm like you, got so many I can't keep track."

"Cheeky tart," he said and disappeared for a minute. "Here, catch." Two bars of chocolate came flying down. "Not be long."

I collected them from the quay and handed one to Teddy. Sweets were still on ration so they were a treat, solid blocks made specially for seamen during the war, nothing on the wrappers but 'Milk Chocolate' and stamped by the customs. Lifeboat rations and out of date now but they tasted great and made me think of sailors cast drift, never knowing if they were going to live or die.

I had been a couple of trips with Uncle Dan but it was new to Teddy and he was all eyes, didn't want to miss anything. A young seaman called Sammy who had been with Uncle Dan a couple of years, threw a heaving line from the stern. Dock workers tied a half-hitch round a heavy mooring rope, Sammy led the heaving line round a winch drum and the mooring rope snaked aboard. Soon it was secured in a figure eight round a pair of bitts.

"Hi, there, Mary." He came to the rail and threw the line again. "Good to see you."

In ten minutes Trader was tied up alongside and the gangway rattled across. She was heavy-loaded and far down in the water so the gangway was almost horizontal, the treads on end. Teddy followed me aboard. The air was rich with the smell of diesel, sausages and fags from a couple of the crew who had just lashed the gangway to the rails. One was Dennis, Sammy's dad, who had been with Uncle Dan in the lifeboats. He had survived uninjured although they said his hair had turned from black to white in a fortnight. He was a stocky, powerful man in stained trousers and a ragged seaman's jersey with the sleeves pushed up.

"Hello, Mary, pet." He gave me a big hug and whiskery kiss. "Does your uncle know you're aboard?"

"Yes, why?"

He shrugged

"He saw us on the quay, threw this down." The chocolate was in bits. I gave him a piece. "Nothing wrong, is there?"

"Not as far as I know. Anyway," he bit off a corner, "joining us again this year?"

"Depends on the holidays. Some of us have to work, you know. I've got school."

"Aye, well, Dan tells us great things. Been in a play, that right?"

"I played a mountaineer. Got killed in an avalanche."

"Big part?"

"Quite big, yes."

"Good for you, sounds lively. Anyway, you know your way to the bridge." He turned to Teddy. "Hello, son, you a pal? Grand lass our Mary. Better take care of her or you'll have this crew after your blood."

Poor Teddy, he was half my size and didn't know what to say.

Dennis grinned and put out a hand to rumple his hair but Teddy dodged aside. "See you at dinner maybe." He strolled off with his shipmate.

Teddy and I stood looking down on the foredeck where the hatch covers had been loosened and the derricks hoisted in readiness for discharging the next day. We wandered round for a few minutes then climbed a companionway to the boat deck, and up another to the bridge.

6

Uncle Dan

"Mary, love!" Her Uncle Dan folded her in a bear-hug. Mary got a lot of hugs.

"And who's this addition to your long list of boyfriends?"

"Stop it, Uncle Dan. He goes to St Peter's. I cut my leg when I was picking coal up Strawberry Hill way and his mum patched me up." She showed him the scar. "His dad took me to the doctor and drove me home. He's called Teddy."

"Hello, there, Teddy. Let's see your leg." He bent close. "Been nasty. Healing up nicely."

"Had to be stitched."

"I can see that. I've done a few in my time, he made a good job. What happened?"

"I'll tell you later. Teddy wants to look over the ship."

"Quite right too. Fancy being a merchant seaman, Teddy?"

"I don't know."

"What! An' I give you a bar of chocolate!" He laughed. "Anyway, welcome aboard. I'll leave our Mary to show you around. Agents coming in a few minutes, paperwork!" He made a face. "But you'll stay for stay for dinner, the two of you, then we'll walk over to see your lovely gran." He went to the wing and shouted down: "Hey, Sammy! Tell Big Lenny there'll be two more for dinner, young folk. Tell him to rustle up something they'll like."

Sammy raised an arm.

"Teddy has to get home," Mary told her uncle. "His mum's expecting him."

"Oh! Well, they'll be rigging up a phone at the gangway in a few minutes. Got a phone, son?"

I nodded.

"You can let her know. And I'll tell the agent I need a car, give you a run back. But stay for dinner, Mary, the crew will be that pleased to see you."

And so it was arranged, an adventure and I could tell mum not to worry.

"Got to go." He crammed an officer's cap on his curls, grabbed a sheaf of papers and clattered away down a flight of stairs. I stood with Mary in the deserted wheelhouse.

She looked around, "Might as well start here."

It was all new to me and I loved it: the ship's wheel and binnacle, the speaking tube and engine room telegraphs, the gyro compass, the radar, the spinning clear-view screen, the locker full of flags. And in the chart room behind the wheelhouse the long chart table with its parallel rules, dividers and plotted course from Zeebrugge, the chronometer in its temperature-controlled box, the course recorder, the barometer, the officers' sextants. Then out on the wings the gyro repeaters and bright azimuth prisms reflecting the compass card beneath.

Mary called down to two men on the foredeck and they waved up. "Come on then," she said, "let's have a look at the lifeboats then we'll go down the engine room."

We wandered the the ship for an hour, exploring every locker and piece of machinery from the capstan on the fo'csle head to the steering mechanism and red ensign at the stern. By that time the telephone had been rigged so I phoned home then followed Mary into the crew accommodation. A delicious smell of cooking drifted down the alleyway. She stopped at a door.

"This is the spare cabin, the one they gave me." She rattled the handle but the door was locked. "That's funny, I wonder why."

Sammy was emerging from his cabin. He had washed and changed and was running a comb through his hair.

"Hey, Sammy. Why's the door locked?"

He joined us. "New radar equipment, pretty valuable. Old man reckons this is the safest place on the ship, down here where we all live. Engineer coming next week to install it."

"I wanted to show Teddy. Do you mind if we look in your cabin?"

"Sure, but don't be long, dinner in five minutes."

The cabin smelled of Sammy, not dirty just soap and his work clothes hanging on the back of the door. The porthole was hooked open and a picture of a girl with a baby stood on the locker. His bunk looked cosy. I'd have liked to sleep there with my fellow sailors in their cabins either side, the soft roar of the engines, and the ship rolling in a long swell.

We didn't sit in the crew mess, Captain Pearson ate with with his deck officers and engineers in a separate dining room. Dinner was delicious. Big Lenny, the cook, had planned to fry sausage, egg and chips for Mary and me but someone told him I was Jewish and couldn't eat pork, so we had cottage pie like everyone else, a glass of beer shandy, strawberry crumble, and tea with caramel shortbread.

Through the porthole I spotted a blue Ford Anglia. "He needs it to keep up with his girlfriends," Mary told me beneath her breath.

Uncle Dan had ears like a cat and he heard her: "You know more than you should, young woman." He gave me a broad wink.

But he wasn't driving off to see his girlfriends just yet because after dinner we piled into the Anglia and drove round to visit Mary's gran. She was fond of Dan and gave him a big kiss then put on the kettle and produced a whisky bottle.

"Thanks, Eva," he told her. "Just a drop for the good of my health."

Although we'd just finished dinner, we were soon sitting with cake and cups of tea.

"Off to see yon what's her name after this, I suppose," said Mrs Fawcett.

"Who's that you're talking about?"

"Denise, isn't that her name? A hairdresser?"

"Never heard of her. Though now you mention it there is someone called Chrissie wants me to call in – or is it Caroline? I know it begins with a C. But she's a primary teacher."

"Oh, you're dreadful!" She slapped his arm but she was laughing. "Don't be listening to him, you two, he's a thoroughly bad influence."

We asked about his recent voyages and he told us about eating apricots in Spain and going up through the Baltic into Russia, ice coating the shrouds, soldiers patrolling the streets with rifles on their backs.

"I'd love to go again," Mary said.

"Any time, sweetheart," he told her. "Don't have to be away the whole trip, we can fly you home. Depends on your summer holiday and if my favourite gran can spare you."

"I'm not stopping her," Mrs Fawcett told him. "School comes first but if the dates work out there's nothing here holding her back. Same as going off to guide camp. I was fine the last time and I'll be fine again."

"Oh, Gran." Mary went behind her chair. "Won't you miss me just a bit?"

"Not at all," she shook her off. "Give me a bit of peace!"

But she loved her to death and gripped Mary's hand with her old fingers.

"You too, Teddy," said the captain, "if you'd like to come. Haven't got another spare cabin but I'm sure we could fit you in somewhere."

"Thanks." There was nothing I would enjoy more and felt the colour rising in my cheeks. "But I'm going to Vienna with mum and dad."

"Vienna!"

"The Nazis took over grandad's factory and the house. Mum's going over to try and get them back."

"What, your mum's – ?"

"Austrian," I said. "She came over before the war and married dad. All the rest of the family got sent to the gas chambers. At least, we think so."

There was silence then Mary's uncle – I'll call him Uncle Dan – said, "Did you know them?"

"I met them when I was little but I don't really remember, and we couldn't go back after the Anschluss. Or maybe we could have gone back but might not have got out again. It wasn't safe."

We chatted a while longer then Mrs Fawcett said, "Time to take Teddy home, Dan, his parents will be getting worried. And there's school tomorrow."

"Couple of clever kids," he said. "I never got to St Peter's."

"Ah well, your talents lay in another direction," she said. "You're a famous seaman, captain at thirty-one."

"Not to mention Denise and Chrissie," said Mary at which everyone laughed. "Or is it Caroline?"

*

Ten minutes later I was home and Uncle Dan came in to meet my mum and dad.

They liked him very much. Dad brought out the whisky and Uncle Dan repeated his offer to take me a trip if they approved. They didn't say yes and they didn't say no. They said they would think about it.

7

The Man in the Barn

That was Sunday and I only saw Teddy once in the next fortnight. I was busy at school, we had the end of term exams and I was writing a story for a competition in the Eastport Chronicle. Mrs Wardman, my English teacher, had spotted it and thought I should have a go. I was writing a story based on my dad, a man who could never settle into a job in peacetime and became a criminal with a prison record. My dad's name was Frank, I called this man Louis Goldman and set it in another town. I gave him a Jewish name because of Teddy but it didn't feature in the story. When war broke out he joined the army and did well until he was killed by a shell trying to save injured comrades. I called it The Hero.

Also I was in the school drama group which was giving a performance of Shakespeare's Julius Caesar after the summer holiday. Mrs Jamison, the teacher responsible for drama, had trained at RADA and before her marriage, at that time called Vivien Banks, she had appeared in several productions at the Old Vic and elsewhere on the London stage. She was lovely and it was fun but she set high standards and was very strict. Woe betide the girl who missed a rehearsal or did not know her lines. As a result our plays and musicals were among the most important events of the school year and highly regarded, not just in Eastport but further afield.

Mrs Jamison had cast me as Lepidus, a minor character, but when Audrey Fraser, a sixth-form girl, moved at short notice to the south coast, she asked me to step in and play Marcus Brutus, one of the leads. I was astonished and more than a little scared because the girls who were playing Marc Antony and Cassius, the other two leads, were also in the sixth form. I told Mrs Jamison this and she said she had thought about it but if I really didn't want to play Brutus she would ask one of the others. So I took a deep breath and said I would give it a try. I heard later that I wasn't her first choice of a replacement, she had asked Jennifer Blyth, but she was working for an important scholarship exam and had to turn it down. Anyway, it was a great part and we rehearsed after school on a Tuesday and Thursday.

*

When Teddy was invited to join me on a holiday trip to the continent, his parents wanted to know more and look over the ship, so Uncle Dan invited the whole family for tea. Gran and I joined them so it was quite a party.

"If Teddy does come along," Uncle Dan said, "we haven't got a spare cabin but there's a locker at the end of the crew alleyway, bigger than a cabin probably. We can clear out the gear and put a bunk in. There's no running water but it's only a few steps to the washroom."

We inspected it and were taken right through the ship from the bridge to the oily steel deck of the engine room. The cabin I thought of as mine was open now, the bunk made up except for blankets, the radar equipment gone. "They gave it to one of the new ships," Uncle Dan said crossly. "Left us with the set we've got already."

"Surely you're lucky to have radar at all," Mr Cohen said, "it was only developed a few years back."

"Aye, and it does well enough, but that doesn't mean we'd not like the bang up-to-date stuff if we got a chance."

We didn't stay long because we'd had tea in the officers' mess and the steward had to set the tables for dinner.

"We're not saying yes, Teddy," his dad told him as we came away, "let's just say it's more of a yes than when we left the house. It all depends on Dan's schedule and," he gave Teddy one of those looks I reckon dads practise in front of a mirror, "what the teachers have to say in your end-of-year report." It was a chance too good for him to miss.

Teddy rolled his eyes. "I knew you'd say that. It's blackmail. But if they say I've been working hard can I go?"

"Let's see the report first."

Uncle Dan laughed. "He's got you there, son. But I need a bit of warning so we can scrub out the locker and put a bunk in. If you're going to Vienna next month I suppose you've got a passport?"

That was the last time I saw Teddy for a fortnight, three weeks nearly, but while I was busy at home and Uncle Dan sailed on to Hull and Southampton, strange things were happening up Strawberry Bank. Someone had begun stealing from…But I'll let Teddy tell you about it.

*

Yes, I'm going to write this bit because Mary wasn't there:

Monday was wash day. Mum had a woman to help her about the house, Mrs Wilmot, she was lovely, and all morning they were boiling and scrubbing and wringing in the brick outhouse. The air smelled of washing powder and clouds of steam billowed from the door. After a cup of tea and a sandwich in the kitchen, the clothes were pegged on a line across the back garden. On dry days, certainly in summer, they hung there until after tea, but now mum discovered that clothes had gone missing. Dad's clothes: a shirt, a vest, two pairs of socks. She hunted, had they fallen, been dropped in the kitchen? No, she remembered hanging them on the line, the clothes pegs were still there, they had been stolen. Someone had walked through the front garden, or climbed the back fence as Rachel and I did to get into the big field, and taken them from the washing line.

Who would do such a thing? A tramp? But no tramp had been seen. One of the men picking coal? But they were all decent fellows. Not a neighbour for they were missing clothes too, men's clothes: trousers, a jersey, muddy shoes from outside the back door.

Nothing like this had happened before, then at bedtime the next day Rachel ran downstairs and said she had seen a light in the old farm buildings at the top of the field. I have told you that we lived in the top house up Strawberry Bank. Beyond us this enormous field rose to a crest then dropped away to woods and the pit heaps where Mary had gone picking coal. Sometimes the field was a pasture for cows, sometimes planted with turnips or, as it was that summer, a sea of waving corn. The buildings stood at the top, silhouetted against the sky. They weren't near the farmhouse, that was half a mile away, these were just field barns, very old and falling down now. Mr Moorhead, who owned the farm, used them to keep bits of machinery out of the rain and store a few bales of straw. He didn't mind Rachel and me playing there as long as we didn't trample his crops or start a fire. We went up quite often and trapped pretty field mice, not to hurt them just to see them, and made dens in the bales, and listened to pigeons cooing in the rafters. Swallows made nests and we watched them swooping in and out, beaks full to feed the gaping yellow mouths that poked above the edge.

But now there was a stranger up there in the darkness, lighting a fire it looked like, although the flames were quickly hidden. Mum said, "You're not to go up there again, either of you, do you hear! Not until your father or some of the men have been to see what's going on." Dad said he'd go up the next day after work and after a lot of persuasion he agreed that I could go with him. "I'm not some little kid," I told him, "I'm nearly fifteen."

It was early July and the sun was still high when we set off about six. We went the way Rachel and I always did, over the back fence and round the side of the field. She was furious mum wouldn't let her go with us. It only took five minutes and we went quietly so we could get a good look at whoever it was before he ran away. A dry track led from the road but we went the back way, through seeding grasses, and tiptoed to a hole in the wall which had once been a window. There was no one there. We crept to a second crumbling hole. No fire was burning but the air smelled of smoke and charred sticks lay in a rough stone hearth. A bed of straw lay against the opposite wall. A man in his thirties or forties sat upon it, resting his back against the stones. He hadn't shaved for several days and his hair was rough. I thought I recognised dad's shirt. He was holding a stick and cutting at it with a pocket knife.

Dad and I stood watching. The man was well-built, a bit over average height, with a head of thick brown hair greying at the sides. For a minute we were silent, the stranger concentrating on his carving, then suddenly, as if some sixth sense warned him that he was being watched, he looked up and saw us at the window.

For seconds no one moved. He was a strong fellow and I'm sure would have been well able to defend himself but he was more frightened than threatening. In a shower of little wood chips he sprang to his feet, snatched up an old army rucksack and headed for a window space on the far side of the barn. He was halfway through and preparing to jump down when he hesitated and looked back at his camp. A few objects remained, things he might need when he moved on:

a small blackened saucepan, a plate, a mug, a spare pair of shoes. Briefly he crouched in the gap then stepped back into the barn.

"Do you mind if I collect a few things? Don't want no trouble, only be a couple of minutes."

"Sure," dad said, "take your time."

The man tucked his few possessions into the rucksack and a grubby cotton bag with a drawstring. "I done no harm, nothing for the kids to be scared about." He turned to me "You come up here sometimes? Bit of a den and a few sweetie papers in the bales over there."

I nodded mutely.

"Here." He rooted in his bag and pulled out a carved wooden rifle, a British army Enfield about six inches long. "Present from me."

"Thankyou."

He shrugged his rucksack comfortable and was heading for the window again when dad called him back: "Bit of a tough time, eh?" He felt in his pockets and pulled out some folded banknotes and whatever coins were there.

The man was uncertain.

"Come on," dad said, "I've seen enough in my time. I'm sure you can use it."

"All right," the man said. "Thanks very much."

He tucked the money away and nodded. He was an intruder, a man who didn't belong, and from the moment Rachel spotted his fire I had seen him as a threat. But he'd been nice, giving me the rifle and all, and as he heaved himself back into the window space, I felt sorry for him. Beyond lay fields and woods, a few pit heaps and mile upon mile of empty countryside. Dad and I had driven him from his place of refuge. I was glad it was a warm, dry evening. Even if he had to sleep under a hedge he would be all right, that night anyway.

He looked back, his eyes a striking blue. "Thanks."

"Good luck," Dad said. "I hope it goes well."

"Aye, well that's two of us. Ta-ta." He jumped down into the grass and the wall hid him from view.

As we went into the barn a smell of sweat lingered in the air. "Poor chap," dad said. "There's a lot like that wandering around Europe."

"Like what?" I said.

"Nowhere to go, broken home maybe. Wife and children killed by a bomb? Seen his mates burned alive? Who knows."

"He looked all right," I said.

"You reckon? Did you see the look in his eyes?"

"Not to notice."

"Something's happened, I've seen it a hundred times. Poor fellows been at sea, in the army. Seen things nobody should have to see, terrible things. Brain can't take it. Come home and the memories won't go away. Can't cope with the kids. Wife's found somebody else. Loses his job."

"What will happen to him?"

"Who can say? Sleep rough for a while, meet some others, hit the bottle. If he's lucky find a doctor, meet a good woman, get back on his feet. Seemed a nice enough sort of chap, let's hope so."

As we emerged into the evening sunshine we saw him heading down the hill, not back towards town but out into the country. I held my little wooden rifle and felt guilty. Had it not been for us he would be safe in the barn, cooking something on his fire, sleeping on his straw bed with swallows and field mice for company.

*

This was Teddy's story and I didn't hear it until several days later. I felt so sorry for the man and it made me think of my dad, dead in France, wondering how he would have coped with coming home to me and gran. Would we somehow have lived together, the three of us, or would he have qualified for a house, maybe a prefab or one of those little semi-bungalows in the new estates? He'd have looked for a lady friend, I was sure of that. He'd been close to a woman called Brenda, but I wouldn't have gone to live with him. I could never leave gran, it was unthinkable.

In the meantime it was the end of the summer term and I was busy all day, every day. Rehearsals for Julius Caesar were full steam ahead but held off for a fortnight for the end-of-year exams. Although the girls' school and the boys' school looked identical, separated only by the dining hall, they were independent. The boys put on plays with the women's parts played by boys whose voices hadn't broken yet, as it was in the time of Shakespeare. In the girls' school the men's parts were played by girls and it worked very well. In January we had presented The Ascent of F6, a modern play about climbing a peak in the Himalayas which had been a great success. Julius Caesar, in which nearly every character was a man, was ambitious and due to be staged in October.

As I have told you, Brutus, the part I had taken over, was one of the leads and I loved it. He is a complicated man, a friend of Caesar, the conquering hero, but is drawn into the plot to murder him. As his boyhood friend, I am the most treacherous of the senators to plunge my dagger into Caesar's chest, the fatal blow at which he looks up and speaks his heartbreaking line, 'Et tu, Brute!' Following the murder I have a long speech to the crowd, 'Romans, countrymen and lovers', seeking to explain my actions but Mark Antony rouses them to a mob wanting revenge and I am forced to flee for my life. Later I am accosted by Caesar's ghost, and at the end of the play, after much slaughter in the battle of Philippi, I have to commit suicide by running on my sword. In the final tableau, as I lie dead on stage, Mark Antony declares 'This was the noblest Roman of them all', for everything I had done was for the good of the Roman republic, and I am carried off in honour by the soldiers. I had learned my lines and went about the house waving the bread knife in the air and declaiming them to gran. I couldn't wait for the costumes to arrive, the magnificent toga I would be wearing, the leg straps and sandals, the armour, the sword and helmet. It was exciting but when I thought of performing it before a packed audience, I was so terrified I felt sick.

As well as the play, now the exams were over, I was writing 'The Hero', my story for the competition. It was nearly finished and gran, who always told me the truth, said that she liked it. I had been sent a form for Mrs Wardman to complete and say it was all my own work.

And Uncle Dan had sent a telegram that he was going to be in Rotterdam the second week in August and hoped I would be able to join him. We would be heading up through the Kiel Canal into the Baltic, calling at Helsinki and Leningrad, possibly Stockholm on the way. If I'd like Teddy to come he was welcome and Uncle Dan or one of the crew would meet us off the ferry in a taxi. When I had sailed with him last summer, I'd enjoyed working with the sailors but it would be good to have Teddy along. The Russians wanted a crew list so there wasn't time to wait for Teddy's school report but his dad said he could go anyway. And he'd suddenly started growing. Maybe I was just getting used to him but already he looked bigger than the boy who had skated up when I had my accident with the pram.

8

Vienna

I haven't told you about being Jewish. It wasn't only Nazis who hated the Jews, we were mistrusted and looked on as a race apart all over the world. Not by most, I hope, but enough to make life difficult sometimes. This was true of Britain the same as other countries. Some people wouldn't go to dad, for example, although he was a brilliant dentist. And I had been shouted at in the street: "Get out of it, you dirty Jew!" This was rare for me because with my sandy hair I don't look Jewish, but the children at school knew and Michael Berg, who was in my class in primary school, was shouted at quite often.

He wasn't a particular friend but one time when we were walking home together, this led to a fight in which we came of worse. Two against five, some of them older boys, it wasn't surprising. After the name-calling Michael, whose family were much more orthodox than mine, shouted back bravely, "Get out of it yourself, you dirty Christian!" The gang flew at us and we might have been badly hurt if a couple of men had not waded in to break it up. As we picked ourselves from the pavement and the roughs slouched off, I heard one of the men say to Michael, "You're asking for it, shouting things like that. You should know better." Michael stared at him, what was the difference? I am sure he went to the synagogue more often than those boys went to church.

Being Jewish was one thing, being a German Jew was worse. My mum wasn't German, she was Austrian, but after living in England since before I was born she still had traces of an accent. Not only that, she looked Jewish, the same as Michael, although he was heavy while mum and Rachel were slim and pretty; no, not pretty, they were beautiful. After all those years in Eastport, doing voluntary work in the hospital and driving an ambulance right through the war, she still met hostility, a woman muttering in a queue or an offhand shop assistant, and came home upset. As if she had not suffered enough, her entire family wiped out in the Holocaust.

When she married dad and came to live in England, mum had trained as a language teacher and St Peter's would gladly have employed her. Although as a girl she had spoken Viennese German, she had needed pure German for her work with the State Opera. Also, as I have told you, she had studied at the conservatoire and was a brilliant pianist, which was why she had been employed by the Opera House. But after we were born her love was all for her family, we came first, and dad being a dentist we did not need the money so she only went to St Peter's occasionally for conversation classes with the senior pupils. Rachel and I had learned German from the time we were in our prams, just as we had learned English, and both spoke it fluently which wasn't being clever, it was just the way we had been brought up. Rachel was still in primary school but I didn't take German classes at St Peter's, there was no point, although I read the set books so I could help other boys with their homework, in return for which they helped me with Latin.

Although mum practised the piano for an hour every day, she only played publicly for charity concerts or if a distinguished singer or choir were coming to Eastport and they needed an accompanist. Rachel was a terrific pianist, streets ahead of me. In that respect I was a big disappointment although I could read music and had my grade three, but was nothing like as good I should have been at fourteen. What I wanted to do was play a trumpet in the school band.

There was a second reason why mum didn't want to work at St Peter's. We had just lived through the devastation of World War 2 and many pupils had lost lost dads and uncles in the fighting. Others had family and friends who had been bombed out of their houses. Factories and shipyards had been destroyed. Food was still rationed. For as long as people could remember, newspapers had had carried stories of death and disaster, pictures of blazing ships and overturned tanks, worn-out soldiers, and more recently photos of the skeletal survivors of concentration camps and the rail tracks leading to the showers and ovens of Auschwitz. The war had in some places been literally a Hell on Earth, and pupils did not like it when a smartly-dressed woman with an accent appeared in their classrooms, talking to their teachers as if she were one of them. They knew she was my mother, at least the boys did for she came into both schools, but she was a German, right? If she hadn't fired the rifle or dropped the bombs herself, she had brothers and cousins who did. She was one of the enemy. Maybe she was a spy. Were boys and girls with no dads, with brothers who had lost their legs, with uncles in the burns units, expected to smile and be polite? No one said or did anything but she could see it in their faces.

What was mum to do, protest her innocence? Absolutely not, she was a private woman, so she left. On her last morning the headmaster asked to see her in his office. He had noticed the way some boys and colleagues looked at her, he had heard what was being said privately. Anywhere, he told her, this was unacceptable, let alone in a distinguished school like St Peter's that prided itself on on tolerance and being a civilising influence. This was the way of the Nazis, this was what we had been fighting against. He wouldn't have it and proposed to set the record straight at morning assembly in a few days' time.

Mum was outraged: "Absolutely not! I'm not going to have my life raked over in front of hundreds of schoolchildren. If the facts leak out, if they become known in the way of things, well and good, but that is *not* the same thing as making an apology for us. And what about Teddy? We're not the only family that's been accused unjustly. For goodness sake, it might end up in the papers. I don't know how you can even think of such a thing."

The poor headmaster, he had meant well. I only found out because that evening mum was telling dad about it in the kitchen and speaking a little more loudly than usual. Rachel signalled to me and we listened at the door. Dad caught us at it and we fled but no more was said, in our hearing anyway. Mum left the school but returned a few years later by which time the facts had become known and the atmosphere had changed.

*

At the start of the summer holiday, mum, dad, Rachel and I drove to Hull and caught the ferry to Rotterdam. From there we took a train to Vienna.

The previous summer mum had written to a firm of solicitors in the city. To her relief they were still in existence and more than that, Otto Müller, who had been my grampa's friend and legal advisor, had survived the war. He was delighted to hear from her and she learned that with the Nazis gaining ever more power and the future uncertain, grampa had made a cast-iron will which Mr Müller still had in his possession. In it he left everything to mum, the house and all its contents, the factory, his stocks and shares, knowing that in the event of any member of the family surviving, she

"I grew up here. My father used to own this house. As I said, I wrote to Herr Ebner a while ago."

"And as I understand it, he replied to you."

"Yes, he did. And the last thing I want is any unpleasantness but the house was taken over by the SS. Papa is dead now, in Mauthausen, and so are the rest of my family. But before he was taken away, Papa made a will leaving everything to me."

The woman's face hardened, "And I understand you're claiming that it still belongs to you."

"Legally it does."

"Well, we bought it from the previous owner, we paid a very good price, and that being the case it belongs to us now. My husband explained all this in his letter. I take it you received it?"

"Yes, and I replied. But you see, I don't accept that. I believe you bought it from Major Kramer, an officer in the SS."

"You'll have to ask my husband about that."

"I have no need to, I know what happened. Having sent Papa and the rest of my family to the concentration camps, along with all the other Jews in Vienna, he just moved in. He paid my family no money, there is no record of it, he just took it."

Frau Ebner's husband called from inside the house: "Who is it, Greta?"

"'That Jew woman, the one who wrote to you from England."

"So if you bought it from him," mum continued, "I'm afraid you are in the same position as anyone else who buys stolen property."

"And what do you mean by that?"

Herr Ebner appeared in the doorway, a bull of a man in braces, his shirt not fully buttoned.

Mum drew a shaky breath. Dad spoke for her: "It wasn't his to sell. I'm afraid you've lost your money, unless you can trace him and get it back. He may have thought, you may have thought, that everyone in the family was dead, but they're not. The house belongs to my wife."

Herr Ebner bristled up, a bully, a man accustomed to getting his own way. "You can think what you like. I don't know what sort of lawyer you spoke to, probably some back-street shyster, one of your own persuasion. I am represented by one of the top lawyers in the country, and if you think you're going to shoehorn me out of this house that I paid good money for, you've got another think coming." He made to go indoors. "Come along, Greta."

"We'll see you in court then," dad said in his broken German.

"If you want to take it that far," said Herr Ebner. "If you can afford to."

"Oh, I think so." Dad put a protective arm round mum's shoulders. "This is my wife's family we're talking about. After the Shoah, the whole Jewish community will back us up."

The door swung shut but before it closed finally they heard him say to his wife: "Judenschwein! Pity the SS didn't get to finish…Do us all a favour."

As they returned to the car, mum took dad's hand: "Thank you, David."

"What?"

"Just for being there."

"Where else would I be?" He kissed the top of her head. "That man, Herr…"

"Ebner."

"What a brute! At least we didn't come to blows, though it would have given me a great deal of pleasure to punch him on his piggy nose."

She smiled then her face crumpled. "Seeing them both

standing there. In our hall." Tears were never far away and now she began to weep. Dad said nothing, just hugged her tight.

Rachel and I had left the car and now we ran up the drive. For my whole life my mum had been a tower of strength, loving me whatever I did, solving my problems, comforting me when I was upset. Now she needed the hugs and we gathered round, a tangled family amid the shrubs and flowers of the lovely garden. Looking towards the house I saw Frau Ebner watching from the bay window.

"Right," dad said as we broke up and continued to the car. "That's that done, worst over. Factory this afternoon, see if there's anything left standing. What now?"

"I'll tell you what I want." Mum took a deep breath and scrubbed her eyes with her handkerchief. "The biggest and best ice-cream the city has to offer. See if Enrico's survived the bombing. That suit you two?"

"Yeah!" We piled into the car.

"It's at times like this," dad said, "I know why I married you."

"Other times too, I hope," she said briskly. "Never mind all that, where's my ice-cream?"

9

Sailors

I can't understand people who say they get bored. Every morning when I wake there are things I want to do and usually things that need to be done. That summer Gran wanted the living room painted and papered, she always likes the house smart, so for three days we were busy with that. And I had to finish my story for the Chronicle and get the entry form signed by Mrs Wardman. Then Archie's grandchildren came on holiday so he asked me to look after the deck chairs for a week which suited me because I'd need some spending money when I went away with Uncle Dan. I baby-sat for Denise a couple of nights. It was a terrific year for films and I went with gran to see Easter Parade and Laurence Olivier's Hamlet. A couple of times I met friends from school and we saw Oliver Twist and Scott of the Antarctic. The sun shone so I went a walk round Strawberry Hill, picked a jug of wild raspberries and explored the barn where Teddy had seen the tramp. Two or three times I took the buggy to the south beach and brought back sacks of sea coal.

There was no shortage of things to do but it was a bit lonely sometimes so it was good to have Teddy home. On an afternoon of wind and sunshine we took his kites to the hill. Lying in the summer grass he told me about the vile Herr Ebner who had behaved like a Nazi and they were taking to court to get the house back. The burned-out factory, he told me, was being rebuilt as a school, not shops as they had been told. And they had been to a theatre for a performance of La Traviata, my favourite opera. Singers from all over the world had performed free to help rebuild the famous Vienna Opera House which had been badly damaged. Because Mrs Cohen used to play for the Opera and the director knew she had lost her family, they were given a box right next to the stage. I was green with envy, especially since Teddy didn't like opera much and I thought it was the most wonderful music in the world.

After Vienna they had spent a week hillwalking in the snow-capped mountains near Innsbruck. As a result of this, beaten by sun on the high hillsides, Mrs Cohen and Rachel were several shades darker and Teddy's sandy hair was bleached, his eyes even bluer in his brown face. No one could have guessed he was Jewish. If the Nazis had still been in power, they would have made him a member of the Hitler Youth.

Lest you should wonder about this, in a discussion some time earlier about Jewish and Catholic traditions, Teddy had told me that as an eight-day-old baby he had not been circumcised. This was rare but despite the laws of the Torah, his father did not agree with it. Consequently, even if he had been physically examined like all children who became Hitler Youth, there was no way of telling he was a Jew. Only his family name proclaimed otherwise.

On the third of August, while they were still in Austria, Teddy had his fifteenth birthday. To celebrate, he set off with his dad after an early breakfast and spent all day climbing in the high mountains, right up into the snow, and came down for a family feast in the Gasthaus where they were staying.

*

Five days after the Cohens' return, while most of Eastport was still asleep, Mr Cohen set off back to Hull, this time for Teddy and me to catch the Maid of Utrecht, the North Sea ferry that would take us to Rotterdam at the start of our holiday with Uncle Dan. Gran had given me as much spending money as she could afford, I had my money from the deck chairs, and Mr Cohen gave Teddy twenty pounds. Apart from scout camp it was the first time he had been away from home.

Dock workers threw off the mooring lines. As the ferry moved out and the propellers churned up clouds of silt from the bed of the harbour, we stood waving to his dad and Rachel until the swinging ship hid them from view.

We were on our own.

*

Although Teddy spoke German and we both knew a bit of French, neither of us had a word of Dutch so when we descended the gangway in Rotterdam the notices were a mystery. It wasn't a problem because Dennis was waiting with a big placard as we came through customs. Uncle Dan couldn't meet us because he was busy with paperwork. As we walked to the car, Dennis told us there had been a change of plan: North Sea Trader had been sent to Amsterdam at short notice to pick up a cargo of grain and machinery. Instead of Russia we were going to Norway. It would be a fine run up and the fjords were beautiful, he hoped we wouldn't be disappointed. I was a bit because I had been reading about the terrible siege of Leningrad and I had hoped to go to the ballet. What I was looking forward to most, though, was just being aboard ship again with the blue ocean on all sides, working with the crew, taking a turn at the wheel, and rocking in my lovely cabin when I went to sleep.

It was a ninety-minute drive to Amsterdam. Scars of

the bombing and German occupation lay on every side: craters and twisted machinery, ships scuttled in the canals, the skeletons of great buildings. I had seen films of war-torn London and we had had our share in Eastport, but driving on roads scarred with the tracks of Nazi tanks, along streets where they had marched in their jackboots and dragged people from their homes, sent families like Anne Frank's and the Olswangs to the concentration camps, brought the horrors of it flooding back.

"Give it a year or two," Dennis said, "the fields will be bright with tulips as far as the eye can see. They're a hard-working people, the Dutch, it won't take long." He glanced at Teddy in the driving mirror, "Memories will take longer."

It was evening and the floodlights were on as we drove through the dock gates in Amsterdam, wound between cranes and railway wagons very like Eastport and drew up at the gangway. Half the crew came running to meet us:

"Hello, darling!"

"Good to see you boy, welcome aboard!"

Straightway they relieved us of our luggage and led the way to the messroom where Big Lenny served up sausage, egg and chips – beef sausage because of Teddy – home-made bread with lashings of butter, and big mugs of tea.

I was tired and after lots of hugs and a laugh I went to my cabin and crashed out straight away. Teddy was so jazzed up he was sure he would never sleep. His cabin had been made ready, the bulkheads scrubbed, a bunk installed and mats on the deck.

"OK in here, Teddy, boy?" Dennis took him along. "Bogs and showers down there on the right."

"Yeah, great!" Teddy looked around.

"Towels and sheets, you can make up your bunk the way you like it. Anything you need, there's usually someone around." Like other cabins, the door was hooked open, the entrance covered by a curtain. "Right then, I'll leave you to settle in."

Mrs Cohen thought her children should help around the house, wash the windows sometimes, do the washing up and every Sunday strip their beds. It didn't take Teddy long to spread the warm red blankets, hang up a few clothes and stow his suitcase in a corner. Feeling restless and a little scared, he went out on deck. Sammy, who was a talented artist, had been working on a painting of a favourite pub for his girlfriend and found him on the foredeck.

"Hi there, Teddy, couldn't sleep?" He sipped a mug of tea.

"I haven't been to bed yet, just having a look around."

"Do you know what time it is?"

"I wasn't sleepy."

"Aye, well. Best get your head down anyway. I bet your mam wouldn't like you wandering round a ship in Amsterdam this time of night."

"Yes, all right." Teddy looked around. "It's exciting, isn't it?"

"I guess at your age. Mind, I was only fourteen when I left school and come away with dad and the captain. I love it, not that I wouldn't rather be home with my girlfriend sometimes."

"I thought sailors had a girl in every port."

"Now then, what kind of talk's that? I don't think Katie would like to hear you say that." He sipped his tea.

"So is it not true?"

"Never you mind," Sammy hid a smile. "Off you go. Night-night."

As he went in he saw Teddy heading to the washroom with a towel and his toothbrush. Five minutes later he tapped on Teddy's door and looked through the curtain. His clothes were thrown over the back of a chair and he was fast asleep. Sammy pulled the blanket to his chin and came away.

*

I changed my skirt for dungarees, tied my hair back and we helped with the painting and greasing, holystoning, repairing tattered flags, checking the lifeboat stores, all the work of the crew. Teddy was great, always willing and worked like a deck boy. When he cut the palm of his hand on a wire and the mate had to bind it up, he kept right on working until the bandages were filthy and falling off. The sailors told him to jump school and stay to work with them. At morning and afternoon break we gathered in the crew mess for tea and tabnabs, as they called the pastries provided by Big Lenny. We ate lunch with the crew also, but for dinner we tidied ourselves up and joined Uncle Dan and his officers in the dining room and were served by a steward.

I loved every minute. For two days we loaded bulk grain and farm machinery in Amsterdam. The weather turned hot and on the second night there was a terrific thunderstorm. Teddy and I stood under a canvas awning with Big Lennie and one of the crew to watch the bolts of lightning illuminate the harbour and hear the sky ripped apart by thunder.

"Look!" Big Lennie held out his arm. All the hairs stood on end.

The second sailor, an AB called Plum, pointed to the mast. The metal cross-trees of Trader and the masts of some other ships, glimmered with violet light. "St Elmo's fire. In twenty years at sea I've never seen that before."

"I have," Big Lennie said. "One time in west Africa."

It was tremendous, as if nature had put on a display just for Teddy and me.

Next morning we sailed west along the North Sea Canal and out through the locks at Ijmuiden into the North Sea.

*

In Amsterdam, Uncle Dan had taken us to the war-damaged Rijksmuseum and the Royal Palace, we had been a cruise on the City Canal, and eaten big Dutch pancakes the size of a dinner plate. But this was what I liked best, out on the open sea with spray flying and the wind blowing my hair.

Our course from Holland to the west coast of Norway lay almost due north. Although Trader had automatic pilot, when there were fishing boats and small coastal vessels about, a helmsman took the wheel. Once we were clear of land and the traffic round the Dutch coast had thinned, Uncle Dan told Teddy to get himself cleaned up and take over.

"But I don't know what to do," Teddy protested.

"Of course you don't," Uncle Dan told him, "Sammy here will show you. Come on, chop-chop."

So Teddy, in his grey school trousers and a jersey, took his place at the ship's wheel and was given his first lesson in steering:

"It's not like a car," Sammy told him. "That travels on a hard road, a ship travels on water. Turn the wheel to port she'll start swinging – and keep on swinging. To stop it you have to turn the wheel the other way and bring her back on course. We're steering 358, so you need to…don't be frightened of it…good, now steady her down…line the jack staff up against a cloud…not your fault…the wind and current…a bit more rudder…watch the gyro…good for you."

I had taken the wheel when I sailed with Uncle Dan the year before. It wasn't easy but Teddy picked it up quickly. Uncle Dan came to see how he was doing. Sammy took him aside, "The boy's a natural," he said out of Teddy's hearing. "Four degrees either side, that's very good in this sea. If it gets to five he's cross with himself. I couldn't do much better myself."

Teddy looked round as Uncle Dan came and stood beside him. "How are you liking it?"

"It's good," Teddy said. "Keep veering to port."

"That's the wind, lucky we're heavy-laden. Sailing in ballast, high out the water, it's much worse. Sammy says good things about you. Want to pack it in or do another half hour?"

"Another half-hour, I'm just getting the hang of it."

"I'm sure Sammy won't mind." He looked round. "OK, Sammy, get yourself a mug of tea. I'll stay here till you get back. You can keep lookout."

When Teddy had finished, Uncle Dan set me to do an hour which I always enjoyed. Teddy had missed his tea and tabnabs which was a pity because Big Lenny had made Dutch pancakes which were even better than the ones we had eaten in Amsterdam. Not a scrap was left so he took Teddy to the galley for hot chocolate and chips.

10

Party Time

It took a day and a half to sail to Bergen. The sky stayed blue but the wind strengthened from the west, making Trader pitch and roll in the mounting waves. Spray flew from the bows, drenching the foredeck and smacking the windows of the bridge. Luckily Teddy and I were good sailors and didn't feel sick. "Look!" he pointed to a crested wave that raced towards us, exploded against the ship's plates and sent a sheet of water halfway to the cross-trees. An edge was raised along the dining tables and the cloth was damped to stop the plates sliding around. The crew complained but I loved it, rocking in my bunk that night with the ship creaking and the door curtain swaying in and out.

The next morning I was still in bed when there was a knock at the door, a voice called, "Are you decent?" and Teddy appeared through the curtain. "Come on, lazybones, you can see Norway."

I pulled a jersey over my nightie and joined him on deck. The sun shone, the sea sparkled with white horses, and far off on the starboard bow a range of mountains appeared above the horizon.

After breakfast we helped the crew make ready for discharging. There wasn't a great deal to do because the heavy machinery we were carrying would have to be lifted out by crane and the bulk grain would be discharged by an Archimedes screw. All the same, the blocks had to be greased and checked and the derricks made ready for hoisting when we got into calmer waters. In the mid morning, when work stopped for tea and tabnabs, Teddy and I went for'ard to see the spray and got soaked to the skin. We took great care and were trying to keep under cover when a rogue wave roared in from an unexpected direction. Whop! The spray landed smack on our heads. Gasping and streaming, we headed to the washrooms.

I took a quick shower to wash out the salt, and was sitting in my cabin towelling my hair when something in a corner caught my eye. I don't know how I hadn't noticed it before because although it was tiny it was plain to see. Anyway, I picked it up and found it was a chip of wood. Something about it was familiar, then I realised it was exactly the same as the chips I had found in the barn above the Cohens, scattered by the tramp who had given Teddy the little wooden rifle. How had it got here? I remembered picking some up. Had they found their way into a pocket? Most of my skirts had pockets in those days, internal pockets if they were wool, patch pockets if they were cotton. The skirts I had with me had been washed but I checked, just in case, but the pockets were empty. I examined it, just a common chip of wood, and decided I was being stupid. It might have been used in packing, maybe that radar equipment Uncle Dan had told us about.

All the same, once I was dressed I showed it to Teddy who searched his own pockets and the turn-ups of his trousers but there were no more.

We hung our wet clothes in the drying room and the deck boy, a sixteen-year-old everyone called Newcastle, lent me a pair of working trousers streaked with paint. They were too big and I had to turn up the legs and tighten the waist with a length of flag rope, but they served their purpose and I was able to continue working with the crew.

We sailed into Bergen from the west. The fjords were beautiful and the summits of the mountains, some of which were snow-capped even in summer, shone pink in the setting sun.

By the time we were tied up at the quay and Uncle Dan had talked to the agents, it was too late to go ashore, although Teddy and I explored the harbour just to say we had set foot in Norway. Too late to head into town but not too late for the crew of another British ship, the West Wind, to come aboard for a party. Bottles were opened, voices were raised in jokes and songs, tray after tray of sandwiches and hot sausage rolls flowed from the galley. This was a grown-up party, no place for Teddy and me, so we retreated to our cabins.

Not for long. I had changed into a skirt and jumper and was reading in my chair – a story called Cold Comfort Farm about about a family of mad farmers – when there was a knock at my door and Sammy poked his head round the curtain: "Haway, Mary, pet, are you not coming to join us?"

I shook my head. "I don't think so, Sammy. Thanks all the same."

"Come on, everyone's looking for you. It's not every ship's got a grand girl like you mucking in with the crew."

"No, really, I can smell the booze. I'm fifteen! What would Uncle Dan have to say?"

"The old man? You don't think he's sitting up there on his ownsome? He's the life and soul of the party, told us to fetch you." He became more serious. "No need to worry, no one's going to force drink on you. You've got forty dads and brothers on this ship, anyone steps out of line he'd have us to reckon with."

I liked Sammy: "All right, but you'll have to come back in five minutes, I'm not going in there on my own. Tidy myself up and put on a bit of lipstick."

His face lit up. "You're on, darling. I'll get your pal, we need him too." He was gone.

I brushed my hair to a shine. Before she was married gran had trained as a dressmaker and had made me two dresses, bang up to date fashion, in case Uncle Dan took us out to a smart restaurant. I chose the patterned one in case beer got spilled on it, tight-waisted and flared down to my calves. Before the five minutes were up I was ready, clean shoes, my hair held with a clasp, a red rosebud above one ear. Unfortunately my fingers, like the seamen's, were ingrained with dirt and no amount of scrubbing would get it out.

Teddy joined me. Back home at that time, fashion-conscious Teddy-boys wore drape jackets, skinny pants and greased their hair into huge quiffs. Teddy Cohen had nothing but a clean shirt and his best grey trousers. All the same he looked quite stylish, his sandy hair brushed straight up, and I was proud of him as we followed Sammy into the thronging crew mess. Our entrance was greeted with a cheer, sunburned arms gave us hugs. Uncle Dan kissed me on the head: "You look lovely, sweetheart."

It wasn't true, I wasn't born to be a 'lovely' girl, but I'd done my best.

Someone began singing: "Hairy Mary, don't be contrary, give me your answer do…" Voices shut him up.

Room was made for us at a table and Big Lenny appeared with glasses of Coke and slices of cream cake topped with strawberries:

"To go with your red rose, sweetheart. I see you're wearing it above your right ear. You know what that means in the South Seas, you're looking for a boyfriend. Am I in with a chance?"

"Absolutely, " I said. "I thought you would never ask. Except you've got a wife and five children."

"Oh, you don't want to let a little thing like that get in the way," he said.

I laughed and he moved away.

Bottles were emptied and voices grew louder.

A black AB from the West Wind, who must have been drunk when he came aboard, found a seat beside Teddy. "You remind me of my little brother," he said sentimentally and took his hand.

Teddy looked around for help.

"Come on, Ezra." A shipmate led the man away. "You're a nutcase, you are. How can he remind you of your brother?"

"Well he does."

"Rubbish, look at him."

Ezra studied Teddy closely. "What do you mean?"

"He's white!"

"Oh!"

Someone produced a mouth organ and people began singing: It's a long way to Tipperary, You are my Sunshine, We'll Meet Again, rude songs, it didn't matter. Stories of drunken nights in Shanghai, stories of storms, pictures of girlfriends and children. Everyone was happy, everyone was your friend. The party spilled out on deck.

At one o'clock Uncle Dan suggested it was time Teddy and I went to our beds. I lay in the comfortable dark listening to the voices. Music, shouts and laughter rang down the alleyway and out across the sleeping waters of Bergen Bay.

11

Remembering Dad

I don't know what time the party broke up, but when I woke at three and turned over in my bunk, the ship was quiet.

At eight the shore gang came aboard and we began discharging but Uncle Dan sat white-faced in his cabin, hung over and crabbed. "Do what the hell you like, darling, just try not to fall off the jetty or get yourself killed and leave me alone. We'll go ashore after lunch." A bottle of Alka Seltzer stood on the table. He tipped two into his palm and went to the bathroom for water.

At two o'clock, much recovered, he led us ashore. We saw the deep-water U-boat pens that had housed the Nazi submarines which caused such devastation in the north Atlantic during the war and almost brought Britain to its knees. It was likely one of these, Uncle Dan told us, standing on the edge, that had sunk the Boadicea in February 1942 and left him in charge of two lifeboats in a bitter north-easterly gale, eight hundred miles from land.

The city was surrounded by mountains and in the past there had been cable car rides to the summits, but allied bombing and the retreating Germans had destroyed the pylons and they had not been repaired yet.

Yet Bergen was returning to pre-war life: Bryggen, the ancient heart of the city, was gay with paint. We went to the famous fish market and watched sea fish swimming in tanks.

I felt sorry for them and couldn't look when housewives pointed to the ones they wanted and the fishmonger scooped them out with a net and killed them on his slab. Buckets were full of slimy red entrails.

Uncle Dan teased me: "Show me which one you fancy and I'll get Big Lenny to cook it for your tea."

"Oh, don't!"

*

After an hour it was time for ice-cream and we sat in a cobbled square. A blue and white awning shaded us from the sun and a breeze blew from the harbour.

"Enjoy the party?" Uncle Dan rolled a cigarette. "Not too grown-up for you?"

"No, it was great."

"Needed a few girls."

"You and your girls! You were drunk."

"Indeed I was not. What a terrible thing to say to your uncle."

"Not to mention hung over," Teddy said and Uncle Dan cuffed him lightly across the head. "I'm captain here. You watch your mouth or I'll clap you in irons and put you down the chain locker with the rats."

We swapped memories of the night: "Party like that," he told me, "right up your dad's street."

"Yeah?"

"He liked a party did Frank."

"I didn't know that."

"Frank? Oh yes, life and soul. Back home he tried to behave but catch him in a pub with a few pals he was a different man."

"I only knew him when I was little and he worked on the dry dock. Then he went inside and I didn't see him much after that. Mum used to get the bus through to Durham."

"I thought you went."

"Just the once, I got frightened. I was only six or seven and it gave me nightmares, trapped behind bars with all those bad men. I used to wake up screaming."

"Poor you!" He thought about it. "But after he joined the army he must have come home on leave."

"I remember him coming in the door. He seemed enormous and he smelled like soldiers on the buses. After I got used to him he read me bedtime stories and took me to the pictures, but he spent more time in the Anchor than he did with us. Gran never talked about it but he had a woman friend. Brenda, she was called. I found a letter."

"Aye, Brenda. Never one for domesticity, our Frank."

"Seems to run in the family," I said.

"Now, now! No need to get personal. Anyway, his situation and mine were different."

"You were on the run from Aunt Winnie."

"You said it, sweetheart, flat out, but he'd lost your mum. Hit him bad that did."

"I should hope so, she was his wife."

"Yes, but I mean, despite everything he really loved her. And after she'd gone there's him still in jail and you with your gran down there in Wherry Row."

It wasn't the way I remembered my father, mourning in prison. I remembered him as a selfish bastard. He should have thought about mum before he took to burgling. "Hit him bad, did it? He never said, he hardly ever mentioned her."

"Maybe it hurt too much. Anyway, the war was on by then and straight after he got out he had to join up. That's why they released him."

"Gave him enough time to find Brenda."

"He knew her already, she used to visit him in jail. You know, fags and newspapers for the prisoners."

"I never knew that."

"Yeah, so after he got out he went and looked her up. Bit of company."

"He had us."

"It's not the same, sweetheart. Kiss and a cuddle. He couldn't take you and Eva to the Anchor."

"I realise that, I'm not two years old." An old thought returned. "I don't suppose they had any children? I don't have a baby brother tucked away somewhere that I know nothing about?"

"Of course not."

"How do you know?"

"I'd have heard about it. He'd have told me."

"He'd have told you? When would he have told you? He was in the army and you were away at sea."

He shrugged. "In his letters, I suppose."

"So did he write to you? He never wrote to me, except a couple of times and that was all about the war and his pals in the unit. Half of it was blacked out by the censors. We never even knew if he was in this country."

"He'd hardly have told you about Brenda." Uncle Dan stubbed out his cigarette. "Don't be too hard on him, the war took us different directions."

"Yes, well he'd just come out of jail and you won the George Cross." His damaged hand lay on the table. I rubbed my thumb over the stumps of his fingers. "You were a hero."

"Didn't feel heroic at the time, just bloody awful, trying to stay alive." He drew his hand away. "I'm sure other seamen found themselves out there, they'd have done exactly the same thing. We survived somehow, we were lucky."

"That's not what it said in the citation, it was in the papers."

"Aye, well, you don't want to believe everything you read." He didn't like talking about it. "To get back to your dad, when was the last time you saw him?"

"They let him out for a few days when mum died, then he stayed a couple of weeks between prison and the army. It was like having a giant in the house but he was nice. He used to cuddle me and give me rides on his back. but he was hardly ever there. Then he got embarkation leave after they'd been training in Scotland. After that there were just these two letters, then the telegram to tell us he'd been killed."

"So you were what – seven?"

"He brought me a banana, I'd never seen one before. But he was only there a couple of days. Left his kit in the bedroom and swanned off. Gran said he'd been called away but I knew there was something fishy about it. He'd gone to stay with his girlfriend. She was called Brenda."

"She's married now."

"Yeah?"

"Couple of years back."

"How d'you know that?"

"Just the way you do, I haven't seen her or anything Pub talk."

"About my dad?"

"Among other things."

"He was a sod to mum and me, but he did OK in the army, made up to corporal."

"Army give Frank what he needed: plenty of action, bit of discipline, company."

"Gran and I went over to see his grave. You know, after they'd moved him to the war graves cemetery."

"What's it say on the stone?"

"Same as all the others: regimental badge, his name, corporal, aged 33, and the date he was killed. All these white stones, rows of them, hundreds, right up the slope to a line of trees. Beautiful."

"You sent me a photo."

"Different from the shell hole where he was killed."

"Nicer to think about."

My ice-cream was long finished. "I know what I've said about him but he was my dad and that. It would be good if he was buried nearer home then I could put flowers on his grave sometimes."

"Good for you." He chased a beetle with his fingernail.

"Did gran tell you what happened? The major wrote a letter: they were advancing on this wood, the Bois des Sangliers[1], and walked into an ambush. The Germans were dug in, machine guns and heavy shelling. A lot of men got killed. Next day the Germans gave them cease-fire for a couple of hours so the burial parties could go out. Knew it was my dad straight away because his pay book was in his pocket and his initials were on his signet ring. Dog tag round his neck. Major said he was a good corporal, popular with his men, died bravely in the counter-attack."

"I'm sure he did."

"They buried him where he fell. Sent back his wallet and the ring and a few other things. Left the dog tag for when they moved him later. It would be awful if he'd just disappeared, blown to pieces, gone to the camps."

I saw Teddy looking at me. "Sorry, Teddy, like your grampa, yeah?"

"And my aunties, and my cousins."

"Yeah, I'm sorry, but you know what I mean. It was the most terrible thing in the history of the world but you do know what happened, they've got books and memorials and long lists of names. If my dad had vanished without trace we'd never know, keep wondering if one day he'd turn up at the door when he's been dead for years."

Uncle Dan said, "What's brought all this on?"

"I don't know. Just being over here, I think, all the war

---

1 Wood of the Wild Boar.

damage. Ruins everywhere, Amsterdam, here in Bergen. Those ships on the rocks. The U-boat pens. All the bombing. People rounded up and shot. It's everywhere."

"So it is."

"When we went to dad's grave, there's this soldier right next to him, a private in the DLI. He was just seventeen, seventeen and two weeks. There's boys in Teddy's school older than that."

"To some lads it seemed like an adventure, they lied about their age." Uncle Dan gathered up his cigarettes.

"It's just so awful!"

"You don't have to tell me." He rose. "But the war's over, thank God, we've got to look ahead."

"It was you started it." I drank off the milky stuff in the bottom of my dish.

"Me? I didn't start the war. What do they teach you in that school? Hitler invaded Poland."

"Very funny! Ha ha! You said my dad would have liked the party."

"So he would. Come on, Teddy, let's see what other delights Bergen has to offer."

A pretty blonde waitress came to clear the table. Uncle Dan pushed in his chair and gave her a smile. "Thank you." He was a handsome man.

She looked at him and giggled.

"Honestly!" I pulled him away. "You're a disgrace."

"Why, what did I do?"

"You know perfectly well. You're not fit to be let out."

He laughed.

Which made us all laugh.

A young woman with a child and a basket of shopping looked towards us. Uncle Dan gave her a wink.

She smiled and kept walking.

We headed for the harbour where Teddy wanted to

visit a famous castle. It was closed. Like the interesting buildings in the whole of Europe, it seemed, the Bergenhus Fortress had suffered war damage. The Nazis had used it as a headquarters until a ship loaded with two hundred tons of explosives blew up in the harbour. The whole neighbourhood had been flattened. It would take years for the ancient towers to be repaired.

Unsure what to do next, we watched a trawler chug in from the North Sea. The fishermen waved to a cargo ship.

"I've got an idea," Uncle Dan said. "It's time we had a lifeboat drill. How if I organize one for tomorrow? We can take a boat and go fishing."

12

Into the Fjords

It was the best holiday of my life. Did Mary tell you that after Amsterdam and Bergen we sailed on to Trondheim? I would have enjoyed a storm, a real storm this time, with the ship pitching and waves crashing down the foredeck but we had perfect weather, the sun baking hot and snow-capped mountains far-off to starboard. We took off our shirts to work on deck – not Mary obviously – but after an hour I had to cover myself up again because unlike the crew I wasn't used to the sun and would soon have been burned. So I didn't get brown but the cut on the palm of my hand became infected.

"You're a fine one," Mary said, "telling me I'd have to get my leg off when I fell over that bloody pram, now here you are squeezing out the pus."

It was my own fault, I should have taken more care. Uncle Dan, who was responsible for the crew's health, cleaned it up and put on a fresh dressing. It throbbed a bit but wasn't too bad and wearing a clean rubber glove I was able to continue working on deck.

We off-loaded some grain at a small port north of Bergen, little more than a jetty and a few farms carved out of the forest, then sailed on to Trondheim far up the fjords. Uncle Dan showed us round the beautiful, war-damaged city. Even in Norway, we discovered, the Nazis had established concentration camps. There had been over a hundred, including one at Falstad, just a few miles to the north, right up there by the Arctic Circle. Some were further north still. "Poor devils," Uncle Dan said, "but we don't want to brood on those unhappy times, not on your summer holiday. I have a much better idea."

When we got back to the ship we unlashed the tarpaulin from the number one starboard lifeboat which had an engine, and prepared it to spend a whole day exploring remote fjords, right up into the heart of the mountains. We had taken a lifeboat to go fishing in Bergen but this time we filled the tank brim full with petrol, took an extra can, mountains of cakes and sandwiches, flasks of coffee, bottles of squash, and set off directly after breakfast.

Lifeboat equipment has to be kept in tip-top condition as no one knew better than Uncle Dan, but Sammy came with us in case of problems and we needed a second man to row. I couldn't row because of my hand and in any case I had only ever rowed in the park at home but Mary said indignantly, "I can row! I take over from Barry sometimes and row the ferry."

"I know you can, sweetheart," Uncle Dan said. "You rowed last summer and you're very good but we'll take Sammy anyway."

I will never forget that day, sun dancing on the water, shaggy mountains to port and starboard, sailing far up the fjords, not the big fjords where tourists go but little fjords that branched off to the side, nosing between rock walls, ducking beneath branches, then out again into great panoramas where it seemed that no man had ever set foot. A couple of times we tied up to rocks and trees and went ashore. We had brought shorts and climbed the rocks to leap twenty feet into clear, deep water. It was too cold to stay in long so we sat on the baking rocks to eat lunch, skin tingling as the sun dried the icy drops on our shoulders.

There was no hurry to return and it would have been

brilliant if we could have put up tents and camped on the shore, but at length we had to head back. You cannot go anywhere in a hurry in a lifeboat and we took our time, investigating inlets we had not visited on the way up.

A fissure in a rock wall lay directly ahead. "Keep to starboard," Uncle Dan told Mary who had the tiller. We slid through, jagged underwater rocks to port, and emerged into a broad fjord. "See that cottage." He pointed to the far shore. "Head for that, I've promised to give someone a lift."

Although it looked quite close it was over a mile and even in those perfect conditions, with an afternoon breeze at our backs, it took twenty minutes.

"My oldest friend in Norway," Uncle Dan told us.

"Ingrid Johannsen?" Sammy said.

Mary smiled.

"Nothing like that, you vulgar creature," Uncle Dan said. "She's a wonderful old lady. Her husband, Carl Johannsen, was captain when I was a young officer. Taught me everything I know. Retired just before the war. A true patriot. When Germany over-ran the country he joined the Resistance."

He pressed a button and a loud foghorn shattered the peace: Barp! Barp! Barp! "Let her know we're on our way.

"It wasn't just Carl joined the Resistance, Ingrid as well and their son Sven. Hiding out in the mountains and blowing up troop trains and bridges, smuggling allied soldiers out of the country, sailors who'd been torpedoed and made it ashore. Carl and Sven got captured but Sven managed to escape. Carl was tortured and shot. Ingrid became one of the leaders and stepped up the raids. The Germans sent out search squads and put up notices offering a reward for information. No one betrayed them, of course, and she doesn't talk about it but time and again she escaped by the skin of her teeth. A very brave woman. I admire her enormously."

Sammy nodded. "Got a medal, didn't she, from the king?"

"That's right, the War Cross, but she wouldn't accept it, not unless the others got one too."

"Did they?" I said.

"One or two. They were all brave."

A pod of dolphins had appeared and gambolled round the bow.

"What about Sven?" Sammy asked. "Still working on the trawlers?"

"He's got his own now, the Narwhal, doing very well. Due in Trondheim tonight, that's why we're picking up Ingrid. She wants to see him and spend a couple of days with her grandchildren."

"Most Norwegians up this way have got their own boat," Sammy said. "Is that not hers?"

A small boat rocked at a wooden jetty.

"Yes, she sails into town sometimes, does a bit of shopping, but they might come back with her and it's not big enough. She likes a drop of Scotch, there's a couple of bottles in my bag. I need to have a few words with Sven anyway."

I don't know what I expected of this Resistance heroine with a taste for whisky, maybe a lean, brown-faced woman with iron-grey hair chopped short and wearing a pair of men's trousers. But the woman who met us on the jetty was small, plump and pretty with curly blonde hair. She wore a pink tweed skirt and an embroidered blouse.

"Danny!" She wound an arm round his neck and planted a warm kiss on both cheeks.

"Hello, Ingrid. My you're looking well. Must be all the hard work, or have you found yourself a toy boy?"

"Indeed I have not! We're not all like you, you Lothario."

Although she spoke with an accent, her English was perfect. A small suitcase stood on the jetty with a basket of home-made biscuits and fudge for the children. Two goats thrust in their noses. She shouted and they stared up with yellow eyes.

"Are you leaving them loose?"

"They'll be safe enough. Fionn will look after them, won't you my hero?"

A grey Irish wolfhound stood watching. He pressed his whiskery head against her side and she rubbed his neck. "My neighbour will come down to feed him, see everything's all right. Now," she turned to Mary and me. "Yours, Danny?"

"No, and behave yourself. This is Mary, Frank's girl, that I've told you about."

"The clever one, goes to that school?"

"That's right."

"Hello, Mary, I'm pleased to meet you."

"Hello." Mary blushed.

"Your uncle's very proud of you."

"And this is Teddy, he's a friend of hers, goes to the same school."

"Hello, Teddy. My, with that colouring you could be a Norwegian boy."

Suddenly my chest was tight. Already I had been told I could have passed for a German, one of the Hitler Youth. But I wasn't, my grampa and aunties had been taken away. "No," I said. "I'm Jewish."

There was a brief pause then Ingrid said, "Well, you could be both, but proud of your family, good for you. That's what we were fighting for, the right of boys like you to say things like that." To my embarrassment she put a hand round the back of my head and kissed me on the forehead.

"A grand worker," Uncle Dan said. "And this is Sammy, a most excellent member of my crew. His father's with me too, Dennis."

"I think you've mentioned him before, wasn't he in the lifeboat with you? The one who took off your fingers?"

Took off his fingers?

"That's right, he did a grand job."

"Father and son, like my Carl and Sven." Ingrid held out her hand. "My, you're a good-looking fellow. Turn the girls' heads I have no doubt."

"Not a bit of it," Uncle Dan said. "A good-living lad, Sammy, got a steady girlfriend up in Newcastle."

"Lucky girl," Ingrid said. "Now, this is me ready, are we – what's this?"

Uncle Dan had produced the bottles of whisky.

"Oh, Danny! How kind of you! Highland malt, my favourite. Oh, everyone's so good to me. I'll take one for Sven."

"Indeed you will not, he can buy his own. These are for you. Shall I take them up to the house or stash them somewhere?"

The house was a hundred yards up the hillside, a wooden house with a strong, steep roof to support the snows of winter. "I'll put them in the meat safe." She went to a box buried beneath rocks and earth and ferns to keep food cool when it was delivered from town. "No one will touch them."

We took her bags and the old lady stepped briskly aboard. "This is very kind of you, Danny."

"Nothing too good for you, sweetheart." He switched on the engine. "You want the tiller, Teddy?"

Happily I settled myself in the stern. The late afternoon sun blazed down, the calm waters of the fjord parted round our bows, the forested slopes were dotted with houses. Steering was easy and Uncle Dan left me to it until at length, as North Sea Trader came into sight among the other vessels moored in Trondheim Havn, he pointed to a slipway: "Pull in over there."

"No need on my account," Ingrid said. "I'm perfectly capable of climbing a lifeboat ladder."

"I'm sure you are, darling," he said, "but Sammy can take her back, I want to have a word with Sven. And I want you all to come for lunch one day, I'll get Big Lenny to lay on something special."

*

It was a wonderful trip but after three days in Trondheim Uncle Dan got orders to sail on to Tromso up in the Arctic Circle, then round the North Cape to Murmansk in Russia. I should have liked to stay aboard, not gone home until the last day of the holiday, not gone back to school at all, but after twelve days Mary and I had to return to England.

On the last night Uncle Dan said, "It's been good to have you with us, the men like it. If you're free next summer, come again."

The crew threw a party for us, at least it was for us at the start but sailors arrived from other ships and it got a bit boozy. Unexpectedly Uncle Dan gave each of us ten pounds. "You've worked like the crew," he said, "you've got to get your wages or I'll have a mutiny on my hands."

So I left North Sea Trader richer than I arrived, or I would have done but Mary and I walked into town and bought Uncle Dan a terrific troll with wild hair, an ugly face and big hairy feet. "We thought he looked like you," Mary said and he chased her round the deck: "Better not let me catch you, you cheeky witch, or I'll have you keelhauled, string you up to the yardarm, feed you to the sharks!"

"There aren't any sharks."

"We'll rustle some up specially."

But leaving Trader was not the end of our adventures for Sven was giving us a lift to Newcastle. So twelve hours after we had bid a sad farewell to Sammy, Dennis, Big Lenny and all the rest who had become our friends, we found ourselves aboard the Narwhal, watching as the nets were hauled, bulging with two tons of flapping cod, haddock, halibut and every other fish that swam in the depths of the North Sea. A young trawlerman moved into the fo'csle to make room for us and I slept in a bunk above Mary in his tiny, hot, fish-smelling cabin. Sou'westers and oilskins, covered in fish scales, hung in the alleyway.

The crew made us welcome although only Sven and the engineer spoke English. Sven was everything a young Resistance hero should be and he was handsome, or would have been were it not for a scar that crossed his face from his left eyebrow to his jaw caused, we learned later, by a German bayonet during a skirmish in the mountains. His mother had knifed the man, two others were shot along with a Resistance fighter, but the rest escaped with their lives.

A wind got up and the little Narwhal pitched and rolled. Spray rattled on deck and smacked the windows of the bridge. Far from being sick, Mary and I both loved it. There was nothing we could do to help for the gutting knives were very sharp and the work was dangerous, but we joined the crew on deck and watched the screaming gulls fight for the innards as they slopped from the freeing ports and turned the sea red.

When a trawler is in the fishing grounds, work goes on for twenty-four hours a day, so Mary and I rose in the middle of the night as they fished and gutted by floodlight, and joined them in the mess at three in the morning for delicious hash and giant mugs of tea.

The weather worsened to the point that fishing had to be abandoned, so the gear was secured and the Narwhal sailed on into Newcastle. At six-thirty on a wet August morning we tied up at the fish quay .

Dad and my sleepy sister there to meet us. Sadly, for the adventure was over, we said goodbye to Sven and dumped our suitcases in the boot of the car.

"Well," Dad said as we drove away, "I don't need to ask if you've had a good time."

He was right but I was tired. The crew had gone to their bunks but Mary and I, not wishing to miss anything, had stayed up half the night again, watching as the black waves bore down upon us, the lighthouses flashed and the lights of the city came closer, blurred through the streaming windows of the bridge.

"I wouldn't mind a holiday like that myself," Dad said, "up through the fjords and trawling in the North Sea."

We left the quayside and drove up cobbled streets into the city centre. Some were blocked with building work and we had to make a detour. Gaps in the houses, the rubble red with fireweed, showed the bombing in Newcastle to be little different from what I had seen in Amsterdam and Vienna. The shipbuilding yards of the north had been the target for a heavy and sustained blitz by the Luftwaffe.

The roads were almost deserted as we headed south over the Tyne Bridge and out into the rolling English countryside. Mary sat in the front. I sat in the back with Rachel who had woken briefly to greet us as we left the fishing boat and was fast asleep again.

"Well," dad looked at me in the driving mirror. "It's good to have you home."

"Thanks."

"Are you going to tell me about it?"

I leaned back against the upholstery. The cut in my hand gave a little stab. A hundred memories crowded in upon me.

"Later," I said.

But Mary said, "Thanks for coming to pick us up, Mr Cohen."

"You're welcome, Mary love."

"You must have got up very early."

"Rachel too, she insisted on coming. Never forgiven us if we'd left her sleeping." He glanced behind and smiled. "Anyway, it's been a success?"

"Yes, it was brilliant. Have you been to Norway?"

"Once," dad said, "to Oslo, but only for a couple of days, a dental conference."

"We didn't go to Oslo but Uncle Dan took us all over." She shifted to face him. "You know you drove us to Hull? Well, when we got to Rotterdam we couldn't understand a word but Dennis, he's one of the crew, he was waiting at passport with a big placard and he drove us…"

Her words washed over me. I rubbed the steam from the window. It was good to be home.

raspberry jam in the middle and pink icing with hundreds and thousands. I took a bite.

"Is anything else missing? Have you checked?"

"No, nothing, I've been right through the house."

"You'd think he would have taken the wireless, your good necklace." I looked round the room. "That lamp's worth a few bob."

"I just don't know, love. He took the money and that's all."

The cake was delicious. "Was it just you or did he do any of the other houses?"

"Number fourteen, when she was out at the shops, and old Mr Wilson in twenty-three. But they both had windows broken at the back and he took the kind of stuff you can hock."

"Have you told the police?"

"Of course, that nice Constable Banks came round. Apparently there's been a spate, two houses in Jamaica Terrace."

"What about the insurance?"

"I've written but there hasn't been time. I'm that annoyed! Josephs have got a sale on and I wanted to buy you a new wardrobe."

"It doesn't matter, Gran, I love my old one." I took her hand and felt the frail, bird-like bones."

"That cracked mirror."

"Adds a bit of character. Better than some shiny new piece from a showroom."

"You're that good, Mary. But I'll tell you what!" She sat up and showed her old fighting spirit. "He'd better hope the police catch a hold of him first because if I do I'll…"

"Bash his head in with the frying pan," I suggested.

"Something like that," she said and we both laughed.

*

Two days later a letter came from the Eastport Chronicle telling me that my story had been included in a short list of seven. I showed it to gran, who had finished her housework and was taking out the flour to bake scones. She was delighted for me but said, "I thought you were going to brush the yard and scrub out the lavatory, that's if you can get your head through the back door." I laughed and kissed her on the cheek.

An hour later, waiting for the scones to cool, we were sitting at the table playing chess – gran used to play in tournaments and was coaching me – when there was a knock at the door. It was Teddy who had come down with photographs from the trip. He had asked the chemist for two sets of prints and gave one to me. I moved the chess board aside and we gathered round. Memories came crowding back: there were the crew and the locks at Ijmuiden, Teddy on the wheel, the fish market in Bergen, the parties, Sammy leaping into the fjord, the trawlermen gutting fish, spray exploding from the bow, and all the rest of it. It was like living the trip all over again.

"Well," gran said as we came to the end, "I wouldn't mind doing that myself. Don't see why you young folk should have all the fun."

"You should ask Uncle Dan," Teddy said.

"You think so? Somewhere warm, southern Italy, Africa. Yes, that would be very nice." She tested the scones and put on the kettle. "Leave the winter behind."

"Gran's been burgled," I told Teddy. "While we were away, all her savings."

He was startled.

"No sign of a break-in. People along the street as well."

"Hey, so were we. Only some clothes off the line but neighbours had windows smashed. Things that could be sold: silver, radios, binoculars. During the day while people were at their work. Just down from us, old Mr Maltby was ill in bed and heard him. Chased him through the garden but he got away."

"What did the police say?"

"Only that there had been a rash of break-ins. We told them about the man in the barn but he seemed a nice chap. Dad felt sorry for him and gave him some money."

"Gran's furious, going to kill him, she says."

A voice came from the sink. "No I did not."

"Bash his head in," you said. "Same thing."

"Deserves it, the rotter, stealing from people that have worked hard all their lives. He should get himself down to the Labour Exchange. Plenty of work with all the construction."

Gran had worked hard all her life and had no time for slackers. My grandad had been an architect. In the First World War he was an infantry captain, killed in the mud of Passchendaele, leaving gran with two children, my mum not much more than a baby and an older boy called Brian. Grandad's name, Arthur Leonard Fawcett, was engraved on the First World War memorial in the square outside St Matthew's, just as my dad's name, Frank Edward Pearson, was engraved on the memorial for men killed in action during the Second World War. When Brian was six he died of meningitis and although gran never spoke about it, I know it broke her heart. His picture, along with that of her young husband and my mum, stood in silver frames on the chest of drawers in her bedroom. So gran, having no money and living in a rented house, brought my mum up on her own, working as a secretary in the Town Hall and hurrying home every night to look after her. She had a hard time but all was well until mum was eighteen when one night after a dance she fell for the careless charms of my dad and found herself expecting a baby. Gran had no time for my dad, especially when my mum, who had dreamed of going to university and becoming a history teacher, had to settle for being the wife of a feckless shipyard worker. Sometimes, when dad had drunk the housekeeping money, mum worked as a cleaner in Charlton's, the store down Port Street. Then he lost his job for thieving, as I've told you, got into bad company and was sent to jail for burglary. When the Second World War came along, mum wanted to do her bit and went to work in the munitions factory where she was killed in that big explosion, so gran lost both her children. Dad redeemed himself by becoming a soldier who rose to corporal then he, too, was killed, so I became an orphan and gran was left with another girl to bring up on her own. My dad's photo did not stand in gran's bedroom but it stood in mine, a handsome young soldier beside his wife, my pretty mum, much prettier than great big me with my strong arms and thick legs.

Teddy couldn't stay for lunch, so gran put some scones into a bag and I walked him up into town to catch the bus home.

14

Day at the Beach

It was the last week of the summer holiday. I'd had a wonderful time, why did it have to end?

On Tuesday, making the most of the last few days, I met some boys from school and we took a tram to the beach which was the end of the line. There had been rain but now the sun had returned and we spent all day swimming and exploring, kicking a ball about, eating sandwiches, buying ice creams and generally mucking about. By four o'clock, although we had put on shirts, our legs were getting sunburned and it was time to go home anyway. So after a rinse under the freshwater showers, we went to a quiet place and wrapped towels round our waists to change.

A ramp led to the lower promenade, then a long flight of steps, known locally as the Goat Steps, led to the upper promenade with its footpaths and lawns and bandstand. Halfway up I happened to look down and saw Mary at the table by the deck chairs. I wondered why because she wasn't normally there on a Tuesday. She looked lonely although I am sure she was not because as always, she was deeply engrossed in a book. I didn't stare but she looked nice in a blue print dress with short sleeves, a straw hat and sunglasses.

Gerry, who is a bit of a loudmouth said, "What are you looking at?"

"Nothing," I said, for I knew what the others would say, even though I'd told them about Norway: "Woo-ooo! That your girlfriend?...Big, in't she?...Where'd you meet *her*?"

They were good pals but having seen Mary I wanted to go back. As we reached the top I felt in my pocket. I knew I had money but wasn't sure how much.

"I'm going to leave you now," I said. "Got to do some shopping."

They stopped. "You never said."

"Yeah, I forgot. It's my mum's birthday on Friday, I've got to buy her a present."

"Where are you going to get a present down here?"

I looked along the front: "Kean's." It was a shop that sold women's things, scarves, perfume, handbags, catch the tourist trade.

"I thought you hadn't got much money."

"I don't have to buy it today," I said. "I'll come back if I see something." It was an obvious lie and I felt myself blushing.

They looked at me.

"I'm not going into Kean's." Gerry said. "It's full of women's underclothes and stuff."

"That's cos you're such a kid. See you anyway," I started across the road. "Give you a ring."

As I reached the pavement I looked back and they stood watching. I raised a hand and turned into Kean's with a sense of dread. Gerry knew more about it than I did because dummies were dressed in bra's and pants, others wore jackets and skirts. High-heeled shoes stood on stands, the air smelled of cheap perfume. I guessed it was cheap because it smelled horrible and if my mum was going out she smelled lovely.

"Can I help you?" An assistant made me jump. She was a fat girl with false eyelashes, one eye hidden by bleached Veronica Lake hair. She wore shop uniform, a tight black skirt with a black, white and green blouse.

"No, I was just going to have a look. It's my mum's birthday."

"What sort of thing are you looking for?"

In acute embarrassment I tried not to look at the dummies. A glass case contained necklaces: blue stones, green stones, silver and gilt.

"Something like this?" She opened the case and took one out. My mum would not have worn it in a million years.

"Yes," I lied. "That's nice."

She turned it to catch the light, her fat little fingers adorned with rings.

"How much is it?"

She examined the label. "Eight pounds, five shillings."

"Oh, um…" Beyond the window I saw that my friends had gone. I grasped my towel firmly. "The green one, is that the same price?"

As she turned to the case I fled, out the door and into an alley alongside. It was a cul-de-sac, I was trapped. Holding my breath, I stood among the dustbins.

When she failed to appear, I crept back to the pavement. No sign of the shop assistant but I could outrun her. More important, no sign of my friends either. Greatly relieved, I felt in my pocket. Rinaldi's was only a few shops along. Mary had looked so lonely I wanted to buy her an ice-cream and take it down to the promenade. Carefully I counted my coins. There was enough for one ice-cream and the bus home, or two ice-creams and a long walk. I decided it would be better to buy two ice-creams so she wouldn't think I was short of money. So I went into Rinaldi's, not in my trunks this time, and stood at the ice-cream counter.

"Hello, love. Third time today isn't it? You must be made of money." She opened the lid of the freeze box and a swirl of cold air rose into her face.

"Two, please." I pointed to the small cones. "Vanilla and strawberry."

"My, you like your ice-cream." She dug her scoop into the rock-hard vanilla. "Pals not with you this time?"

"They had to go home."

I had miscounted, I was a halfpenny short but the woman let me off: "We'll not go broke for a halfpenny, love. You enjoy your ice-creams – or is one for somebody else?"

"Thank you." I didn't reply and hurried from the shop.

The sun seemed hotter than ever. Shielding the ice-creams, I hurried across the road and ran down the long flight of steps to the lower promenade. Mary sat as I had seen her:

"Oh, hi, Teddy" Her eyes brightened. "Is one of those for me?"

"Which one do you want?"

She considered. "Strawberry." Her tongue caught the pink trickles. "Lovely! Just what I wanted." She smiled mischievously. "Does this mean I'm your girlfriend?"

What should I say? "I just thought you'd like an ice-cream. Sitting down here in the sun."

"And so I do."

She shifted her heels from a chair and I sat down. "What are you doing here on a Tuesday? I thought it was only Saturday when what's-his-name goes to the match."

"Archie," she said. "Any time he's away if I can. His granddaughter got her tonsils out yesterday, I'm doing a couple of hours so he can pay her a visit. Back around five." She glanced around. "Down here by yourself?"

"No, I came with some friends, they're away home. I stayed on a bit."

"And bought me an ice-cream. Thanks."

My eyes fell on her book, a huge stately home on the cover. "What's this you're reading now?"

"Brideshead Revisited, it's terrific. All about this rich, titled family that's falling apart. She marked the page with a tram ticket. "I wish I could write like that."

"What do you mean? You're in the what-do-you-call-it for the competition."

"The short list. Thanks, but it's not the same thing."

"Nonsense," I said and read the author's name. "Evelyn Waugh, when you're her age I'm sure you'll write much better."

She didn't tell me that Evelyn was a man. "Anyhow, you always ask what I'm reading, what about you?"

A fat man brought two chairs back and Mary returned his deposit.

She had shamed me from Biggles which I still liked best. "The Thirty-Nine Steps and a book about building your own radio. I've made a crystal set."

"Good for you, I couldn't do that in a month of Sundays. Does it work?"

It wasn't true, Mary could do anything I could, but it was nice of her. "Yes it works," I said, "but you have to be careful with the cat's whisker. Get it exact and you can hear perfectly, move it a tiny bit and you've lost the whole thing. Last night I listened to—"

"Hey, lover-boy!" A voice like a crow reached us from the top promenade. "Did you get your mum's birthday present?"

I looked up and saw them hanging over the safety rail. "This your girlfriend? This the one you went to *Norway* with?"

"Big, in't she!"

Gerry blew a kiss and they fell about laughing.

I was embarrassed but if he had expected Mary to be put out he was mistaken: "Cheeky oik! They your friends?"

"Yeah. Not him so much but he's all right."

She laughed and blew a kiss in return. "Come down here they can give us a hand."

"A hand?"

"Put the deck chairs away. Leave them out all night, there'd be none left." She beckoned for the boys to join us.

"Where d'they go?"

"The chairs?" She pointed to heavy green doors in the back wall of the promenade. "Save Archie the bother. They can collect any left on the beach."

"You got a key?"

She patted a big iron key hanging at her waist and beckoned again. The boys were uncertain.

"Come on," she shouted. "Scared we're going to beat you up?"

They talked about it. While we were waiting she opened the doors, revealing a huge gloomy space with pillars and dark recesses like the vault of a church. The floor was strewn with sand and grit. Racks of deck chairs stood at the near end.

"Come and see this." A torch lay on an old black frame. Nibbling the cone of her ice-cream, she led the way into the shadows.

My eyes hadn't adjusted and I bumped into a pillar.

"There." Mary shone the torch at the top of a wall.

Gradually I made out a mass of fuzzy shapes hanging from the ceiling.

"Bats," she said. There were dozens, hundreds. "Come down at night you'll see them flying round the street lamps."

I had seen bats flitting round the trees on Strawberry Hill but never sleeping or in such numbers. I had seen their droppings, too, on top of the car. For a long time I thought they were mouse droppings and wondered how they'd got up there, but here the ground rustled under my shoes and the air smelled musty.

Mary shone the torch down. It wasn't offensive, just like fine dry soil. "The insects come and eat it up," she said.

For a minute we watched them. The bats didn't like it, shivering their silky wings, turning their little heads this way and that.

"I've walked past a hundred times," I said, "but I never even thought of anything like that."

"Why would you," she said, "everybody sunbathing and splashing in the sea?"

"It's another world."

"So it is," she said and had obviously been thinking about it. "We all live in different worlds."

"Like foxes," I said, remembering a vixen and cubs I had seen in the garden. "Or those insects."

"Not just animals, people," she said. "While we're down here, Archie's granddaughter's lying in hospital, women are working in factories. your dad's drilling teeth in his surgery."

It had never occurred to me. "Uncle Dan and the crew over in Russia," I said.

"People in Africa living in grass huts."

"People in concentration camps when we were at school."

"My dad in France."

As we emerged the sunlight hurt my eyes. People were waiting to return their deck chairs. "Sorry," Mary handed back their deposits, "we had to go into the shed for a minute."

"That's all right darling, you're doing a grand job." A couple of men gave her a tip.

My friends had arrived and stood by the table. They weren't used to talking to girls.

"Hello," Mary said. "What's your names.?"

` They introduced themselves.

"Which one of you blew me a kiss?"

"Me," Gerry said.

"Cocky little sod aren't you?" she said and took my hand. "But I'm sorry, I've already got a boyfriend, you'll have to find a girl of your own. Handsome chap like you, shouldn't be a problem."

She was right, Gerry was good-looking. He was pleased.

"Right then," she said. "Are you going to give us a hand? All these chairs got to be stacked away in the shed. And those left on the beach got to be brought back. I'll give you sixpence for each one." This was generous but it still left her with sixpence profit. More important from my point of view, it meant they wouldn't tease me when we got back to school.

"Make a good job of it, I'll show you the bats."

15

The Soldier's Return

The long summer holiday came to an end and on Monday, 6th September, we went back to school. I was now in the Upper Fifth, last stop before sixth form. Later that year I would sit my School Certificate but long before that, in a mere six weeks, I was due on stage for the first night of Julius Caesar. It was a big production, there was a lot to do. Rehearsals resumed at four o'clock the very next afternoon.

The scenes Mrs Jamison had pencilled in for that day involved Brutus, so I had to stay until the end which meant I didn't get home until six. The second I opened the door I smelled cigarettes and when I went into the living room I discovered that gran wasn't there and a man was standing by the fire. I recognised him instantly, even though I hadn't seen him for four years.

His photo stood in my bedroom.

It was my dad.

I got such a shock that for a moment I felt dizzy and had to sit down.

But my first words as I recovered were not, 'Where the hell have *you* been?' or 'We thought you were dead.'

"Where's gran?" I said.

Even after four years his voice was familiar: "Not got a word for your poor old dad?"

"No, I haven't," I said, surprised at the bitterness in my own voice. "Where's gran?"

"She got a bit of a shock," he said. "The woman two doors down phoned the ambulance. They've taken her into hospital."

"Hospital!" I sprang to my feet. "How is she? I'm going to see her!"

"No, love, don't rush out."

"Take your hands off me! You bastard! How is she?"

He stood back. "She's OK, I think. Just got a bit of a shock seeing me. I never thought that would happen."

"You never thought – ? What did you expect to happen, turning up here like a ghost? She thought you were dead! Think she'd have the kettle on just in case you rose from your grave and came visiting?"

"I don't think she's bad. They just want to keep an eye on her."

In a whirlwind I ran to my bedroom and threw off my blazer. There was a jacket on a hanger and a scatter of coins in a drawer. I grabbed a handful and was starting back when I paused. If gran had been taken into hospital as an emergency, she wouldn't have her personal possessions. A small suitcase lay on top of her wardrobe. Quickly I threw in some things she might need and hurried back to the living room.

"Don't you want to – ?"

"When I come back," I said. "Which hospital?"

"Royal Infirmary."

"I don't suppose you know which ward."

"Sorry."

"I should bloody well hope so."

Standing there in an ill-fitting jacket and crumpled trousers he seemed beaten. As I hurried past he caught at my sleeve. "Don't tell anyone."

"I wrenched my arm away. "What?"

"That I'm here."

"How do you mean?"

"You and Eva, you're the only ones know."

"What about Mrs Jennings?"

"Two doors down? She's new, I told her I'd come to look at the sink."

"And the hospital?"

"Called myself Mr Harrison."

"Oh, for God's sake!"

"If you spread it around there'll all sorts of trouble."

I stared at him. "Nothing's changed, has it? Five minutes back and you're dodging the police, using an alias, dragging me and gran into it. Well, whatever you've done I don't want to know about it. All right? I don't bloody well care."

The door banged behind me.

"Everything all right, love?" Mrs Fentiman called across the road.

"Yes, fine," I said. "Gran's had a bit of a turn, she asked for a few things."

"Only I saw the ambulance."

"Yes, but she's all right." Nosy cow! "Excuse me, I've got to run."

"There was this man with her."

"My uncle, he'd come to look at the sink. I've really got to go."

As I ran up the road I could feel her mean little eyes following me, her mean little mind trying to work it out.

*

Ward 14 was on the first floor. Gran lay on the right, second from the far end in a ward of sixteen women. She looked small and frail in a hospital nightgown that was too big for her. Her name, Eva Mary Fawcett, was chalked on a board behind her head. Her hair was loose, her false teeth stood in a glass of water. Hospital charts, hidden from gran but ready for nurses, hung at the foot of the bed. Her eyes opened at my footsteps.

"Oh, hello, Mary, love."

"Hello, Gran." I kissed her cheek and fetched a chair.

"This is a turn-up for the books, eh?"

"How do you feel?"

"I'll live. Put off the four-minute mile till tomorrow. Tell you what, though, I'd feel a lot better with my teeth in."

"But when did he turn up?" I asked a while later.

"About half two. I'd washed the dinner dishes and was just having forty winks when there's a tap at the front door. I thought about leaving it because I'd had a busy morning but anyway, there he was in a jacket and trousers looked like he'd got them out the bin lorry, smiling that smile of his – you know, 'sorry but I'm good at heart and you'll forgive me won't you?' I know he's your dad, love, and I don't want to speak ill, but it makes me want to slap his face. I got such a shock I nearly passed out. I mean, we were officially told he'd been killed, we went to his grave, now here he is back from the dead. If he hadn't stepped in smartish and caught me, I'd have landed on the floor. Anyway, fair do's, he helped me to a chair and made a cup of tea."

"He smelled," I said. "Dirty."

"He certainly did, very ripe. Been sleeping rough, I reckon."

"He could have had a bath at the swimming pool, only costs sixpence or a bob."

"I suppose. Still, that's easy put right, as long as he's got no sores or infection."

I thought about it, this was my dad. "But what's he doing here? Is he a deserter?"

"I don't know, love, we didn't have time, but I should think so, don't you?"

I had read a piece in the Telegraph about gangs of

deserters, British, Russians, Poles, Germans, roaming the streets of Naples and Berlin. They were crooks, many armed and violent, hundreds of men cast adrift in the ruins of war-torn Europe. If they were soldiers they wouldn't be shot for desertion, as men had been in the First World War, but they would be taken to court and probably end up in jail. Even if they were suffering from shell-shock, men who had fought on and lost comrades, the families of dead soldiers, men in pubs, would not be sympathetic. So they stayed away, wives and children never knowing if they were alive or dead. Except my dad, of course, everyone thought he *was* dead.

"Do you think he's one of them?"

"I don't know, love. Like I said, we didn't get to talk about it, I got such a shock just seeing him there. Not like me but we'd been to his grave and everything. Next thing I'm sitting in a chair, there's ambulance men all over and they're bringing me in here. He might have said something, I don't know. You'll have to ask him."

"He told me not to tell anyone."

"That sounds about right."

"Do you think he'll be staying?"

She arranged her blanket. "I suppose he might for a while unless he's got other plans."

"He can't go back to Brenda anyway," I said. "She's married."

"How do you know that?"

"Uncle Dan told me."

"Well, goodness knows. Maybe he'll take up with some other woman. Apart from the stubble and smelly clothes, he's still a good-looking man."

A nurse came round with a tea-trolley. "Thanks, dear," gran said. "Just what the doctor ordered. Can I have one of the custard creams?" As the nurse was heading to the next bed gran called her back. "It's a bit of a cheek but do you think you could run to a cup and a biscuit for my granddaughter here? A bit of a kerfuffle at home, she's had no tea."

The nurse eyed me. "Yes, sure. Here you are, darling. Do you take sugar?" She passed the biscuits. "Go on, take two."

We sipped and nibbled then gran said, "I don't like to say, Mary, he's your dad, but I've been lying here with nothing much else to occupy my mind. I think we can have a pretty good guess where the money went."

Although I had been in a bit of a panic, I'd had the same thought myself. Not just gran's savings but the neighbours. It fitted perfectly: he knew where she kept the spare key, the others had had their windows broken, he had spent time in jail for burglary.

"What are we supposed to do?" I said.

"You tell me, love."

"We can't shop him."

"No, we can't, I'm sure he realises that. I think the best thing's do nothing, not for a few days, see how it works out. He can sleep on the settee, I'm not having you give up your room."

"Do you know how long you're likely to be in?"

"Home tomorrow, I should think. Or the next day. It was just a little turn."

*

But gran wasn't home the next day, or the day after. My dad's return had given her a bigger shock than she realised and the doctors discovered a deep-seated infection in her lungs. She'd had a bit of a cough for several weeks: "It's nothing, love, just a summer cold." But it was more than that and triggered by the shock and perhaps the unaccustomed stay in bed, the infection flared up and gran, who was always so fit and energetic, the linchpin of my life, developed a fever. For ten days she was a sick old lady.

Visiting hours were from seven until eight and I went in every evening. One day a woman from the council called me into an office:

"Mary, isn't it?" she said. "How are you getting along?"

"Fine."

She shuffled some papers and found mine. "Just the two of you, is that right?"

"Yes."

"Does this mean you're living on your own now?"

"No," I said. "My uncle's with me. He brought gran in, remember. And we've got good neighbours. Anyway, I'm fifteen, I can look after myself."

And with me being so big and capable, and so many children needing care and housing after the war, she was glad to leave me alone.

"Just give us a call if you need anything," she said.

"Thank you," I said, thinking I'd rather live on crusts and water for a month than have the council interfere in my life.

*

Before I got home that first day dad had taken a bath, sitting before the fire in the zinc tub we had used for as long as I could remember. His clothes were so dirty he had bundled them into a ball and left them in the shed where gran did the washing. Since he could hardly be naked when his daughter came home, he had pulled on my brown dressing gown. I have told you I am big, the biggest girl in my class, but I am not as big as a sturdy six-foot tall man and I hated to see his hairy chest, his strong wrists protruding from the sleeves and his big white knees where the front had fallen open. He had washed his hair but his cheeks were scruffy with stubble.

He gave me some money and I went to the Mission to Seamen down at the docks. I knew Steve who ran it, a young fellow with an eye-patch and clumsy artificial foot who had been blown up in a destroyer on the Malta convoy in 1942. He found me trousers, a shirt, shoes and other clothes in slops, and sold me a razor and shaving soap. I told him my Uncle Jack had turned up unexpectedly and was in a bit of a mess. Steve was a great chap who did everything he could to help and didn't ask questions.

When I got back, dad had the potatoes on. A pot of stew gran had made that morning filled the room with mouth-watering odours. This was a treat she couldn't make often because it took most of our meat coupons for an entire week. Two bottles of beer which dad had brought with him stood on the table.

"Keep an eye on the stew, pet," he said and went through the house to get dressed. The clothes from the Mission were crumpled, threads pulled in the jersey, the trousers too short, but they were clean and at least he no longer smelled.

"I'll have a shave later. You're a good girl." He went to give me a dad's kiss but I pulled aside. I could see he was hurt but I didn't care.

Dinner was delicious I only had a small helping because I wanted to keep some for gran when she came home, which at that time I hoped would be the next day. Not so my dad who devoured two platefuls and when he had finished wiped round the empty stew pot with a crust of bread. "I know, darling," he said, "but I was starving. I'll rustle up something tasty for Eva in the morning."

That night he slept on the settee but the next day, when I heard that gran wouldn't be coming home for a while, he moved into her bedroom. Her treasured photos went into a drawer along with some pretty embroidered mats and were replaced by worn socks, fags, a lurid paperback and empty teacups. It was horrid, smelling his ashtray after gran's lavender, hearing him snore if I woke during the night, and the couple of times I looked into the room before going to school, seeing his big male head on the pillow instead of gran's white curls.

He never went out, not to start with, terrified that neighbours and men he had known in the past would recognise him.

It was on the second evening, after I had come home from the hospital, that he told me what had happened in France.

16

Uncle Jack

I was eating breakfast when the phone rang. Mum took it in the hall. It was Mary: "Hello, Teddy? Look, I'm afraid I won't be able to come tonight."

"Oh, that's a pity."

"Will you tell Rachel I'm sorry."

It was my sister's birthday and she wanted Mary to see her hamster, Toffee, in the terrific cage my dad had made. After tea we were planning to play Cluedo.

"We were looking forward to it," I said. "Has something happened?"

"Gran's been taken into hospital. I'm going to visit her."

"Has she had an accident?"

"No, it's a chest infection but they're keeping her in for a day or two."

"I didn't know she was ill."

"It came on suddenly."

"Is she bad?"

"I hope not."

"Golly! Well give her my best wishes."

"I will."

"That means you'll be on your own down there."

"I'll be fine."

"Is there anything we can do?"

"Not really thanks. Look, I've got to run or I'll miss the bus. Bye."

The receiver clicked. I stood for a moment then went back to my cereals.

Rachel was disappointed.

Mum was concerned: "I hope her grandmother's not seriously ill. She sounded upset."

"She did a bit. What time's visiting?"

"Seven, isn't it?"

"So she'll have to go home after school. Shall I go down?"

"If you like, Teddy, that would be kind of you. Have you got bus money?"

I felt in my pockets and she gave me two shillings. "I'm not sure what's for tea but if it's hot I'll keep something back."

So when the school bell rang at four, I ran to the bus stop with the rest of the boys and caught the bus into town. It was a ten-minute walk to the Waterman's Arms down by the docks then a right turn into Wherry Row. Mary's house, as ever, was bright as paint with fresh curtains in the windows, autumn flowers in the garden and the front path spotless. I turned through the gate and stopped in my tracks. There was a man in the front room. I only saw him for a second because he was hidden by window dazzle and disappeared into the hall, but he didn't look like a visitor because he was in his shirt sleeves. I stood with my hand on the gate post. Who could it be? Mary had said nothing. Uncle Dan's ship wasn't in port. Should I just go away? I decided against it and continued to the front door where there was a polished brass replica of the lion's head knocker at Durham Cathedral. My *rat-tat* sounded shockingly loud in the silence of the street. For a long time no one answered although I heard movement, then the door opened to reveal Mary looking very hot and bothered.

She was startled to see me and glanced anxiously over her shoulder. "Oh, hello, er, Teddy." Far from inviting me in, she filled the gap and after a moment's hesitation joined me outside and pulled the door shut. Her hair was untidy, she looked upset. "You've not come down this time before."

"No, but you said your gran's ill and we wanted to know how she's keeping, if there's anything we can do."

"Thanks but not right now. Something gave her a bit of a shock and she took a turn. Then this infection flared up in her chest. But they've got her on that penicillin you read about and they say she's going to be OK. I'm going up after tea."

She looked back at the door. "Sorry I can't invite you in but I've got this mound of homework and I'm just making something to eat."

It was obviously a lie and she blinked as if to hold back tears.

"Come on, Mary," I said, "this is Teddy. What's it all about?"

"How do you mean?"

"What's wrong?"

She rubbed her eyes with a knuckle. "I can't tell you."

"Yes you can, you can tell me anything. I saw him."

"Who?"

"The man, he was in the front room. Who is he?"

She drew a shaky breath. "My Uncle Jack."

"Uncle Jack?"

"I'm not supposed to tell anyone, he's in a bit of trouble. Staying a few days until the fuss dies down."

"You've never mentioned him. I thought Uncle Dan was your only relation, apart from your gran, of course."

"He's not my full uncle only a half uncle. We haven't heard from him in years."

"Is he the one gave your gran a shock?"

She nodded, glad I accepted it so readily. "Don't tell anyone."

"Of course I won't tell anyone, not if you don't want me to. What's he done?"

"I'd rather not tell you." A tear which had been trembling on her eyelashes spilled down her cheek.

Until then I had looked on Mary as a friend, a special friend and a girl of course, but like my best pals at school. Now she broke my heart. I wanted to hug her and tell her that everything would be all right.

"Are you OK? Mum says would you like come and stay with us? I suppose not if you've got your uncle here."

"I'll be fine." She sniffed and rubbed her eyes. "Sorry, Teddy, I've got to go. Will you tell her thanks. I'll see you soon." She started towards the house then turned back and kissed me quickly on the cheek. Next second her hand was on the door.

"Bye." As she stepped into the hall I heard a sob then she was gone.

I stood frozen, first by the kiss then the rank awfulness of whatever seemed to have happened. For a time I stared at the green door and the curtains of the front room then returned to the pavement. What on earth could I do? In a turmoil I walked to the end of the street. It was a poor street of small terraced houses. Many were shabby, dead grass and weed in the gardens, litter in some. A little boy in a vest and no pants played in the gutter. Mary's house was one of the few whose owners took pride in their appearance. All this I saw but scarcely registered, my thoughts full of what I had just heard.

I was about to turn into High Street East when there was a shout at my back: "Teddy! Teddy!" Mary came running after me. "Oh, Teddy!" Gone was the clever, courageous, outgoing Mary I knew. Her hair was tangled, her eyes red with weeping. "I'm so sorry!" She felt for a hankie, didn't find one and scrubbed her nose with a wrist.

"It's OK," I put an arm round her shoulders. "Sshhh! It's all right."

"No, it's not all right. It's anything but all right. I've been lying to you and I can't bear it!" She looked into my face. "Can you come down tomorrow morning? Or I'll come up. No, you come down. Your mum's lovely but she'll want to talk about it. I just want to tell you."

I didn't need to think, this was Friday, the end of the school week. "Not tomorrow, not in the morning anyway, we go to the synagogue. It's the one thing dad insists on. I could come in the afternoon."

"That'll do, thanks. We'll go for a walk."

I looked her in the face. "Are you all right? I can see there's something wrong but are *you* all right? You've not been hurt?"

"No, it's nothing like that but I'm *so* sorry. About two o'clock?"

"Yes, sure."

"Thanks." She managed a smile. "See you then."

I took her hand. "Is it OK if I tell mum and dad?"

"Yes, of course. I've not done anything wrong, I just don't want to meet them, not right now."

Halfway up the street a woman stood looking towards us. Another woman watched from behind the curtain. Mary waggled her fingers. "Mrs McConnell, nosy cow!"

"They'll be wondering what it's about."

"They certainly will." Her eyes twinkled, the old Mary making a brief appearance. "I'll tell them I've got a bun in the oven."

I was shocked.

"Oh, come on, Teddy, there's a girl younger than me had a baby in Cotton Close just a few months back. Give them something to talk about. How do you feel about being a dad?"

"But you're not going to have a baby."

"Say it was a false alarm."

She had taken my breath away. Then for the benefit of Mrs McConnell she kissed me again, on the lips this time.

"Thanks for coming." In better spirits she turned back along the pavement. "See you tomorrow."

As I walked up into town my feelings were a riot. She had said she kissed me for the benefit of her neighbour. It had been very nice and filled me with a hundred sensations, but if it was because she liked me as a boy, I was out of my depth. A dad? I wasn't sure I was even ready for a girlfriend.

*

I wore gym shoes because I thought we might walk on the beach, and old grey trousers in case we went for a paddle. Apart from my best Saturday trousers and my school trousers they were all I had.

Mum looked at me critically: "What a rate you're growing, Teddy, you're showing two inches of sock there. It only seems like yesterday those trousers were hanging over your shoes."

"Are they OK? Do I look stupid?"

"Of course not. You look like a handsome boy who's growing up fast."

Handsome? She'd never said that before.

"Be sure to tell Mary we're thinking about her and any time she wants to come up here she'll be very welcome." Mum had baked rock cakes and set a bagful on the table. "I'm sure they'll not go amiss. Do you suppose this Uncle Jack's expecting her to cook for him?"

"I've no idea."

"She's got enough on her plate already."

"Maybe I'll find out." I had said nothing about the kiss, it wasn't the sort of thing you tell your mother. "She was in a terrible state. Whatever's going on it's not right."

"Well, I hope it's not as bad as you think. And remember, dad and I are always here if she needs a hand."

*

As I turned into Wherry Row on Saturday afternoon, that was the thought that ran through my head, that and the confused memory of her kiss. Mary was looking for me and before I could knock she came trotting down the steps with a smile.

"Hi."

"Mum sent these." I held out the bag.

"Thanks. Oh, rock cakes, terrific. She made them before." She took one, gave one to me, dropped a couple into a bag and left the rest on a chair. "That's me away," she called through the house. "Back around teatime. I'll try not to be late."

The door shut and we set off down the pavement. No faces appeared at the windows so we didn't hold hands. I was relieved although the memory of Mary's soft lips had remained with me, as had the scarcely believable thought that one day I might become a dad.

"I thought we could take the ferry and walk out the North Pier," she said.

"Wherever you like, I've only been once since they took down the barbed wire."

"Or get a couple of deck chairs from Archie."

"You're not on today?"

"They're playing away."

We walked through streets whose names were a record of Eastport's trading history – Flour Lane, Trinidad Street, Chandler's Row – and emerged at a chain link fence beyond which lay the cobbles, warehouses and rail wagons of the South Dock. Work had stopped for the weekend. The cranes and derricks stood motionless apart from the sway of cargo hooks in the breeze. The only people in sight were a group of seamen leaning on a rail and a watchman at the door of his shed. Seagulls hunted the ground for scraps and quarrelled over a perch at the head of a crane.

Mary knew the watchman. "Hello, George."

"Hello, there, Mary pet. Heading for the beach?"

"Something like that."
"You enjoy yourself. How's that gran of yours?"
"Fine, thanks. I'll tell her you were asking."

*

The ferryman's hut, like his hut on the North Quay, stood by a flight of stone steps that descended to the river. Two ocean-going ships, the Marguerite and Polish Princess, were moored above and below, squeezing it in like an orange pip. We stepped over mooring ropes and saw Barry, the ferryman, mid-river and rowing towards us with two passengers in the stern. It was high tide again, the brown water high up the harbour walls and stirring uncertainly with deep swirls and hidden currents. At ebb tide when the river was emptying, the current ran swiftly. I remembered standing with mum and Rachel, throwing sticks into the water and running to keep up.

The breeze blew Barry's white hair; his passengers covered their chests although it was not cold. Soon the little ferry was drifting up to the steps and Mary ran down to catch the painter. Carefully Barry handed his passengers ashore and followed them up to the quay.

Hello, Mary darling. Where are you and the boyfriend off to this time?"

She didn't correct him. "I thought we'd go out to the lighthouse."

"Perfect day for it. Give us five minutes for a fag and I'll take you across."

"Can I row?" She gave him a rock cake. "Here, Teddy's mother made them."

17

Flight

"Your dad?"

I nodded

"Your *father!*"

"Yeah." I wasn't sure how Teddy would take it.

"So there's no Uncle Jack?"

"No."

"But you went to your dad's grave, you and your gran."

"You don't have to remind me."

"In that military cemetery, over in France."

"Yes."

He thought for a moment. "Well if it's not your dad's grave, whose grave is it?"

"I don't know, nobody knows."

I had chosen a spot where we could sit and talk. On a few acres of flat ground between the river and the North Pier the council had planted flowerbeds and put in a couple of iron seats. Two old people sat on one, we took the other.

"Well what?" Teddy didn't know what to make of it. "Has he killed somebody?"

"No, thank God! Don't make it worse than it already is. He's a deserter and they've buried somebody else in his place."

"Somebody else in his place?"

I drew a deep breath. I would have to tell him the whole story, there was no other way to explain it, and I was glad. I couldn't tell gran when she was ill in hospital and I needed to tell someone so I told Teddy, just as dad had told me, only without attempting to justify it as he had done. I wasn't a soldier, I hadn't been in the heat of battle with comrades dying all about me, knowing that any second it might be my turn. Even so, I thought, it was a cruel, calculated act.

But before I plunged into the story, there was something else I had to tell Teddy: "You've met him actually."

"Pardon?"

"My dad, you've met him."

"I've met your dad? When?"

"During the summer holiday."

"I met your dad during the summer holiday? I never met anyone during the summer holiday. Apart from the crew of the ship, I suppose, but he wasn't one of them."

"No, not the crew. But you did, and you told me all about him."

I had no idea what she was talking about.

"Up in the old barn," she said. "Above your house. You and your dad."

He stared at me then the penny dropped. "You mean the tramp? The man who was living there?"

"He give you that little rifle he'd whittled out of wood."

"That was your dad?"

"He was hiding out," I said. "He had nowhere to go."

"Dad gave him some money."

"Sounds about right. He broke into our house; well he didn't have to break in, he knew where the key was hidden. He was the one took took gran's savings."

I could see Teddy hesitating. What could he say? This was my father.

"He took your dad's shirts as well, I'm sorry. And he broke into houses. He did the same down our way when people were at their work. He knew how to go about it, you see. Mum used to visit him in prison. I told you about it."

I took a deep breath. It was something I had lived with all my life and kept locked away. Other girls' dads were shopkeepers, doctors, bus drivers. My dad was a burglar, a jailbird. It was hard to say. Despite the life I lived with gran, despite winning a place at St Peter's, the shame was always there. For a year or two in the army he had redeemed himself but now he was back to his old ways although, to be fair, it was from desperation.

"We nearly met him before that," I said.

"Yeah?"

"On the ship. Remember the first time we went aboard?"

"When?"

"Uncle Dan threw down a bar of chocolate. I was showing you round and when we came to the cabin I'd been in before it was locked."

"Yeah, there was some radar equipment in there."

"No, my dad."

"Pardon?"

"Not radar equipment, my dad. He'd been on the ship for a few weeks. Saw us on the dock and got a hell of a fright. Locked himself in."

Teddy looked cross. "So no Uncle Jack and no radar parts?"

"Don't blame Uncle Dan, what else could he do? His brother that everyone thought was dead turns up out of the blue. Gone AWOL sometime after D-Day and been hiding out in Europe for years, He wants to get back to Britain. Uncle Dan's not going to shop him to a boy he's just met that minute."

"I suppose."

"Then when dad arrived back in England he'd got nowhere to go, so Uncle Dan let him stay aboard for a couple of trips, passed him off as one of the crew, gave him that cabin. But the crew didn't like it, they'd suffered in the war like everyone else. Dennis had been torpedoed with Uncle Dan. Big Lenny, the cook, he'd lost his oldest son, just seventeen. And here's this deserter taking advantage of his brother's good nature, forcing him to cover up to passport control. And when he had to lie to you and me about the locked cabin it was the last straw. They told Uncle Dan they wanted him off so he had no choice, dad had to go.

"I suppose that's when he turned up at your house and broke in," Teddy said. "Then we found him living rough in the barn."

"Anywhere he could find a place. So when we went to Norway I got my cabin back. He'd been at the carving like when you saw him. I found that chip of wood, remember."

Teddy said, "How did he know where I live?"

"He'd been hanging about the docks, lived there most of his life. He'd always been a smart dresser so in case someone recognised him he changed his appearance: shabby clothes, sailor's bonnet, glasses, let his whiskers grow. He saw me head off with you one time and wondered where we were off to, so he caught the same bus. We went upstairs, he stayed down. Followed us up the road."

"That's how he found the old barn."

"Suited him perfectly, at least until you and your dad showed up."

I saw Teddy looking at me, wondering how it felt to have a dad on the run, a dad who robbed the neighbours, a dad who was scared to be recognised.

He never owned up to the burglaries, not only round Wherry Row but up Strawberry Bank and goodness knows where else. I never asked but there was no doubt he was responsible. And if Teddy wanted to know how it felt I could have told him simply enough, I couldn't bear it! Gran had very little money but she was scrupulously honest, we lived good, hardworking lives, and what my dad had done made me deeply, deeply ashamed, so ashamed that if anyone had discovered the truth I think I would have wished to die.

*

But going back to the war:

He had done well in the army. Although an untrustworthy husband, a man who preferred the pub to his own home and had finally landed in jail, he was a good soldier, promoted to corporal and popular with the men. I could readily understand it for he was a man's man who enjoyed action and a few beers, well-built, easy-going, and if he could make life easier by cutting a few corners, why not? Anyway, he was there with his battalion when they landed on the Normandy beaches on D-Day, got a foothold in France, and began driving the Germans back to where they'd come from. Crowds lined the streets, cheering as they marched through villages. But it wasn't all beer and pretty girls, there was heavy fighting – artillery, mine-fields, infantry, hand-to-hand – right up through France to the Belgian border.

After a while, I don't know how long, five or ten days, his battalion reached this place, the Bois des Sangliers, wood of the wild pigs. They thought they had the Germans on the run but it was a bluff, the Germans were enticing them to this location where they were deeply entrenched with artillery and machine-gun nests hidden among the trees. First thing dad's company knew about it, there's a terrific bombardment. No chance of counter-attack, all they could do was look for a bit of shelter, hunker down and wait until it eased up.

Well, dad's terrified, reckons his time's up, especially when a big shell lands just a few yards away, half burying him and blowing some of his company to kingdom come. It left a huge crater, so once he's dug himself out he crawls inside and hides. Then he sees a man he knows lying dead, and another with half his head blown off lying further over.

An hour later the order comes to retreat and reassemble, wait for back-up and they'll make an attack first thing in the morning. Well, dad's got it into his head that this time he's going to cop it, so what's the point? Who's it going to help if he's lying there with his legs blown off and a hole in his belly? So he decides to scarper, go AWOL. But if he does that they'll come looking for him, maybe not right then but sometime. They'd let him out of prison to to join up, so if next thing he's a deserter they're not going to be too pleased. He wouldn't be shot like soldiers in the First War but he'd end up back inside, maybe for a long time.

"I saw a film about that," Teddy said, "a soldier in the First World War that got shell shock. What he saw, his pals killed and dying, the noise of the guns, he had a mental breakdown. When he walked away because he couldn't take any more, they said he was a coward and put him in front of a firing squad."

"We read some war poems in Mrs Wardman's class," I said, "She'd lost her dad in the trenches, she was in tears. I think if I'd been there they'd have had to shoot me too."

I broke the last rock cake in half. "Anyway, there's my dad in the crater, covered in mud and blood, and he sees a way out, a way they'll never come looking for him. He fakes his own death."

"Yeah?"

"Here's this soldier, not his pal the other one, and he's unrecognisable like I said, half his face missing. But he's got dark hair and he's more or less the right height, so dad reckons if he swaps dog tags they'd reckon it was him."

"I know about dog tags," I said, "I've got dad's. That little identity disc they had to wear around their necks."

"That's right, so dad cuts it off this dead soldier and

replaces it with his own. But there's other stuff as well, so he goes through his pockets and takes his wallet and whatever else, fags, photos of his kids, wedding ring, army pay book, and replaces these with his own as well."

"Why would he have his pay book?"

"I asked dad. It's not just pay, it contains all your details: service number and religion, the date you joined up, medals, next of kin, even your will. Soldiers have to carry it all the time, top right pocket of your battledress so if you're killed they don't have to search for it."

"Did your dad have photos of you and your mum?"

"I don't know but the other chap did, his wife and three kids playing in the garden. His mum and dad as well, I think."

Teddy thought about it. "Your dad was a corporal, right?"

"Yes, I told you."

"So he'd have a corporal's – what do you call those things on your sleeve – chevrons. If the other soldier was a private —"

"But he wasn't, didn't I say? He was a corporal like dad, that's what gave him the idea. He wouldn't have to swap jackets. It was all bloody, I think it would have been impossible."

Teddy nodded. "But if he set him up like you say, how would anybody know who he was?"

"Well they wouldn't, they'd think it was dad."

"Yes, but who he was really?"

"I don't know." It troubled me.

"That's terrible! Your dad's stolen his identity. The poor soldier's lying dead in that shell hole and no one will ever know. His wife will be waiting for letters and he's disappeared off the face of the earth."

"I know, but dad wasn't pretending to be him, he just wanted people to think he was dead."

"I realise that and I can understand why, all those men dead and wounded, knowing any second it might be your turn. It must have been hell. Still, he had this chap's papers. Once he'd got away and the war was over, he could post them to regimental headquarters or somebody, let them know what happened."

"No he couldn't," I said. "He lost them."

18

The Road to Wherry Row

The barrage continued, dad told me. The order came to withdraw and reassemble but it was impossible. Never knowing if the next mortar shell or machine-gun bullet might kill him on the spot, he hunkered down in the mud with his two dead comrades.

At last the barrage relented enough for him to make his escape. Muffling his face between his helmet and army cape, he made his way back to the company and indicated that he was going behind a hedge for a call of nature. Nobody was interested because the ground was littered with bodies, dying and injured soldiers crying out in pain, praying for medics to come with morphine and give them relief.

Beyond the hedge was a patch of woodland, not the Bois des Sangliers but a copse a couple of minutes away. A score of soldiers were hiding there but they were too concerned for their own safety to bother about a British corporal hurrying through the trees. Perhaps they guessed he was carrying reports to officers behind the lines.

Steadily the shouts and bursts of machine-gun fire were left behind and he discovered he was on a farm track. On either side lay fields of wheat and maize, and a short distance ahead a dirty white farmhouse with shattered walls. Far away an endless convoy of military vehicles moved along what appeared to be a main road. He thought he recognised a turreted building that had acted as regimental HQ. It seemed a good idea to avoid it and to avoid the farmhouse also. He still carried his rifle but which way to go? With British forces advancing from the Channel and the Germans retreating northwards, dad decided to head east, deeper into France.

That evening he succeeded in buying bread and rough red wine in a village. The French were happy to assist their liberators and he spent the night among bales of hay in a barn.

As Teddy and I talked, a second old couple arrived among the flowerbeds, one leaning heavily on a stick. They were disappointed to find us occupying the seat so we gave it to them. A chain of concrete pillboxes had been built along the shore to repel any attempt by the Germans to make a seaborne landing. One of these stood nearby. We walked to the seaward side and sat on rocks with our backs to the wall and the rifle loopholes overhead. The wind was fresh and out on the open sea white horses crowded together but here, sheltered by the pier, little waves tumbled ashore and broke on the sand.

"Dad headed for Paris," I said. "It was still occupied by the Germans but the Allies were closing in. He needed to get rid of his uniform, so by spending a few francs and stealing from washing lines like he did here, he dressed himself in a stained pair of corduroys, an old jacket, a peasant's shirt and all the rest so he would fit in.

"After a few days he got a job on a farm. There was a shortage of labour so he helped the farmer to bring in the hay, repair his barns, clip the sheep, that sort of thing. He could work hard enough when he wanted to. What he told the man about himself I have no idea but there was no hiding the fact that he was a British deserter. Anyway, he was out of the fighting and he got his food and a few francs in his pocket so it suited him well enough."

Every bulletin on the radio, the farmer told him, brought

news of allied advances and the German retreat. There were stories of Nazi atrocities, whole villages machine-gunned and burned, mass graves found in woodland. It wasn't long before the Allies – British, Americans, Free French, soldiers from all over the free world – were fighting on the outskirts of Paris and dad left his job on the farm to join them. In August, two months after D-Day, the first tanks rolled into the city. The people of Paris rose up against their brutal oppressors: roads were torn up to form barricades, trees were cut down, vehicles set ablaze. Anyone who had a rifle went to the window and fired into the street. Dad joined them, along with thousands of others, deserters, escaped prisoners, everyone who had reason to hate Hitler. The dead and the dying, men, women and children, lay among the rubble. Hanged German soldiers swung from lamp-posts.

It was over in a week, Paris was liberated. There were scenes of great rejoicing, rifles were fired into the air, women hugged the victorious soldiers But peace did not come with victory, not at once, for war had destroyed the established order. Too many families had been torn apart, not just in France but throughout Europe and much of the world; too many people were dead; too many buildings had been destroyed. Millions of refugees wandered the land with nowhere to go and no idea what to do.

In this great melting-pot people clung to what little they knew and what little they had. In my dad's case this was a gang of deserters and refugees – British, Americans, French, Poles, Greeks – who established themselves in the vault of a ruined church a few miles from the city centre. They were armed, they were powerful and many, who had been brutalised by the war, who had seen their families murdered or transported to the labour camps, were ruthless. My dad was not a violent man although he had been in prison, but he was willing to follow the leaders. If a raid was planned on a warehouse or a railway yard, he did whatever he was told. That way he survived, that way he had drinking companions and the company he craved.

For a year following the fall of Paris all went well – but theirs was not the only gang. In the chaos that followed Germany's defeat, as the Third Reich broke up and the Nazi leaders – Hitler, Himmler, Goebbels and the rest – committed suicide or fled, similar groups were to be found in cities throughout Europe. In Paris there were several. Fights were not uncommon and with an endless supply of weapons left over from the war, there were many deaths. Bodies were left in the street where they fell, prisoners had weights tied to their feet and were dropped into the River Seine in the hours of darkness. Either way, what did the authorities care about a few thugs and gangsters killing each other when so many millions had died at the hands of the Germans?

My dad's group called itself Les Fils de la Guerre, the Sons of War, and clashed in particular with a Russian gang that lived in a labyrinth of tunnels beneath the city streets. Both wanted control and there were running fights and murders that came to a head eighteen months after the liberation of Paris when they clashed over protection money to be paid by a cigarette manufacturer. There was a meeting of leaders which became heated, insults were exchanged, knives appeared and in a moment the Dutchman who led Les Fils de la Guerre lay dead with the handle of a dagger protruding from his neck. His followers were hidden nearby, many were armed, and in no time a pitched battle was in progress up and down the banks of the River Seine. It was February and the afternoon was loud with the noise of gunfire. Bodies littered the ground, figures fell from the bridges. It was a sensation, carried on the front pages of newspapers throughout the world.

The gendarmerie could ignore the gangs no longer and moved in to break them up. My dad lost everything, his money, his clothes, his papers, all the possessions he kept in his corner of the vault beneath the ruined Église Saint-Martin which had been the gang's headquarters.

Where was he to go? With a young companion named Hamish, a private in the Black Watch who was also a deserter, he fled south. Sometimes they found work in the vineyards, sometimes they stole, but came at last to sunny Italy and there, in a small port on the Adriatic coast, they found jobs as fishermen.

Dad was happy, he liked the work and he liked Italy, the wine flowed and all went well until after a while Hamish met a girl called Greta. He was a handsome young man, she was beautiful and affectionate, too affectionate, for after a while, to Hamish's dismay, she discovered she was expecting a baby. They would have fled again but Greta had five brothers, all powerful fishermen, and they gave Hamish a beating that put him in hospital for a week. More than that, if he did not marry Greta within a month they promised to hunt him down, cut him into pieces and send him home to mama in a parcel. Hamish believed them and as soon as he could walk, still on crutches, he escorted the beautiful Greta up the aisle, started work with her brothers, and dad was left on his own.

What was he to do now? Italy had been fun, but living alone in the shack he had shared with Hamish, he realised that he was tired of Europe and struggling with languages that were not his own. He wanted to go home. So for six weeks, walking, hitching lifts in lorries or on carts, sometimes working for a few days, he made his way north. A letter to the shipping office in Newcastle brought news that Captain Pearson was still commanding SS North Sea Trader and it was due to pick up cargo in Bordeaux in early June, so that is where he went.

Uncle Dan was as astonished as gran and I to find his brother alive. And when dad asked for a berth to get back to England he could hardly refuse. But where was he to go when he got there? Officially he was dead: gran and I had been informed, his military records must say the same, and somewhere there was a report of the scene he had staged in that shell hole by the Bois des Sangliers. If that were not enough, his name was inscribed among the fallen of WW2 on the town cenotaph, it appeared in the Regimental Book of Remembrance, and we had visited his grave in the Commonwealth War Graves cemetery close to the Belgian border.

He pleaded with Uncle Dan to let him stay aboard until he had worked out what to do. Uncle Dan didn't like it, he had a distinguished war record and so had several of the crew. What dad had done was despicable but Uncle Dan felt he could not refuse his brother and so, as the ship sailed on, my dad stayed aboard, passed off illegally as one of the crew.

He was there that first time we went aboard, as I had told Teddy. Luckily he saw me before I saw him and rushed to his cabin. He was in there when I rattled the door and found it locked, but following that incident the crew insisted he had to go. His charm had worn off, they were tired of him abusing his brother's kindness, they did not like covering up and lying to Teddy and me. So the following morning, carrying his few possessions in a rucksack, he walked down the gangway for the last time and stood on the cobbled South Dock in Eastport – the dock where, in a few months, so much was to happen.

Where was he to go? What was he to do? Nothing had been decided. 29 Albert Street, where he had lived with my mum, lay half a mile away. 17 Wherry Row, where I lived with gran, was a little nearer. Unsure of his reception, he felt in his pocket and lit a fag.

Part 2

19

An English Jew

Teddy and I left the pillbox and walked on, past the spiked railings and remaining coils of barbed wire, out onto the mile-long North Pier with its towering red-and-white lighthouse.

Teddy buttoned his jacket. "But your dad didn't go to the house did he? Not right then."

"I don't think he dared," I said. "Scared what he'd done, scared what gran might say to him, scared of being recognised. He had a few quid so he went to a lodging house the far side of town. Got himself a pair of specs, stopped shaving. I told you."

"A bit scruffy for anywhere decent. Maybe they thought he was a spy."

"He was spying on me anyway. It was only through Uncle Dan he knew gran and I were still living there, we could have been bombed out for all he knew. Came down early and saw me head off for school, watched gran go out shopping."

"That's how he knew when to break in."

"He didn't have to break in, he knew where she kept the spare key."

"He broke into the neighbours."

"Up your way too. He followed us like I said."

The wind had freshened as we left the land. A wave flung spray across the cobbles. "It was that day we flew the kites up Strawberry Hill. He was watching us. He told me."

Teddy made a face. "They were hopeless, ten minutes and they were in bits."

"You always put yourself down. They were fantastic at the start and now you've got that new design. Anyway, that's how he discovered the old barn. Suited him perfectly: no chance of bumping into people he knew, twenty minutes to the Pit Pony. He'd have stayed longer if Rachel hadn't spotted his fire."

"Dad gave him money. Is that why he didn't break into our house?"

"He took clothes."

"That was before. Old Mr Maltby that chased him, he's had to go into hospital."

"Yeah? Was that because of dad?"

Before he could answer a rogue wave hit the pier with a loud *crack* and flung a deluge of spray that drenched my back and hit Teddy smack in the face. He stared at me, shocked, seawater streaming from his chin. I laughed and after a moment he joined in. He was a pretty good sort of boy, all things considered.

We were the last allowed on the pier that afternoon but they didn't turn us back and we got to look over the lighthouse which is terrific. I had been before, my mother took me before the war but I couldn't really remember. Teddy was fascinated and had lots of questions: how was a little lamp magnified a million times until it became a blazing beam visible as far as you could see with the curvature of the earth? How far was that? How did it flash at timed intervals? When it only gave ships a direction, how did they pin-point their exact position? I was very impressed.

And he showed me a third time that afternoon that he was a special sort of boy when we got back to the mainland. Although he was a Jew and I was a Catholic it made no difference. Gran and I went to mass every Sunday morning.

Like every Catholic girl of my age I had been baptised and confirmed, I went to confession, took communion, said my rosary and made the Stations of the Cross. Teddy, as a Jewish boy, had celebrated his bar mitzvah and was thus, at the age of fifteen, considered a man with all a man's responsibilities. He sat with the men at the Shabbat service in the synagogue on a Saturday morning. He wore the kippah. He celebrated Hanukkah, the Jewish Festival of Lights, and other Jewish holy days. There were certain foods he should not eat. Otherwise Teddy, with his fresh colouring and sandy hair, was no different from the five hundred other boys who attended St Peter's

Yet if he had lived in Europe in recent years, the Nazis, who wished to wipe every last Jew from the face of the earth, would have sent him to the gas chambers along with the rest of his family and burned his body to ashes.

The Nazi hatred was diseased and extreme but throughout history and in many countries even then, the Jewish community was looked on with distrust and suspicion. To my shame, it was like this in Britain. Sarah, a girl I knew in school, who was beautiful with dark Jewish looks and could not have been kinder, was denied friendship by a few and deeply upset although the school did everything it could to stamp this out. Teddy, too, was subjected to occasional comments from boys who knew his background. "Jew boy", they called him, and "Dirty Jew", but he had learned to live with it and not make matters worse by protesting. That afternoon, as we returned from the lighthouse, he was about to encounter much worse hostility.

The sun shone, the sea sparkled, the only shadows in our lives were my dad at home and gran in the hospital. The beach, where people lay on their towels and went swimming all summer, was a five minute walk from the pier and we followed the tide line, heaped with weed and stinking of the sea. We were about midway when a gang of five boys came trailing towards us and recognised Teddy. They had been to the same primary school, some in the same class, but were very different. Although Teddy's mum said he was growing at a great rate and I had noticed this myself, he was still shorter than an average boy of his age and lightly built with thin wrists and bony knees. To the casual observer, as I have said, he didn't look Jewish but these boys knew.

One, who appeared to be the leader, saw someone to victimize and brightened up. "Well, if it isn't our little Jewish friend. Hello, Abraham."

"Hello." Teddy tried to walk past.

They stood in our path. "Who you been robbing today then?" He sniffed as if his nose was running and looked round for approval.

"Oh, grow up, Peg." Teddy stood his ground. "Change the record, that's what you were saying back in primary."

"An' I'll keep on saying it, cos it's true, rob you blind. Any rate, who you calling Peg?"

"You if the cap fits," Teddy said. "Who are you calling Abraham?"

I was impressed. Peg, if that was his name, was twice Teddy's size with bold eyes and thick black hair. He stood as if he wanted a fight.

"You'd better watch what you're saying," said another of the gang.

"Dirty Jew," said a third.

Teddy smiled. "Hello, DB, you still hanging round? Brushed your teeth the last couple of years?"

The boy's face, red with acne, grew redder. He stepped forward angrily.

I was puzzled: Peg? DB?

"You want a doing?" Peg said. "You asking for it?"

"Not specially," Teddy said. "We just want to get past."

"We just want to get past! Will you listen to yourself." He turned his attention to me. "Who's this then?"

I spoke for myself. "Someone who just wants to get past."

"Ooh, cheeky! He your boyfriend then?"

"None of your business."

"You want to get someone with a bit more beef on his bones."

"You mean a big ox like you?"

"Yeah."

"You're not serious."

"Why not?"

"Cos you're thick and stupid. I'd rather go round with a dead dog than you."

He was taken aback. Peg wasn't used to people talking to him like that. I hoped I hadn't earned Teddy a beating.

The boy who had spoken earlier said, "Some Jew doctor tried to set up in the next street to us, *Dr Levi*," he mocked the name. "No one will go to him."

"Quite right an' all. Got their heads screwed on."

"Ask me, Hitler had the right idea. About the Jews, I mean."

"Well said, Ringo." Peg regained some composure. "Give this place a good clean out. Set up a few of them camps."

I'd heard the phrase 'white as a sheet' but never seen it until that moment. Teddy froze, the blood drained from his face, and with a scream he flung himself at the bigger boy. "You stupid, ignorant pig!" His thin fists hit Peg in the face, hammered him on the chest. Taken completely by surprise, a tomcat attacked by a mouse, Peg put up hands to defend himself, caught his heel and crashed heavily to the ground. Teddy kicked him, fell on him, and would have continued the beating if two of the others had not pulled him off. One did his best to hold him, for Teddy was out of control, and the other punched him viciously about the body, two, three, four times.

I was outraged and waded in myself. A white stalk of seaweed, thick as a club, lay at my feet. I swung it at their heads. One staggered back, blood running from his cheek. The other let go to defend himself. A fourth boy joined in. Peg pulled himself from the ground and charged at me. I whacked him with the root of seaweed then it was torn from my grasp and we were fighting hand to hand. Although I am a girl I am strong but Peg, a powerfully-built boy, was stronger. We struggled face to face then a group of men who had been kicking a ball about came running.

"Let go of her! She's a girl for God's sake." They pulled us apart. A man with a naval beard pulled DB off Teddy and flung him aside.

"What the hell's going on? Five big lads and the two of them. First you wouldn't let them past, now this. What kind of animals are you?"

Peg protested. "We was just talking then he flew at me. He's off his head."

"No reason, I suppose."

"He's a madman."

Teddy had been punched in the stomach and was close to vomiting. He struggled to get at him.

"Come on, son, quieten down. Well?"

"Yes there's a reason," I said. "Teddy's Jewish, lives up Strawberry Bank. His mother comes from Austria. The Nazis sent her whole family to the gas chambers, Teddy's grandad, aunties, everyone. Took all their property." I pointed at Peg. "He said they should do the same thing here. So Teddy went for him."

"That right?"

Peg shifted uncomfortably. "Bloody Jews. They're everywhere."

One of the men said, "I'm a Jew. Are you planning to get rid of me?"

There was no answer.

"I know this lad anyway, we go to the same synagogue. His dad's a dentist, nice family."

One of the others had Peg by the collar. He gave it a twist. "I got a good mind to take you to the police station, the whole lot of you. Bloody Nazi attitudes. That's what we just fought a war about."

"Aye, I just spent four years in the DLI," said another. "Lost my brother. Saw my mates killed. For what, to protect scum like you?" He surveyed the group. "I'd like to drop you off the Tyne Bridge."

They looked away, stared at the ground. DB shot a look of pure hatred at Teddy.

A fit-looking man in white shirt sleeves and black trousers took over. "Gerry says take you up to the police station. Well I'm a cop, Constable Brownlee, nothing easier. And I'll tell you what, if the Chronicle gets a hold of this you'll be front page, probably make the nationals. Your mam and dad will never be able to hold their heads up again. But I'll not this time, I'll give you the benefit of the doubt. Assume you're not evil, just pig ignorant. Still at school are you?"

"Leave at Christmas," Peg muttered.

"But still at school, yeah? All right, I'll speak to your head teachers and a team will come out and give a lecture. Show you a film, see what the Nazis did, to the Jews along with everything else, make sure all the senior ones know. And you'd better be there cos I'll be checking, else I'll go to the editor and your parents. And any repeat of what happened today, *any* repeat, I'll take you to the courts and you'll end up in Borstal. You'll not get a job, it'll be on your files till the end of time. You understand? And you two," he spoke sternly to Teddy and me, "they trouble you again you're to let me know. Cos it won't only be you, there'll be others and we've got to stamp it out." He turned back to Peg. "What the Nazis did over there, Auschwitz, Belsen, the mass murders, it's the most wicked thing in the history of the world, and ignorant scruffs like you are saying we should do the same here." He drew a deep breath. "Right, give me your names and addresses." He jogged to a pile of jackets and returned with his black police notebook.

Another of the men said, "You dying over there, you with the blood on your face. Let's see you." He wiped the blood aside. "Go on, you great baby, it's nobbut a scratch."

He pushed the boy away. "Tell your mam you were attacked by a girl."

"And if she wants to complain," Constable Brownlee looked up, "she'll find me at the police station. I'll get someone along from the Chronicle."

20

A Wild Streak

Teddy stood on the path. "Are you sure?"

"Yes, I told him you would be coming back." I turned the key. "When you meet him you'll like him."

"Yeah?"

He followed me into the house. Dad had set the table for tea: bread and margarine, jam, a tin of corned beef, tomatoes and Teddy's rock cakes.

"Hello, son." He was anxious but hid it well. "Mary's told me a lot about you."

"Hello."

"Here, give me your coat." Teddy pulled it off. "Feels a bit damp, I'll hang it by the fire."

I don't think they were ever at ease, not completely, but dad boiled the kettle, we sat at the table and in time they stopped casting hidden looks at each other. The bread had doughy bits in it and the marge was greasy but gran's raspberry jam made up for it.

"Here, pass us your cup." Dad gave Teddy a fill up. "Tell me again, that big boy, the one you had a fight with, why's he called Peg? He doesn't sound very girlish."

"Back in primary he had this snotty little nose," Teddy remembered, "always sniffing. And you could see his teeth, little stumpy teeth with gaps, looked like pegs. If he'd been OK nobody would have said anything but he was a bully and a thief, so everyone called him Peg – or Snotty."

"What about DB?" I said.

"Death breath," Teddy said. "He was a weed and he had this terrible breath, never brushed his teeth. Hung around with Peg for protection, a nasty couple. Some people called him PG – poison gas."

Dad laughed, "You're a clever lad, went on to St Peter's like our Mary. What happened to them?"

"No idea. They've shouted at me a few times in the street but you just walk away. They told that policeman they went to North Park."

"Will they come after you?"

"I shouldn't think so. He fairly warned them off, the courts and reports in the newspapers and that."

"Toe rags," dad said, overlooking the part magistrates had played in his own life. "Any idea where they live? Give them a clip round the ear, see how they like it."

"Dad, no," I said.

"Teach them a lesson."

"You'll end up in more trouble."

"Don't you believe it, girl."

"Well I don't know where they live anyway, and I wouldn't tell you if I did."

But I had no doubt that dad might do what he threatened, there was a wild streak, a recklessness in him. He was thirty-seven at the time and being on the run had kept him fit. He was always a sharp dresser and he'd washed and pressed all his clothes, even the things I had scrounged from the Seaman's Mission. He was proud of his looks, always fancied himself, though right then his hair was too long and his whiskers were scruffy.

"I like your shirt." Teddy said.

Dad smoothed his chest. "Yeah, got it in Italy before I come away. Nice."

Was it the shirt he had stolen from the washing line? I guessed so.

He leaned forward. "Turn up for the books, you and our Mary being such pals. Still got that Enfield I give you?"

"It's on the kitchen window sill. I'm thinking about painting it."

"It'll look good. I'll make you a sten gun to go with it."

Why did dad tell such lies? He knew Teddy and I were friends, he had seen us on the ship, followed us up the road.

"Gran needs some things," I said. "I'll get them from her room."

There was little sign of gran in there by this time, dad had made it his own. Trousers hung on the back of the door, a heavy grey jersey was folded on the chair, freshly-polished shoes I had unearthed from a box at the Sally Ann stood under the bed. The room was tidy but it smelled of socks and fags. Gran's clothes lay in the chest of drawers, neatly folded among sachets of lavender. I collected some underwear and two nighties, pretty bed socks and a few other things, and put them in a shopping bag.

When I returned to the living room they had left the table. Teddy was looking through my battered copy of Julius Caesar. My lines as Brutus were marked in red with pencil scribbles wherever there was space. "You've got some big speeches," he said: *"Romans, countrymen and lovers…"*

"hear me for my cause and be silent that you may hear," I continued. "Maybe you'll read with me sometime."

"I wouldn't mind."

"Her mum was a great actress," dad said. "That was the first time I saw her. Lady Macbeth in a black wig. I went with the girl I was courting at the time. Scary, all those speeches about night and death, washing the blood off her hands. She went to St Peter's as well, you know."

Teddy nodded and said quite bravely, "Yes, Mary told me. She was clever, wanted to be a history teacher."

"Yeah, well." He had the grace to be embarrassed. "Way things work out."

"What do you mean, the way things work out?" I couldn't keep quiet. "You got her in the family way. Mum was seventeen, she knew nothing about it."

"Yeah. OK. Not in front of the boy, right?"

"Well, don't make it sound like an act of God or something."

"Fair enough." Dad drew a deep breath. "I'm sorry, is that what you want me to say? You think I haven't thought about it?"

"I don't know what you've thought about. Seems to me there's a lot of things you haven't thought about."

"I can tell you something I have thought about." He looked me in the face. "Maybe it shouldn't have happened but it did and I'm glad you're here."

"Well I'm glad I'm here too," I said. "And gran's glad and mum was glad. And it wasn't your fault the munitions factory went up. But it wasn't what she planned."

"No, it wasn't." Dad looked at the mantlepiece where we kept two snapshots of mum in a small hinged frame. She had fair hair which she kept short and loose. In one she wore the overalls for her work at the factory; in the other she sat on a fence in the country, blown by the wind and laughing. She looked very young. "But I told you last night," he said, "she was planning to go to college when the war was over, when you'd grown up a bit. She was studying."

"Do you think I didn't know? If I couldn't sleep when I was little and came through, she was always reading in her chair, or sitting at the table there with some book in front of her."

"So she was."

"How would you know? It was this house, that chair, that table. She'd moved in with gran. You were in Durham jail."

Dad glanced at Teddy.

"It's all right," I said, "he knows."

"She was always like that," dad said. "When we had the house in Albert Street, always at her books."

Teddy said, "Mary takes after her, she's clever too."

"I wish I did," I said. "Gran's kept some of her school books, she was cleverer than me. If we have a French essay or something, I pinch bits."

Dad picked up my dog-eared copy of the play. "Go on, give us one of your speeches."

I turned away, "Not right now, we're going to the hospital. I want to pick some Michaelmas daisies and a bit of green."

"Later, maybe?"

"If you like."

"Give her my love."

"Your love?"

"Of course."

"All right. You'll be here when I get back?"

"Depends what time. I've got to go out."

"You've got to go out?" I looked at him. "Where, that pub the top end of town? What's it called, the King and Country?"

"I do sometimes go places other than pubs. No, I got to meet someone."

"Meet someone? Who?"

"No one you know."

"Oh, my God! You're going to get into trouble again."

"No, I am not going to get in trouble *again*, as you so kindly put it."

"Well I certainly hope not, it's bad enough already: you only go out in disguise, everyone thinks you're dead."

Teddy was embarrassed but I was beyond caring. "Where are you going to meet this mysterious *someone?*"

"Not so mysterious. Up the coast a bit."

"Up the coast a bit? It sounds pretty mysterious to me. Up the coast a bit where? And what about coming back, how are you going to cross the river?"

"He's got a car."

"And a few dodgy petrol coupons?"

"He might." Dad looked at me with those guileless blue eyes. "You're very hard."

"What do you expect? You turn up out of the blue…"

"Come on, darling!"

"Well!"

"Anyway, what is this, the third degree? I'm your bloody father, have I got to tell you everything?"

My heart was thudding. Who was this friend with a car? Where were they going? If they were heading 'up the coast' were there more of them? So many questions and he had only been home two days.

I didn't pursue it and went to the drawer for the big kitchen scissors. Teddy followed me into the garden where gran had a clump of Michaelmas daisies, bright purple and high as my chest. I cut a small bouquet and some green shoots to go with them. I knew gran would like it and hoped she was feeling better.

Teddy said, "You OK?"

"Yeah, sorry about that. Just find a bit of paper for these and we're on our way."

21

I Like a Windy Day

I was shocked to hear how Mary spoke to her father. She swore sometimes, not bad words but more than I did, and she had a bit of an Eastport accent, but talking to most people and certainly to my parents, she could not have been more polite. My father was a very different man and I was proud to be the son of Lieutenant David Cohen, RAMC, who had survived some of the great battles of World War 2 and gone out into the front line and no-man's-land to care for injured soldiers and bring them back to the dressing stations. Mary's father, in contrast, had fled the fighting and stolen the identity of a dead soldier, a man with a wife and children who would never know what became of him. He was a thief who had been to jail for burglary and was now in hiding. If, or more likely when, he was captured, public disgrace lay in wait, not just for himself but for his family. If this had been my father, even though Mary's dad was a well-built and likeable man, I also would have been bitterly ashamed.

Anyway, carrying the purple daisies and a bag of freshly-ironed clothes, we took the bus through town and got off at a stop outside the hospital. Mary led the way along the antiseptic-smelling corridors to Ward 14.

Mrs Fawcett lay asleep, her mouth open and a trickle running down her chin. I knew her as an old but pretty woman; now her hair straggled on the pillow and her teeth stood in a glass by the bed.

Mary didn't like to wake her. "She'd be disappointed to miss you," a nurse told her. "Maybe not stay too long."

"Hello, Gran." Mary spoke softly.

The old lady stirred and coughed. Her eyes cracked open and when she saw Mary she gave a sweet smile. "Oh, hello, Mary, love." Briefly she struggled to sit up then sank back. "You've brought Teddy with you. Hello, love."

"Hello, Gran," I said."

"Ooh, gran! And you've brought some of my daisies. Let me see."

She buried her face in the purple flowers. The nurse brought a vase and Mary arranged them on her locker.

Abruptly Mrs Fawcett realised she was toothless and covered her mouth with a hand. Mary passed her the tumbler and she slipped in her big pink denture. "That's better. Sorry, love."

"Don't be silly," Mary said. "How are you feeling?"

The old lady coughed again. She was always so vigorous but now her lungs were choked up. "A bit tired, you know. Nothing to worry about. This new stuff, penicillin. The doctors say it will do the trick, just take a few days." Her eyes closed wearily then opened again. "Never mind me, there's a whole hospital looking after me, what about you?" Another cough and a wheezing intake of breath. "How are you getting on with your dad?"

"OK most of the time. He's very kind, at least he means to be. Porridge and toast for breakfast, sees me off to school."

"Really?"

"Yeah, and he's fixed those tiles in the hearth, scrubbed the yard, made mince and tatties for dinner."

"Goodness!"

"But he's up to something, I don't know what." Mary told

her about the mysterious man with a car. "I hope he's not going to get into trouble again."

"Well, if he is there's nothing you can do about it." Mrs Fawcett picked at her blanket. "I never say things about your dad, sweetheart, but he's a tricky beggar, a law unto himself. Charm the birds off the trees but he's got a wild streak. Gets into bad company. Your mam never knew what he might do next."

These were family matters. It made me uncomfortable.

"Where's he sleeping?" gran asked.

Mary hesitated.

"It's all right, taken my room has he? Makes sense while I'm in here. He'll move out when I come home. Maybe look for," she struggled for breath, "a place of his own, somewhere we'll not be breathing down his neck."

"Another Brenda."

"Aye, well he's got an eye for the ladies, right enough." She smiled. "A lot of women lost their husbands in the war, their boyfriends. Who knows, once he gets chatting in one of them bars he keeps in business? He's certainly a good-looking man."

"Not these days; he's growing this scruffy beard, thick specs, clothes I got from the Seamen's."

"Sounds like all he needs is a false nose and ginger wig."

Mary laughed. "And he's walking like a sailor, you'd hardly know him from a few yards off. Doesn't risk the street though, goes out the back and walks up into town. Takes the bus to that pub out by Drake Park, you know, the King and Country."

"Looking like that? Your granddad and I used to go to the King when we were courting." She smiled at the recollection. "He'll certainly find a few bonny lasses up that way. Anyway, no point—" her thin shoulders shook with a bout of coughing, "no point jumping the gun, let's see what happens. It's not going to affect us, love. I'll be out of here in a week or ten days, then your dad can make his own arrangements." She took Mary's strong hand. "If that's what you want."

"All I want is you home again. Things back to the way they were."

"Well, whatever else, he is your dad. I just don't want you caught up in any of his shenanigans."

"Me neither," Mary said, little knowing how soon that was going to happen. She hoisted her shopping bag from the floor. "I brought some clean clothes."

"Oh, thanks, love. There's a few things need washing in the locker." She watched as Mary busied herself then turned to me. "It's kind of you to come, Teddy. I'm sure you have more important things to do than visit an old woman in hospital."

"I was down at the house. We'd been for a walk."

"That's nice. Where did you go?"

"Along the pier."

"I'd rather be down there than stuck in here."

"When you get better, Gran," Mary said.

"It was windy," I said, "spray flying right over. Mary got soaked."

"Hit Teddy smack in the face. He was dripping."

"I wouldn't mind a shilling for every time that's happened to me. I like a windy day."

It was nice to hear the old lady say it, lying there in hospital.

"Teddy had a run-in with some louts," Mary said. "They'd been at the same primary school. Called him Abraham, said horrible things."

"Oh, my goodness!" said her grandmother.

"You know his mother's family were sent to the concentration camps? They said the same thing should have happened to him. It led to a fight."

"I'm not surprised. Oh, love! I hope you weren't hurt."

"No, I'm all right," I said and it was true although when I put on my pyjamas that night my ribs were crimson and purple.

"It's the big one that got hurt," Mary said, "a brute called Peg. You should have seen the way Teddy went for him."

"Some men came and broke it up," I said. "One was a policeman and he took everybody's name."

Mrs Fawcett was anxious: "Aren't some people just awful! Do you remember that nice Mrs Berg in Candlemakers Row, Mary? Husband had that little paper shop? They had to move away. And then there was Mr Rowland, came round with the dust cart…"

I didn't really want to talk about it.

"I think that's it, Gran." Mary rose from the locker. "Anything else you're needing?"

"Not that I can think of."

Mary had brought her a small bar of chocolate, all she had coupons for. Three years after the war sweet rationing was still in place. Mrs Fawcett handed it back: "You take that, love."

"Nonsense, you like a bit of chocolate." Mary put it on the locker.

Her words gave me an idea. I had never been in hospital; when I'd had my tonsils out it was on the dining-room table. But when mum had an operation – it was never properly explained to me but something to do with babies – dad somehow got hold of a bunch of grapes and a box of chocolates. I would have liked to do the same for Mrs Fawcett.

"How's your play coming along?" she said to Mary.

"It's looking good. Teddy's going to help me with my lines."

"You know your lines, you knew them before the summer."

"Yes, but my prompts and everything."

"If you feel you need it, but you've got nothing to worry

about, love. Your mam was good, I think you might even be better." She was tired, her eyes kept closing. "I'll be that disappointed if I can't come."

"Not as disappointed as I'll be, Gran. But we're going now, we'll talk about it tomorrow."

"You don't need to come every day." The old lady put on a show of liveliness. "You stick in with your homework, that's more important. I'll be fine."

"I'm sure you will but I'll be here anyway. There's time for both." Mary gave her a kiss. Gran looked at me pointedly so I did the same, and we came away.

She waved cheerily as we got to the end of the ward, but when I peeped back a few seconds later, her head had fallen on the pillow and her eyes were closed. She looked exhausted.

22

Chocolates for Gran

We did a swap, homework for sweet coupons. Teddy did German for everybody and sciences for the junior classes. I did Latin and maths and anything the younger ones asked me. We had to keep it secret.

Amanda said on Tuesday, "I've only got one coupon but could you give me a hand with this?" It was a translation from Caesar's Gallic Wars.

She was nice, I would have done it for nothing but we needed the coupons for gran's box of chocolates.

"Let's see." Amanda was a year below me and she had been given a whole page to translate. Most of the girls hated Latin and thought I was mad or a genius because I enjoyed it. Anyway, I wrote the translation on a piece of paper and she copied it into her Latin jotter. "I'd better make a few mistakes," she said, "or Miss Levison won't believe I did it myself."

"I might make some anyway," I said.

"Not as many as me." Amanda was a pretty girl with a lovely figure. I knew her from the drama group where she was playing a soldier, which meant she had to brown her face and put lines on her forehead. "All those rotten Romans!" she said. "I want to play somebody beautiful and glamorous and wear gorgeous clothes."

It was a part better suited to her than me.

Teddy, meanwhile, was helping the senior boys with their

German. The fact that he was Jewish never came into it. Big sixth-formers with broken voices seemed perfectly happy to sit down with this skinny fifteen-year-old who spoke German better than their teachers and had plenty of time to help with essays and translations without making them feel stupid in front of the class.

We took coupons at school but not money although pocket money was not enough to buy the chocolates we had spotted in the sweet shop at the top of the High Street. To earn the money we did jobs after school. "Would you like me to clean the windows?" I asked old Mrs Tankerton across the road. "Would you like me to hose down the yard? Have you got any ironing? Would you like a bag of sea coal?" And Teddy did similar jobs: "Would you like me to chop that box of logs? I'm good at weeding. I can wash the car. Would you like me to paint the gate?"

It had been Teddy's idea and we wanted to do it without help. Sixpence and a shilling at a time the money came in but by Friday night we still didn't have enough. Then Teddy's dad gave him his next week's pocket money in advance so it was Teddy's money really, and we met in town on Saturday afternoon. We didn't go to the shop in the High Street because the assistant was stringy-faced and mean; Teddy remembered she had once cut a sweet in half to avoid giving him more than two ounces. Instead we went to a smaller shop in a side-street, a shop with a striped awning and a tortoiseshell cat sitting in the window.

The woman who owned it was lovely, roly-poly with bright eyes and a flowery apron. When she heard who we wanted the chocolates for and saw the scatter of coins and coupons we had collected, she went through a curtain and returned with a beautiful pound box, cream, blue and gold with a big red bow. "They just came in yesterday," she said. "Here, try one, the manufacturers sent a sample." She held out a small cardboard tray. I chose a violet cream and Teddy took a caramel. We never got sweets like that and they tasted wonderful.

A young boy, perhaps her son, appeared through the curtain and stood smiling shyly. The cat jumped down and pressed round my ankles, purring like an engine. I stroked its ears.

"I think what you've done is just lovely," the lady said. "Good for you." She wrapped the box in gift paper and put it in a carrier bag. "Try not to worry about your granny, I'm sure these will help her to get better."

She had to take the coupons but when she came to collect the money, sorting out the pennies and sixpences and threepenny bits, she said, "I've just remembered, there's a reduction today," and gave us two shillings back. I am sure it wasn't true but it was very kind of her and meant that Teddy and I could go to Gianni's for ice cream and a cake.

*

When we got to the hospital a lady I knew from church, Mrs Browning, was sitting at gran's bedside and on the point of leaving. I saw she had brought flowers and two home-made scones, cut and buttered.

"All right, Eva, it's good to see you so much better. Home on Tuesday. I'll look in to see if there's anything you're wanting." She gathered her gloves. "Now I'll leave you in the capable hands of Mary and – who's this?"

"Just a friend," gran said.

"More than that, Mrs Browning," I said. "He's my boyfriend. We're going out together." I squeezed Teddy's fingers.

She was taken aback but recovered quickly and smiled. "That's nice, love. I didn't know you have a – er—"

"I thought gran would have told you," I said. "We went to Norway with Uncle Dan. He's called Teddy, Teddy Cohen. His dad's a dentist."

She was nice, one of gran's friends, just a bit nosy. "Oh, is that Mr Cohen?" she said.

"I think that's a fair guess," I said.

"Has that practice in Park Street? Our Darcy goes there, she says he's very good."

"Of course he is," I said. "You don't think I'd go out with the son of a rotten dentist?"

"Mary, behave yourself," gran said.

Mrs Browning laughed and turned to Teddy. "And where do you go to school, love?"

"St Peter's," he said.

"That's nice, a clever boy and a clever girl. And do you live down our way?"

"No," he said and gave her a smile. I was proud of him.

You could tell she wanted to know more and I saw her eyeing the carrier bag but she said nothing. Doubtless she would quiz gran next time they met. I wondered if she would come in specially.

"Well, I must be on my way, Eva. I hope to goodness that team wins today. He's like a bear with a sore head if they don't." She settled her handbag. "Bye, Mary. Bye – Terry, is it?"

"Teddy," he said.

"Teddy Cohen," she said, memorizing it. "Right, bye."

"Bye," we said. "Bye, Mrs Browning," and she tip-tapped up the ward on her high heels.

"Mary, you're very naughty to tease her," gran said. "She's a kind woman, she brought me these flowers and made the scones specially."

"Sorry, Gran, she's always such a nosy parker."

"You don't have to tell me, but what kind of a life do you

think she's got with that boor of a husband? And her son's in trouble again. Here's you and Teddy doing so well at St Peter's with your laboratories and playing fields and everything, and her two over there at North Park with their muddy council pitches and those bad boys you were telling me about. She was very nice about it."

"So she was," I said. "What's Billy done this time?"

"Stolen a bike; well, borrowed, she says, but the police have been round."

"Poor her," I said.

"Yes, poor her!" Clearly gran was getting better.

"Tout comprendre c'est tout pardonner,"[2] I said.

"Precisely," gran said. "And we should all remember that."

So that was me well and truly told off.

"It was just a little tease," I said, "Anyway, you're not to be cross because Teddy and I have brought you a present."

Teddy set Mrs Browning's chair against the wall and collected two more because he didn't like sitting on a seat that was still warm. I handed him the carrier bag. "Go on, it was your idea."

He pushed it back. "Don't be daft, she's your gran."

So I took out the parcel, wrapped in paper with a pattern of flowers. "This is from Teddy and me."

She sat forward. "A present, from the two of you? Goodness, what is it?"

"You'll have to open it and find out."

The lady in the shop had tied the paper with green ribbon and fashioned a bow but the knot had jammed. For half a minute gran picked at it but she wasn't comfortable and passed the parcel back. "I don't want to spoil it, love. You have a go."

It wasn't difficult if you took it to the light and I handed

---

2 To understand all is to forgive all.

it back. Carefully gran set the ribbon aside and folded back the paper.

"Chocolates! Where on earth did you…? Oh, I've never seen such a beautiful box, not for a long time anyway. Oh, how lovely! Thank you so much." She held out her arms to give me a big hug and said to Teddy: "Come here, sweetheart, and give me another of those special kisses." So he did and she wound a tight arm round his shoulders. "My, she's going to be a lucky girl that marries you."

Teddy blushed.

"But where did they come from? How on earth did you…?"

So I told her about Teddy's idea, how we had collected the coupons and the money. "He was very strict about it. We had to do it all ourselves, no help from anybody or it wouldn't be the same."

"I think it's just wonderful!" She held the box at arms' length then set it in her lap, still holding it in her thin fingers. She had lost weight in hospital.

"Maybe I could have asked dad, or Teddy's dad would have…"

I don't know if she heard me. Her eyes went from Teddy to me and back to Teddy. Her eyes brimmed with tears. "Oh, Mary, love. You're both so…" She wept.

"Come on, gran." My own eyes filled up and I sat on the bed to put an arm around her. Teddy rested a hand on her shoulder.

"I don't deserve it," she said as her voice came back.

"You most certainly do," I said. "If I had the money I'd buy you a whole chocolate factory."

"Can I have a job there?" Teddy said.

Gran looked up and smiled. "Would there be any left to sell?"

"Prob'ly not," he said.

She scrubbed her nose with a crumpled hankie then gave

it a business-like blow. "Well come on, no good just looking at it." With a thumb nail she broke the seals, lifted the lid and folded back the paper. The rich sweet smell of chocolate filled the air; a dozen shapes, milk and dark, two layers deep. "Goodness, they look so delicious!" She examined the leaflet and chose her favourite, a rose cream, then passed the box to Teddy and me.

They tasted wonderful and we had two each then gran shut the lid firmly. "If you want another one you'll have to come again!"

They were a great success but the chocolates were not, for me, the most memorable event of the afternoon. The most memorable event was to see gran's eyes sparkle again, even though they were pink with weeping, to hear her laugh, and to know for sure that she was getting better.

23

Gold Watches

Gran was in hospital for a fortnight. That was the most important event of those two weeks, but my dad's reappearance from the dead ran it a close second. He tried his best to be kind and helpful but his presence dominated the house. This would have been true of any man but I never knew what to expect. Some days he did the ironing and cooked a meal, other days he was not there at all.

So much was happening at the time that I'm going to have to back-track a bit. You will remember that on the day Teddy and I had the fight with Peg and his followers dad made tea, then Teddy and I went to see gran in the hospital. This was when she was poorly, before the chocolates. When I got home dad had gone out as he had warned me. He had done the washing-up and filled the coal scuttle, but there was no note to tell me where he had gone or when he would be back. There was a faint smell of garlic in the air so I guessed his friend had been in the house, maybe a French or Italian friend.

I sat up until midnight, catching up on homework and some of the work I had swapped for sweet coupons, but he had not returned by the time I went to bed. It had been a long day and I fell asleep at once, but at three in the morning I was woken by the back door shutting and movement in the kitchen. I pulled my dressing-gown over my nightie and went through.

"Oh, hello, Mary, love. Sorry, I was trying to be quiet."

Despite the hour he looked fresh apart from his scrubby whiskers, and although I smelled beer he was perfectly sober. The kettle was on the stove and he was cutting a corned-beef sandwich. "Fancy a cup of tea?"

"Yes, all right." I sat at the table. "Where have you been?"

"I told you, up the coast a bit. Had to see some men I know."

"Some men you know? You haven't been home for four years."

"One of the boys I knew in Paris, before the gang broke up and me and Hamish went to Italy. Greg Williams, Bombardier Williams as was, comes from up Newcastle way. Got to hear I'd spent some time with your Uncle Dan, bumped into one of the crew in a bar somewhere and came to look me up."

"He smells of garlic."

"Aye, well, he stayed on in France for a while. Prob'ly got used to the nosh."

"You never told me about him."

"Well I wouldn't, would I, Eva there in hospital, you a schoolgirl? Not the sort of fellow you invite to the house, introduce to your daughter. What we got up to there in Paris, not something I want to talk about."

"But you went off with him?"

He gave a little shrug.

"Oh, for heavens' sake, Dad!"

"What?"

"I just don't like the sound of it."

"Why, for goodness sake?"

"I'll give you ten guesses. You don't want me to meet this Bombardier Williams. What about the others?"

"Just a few fellows, bit of company."

"A bit of company? I don't like to say it, Dad, but are you talking about a gang of deserters, men on the run with no homes to go to?" I took a bite of his sandwich.

"One or two maybe."

"And what, do you meet in a pub and have a few beers? Some place out in the country no one will come asking questions?"

"Something like that."

"And talk about the old days, what you all did when you were soldiers?"

He poured the tea and added something to his own from a hip flask. "Fancy a proper sandwich?"

"Not right now thanks. And is that it, until three o'clock in the morning?"

"More or less."

"What does that mean?"

"What's wrong with you, Mary? Why have you always got to think the worst?"

"Because I just don't believe you. You meet this crowd of men in some out of the way place to have a beer and talk about the old days? Come on, Dad, I'm not five years old, you're up to something. What is it, you're not housebreaking again?"

"Mary, will you stop it. You're getting a nasty sharp tongue on you."

"Well that's what you did before, what you did when you had mum and me, and you ended up in jail. What are you planning with a gang? Don't tell me it's a bank robbery, knocking off some fag warehouse."

"How many times? I've told you, we just went for a few jars and didn't realise the time. Men who've been in the forces, seen terrible things, got on the wrong side of the law. A few pals in the same spot, looking for a way ahead."

He looked so sincere, his voice was so persuasive. He was my dad, I wanted to believe him, but I just couldn't. After a lifetime of lies and evasion had he really turned over a new leaf? Everything warned me against it: getting my mum pregnant, robbing the shipyard, three years for burglary, setting up the dead soldier, the brutal Paris gang, hiding out on North Sea Trader, stealing from gran, robbing the neighbours, lying so glibly about the shirt. As I listened and looked into his handsome, open face, I felt slightly sick because I never knew where truth ended and lies began.

"Yes, all right," I said, "I hear what you're saying, it's as innocent as a church tea party. But if you and this Greg Williams and all the rest of them do get up to something, for God's sake don't get caught. And keep gran and me out of it."

He was still for a long moment, his tea untouched, his sandwich half-eaten. "I do love you, Mary. I hope you know that."

"Yes, I think you do," I said. "Gran too. I just wish everything wasn't such a mess."

Something like a tear glimmered for a second and was blinked away. Was it genuine or was that, too, a part of the act?

*

That was the last Sunday in September. The following week I had scarcely a minute to call my own. There was school, of course, and every evening I called at the hospital to see gran. We had taken some of the sweet coupons and money in advance so a few homeworks and jobs had yet to be completed. And Julius Caesar was in its final rehearsals, just a fortnight to first night which promised to be a big occasion.

So I was grateful when I came home at about six on the Monday to find dad had dinner ready, vegetables in the saucepan and two lamb chops sitting by the frying pan. The next day, however, when I returned a little earlier with some third-year algebra and an hour's gardening to do for a neighbour, he wasn't there at all. He had promised a cottage pie for tea, my favourite, but instead there was a note on the table:

Mary,
    Sorry but I've got to go out. Might be a bit late. Don't wait up.
    Love,
        Dad

Nothing was ready, no cottage pie, carrots and cabbage still in the vegetable basket. I dumped my schoolbag and looked in the pantry. We had bread and half a block of corned beef left from the weekend, so I boiled the kettle, put on a record of Glen Miller, and made myself a corned-beef sandwich.

Directly afterwards I spent an hour weeding my neighbour's flowerbeds and washing her windows, after which there was just time to iron a shirt for school and polish my shoes before I took a bus to the hospital. I told gran that dad's cottage pie had been delicious and he'd made an apple crumble for pudding. When I got home the maths for Diana and my own mountain of homework were waiting, so much that the clock was striking eleven before I finished. Dad still hadn't returned and as I went to bed I wondered if I would be woken again in the middle of the night. But I wasn't, I slept the night through, and when the alarm went at seven and I padded through in my bare feet, his bed had not been slept in.

He didn't return that day either, and apart from visiting gran I spent a second evening alone. I didn't have time to be bored, there was too much to do, but I was anxious. Where was he? What had happened? There was no one to ask.

Then around midnight, not long after I had fallen asleep, I heard the bump of the back door and footsteps in the kitchen. I jumped from bed and ran through in my nightie.

"Oh, hello, love." His clothes looked slept in, there was a bruise on his cheek.

"Where the hell have you been? That's two days!"

"Yes, I know. I'm sorry, I had to go away. Don't get onto me. Look, I've brought you a present." He dug into his old army rucksack.

"Thanks," I said without seeing it, "but I'm not looking for presents. You're my dad and if you're staying you should be here, not vanishing for days on end."

"Here we are." He unearthed a wad of grubby newspaper, set it on the table and unfolded it. A beautiful wrist watch lay before me with a gold setting and what looked like a solid gold bracelet. Dad laid it against my wrist. The numerals, each with a tiny dot of green, glinted in the light. Could they be emeralds?

"But where—?" The words froze on my lips.

"Do you like it?"

"Of course, but – "

"Nothing too good for my girl. I got one for Eva too." It was buried in the paper. He hunted through several layers and produced a watch as beautiful as the first but while mine was a man's watch or very like it, this was smaller and very elegant, definitely for a lady.

Where had they come from? These were not three-pound watches or even fifty-pound watches from the jeweller's in the High Street, they were the sort of watch you saw advertised in the film magazines, watches from New York and Geneva.

"Don't say a word," dad said. "Don't ask. I gave somebody a helping hand and they were grateful. That's all I'm going to tell you. Nobody got hurt."

"At least tell me where you—" The crumpled newspaper lay on the table. A headline caught my eye:

Tragedie de la natation
deux frères se sont noyés

I pulled it towards me:

Deux garçons de neuf et onze ans se sont noyés dans une rivière gonflée près de Neuchatel. Ils campaient avec leur père lorsque le garçon plus âgé...[3]

---

3   Swimming tragedy: two brothers drowned
    Two boys aged nine and eleven have drowned in a swollen river near Neuchatel. They were camping with their father when the older boy...

"Have you been to France?"

"No, that's just the paper they came in."

I shuffled the pages: Le Figaro. And there was the date: Vendredi, 24 Septembre, 1948. "That's last weekend! You have been in France." I nodded to the fag that smouldered in the ashtray, "You stink of Gauloises anyway."

He sighed, "All right, yes, yes. I've been to France."

My heart was thudding. "What for?"

"I really can't tell you. There's seven of us, I'll tell you that much and Erik – he was with us in Paris – he got a lead on some business that's going to be worth a lot of money. Not for long, maybe just a month or two, but we've sworn not to tell a soul, not even brothers or wives."

He was dead beat, out on his feet.

"Well, it's not on the side of the law, that's for sure," I said. The beautiful watches lay before me. "Somebody gave you these for doing him a favour? What sort of favour's worth watches that cost hundreds of pounds? Not the sort of favour I think gran and I want to know about." I slipped the lady's watch around my wrist and admired it then put it back on the table and pushed them away. "Well thanks, Dad, I know you mean well but I don't want it. Nor does gran, I'm sure. How could I go to school wearing a watch like that? How could she go into the shops? Put them back in the newspaper and find some place to stash them."

"I thought you'd be pleased."

"But where do they come from? Who do they belong to? What have you been doing?"

He started to wrap them up then left them lying. Most women like pretty things, maybe he hoped the dazzle would make me change my mind. His hand was hurting and I saw a cut. A fingernail had turned black. Clearly there had been an accident or violence of some kind.

"How did you get to France anyway?"

"Well I didn't swim." He shook his head. "Sorry again, love, the less you know the better."

I thought about it. "So is this what you'll be doing from now on, heading off to France to do people favours?"

"Sometimes, maybe. Depends if Erik's got a job on."

"And if he hasn't, what? Chat up the talent at the King?"

"Mary, for goodness sake! This is your father you're talking to."

"Come on, Dad, it's no use pretending; you used to spend most of your time at Brenda's but she's married now, Uncle Dan told me. I thought you might be on the lookout."

"It seems to me you know far too much for a girl of fifteen."

"Not about France. Anyway, what are you going to do when gran comes home? She'll want her room back. And she'll not put up with you swanning off every few days and coming back God knows when."

"Aye, well, we'll cross that bridge when we come to it."

"Won't be long. Start of next week I hope."

"That's good to hear." He was genuinely pleased. "Whatever you might think, there's no one in the world I admire more than Eva. She must be making real progress." He heaved himself from the table. "What's in the pantry? I could eat a horse."

24

Home with Dad

When I woke the next morning he was sleeping the sleep of the dead. I made myself some toast and sat by the fire to eat it, catching the last of the warmth from the night before. Burned paper lay on the cinders, fragments of French headlines. I stirred them into dust, and chewing a crust returned to dad's room to have another look at the watches. They were nowhere to be seen. Reluctantly I felt in his pockets but they contained only a bloodstained handkerchief, his pocketknife and some other bits and pieces. I knew he kept some clothes in the top drawer of the dresser. Softly I slid it open: nothing but shirts and socks, carefully folded and smelling of soap.

"In her shoes, love." I jumped out of my skin. Dad had woken up and lay watching me. "Bottom of the wardrobe."

"I just wanted to have another look."

"Why not?"

"I don't want them or anything."

"That's all right."

"No, really."

"Sweetheart, they're yours if you want them. Nothing would please me better."

My face was burning.

"Have a look if that's what you want."

So I opened the wardrobe door which always stuck. The

watches lay in the toes of gran's navy court shoes, the pair she wore to church every Sunday.

He stirred beneath the blankets. "Just somewhere to put them. No one will be coming round."

They lay heavy in my hand. The curtains were closed but even in the half-light the watches were beautiful, or if not beautiful, very fine. I set one on the chest of drawers and examined the other closely. I had never handled such a valuable object but I didn't want it, even though all I had to do was say thanks. I knew gran wouldn't have touched them either, she'd have demanded he took them out of the house immediately. It did occur to me that if he went to a part of the town where nobody knew him dad might have pawned them but it would have been dirty money. I could only guess where they came from and had no idea what 'helping hand' had deserved such a reward or how the face regarding me from the pillow came to have a bruised cheek. I would never again have the chance of owning such a watch but without regret I dropped them back into gran's shoes and shut them away in the wardrobe.

"Thanks anyway, Dad." I shook my head. "They are gorgeous but no."

"Ah well." He smiled and took my hand then drew his arm back under the bedclothes. "I'll see to them. Have a good day at school."

"You'll be here when I get back?"

"I certainly will. Just have another hour's shuteye."

*

It was a busy morning, history, Latin and double physics. I gave Diana her maths and handed in my own homework. Thursday was sports afternoon and I enjoyed hockey but that day I was excused and hurried to Mrs Jamison, who was having a big rehearsal on stage. For a few of us it continued after school, so it was nearly six before I returned home. Dad had cleaned the house, done a washing and made dinner for which I was grateful because I had to visit gran and there was still work to finish on other girls' homework as well as my own. Luckily some was not required until Monday, so I had the weekend to catch up. For dinner he had made mince, mashed tatties and cauliflower cheese, another favourite of mine, with rice pudding and jam for afters. It was delicious and although what I had guessed about his activities 'up the coast a bit' made me sick with worry, he was good company and I was pleased to have him there.

While I was at the hospital he poked through my schoolbag and discovered the jotters of the other girls, not that I was going to write in them but they told me what work had to be done. "What's all this?" he said as I took off my coat and hat. "Who's Moira Jennings and Jane Wilson? They're not even in your year."

There was a plate of biscuits on the table and he was making tea. I thought about lying then thought there were enough lies and secrets in the house, so I told him about collecting coupons and making some money to buy gran the box of chocolates.

"What a girl!" He kissed the top of my head. "Here, let me—" He felt in his back pocket and produced a thin wad of notes.

"No! No!" He was spoiling it. "We've got to do it ourselves, just Teddy and me."

"Come on," he licked his thumb. "A couple of quid. I'd like to help."

"Dad, no!" I pushed past. "We don't want it."

"Why not?"

"We just don't."

"What about your pal?"

"Teddy? It was his idea."
"I bet he wouldn't turn it down."
"Why?"
"Well, you know."
I stared at him. "No, I don't."
He shrugged.

A terrible anger was growing in me. "Dad, don't say another word. Not one, or we're going to have the most terrific row. How dare you say a thing like that about Teddy!"

"All right, all right." He held up his hands in an attitude of surrender.

"He's the one said we had to do it all ourselves. His dad's a dentist, he gave you money that time up in the barn. Do you think Teddy couldn't get it from his dad if he asked?"

"OK, I got it wrong. I'm sorry."

"You said you wanted to give them boys a clip round the ear, the ones called Teddy a Jew and started the fight. You're just as bad yourself."

It was a pity, we had been getting along so well and it spoiled the evening. We ate the biscuits and drank the tea. I settled down to work at the table but dad got his jacket and hat: "I'm just going out for a bit."

"You don't have to go out because of me."

"Mebbe not, I just feel like it."

"Going to the King?"

"Prob'ly, or the Forester's. Don't wait up. Sorry about the upset."

"OK, but I don't know how you can think like that, Dad. You met Mr Cohen. When I hurt my leg back in the summer he took me straight to the doctor for the stitches and brought me home. He was right through the war where the fighting was, bringing in the injured soldiers. And I've told you what happened to Mrs Cohen's family. Don't you think they've had a hard enough time?"

"Yes, I'm sure you're right. But they're not all like that."

"They? They?"

"You know who I mean."

"Well the ones that I know are: the girls at school, Mrs Sherman along the road, Mr Arnold has the shop. Really nice people."

"Stick together, help each other out."

"What's wrong with that? They help other people out as well; Teddy's dad, he helped you out, helped me out. You should hear Uncle Dan and the crew when we went up to Norway, the way Teddy got stuck in, they thought he was great."

"Aye, mebbe then, but you can't pretend they're like the rest of us." Dad tightened his shoe laces. "Saturday morning, hats on their heads, trooping along the pavements like a load of black beetles."

"Going to the synagogue, you mean? Going to church? Good for them, it's the same God. When was the last time you went to mass? More to the point, when was the last time you went to confession?"

He'd become a Catholic to marry mum. Talk of religion made him uncomfortable.

"You must have a fair bit to tell the priest by this time," I said. "Setting up that dead soldier; the gang in Paris you keep talking about; whatever just happened over there in France with your blood-soaked hanky and stolen watches. Take a few Hail Marys to wash that lot out."

"They're not stolen."

"Not by you, maybe, but you didn't get them helping an old lady off a bus."

He thought about replying but decided against it and pulled on a knitted hat. "I'm off then. Ta-ta." He kissed me on the hair and headed for the back door.

"What time will you be back?"

"Don't wait up." The door closed. He was gone.

That was the night he met Reenie at the King and Country and was late home. I normally slept like a log but that night I woke at four and padded through the house to look in his bedroom. His bed had not been slept in. But when my alarm went at seven-thirty, there he was, dead to the world and smelling of beer and fags as if he'd had quite a session. I didn't disturb him and tried to be quiet as I washed and made breakfast.

DAD
8.15, OFF TO SCHOOL. REHEARSAL AGAIN SO I'LL BE A BIT LATE, PROBABLY AROUND SIX. HOPE YOU HAD A GOOD TIME. LOVE,
MARY

I left it on the table and went to catch the bus.

*

It was another busy day, at least until mid afternoon when, since it was Friday, lessons eased off a bit and Mrs Jamison had arranged for some of her actors to come for rehearsal. We didn't use the stage that day because Mr Rankin, who was Woodwork Teacher in the boys' school, was working with a team of senior boys to construct the set. Their presence in the school caused quite a stir and dozens of girls had a sudden urgent need to go to the lavatory so they could walk past the assembly hall and peep through the doors. They were quickly sent on their way but it was noted that some of the younger teachers, fascinated as the girls, found their footsteps wandering in the same direction.

School ended at four but we continued an hour and a half longer so it was six before I hurried past the chipped doors of the Waterman's Arms and turned into Wherry Row. Smoke rose from our chimney, dad was still home.

"Late again, love," called little Mrs Robinson across the road. She was a kind woman, one of gran's friends.

"Yes," I called back. "Only a week till the play, we've been rehearsing."

"Oh, I know. Our Muriel's treating Jim and me. We're looking forward to it so much."

"I hope you'll enjoy it. We're doing our best."

"It will be wonderful, love. The St Peter's Girls are always excellent. You were so good in the last one. I couldn't bear it when you had to climb down that cliff to get the flower and got killed by an avalanche."

"Thanks. It was a good play, wasn't it." I stood by the gate.

Mrs Robinson had lived there for ever: "Eva says you don't think you're as good as your mam. But you are, you know. I saw her in that other play by Shakespeare, the one about the black man. She played his wife and got murdered."

"Othello," I said. "In this one I have to kill somebody, stab him with a dagger and then kill myself."

"Julius Caesar, yes, I know."

"I've got to go, Mrs Robinson. Have my tea then get up to see gran. How's Mr Robinson?"

"Oh, he's fine, it's just his back. He's got these new pills."

"That's good."

She could see I wanted to get away. "Give Eva my love. Tell her I'll try to look in tomorrow."

"I will do, thanks. Bye-bye."

Dance music and a warm smell of cooking hit me in the face as I went through the door.

"That you, Mary, love? How's the day been?"

Our neighbours must have known there was a man in the house. He never went out the front and when they visited gran in hospital she had told them a story not unlike my own about dad's half-brother Jack who was staying for a few nights to keep me company. She was a scrupulously honest woman and they had no cause to disbelieve her. Certainly they could never think it was dad because his death had been announced in the paper and there was his name on the war memorial.

"I didn't put the tatties on in case you were late." He popped the gas and slid the pan across. "You've got a letter."

The table was set, water jug, knives and forks. He had lifted a small pot of African violets from the window-sill and put it in the middle.

A long envelope lay on my place mat.

25

A Letter from The Chronicle

I hung up my hat and blazer and sat at the table. It was an official, cream-coloured envelope with a fine coat of arms and *Eastport Chronicle* embossed in blue and gold. Short Story Competition 1948 was stamped across the top corner in red. My name, Miss Mary Pearson, 17 Wherry Row, Eastport, appeared below in much less distinguished typing.

I had worked hard on the story, put so much of myself into it that I could hardly breathe. For a full minute I stared then slit the envelope with my dinner knife. The folded letter was on heavy, good quality paper:

'*Dear Miss Pearson,*

Thank you so much for your contribution to the Eastport Chronicle *Short Story Competition 1948. We check the provenance of every story that makes it past the first round, and in your case we contacted Mrs Constance Wardman, your English teacher, whom you named as a referee…*'

I hadn't the patience to read the whole letter and scanned the page quickly to find the results. Two-thirds of the way down I found the under-eighteen category:

First place – Mary Pearson – for her story The Hero.

Me? I read it again: Mary Pearson. I couldn't believe it

and a huge lump swelled in my chest. I thought I was going to be sick, or maybe cry. Terrified I had made a mistake I read it a third time: First place – Mary Pearson...

Second Place...

Third Place...

Highly Commended...

I had not heard of them and looked back at my name. Golly!

I glanced over the rest of the letter. Who had won first prize in the senior category, I wondered, the story that was going to be published in a leading anthology? Again his name was unknown to me, but my heart jumped for there was my name a second time:

Third place – Mary Pearson.

There must be a mistake, I hadn't entered the senior section. Perhaps there was another Mary Pearson? No, for there it was again: Mary Pearson – for her story The Hero. Someone must have liked my story enough to put it forward in the Senior Section. And I'd got third! I flopped in my chair and stared into space. Mrs Wardman usually liked the essays I wrote for her, it was she who had told me to apply and I had done my best, but I never really expected—

"Are you all right, sweetheart?" Dad stood beside me. "You're white as a sheet. Is it bad news?"

"It's from the *Chronicle*." My breath was shaky. "I've just – I've just won..." I passed him the letter.

He was delighted. "Good for you! Clever girl!" He gave me a huge hug. "You get that from your mum, not me, that's for sure, not my side of the family."

But as his whiskers scratched my cheek and I smelled beer on his breath, I recalled that The Hero was about him, not as he was now, not my dad the crook and deserter, but my dad the hero, as we had believed, killed among his comrades in the bold push into Germany after D-Day. Not exactly my dad but a soldier very like him. Not a corporal, a private with a different name, but there was do doubt who it was based on. What would he think when he read it and compared the facts with what I had written?

"Have you got a copy?" he said. "Can I read it?"

"I'm not sure where it is," I lied and had an idea. "I showed it to Mrs Wardman, I think it might be in school."

He believed me. "Fetch it back on Monday."

"I will if I can. I think she gave it to Mrs Frobisher."

"Who's she?"

"The head teacher."

There was no way I could keep it from him indefinitely because the *Chronicle* was publishing the winning stories next weekend. There was to be a presentation with a certificate and small cash prize in a room at the Town Hall then the stories would be published in a special edition on Saturday.

I phoned Teddy on my way to the hospital and gran was over the moon: "Oh, good for you, darling!" She squeezed my hands and gave me her special smile. "Do you hear that?" she said to the lady in the next bed who had become a friend. "My clever granddaughter here has just won the story competition in the Chronicle."

"Really, Eva? Oh, well done you."

They were lovely. Gran reached for the box of chocolates which stood in pride of place on top of her locker. "Go on, love, take two. If ever it was deserved…"

*

A bit before ten o'clock I got my second shock that evening. The house was at peace. Soft swing music came from the wireless. Dad had put his carving aside and was reading an American thriller with a picture of a half-dressed girl and a man with a revolver on the cover. I was sitting at the table working a few quadratic equations for Doreen Mathers, who was in the year below me. He had made tea and I was nibbling a digestive biscuit when there was a noise in the yard.

I swung round and dad got to his feet. There was an intruder. With a clatter and an oath whoever it was stumbled into the dustbin. The back door was bolted but the catch rattled and next moment there was a knock. Dad and I looked at each other then he picked up the iron poker, holding it like a weapon, and went into the scullery.

"Yeah? Who's that?"

I couldn't make out the reply but dad knew him and the bolts snapped back. It was a wet night, the man who came in sparkled with raindrops. I had never seen him before. He was younger than my dad and very fit-looking with an auburn beard and alert blue eyes. He shook the drips from his coat and pulled off a woollen hat.

"This is my daughter Mary," dad said. "This is Lucas."

He stepped forward and held out a hand. It was ice-cold and wet.

He wasn't one for small talk. "We have to go," he told dad, the words clear but his accent strong. I learned later that he was Swedish. "The car's at the end of the lane, Pavel is waiting. We must be quick."

It sent a chill through me. We had been sitting like a family in the warm living room, my father had cooked dinner and I had won a competition. All at once this stranger had appeared from the night and was taking him away.

"Dad?" I said.

He looked at me apologetically. "Sorry, love." My insides turned over as I saw that he must do what this messenger told him.

"Give me a minute. I got to change, collect a couple of things." He disappeared into his bedroom.

Lucas looked around the living room and then at me. "So, you are this daughter he so proud about."

I didn't know what to say.

"Always he tell us about you." He looked at my wrist. "You not wear the watch he bring back for you."

"No."

"Big deal he make about these watches. Worth much money."

"Yes. They were beautiful."

"You not have them no more?"

"We don't want them."

"Phhh!" He rolled his eyes.

"They were stolen, weren't they?"

"Maybe." He shrugged. "Long time. Nobody you know."

I didn't like him.

"So, your father, he still have them?"

"I don't know, you'll have to ask him."

He turned to the fire, warming those cold hands. As he leaned forward I saw a lump under his jacket. Something at his belt. A pistol? He pulled it comfortable.

Dad returned, his old army haversack over an arm.

Lucas said, "The watches, your daughter say she not got them."

"She wouldn't take them." Dad opened the haversack and showed a cloth. "Sort it out when we get back." His shoes lay beside the hearth and he sat to pull them on. "Did she tell you she just won a big writing competition?"

"No," Lucas said briefly.

"Going to be published in the Chronicle," Dad said.

"Very good." Lucas didn't hide his lack of interest.

"Award ceremony in the town hall."

"Just a room," I said.

"You ready?" Lucas moved to the back door.

"How long do you think we'll be away?" Dad wanted to give me some idea.

"Two – three days? Who knows?"

"Sorry, sweetheart." Dad struggled into his jacket and tried to give me a kiss. I turned away.

It was a filthy night. Rain rattled on the window. As the door opened a wet gust blew from the yard and I heard the down-pipe gurgling.

"Bye, Dad." All at once I was sorry for him. "Take care."

The door banged shut. He may have replied but I didn't hear. Briefly there were sounds, then nothing but the noise of the wind and the black September night.

I was alone.

26

Grapes and a Pistol

That was Friday.

About ten o'clock on Sunday evening, my work all done and schoolbag packed for the morning, I was sitting with a glass of gran's ginger wine and reading the sad last chapters of Brideshead, when the back gate clashed shut. Unsure when dad would return, assuming he ever did, I had not bolted the scullery door. Following his example, I reached for the poker.

"Hello, Mary, love. Back at last."

He wasn't wet or injured as he had been the last time he came in from the night, he looked in good form. His cheeks were flushed, partly from the cold wind but more likely a session in some pub because his breath was strong.

"It's good to be home." He hung his jacket on the back of a chair and sat by the fire to pull off his shoes. "How's it been going, sweetheart?"

"Fine, I've been busy. Got the last of those homeworks finished."

"Good for you. You're some worker."

"Yeah, well, we got gran her chocolates so that's it done now." I hesitated, "If you don't mind me saying, I wasn't too thrilled when that Lucas person turned up out of the blue and you went off with him."

"Yeah, sorry about that."

"Well, where have you been? Not France, obviously, there hasn't been time."

"I have, as a matter of fact, that's why there was a rush. Greg organised a plane at short notice."

"You flew over?"

"Not a passenger plane, just a little Anson from the flying club. Had a job the far side of the country."

"Where, for goodness sake?"

"A place called Luneville, you'll not have heard of it. Not far from there."

"A job doing what?"

"Sorry, love." He pulled off his socks. "Anyway, never mind me. How's Eva?"

"Home in a couple of days."

"That's good news. Were you there this afternoon?"

"No, some friends from church, I went to the beach with Teddy. Called up tonight."

"Good for you."

He glanced at his haversack. "Have a look in the bag."

"Not another watch?"

"Now, now! They've gone back to the boys. This is something for Eva." He stretched his legs. "Any chance of a cuppa?"

"Any chance you'll wash your feet?"

"Yeah, yeah."

I undid the khaki straps. Right on top, wrapped in another page from Le Figaro, was a big bunch of black grapes. We rarely saw them in Eastport and they were expensive.

"I hope she'll like them."

"I'm sure she will," I said and took one, but as I lifted them out I spotted something among the crushed clothes beneath, a glimpse of metal. I nudged a sock aside and saw it was the barrel of a pistol. It gave me a great fright. I had seen Lucas carrying a gun, at least I thought so, now my dad was. What were they doing, these armed men who crossed back and forth to the continent? The world had been at war for most of my life and there had been soldiers in the streets, occasionally with rifles, but but this was different, the war was over. I was only fifteen, of course, but personally I had never even been close to a firearm except the two Enfield .303s Uncle Dan kept locked in a steel cabinet on the bridge of North Sea Trader in case of trouble.

As I made the tea I resolved to say nothing. "What are you planning to do when gran comes home?"

"I've been thinking about that. There's a couple of boarding houses out by the King, the barman was telling me about them. The Laurels and something else. Not too pricey, do for a few days. I'll check them out tomorrow."

Despite everything, I liked having dad around the house, I was getting used to him. "Not down this way then?"

"Come on, love, how can I? Why d'you think I go all the way out to Drake Park for a drink?"

"We'll see you sometimes, I hope."

"I don't see why not."

"Handy for Reenie," I said.

"What?"

"You met her at the King, didn't you? I assume she lives somewhere out that way."

"Is that right?"

"You were only home five minutes before the milkman. It's obvious you'd be on the lookout now Brenda's married. I thought Reenie might be her."

"You know what thought did."

"So she's not?"

"Never you mind. You're a bloody schoolgirl, what sort of conversation's this to be having with your father?"

"Well, I'm interested. Uncle Dan says Brenda was nice." Actually he had said dad wasn't good enough for her.

"Anyway, what sort of father turns up after four years with his name on the war memorial?"

I carried two cups of tea across and went to the cake tin.

"You're very hard."

"Not really. Gran used to go to the King with grandad when they were courting. Lots of pretty girls round that way, she says."

"I hadn't noticed."

"Why, are you getting old or something?"

"Cheeky cow."

"Well, is Reenie pretty? How old is she, twenty-five? Seventy?"

"She's all right."

"Is that it? I hope any boyfriend of mine would be a bit more enthusiastic." Flour was still rationed but a lady from church had baked a cherry cake for me. I cut two slices. "Anyway, now you're back in Eastport have you had any thoughts about handing yourself in? I was talking to gran about it."

"Goodness, that's a change of subject."

"You can't stay on the run for the rest of your life. Those men you're hanging around with, they're going to get caught eventually."

"How come you know so much about it?"

"Come on, Dad, get real. How can you keep crossing to the continent without people noticing? Heading off at night: there's fishermen about, coastguards, people walking dogs. Somebody's going to report it."

I had been thinking a lot about this: if dad handed himself in as a deserter, the officials might be more lenient than if he were caught smuggling. On the other hand, would they believe he'd been suffering from shell-shock? What he had done out there in France was very calculated. What about his nameless comrade abandoned in that shell hole and everything that had happened since? Uncle Dan would be in serious trouble for a start. There was another problem too: ever since dad was believed to have died, gran had been receiving an orphan's allowance for me from the government. Without it she could never have managed. She had nightmares that when it was discovered my father had been very much alive all those years she would be required to pay it back. It was impossible, she had no money.

"Report it?" he said now. "You could be right but let's hope not. Not yet anyway. We've talked about it."

"And I don't know what the others are like but I didn't like your friend Lucas very much."

"Why, what's wrong with him?"

"I thought he was a bit of a bully. And he was carrying a gun."

"How do you know? Did he show you?"

"I could see it under his jacket."

"Maybe it was something in his pocket."

"Oh, Dad, I keep telling you, I'm not a baby any more, don't lie to me. You've got a gun in the rucksack now."

He glanced across.

"Guns are used to shoot people. If one of that crowd shoots somebody that makes you an accessory to murder. The war's over. You know what they do to murderers."

He was still for a long moment. "Aye, well, you're right, of course. But no one's shot nobody yet. And some of the people we deal with – you've got to be ready to defend yourself." He sank back, his tea untouched. "Anyway, give us a break will you, sweetheart. I've only been in the house five minutes and I was that glad to be home. Got the grapes for Eva and everything. Can we talk about it tomorrow?"

He had come in flushed from the night, full of good spirits. Suddenly he was deflated and I felt sorry for him."

"Yeah, OK. As long as you don't shoot me first." I kissed his whiskers. "D'you fancy a sandwich? I've got a bit of cold ham and a tomato."

"Aye, that would be grand."

27

Ice Cream, Bread and Trains

When I went to bed dad was sleeping in the chair, and when I set off for school next morning he was sound asleep in bed. It was Monday and I left earlier than usual because I had the last homeworks to hand back and I wanted to show the letter from the *Chronicle* to my English teacher.

"Can I speak to Mrs Wardman, please," I said to the grumpy chemistry teacher who answered my knock on the staffroom door.

"Is it important?"

Miserable old bag, I thought, and straightened my back. "Yes, quite."

"Wait here." She shut the door on the hubbub and a moment later her place was taken by the much friendlier Mrs Wardman.

"What is it, Mary?"

"I got this letter from the *Chronicle*." I handed it to her. "It came on Friday."

She read it through and gradually her face lit up with pleasure. "Oh, Mary! Well done. Well done indeed!"

I liked Mrs Wardman and I could see she would have liked to give me a hug. Instead she took my hand and shook it warmly, almost too warmly, I thought she was never going to let go.

"Oh, I couldn't be more pleased. What a wonderful start to a Monday morning. Here, Edwina," she stopped a geography teacher. "You know that short story competition in the *Chronicle*? Mary here's gone and won it. First prize, and third in the adult section.

"Oh, well done, you!" said Miss Ayrton, who didn't teach me that year but had done in the past. "Congratulations! Will we get to read it?"

"They're going to print the winners next weekend," Mrs Wardman told her. "We'll all get to read it."

Mr Ryland, the assistant head teacher, squeezed past, the only man on the staff apart from the janitor. Mrs Wardman caught at his arm but he was late and sped on down the corridor, gown flying.

She turned back to me: "Mary, can I hold on to this until lunchtime? I'd like to show it to some of the others. And I'm sure the head will want to say something in assembly tomorrow. That will be all right, yes?"

I had feared something like this would happen. My cheeks felt hot. I nodded.

"And tell me, how's your grandmother keeping? She had to go into hospital, didn't she?"

"Yes, she took a turn and then a bit of a chest infection. But she's much better now, thank you. Coming home tomorrow."

"Oh, that's good, you'll have been worried. Not only that but Julius Caesar coming up next week."

If only that were all, I thought.

"Will she be all right? Is there anyone at home?"

"Just me, but neighbours will keep an eye on her, and we've got friends from church."

"Oh, that's good. Try not to worry, you've got quite enough on your plate as it is."

"Yes, thanks, Miss."

"I think the head might want to talk to you. And I'll give

you the letter back at lunchtime, just come to the staffroom."

She was so pleased for me you could never guess she'd had such a bad time in the war. Girls had told me that her husband, rear-gunner on a Lancaster bomber, had been shot down over Germany and with the shock she had lost the baby she was carrying.

"Very well done, Mary. I've read it, of course, but I can't wait to see it in print."

She was lovely.

*

Although first night was only a week away I wasn't needed for rehearsals that day, so I met Teddy outside school and we took the bus into town for an ice-cream. Gianni's was famous. Little wooden booths down one side were decorated with pictures of Italian piazzas and blue Mediterranean seas. We had five shillings, so I grabbed a booth while Teddy ordered dishes of the best ice-cream in Eastport with wafers and strawberry topping.

He had news. His mother had been contacted by her lawyer in Vienna and the following week she and his dad had to return for a court hearing. Her claims for the return of the house and furniture factory were progressing well.

"Will you be going?" I said. "You and Rachel?"

"How can we, there's school?"

"So are you staying home by yourselves?"

"Mum would have left us for a night but they'll be away four or five days. We're going to stay with friends."

"Where?"

"You've met them actually. Dr McGregor, you know, the one who stitched your leg. Dad used to play rugby with him."

"He's nice."

"We went on holiday with them last year."

How were we to know, sitting that afternoon in Gianni's. what drama this stay with friends was to lead to, but that was for the future. Right then it raised a matter of more immediate concern: "Does that mean you'll miss the play?" Even though I had butterflies I wanted him there, I wanted them all there.

"They'll be back, we've got tickets for Saturday." He sucked his spoon. "Anyway, what about your dad?"

"We're getting on fine, he went to the pub last night. Still sleeping when I came out."

"Will he have a meal ready?"

I hope so, I've got to see gran after. He's brought her a big bunch of grapes."

"Where'd he get those?"

I shrugged.

Although I told Teddy most things, I hadn't told him everything. He knew about dad going AWOL and turning up again when everyone thought he was dead, but that was in the past. He didn't know what was happening now, the crowd 'up the coast' and crossing to France, Lucas turning up in the middle of the night. I needed to talk to someone but I couldn't tell gran, not in hospital. Uncle Dan would have been the perfect person but he was off on his travels.

"Teddy?" He looked up. "If I tell you something will you keep it secret?"

"Yeah, if you want."

"I mean really secret, it's serious."

"What about?"

"My dad."

"You've told me already."

"There's more.

"Well," he shrugged awkwardly. "OK, but I don't want to know if he's killed someone." It was only half a joke.

"I don't think so."

"For goodness sake! What's he done? All right, I won't tell

anybody, but if it's really bad you shouldn't keep it to yourself, you'll get into trouble."

He was right but it was a struggle, this was my father. In the end I told him everything: the men up north of the river, the plane, the watches, Lucas, the grapes, the French newspaper, the pistols. By the time I was finished the ice-cream dishes were long empty but there was enough money left to buy two coffees and share a cake.

"So these men, you think they're – what?"

"I don't know for sure," I said, "but some were in that gang I told you about in Paris. The leaders got killed and they split up, but a few have joined up again and now they're over here. That's the best I can work out. They've got hold of this boat and they're crossing to the continent."

"Smuggling?"

"I suppose so."

"Stuff stolen by the Nazis?"

"Some anyway."

Teddy stirred his coffee. "That's what happened to the Olswangs, my grampa's family in Vienna. They were quite well off, not rich but they had some nice things, mum says. Grampa had a sixteenth-century menorah that was worth a lot of money, you know, the candlestick we use on holy days. And when mum worked for the opera an old man gave her some sheets of music written in Mozart's own hand, a real treasure. They were left in the house. Nearly everything, I suppose, but when the German's realised they'd lost the war they probably sold it."

"Like those watches."

"Granny had a lovely watch, mum says, and some nice jewellery. She took it with her when they had to leave. Swapped it for food, a few slices of bread, when they were starving. Her wedding ring, everything. A woman who survived knew them in the ghetto."

"That was before…"

"They were packed off in the trains, yeah."

The trains, those photographs that filled the free world with horror. We had all seen them in the papers and on Pathé News at the pictures: soldiers clubbing people with their rifle butts and cramming them into cattle wagons; the helpless faces of men, women and children on the platforms; the grey railway lines that transported them to the camps at Buchenwald, Auschwitz, Belsen, Dachau, Chelmo, Mauthausen, Treblinka, Sobibor, names that turned your blood to ice. The terrible lie, *Arbeit Macht Frei*, works sets you free, cast on the iron entrance gates. And not just those camps whose names are familiar, but hundreds, thousands more. Mass graves in the forests of the east. Pits full of corpses. Bodies piled high. Living skeletons looking through the wire. Smoking ovens, Teddy's aunts and cousins. Teddy himself, looking at me now with his elbows on the table, if he had lived elsewhere in Europe.

"Not just Jews," he said, "gypsies, handicapped people, anyone whose face didn't fit, dragged from their homes, never going back. Whatever they owned, those people, it was there for the taking. If they died at the roadside soldiers robbed their bodies. When the houses were empty they walked in and helped themselves: ornaments, toys for their own kids, whatever they could carry. The treasures, the really valuable stuff, paintings, sculpture, church silver, that was for the officers, loaded into trucks and driven away. Who was to stop them? Here in Britain we escaped and the killing's over, thank God, but the whole of Europe's been torn apart. You see it every day in the papers, long lines of refugees with nowhere to go, their homes and cities destroyed. And there's all this looted stuff in barns and cellars, bricked up behind walls."

"That's what dad's lot are doing," I said, "I'm sure of it. Fetching it over here."

"But this won't be the end of the line. If it's valuable, I mean really valuable, Leonardo da Vinci and so on, there'll be people trying to track it down. So the best thing for the crooks is to get it out of the country as fast as they can, pack it off somewhere there won't be so many questions."

"Like where?"

"Further the better: the States, South America, Australia."

"Via Britain?"

"Why not? Who's looking for Nazi treasure in Eastport?"

"Or little Monkton Parva?"

I was sure he was right, it was what I had worked out for myself. A dirty business, the dirtiest, profiteering from Hitler's atrocities, making money out of death and disaster, the murder of innocent people. It made me sick to think of my dad mixed up in it.

Teddy said, "They can't be working alone."

"It's got to be a smuggling ring of some kind: one lot collect the stuff and bring it to the coast, dad's crowd ferry it across, somebody crates it up and labels it household goods or something, then a ship takes it to – well, wherever."

He scraped sugar from the bottom of his cup. "Did your dad say anything about this boat they're using?"

"A fishing boat, I think."

"Makes sense, something people recognise. Take a time to cross the North Sea though. Maybe they meet a bigger boat a few miles out."

"And pass the stuff across – if it's not too heavy?"

He sat back. "Dangerous business."

"If the sea's too rough I don't suppose they'd even try."

"That's not what I meant."

"You mean trouble?"

"In all kinds of ways."

"Yeah, well dad was in a fight of some kind, I told you. They're a rough crowd, maybe on opposite sides in the war. A lot of money involved. At least no one got shot."

"As far as you know."

"Yeah."

"But I was thinking more about the law, the police."

And the Royal Navy, he might have added, and the coastguard, and people out for a walk. It was a minefield.

Oh, Dad, I thought. You're going to get caught. What's going to happen to me when your photo's on the front page of the Chronicle?

28

Shaking Hands with the Headmistress

I suppose some girls might like being praised by the headmistress and hearing their names in assembly. I am not one of them.

Gran was due home on Tuesday afternoon and I wanted to be there but it was impossible, I had a full day in school and there was a rehearsal at four o'clock. In my absence Mrs Surtees was coming to meet the ambulance and see her settled in, which meant dad had to disappear. He made porridge and toast for my breakfast and saw me off to school, then planned to tidy the house and set the fire, make up gran's bed with clean sheets, and store a few belongings in the bottom of my wardrobe. Afterwards, he told me, he was going to investigate the lodgings he had been told about near the King and Country. One, I remembered, was called The Laurels, I have forgotten the name of the other. Perhaps it would be permanent, at least for as long as he stayed in Eastport, although I'm sure he'd have preferred to move in with another Brenda, If the police caught up with him, of course, he would have to disappear again, but it signalled the end of his stay in Wherry Row.

As I sat with my class in assembly that morning, however, my thoughts were not of my dad or gran but what Mrs Frobisher, the headmistress, would say and what I might have to do. Word had gone out and as we made our way along the corridor some girls had paused to say, "Well done, Mary, good for you!"

All too soon the hymn, the prayer and the notices were finished:

"Now, girls." Mrs Frobisher took off her reading glasses and looked across the sea of faces, "we are always delighted when the pupils of St Peter's do well, either a whole group of you in the national exams or some other enterprise, or just one of you who has distinguished herself in some way." It was awful, I stared down at my knees. "And I have to tell you that we have a very particular reason for celebration today; one of our girls in the Upper Fifth, Mary Pearson, has been awarded first place in the short-story competition run by the Eastport Chronicle. Stand up, please, Mary."

My face on fire, wishing the ground would open and swallow me whole, I did as I was told. I am not one of the beautiful girls at St Peter's, but the night before I had washed my hair and pressed my skirt and blazer, so at least I looked tidy.

"Very well done, Mary," she continued, "I think this deserves a big round of applause."

I didn't have a large circle of friends, just a few girls I got on well with, but equally I don't think I was disliked particularly, and the applause was long and genuine.

"This was for the Under-Eighteen Competition," said Mrs Frobisher," and when I phoned the editor yesterday he told me that Mary had come first out of two hundred and thirteen entrants. And as if that were not enough, her story, which is about a soldier in the war and entitled The Hero, has been awarded third place in the adult section also, although Mary did not enter for that. I have not read the story yet but I look forward to doing so next weekend when the Chronicle will be printing both winning stories, junior and adult, in full, so you'll all have a chance. And who knows, after Mary's success some other budding author among you may be inspired to have a go."

I thought she was finished and sat down with relief but worse was to come. She beckoned me to the stage: "Mary, will you be so kind as to come up here and join us?"

I shook my head in panic.

"Mary?"

I clung to my seat.

My form teacher, young Miss Laval, who was very popular and taught me history, nodded in encouragement.

I was being stupid, in a few days' time I had to face a packed hall on that stage and play the second lead in Julius Caesar. Reluctantly I rose, walked between the rows of junior girls, and climbed the steps.

"Quite an ordeal for you." Mrs Frobisher greeted me kindly then looked back at the sea of six hundred faces. "I am told the Chronicle will be awarding a prize, but I have discussed it with the teachers and we'd like to make a little presentation of our own for bringing honour to St Peter's. Very well done, Mary."

In a daze I shook her hand and took the small package she handed me, tied with a ribbon and bow in the school colours.

"Thank you very much."

Amid more applause, I was told where to stand as one of the teachers took a photo of me shaking hands with the headmistress for the school magazine.

It was awful and years before I could think of it without embarrassment, but gran was enormously proud and they couldn't have chosen a better gift, a black and gold Waterman's fountain pen. I didn't like the nib but the shop changed it and I used that pen for the rest of my schooldays and in the years that followed until at last, to my great sadness, it fell apart and could be repaired no more.

*

When I got home after rehearsal, dad was gone and gran was sitting in her chair, wrapped in her warm dressing gown. The fire was glowing and Mrs Surtees had set a hot-pot in the oven for our tea.

I dropped my schoolbag and ran to give gran a kiss.

"Hello, darling!" She wound her thin arm around my neck.

"How are you? It's wonderful to see you back."

"It's wonderful to be back, I can tell you. They couldn't have been kinder but you want your own home."

"Of course." I tucked back a strand of white hair. "Is there anything I can get you?"

"Not one thing. Just sit down there and let me look at you. How did it go this morning? As bad as you thought?"

"Worse, I'll tell you later." I collected my fountain pen. "They gave me this."

"My, that's a bobby-dazzler." Gran turned it in her thin fingers. "I'm that proud of you, sweetheart."

"And I'm proud of you, Gran." The air was rich with the smell of cooking. "Do you think you'll be able to eat a bit of hot-pot?"

I certainly will, and do you know what I fancy? Your dad's left a couple of bottles of ale, why don't you pour me a little glass. They're by the sink.

It was pure bravado. After a fortnight in hospital she must have felt weak as a kitten but she wasn't going to tell me that.

I smiled and went to do as she asked.

*

Two days later, which was on Thursday, dad called to pick up the last of his possessions. Gran, never one to give in, was in the midst of making a fish pie for our evening meal. He was looking much sprucer than I had described but hardly recognisable as the Frank Pearson who had married her daughter and was my father. To gran's surprise he now sported a neat dark beard, military haircut, spectacles, a tweed sports jacket and cavalry twill trousers. He had rented a room in a lodging house called Oak Lodge, he told her, a ten minute walk from the King and Country, which would suit him excellently for the time being.

I had not told gran about the watches, the pistol or the men who called under cover of darkness. There was no point in distressing her and nothing to be done short of reporting him to the police, which I could never do to my dad. How he would explain his absences to the proprietors of Oak Lodge I had no idea; perhaps he would tell them he was a travelling salesman.

Gran had made tea but he had barely bitten into a slice of cake when there was a knock at the back door. To her astonishment it was a man she had never seen before, "A man in working clothes with a foreign accent," she told me when I got home. "He told your dad there was a car at the end of the lane and they were waiting for him. So he grabbed a mouthful of tea had to hurry away. What was all that about?"

"I've no idea." I feigned surprise. "Did he take his things?"

"No, he said he'd call back in a day or two."

"If he's not here by the weekend, I'll call at this place where he's staying and ask him."

"Mm." Gran looked at me shrewdly. "There's something you're not telling me, Mary. I'll not press you, but if it's something that needs sorting out, you're to let me know straight away."

I blushed. "All right but it'll be OK, I'm sure."

"If you say so. Now come on, I've made a lovely cod pie, your favourite. Off with your school clothes while I dish up." She doubled the tea-towel she used for the oven. "How did the rehearsal go? Did you get the rest of your costume?"

29

St Jerome's

Although she was so recently out of hospital, gran was up at seven as usual on Saturday to clean out the fire and put on the kettle.

"No, no, love," she said when I offered to take over. "You get dressed and away out to Harry's for a copy of the Chronicle, I want to see my granddaughter in print. Better get three while you're at it. Oh, and a pint of milk. Take the money from my purse."

Harry's was the corner shop along from the Waterman's Arms. A rusty tin advert in the shape of a fat, full-sized chef with Bisto printed across his apron stood at the doorway. Yellowed notices advertising long-past concerts and quiz nights decorated the windows. Harry sold everything from fags to paint, baked beans to work boots, and was famous in the dock area, always happy to see you with his gap-toothed smile and whiskery chin. I had known him all my life.

"Aye, you're the famous lass," he said and bobbed his head in delight. "I've read your story. Very good, very good."

"Thanks, Harry," I said

"Your mam would have been right proud." He tapped the ash from his hand-rolled into a tin. "Puts me in mind what it was like in the First War. I was in the DLI like your dad, you know, in the trenches. Copped it in the leg on the Somme." He tapped his rigid knee, his face saddened. "A lot of the boys from round here got killed, you know. Best o' pals, grew up together. Your gran's brother for one, Billy Thomson, a great lad, always ready with a joke. Good footballer too, could have been a professional."

A strong young fellow came in from a van, clashing the bell on its spring. "Have you got Mrs Benson's order?" He was one of Harry's sons.

Harry ignored him. "Aye, he wouldn't be here if I'd bought it. Would you, Dave?"

"What?"

"If I'd copped it in France."

"That you on about the war again, Dad?" he said good-naturedly.

"Only 'cause of Mary's story."

"Oh, aye, I read it when I was sorting the papers. Good story that, pet. I couldn't have written it, I'll tell you that."

"I was just telling her if that shrapnel had got me in the guts 'stead of the leg, you wouldn't be here today."

"Can't argue with that. Or if that destroyer hadn't spotted us off the North Cape back in 'forty-one." Dave had been a gunner in the Royal Navy. He scowled at two young boys who had followed him into the shop and ran shouting to their grandfather. "Them neither. Good thing too, bloody pests!"

"Am I a bloody pest, Granddad?" one shouted delightedly.

"You certainly are," Harry said. "Here, take your hand out o' them lollipops!"

I paid for the papers and milk and left the shop.

Gran had heard the story before, of course, I'd read it to her aloud, but she was enormously proud to see it in print. The Chronicle had given it a whole page apart from the adverts, with my name at the top and a terrific pen-and-ink drawing of soldiers by one of their artists. As a treat gran made bacon and egg for breakfast and we ate it with the paper propped open on the milk jug.

*

I wanted to show the story to Teddy but he and Rachel were staying with Dr McGregor and his wife while their parents flew to Vienna for the court hearing. Mr Cohen and Dr McGregor had been friends since school days. He wasn't Jewish like the Cohens, or Church of England like most people in Eastport, or a Catholic like gran and me. Dr McGregor was an atheist, he didn't believe in God and didn't send his children to church, but he drove Teddy and Rachel to the synagogue for the Saturday morning service. In the afternoon the whole family, six in the car, drove north up the coast and hired a crab boat to see the inquisitive seals and thousands of sea birds wheeling round the cliffs of the Farne Islands.

Who could have guessed that a happy outing would lead within a fortnight to such scenes of drama and death? But as I've said, that is yet to come.

I did nothing so adventurous. In the morning I went shopping, caught up with my homework and listened to Forces' Favourites, a musical request programme, on the wireless. In the afternoon friends from church picked up gran and me in their car and drove to the promenade. For an hour we sat in the warm October sunshine then went to Rinaldi's for ice-cream and a sticky bun. Just four days out of hospital, recovering from pneumonia, it was exactly what gran needed.

Overnight the weather changed, bringing rain and a wet wind from the sea. I was glad it was Sunday because I had so many things on my mind that I wanted to go to mass. The calm atmosphere of St Jerome's, the Latin mass, the ceremony of bread and wine, the words of Christ to his disciples at the Last Supper, never failed to bring me comfort and often resolved a problem. Gran and I always attended mass together but on such a morning it would have been madness for her to venture out, so I pulled on my raincoat and waterproof hat and left her by the fire with her missal and well-read Bible. Luckily it was only a ten-minute walk, for the rain beat on my umbrella and I had to struggle to prevent it blowing inside out.

On Friday evening, in preparation for Communion, I had been to confession with Father Martin. The doorway of the confessional box was covered by a heavy curtain. I went in, crossed myself and knelt on the familiar tapestry stool at the grille. Father Martin had been our parish priest for as long as I could remember; he was a gentle, lovely, elderly man.

Although I understand that God knows everything, and whatever the priest hears in the confessional will never under any circumstances be repeated to another person, I could not bring myself to tell him about my dad, who far from being a dead hero as everyone thought, was living here in Eastport and carrying a pistol. I did tell him, however, that my main problem was something concerning him, and Father Martin behind the grille said, "But your dad's dead, Mary."

"Yes," I told him.

"He died fighting the forces of evil, he's with the saints now. You must know that."

"Yes," I said again.

"And God knows everything he's done."

"I know."

"So what is it you want to say?"

"I can't tell you, Father."

"But you must, if I'm to give you absolution."

"I know," I said again. "I'm sorry."

"It's not me you should be saying sorry to, Mary."

"Yes, I know." I tried to hold back the tears.

"I'll not press you, child, you're a good girl, but in your prayers you must ask for guidance. And I hope you'll be able to tell me about it the next time you come to confession."

"Thank you, Father."

"Take the weight of it off your soul. God wants you to have a clean, open heart. Think on it, Mary."

"I will." I don't know if he could hear me.

"And is there anything else?" he said gently.

I had thought about it. "Not really, just my friend Teddy. He's Jewish and his parents have gone to Vienna to try and get their house back. They're lovely people and it was stolen from them by the Nazis. His mother's the only one left, his grampa and everyone else was sent to the gas chambers. The man who lives there now, he hates the Jews, he's horrible, and I have bad thoughts about him."

"Your poor friend, that's a terrible, terrible story. But Jesus didn't like everybody, did he, not if they were doing bad things. Think of the money-changers. Try not to harden your heart, God knows better than you. It's not easy, I know, but he's got his eye on them."

"Yes, thank you, Father."

"And now, is there anything else?"

"I don't think so."

We were at an end. In Latin, for like most Catholic churches at that time St Jerome's still said the Latin Mass, Father Martin spoke the brief words of encouragement and followed them in English, "For your penance you should say three Hail Marys and two Our Fathers."

"I will," I said.

Then I bowed my head as he made the sign of the Cross and gave me absolution: "Ego te absolvo a peccatis tuis, in nomine Patris, et Filii, et Spiritus Sancti. Amen."[4]

"Amen," I responded and crossed myself in turn.

Finally Father Martin said, "Bless you, child. Go in peace and serve the Lord. Remember me in your prayers."

"I will," I said again and rose. "Thank you, Father."

---

4   I absolve you from your sins in the name of the Father, and of the Son, and of the Holy Spirit. Amen

As I let myself out into the church three others were waiting. I knew one of the women. "Hello, Mary," she said.

"Hello, Mrs Oliver," I did not stop to talk. People never did after confession, she didn't expect it."

Although I had only spoken a few words through a grille I was shaken and felt light-headed, not because of the Cohens, I'd known more or less what Father Martin would say about that, but because of my dad. The corners of St Jerome's were lost in shadow, the magnificent pillars and statues stood round me and spoke of tremendous matters, far beyond the events of my own little life. Three Hail Marys and two Our Fathers: it wasn't much I thought as I crossed myself at the stoup and buttoned my coat at the church door, I would say a whole rosary. What with dad, and gran, and the play, and Teddy's parents, there was a lot to pray for.

A drop of holy water trickled past the bridge of my nose. It was cold and felt nice.

30

The Unwelcome Boy

Rationing did not end with the war but continued for years afterwards. Meat, especially, was in short supply; people who longed for beef and Yorkshire pudding had to make do with potted brawn and cabbage. And so, when I took our ration books into the butcher's on Saturday, hoping for half a pound of mince, I was astonished when Mr Dixon reached beneath the counter and handed me a paper bag wet with blood and containing something solid.

"Here, Mary, love, pop it in your bag quick," he whispered.

I knew better than to argue. "What is it?" I mouthed.

"Never mind, just a little present for a nice and very clever girl."

It was the morning my story had appeared in the Chronicle. "Thanks very much, Mr Dixon."

"Me and the wife were that proud when we read it."

He was a lovely man. Although he never spoke of it, his son Mike, a private in a parachute regiment, had been captured and imprisoned by the Germans. When the camp was liberated by the advancing Americans, bodies littered the earth and Mike, who had been a boxer, was reduced to a skeleton covered with skin. Although he was now married and drove a van for his father, he had never been completely right afterwards.

"Your gran's out of hospital, I'm told."

"I nodded.

"Help to build her up a bit." He smiled. "Now, what is it you're wanting?"

"Half of mince if you've got it." I handed him the ration books. "I think there's enough coupons."

The soggy bag contained a small joint of lamb, a rare luxury, and that Sunday lunchtime gran roasted it and made the most delicious gravy I have ever tasted out of the juices. With roast potatoes and sprouts from Mr Hemmings' allotment, followed by stewed apples and Carnation milk, it was a wonderful Sunday lunch. I began the washing-up but gran chased me away:

"No, no, no, Mary, on you go. You've got that big rehearsal this afternoon – what did you call it?"

"The technical rehearsal."

"Yes, right, well you don't want to be late. I'll do this in five minutes then have a little nap."

It was only two days until the dress rehearsal, and two days after that, on Thursday, October the fourteenth, we had first night. Mrs Jamison had summoned everyone, the entire cast, electricians, designers, stage crew, costume department, make-up artists, programme sellers, everyone, for a technical check and final rehearsal at two o'clock prompt that Sunday afternoon. Other teachers were in charge of most of these, Mrs Jamison couldn't do everything, and the date had been pencilled in months before. Nobody objected because she worked twice as hard as anyone and brought prestige to the school. Some pupils could expect to be home by three-thirty; others, I among them, were told to bring sandwiches because we might be there until seven. It was a long session and a team of volunteers, mostly kitchen ladies and mums, had been drafted in to provide tea and Tizer, home-made lemonade, and whatever sandwiches or biscuits they could afford from their meagre rations.

The school was a hive of activity: a hundred or more girls, technical boys from St Peter's, mums, dads and teachers, hurried along the corridors, buzzed about the stage, and huddled in classrooms with baskets of Roman costumes, big jars of cream and sticks of Leichner grease paint to make us look Italian. In other classrooms clear voices rang out as girls in their everyday clothes rehearsed speeches and movement while friends sat on desks and fed them their cues. Pupils from the photographic club took shots to display in the vestibule on opening night. And here, there and everywhere, with her clipboard and bursting notebook, Mrs Jamison offered a smile and helping hand to anyone who needed it, a tower of strength to us all. In her earlier life, as Vivien Banks, she had been an actor on the London stage. We were enormously lucky to have her on the staff, so dedicated and enthusiastic, with all that RADA training and experience to draw on.

In Shakespeare's play, Brutus is a nobleman who kills his lifelong friend, Julius Caesar, whom he loves, fearing he has become so powerful that he might anoint himself Emperor. Although Brutus does this for the good of Rome and it leads to his being called 'the noblest Roman of them all', it is a treacherous act which eventually leads to suicide by running onto his sword which I had to perform centre stage. It is a long play and in the slightly shortened version we performed at St Peter's Brutus was not the star part, that was Mark Antony, but along with Cassius it came a close second. Many times with Mrs Jamison I had rehearsed my famous speech in Act 3, 'Romans, countrymen and lovers', and my big scenes with Cassius and the other murderers, but there were shorter scenes that I hoped to rehearse a final time, for example my encounters with the ghost of Julius Caesar, and my lifeless body being carried off-stage at the end. Mrs Jamison, professional to the last, was aware of this and they were pencilled into her notebook.

That afternoon, for the first time, I got fully made-up, my face, arms and legs browned, black wig and short curly beard, heavy eyebrows and eye liner. Miss Grant, who was in charge of the costume department, helped me with the three outfits I was to wear: for domestic scenes a white, knee-length tunic; for ceremonial occasions a magnificent white toga edged with purple; and for battle scenes a tremendous helmet with a crimson plume, an ornamental breastplate and sandals with straps that criss-crossed my calves. When engaged in the fighting, I carried a decorative leather shield on my left forearm, and in my right hand an officer's stabbing sword.

When I saw my reflection in the full-length mirror set up in the dressing room, it was hard to believe this was Mary Pearson, a schoolgirl from Wherry Row down by the Eastport Docks. Suddenly I was terrified, in just two days I would be on stage, the hall would be packed. Could I make an audience believe in this powerful man, or would I fail horribly and be an embarrassment to myself and everyone else?

Mrs Jamison had warned us that some pupils might not be going home until seven but I stayed behind to help tidy up and in the event it was nearly eight o'clock before I left the school. It had begun to rain but as I stood at the bus stop the father of the girl who was playing Casca, another lead, stopped to offer me a lift in his car, not just into town but right to my front door.

*

Monday was planned out, I knew exactly what I would be doing, or so I thought. In the morning there would be normal teaching. In the afternoon I was to go to the hall for a final run-through before the dress rehearsal in front of the whole school the following day. Some of my teachers complained that I would miss important lessons but they had given me catch-up work for Potato Week which followed directly after, and since Mrs Frobisher had given permission, there was nothing they could do about it.

We wore our normal school clothes and all went well until cross-patch Miss Bird, who taught me maths, brought a message that a 'boy' had entered the school unannounced and wished to see me. It was important, he said, and he had been shown into an empty classroom close to the secretary's office. Boys, such as the senior boys who had been constructing the set, rarely appeared in the school and were the subject of much interest and speculation. I didn't like Miss Bird whose name, going by her appearance, should more properly have been Miss Toad. It was said she was a very clever mathematician and she was nice to me because I was good at her subject, but to those girls who found maths difficult, particularly if they were pretty, she was sarcastic and unkind. More than once I had seen a lovely girl who was doing her best reduced to tears. Anyway, I apologised to Mrs Jamison and followed the squat figure of Miss Bird to the classroom where they had put 'the boy' as she called him with something not far from disgust. She left me at the door but could not resist saying: "We don't encourage boys calling like this, I hope it's not going to become a regular occurrence. Mrs Frobisher is very much against it."

Cow! Did she dislike all males, I wondered, or was she bitter because none had ever wanted to marry her? "No, Miss Bird, it's never happened before. He'd only call if it was something really important. Thank you."

It had to be Teddy, there was no other 'boy' in my life, but what could he want? He was staying with Dr McGregor, his parents were in Vienna. What could be so important he would call me out of rehearsal? I let myself into the classroom. Although I had announced elsewhere that Teddy was my boyfriend he wasn't really, but Miss Bird hovered outside the door as if she wanted to catch us kissing. "Thank you," I said again, this time pointedly, and she moved away.

"Hi, Teddy. What is it?"

"Sorry to call. Hey, that woman's a bit of a dragon."

"Yeah, no one likes her." The chairs stood on desks to help the cleaners. I pulled one down. "What is it?"

Teddy sat opposite, a desk between us. "You know Dr McGregor where Rachel and I are staying? He stitched your leg."

"Yeah, we talked about it."

"Well on Saturday afternoon he drove us all up the coast to Monkton Parva, and we took a crab boat out to the islands. It was great, all the seals and the seabirds and—"

"Yeah, yeah, but what?"

"Give us a sec, I'm just coming to it. When we came back we wanted a cup of tea but everywhere was shut except for a sort of café behind the boat houses, you know, up that twisty lane. A bit scruffy, just a big shed and a cinder area with a tin roof and tables for tea and that. Mrs McGregor went to see what they could give us and there were some men had pushed a couple of tables together and they were sitting with empty beer glasses. It was a nice afternoon and I guessed they'd rather be outside than in the shed. Good view over the harbour."

"Yes, and—?"

"You're very impatient!"

"Teddy, I'm in the middle of a rehearsal!"

"All right, well will you just listen! I wouldn't have taken any notice but there was an empty chair, one of them had gone to the gents, and where he'd been sitting there was some stuff on the table. A bit of a jumble, then I saw it was a packet of French fags and a penknife and a bit of wood he had been carving. Chips of wood all over the cinders."

"Oh, my God! My dad?"

"That's right. I waited for him to come back and I'm sure

it was. I've met him a couple of times, up in the barn and when he made tea after we'd had that fight with Peg. But he looked different, he's grown a beard, like you said, and his hair's down over his forehead. And it was different clothes, but I'm sure it was him."

"Did you say anything?"

"Well, I couldn't. Nobody knows anything about your dad, they think he's dead. The men he was with looked a bit of a tough crowd. Some didn't look English. I can't say why, they just didn't."

I remembered Lucas who had called in the middle of the night and carried a revolver. "Did dad see you?"

"Not to recognise. I tried to listen but they were too far away so I went to the gents myself, getting as close as I could. They were speaking English, nothing important, just something about heading back and what they were going to have for dinner. But one of them said something in German: 'Wieder blutiger Fisch'."

"What does that mean?"

"Bloody fish again. They must be sick of it. I saw one chap looking at me, wondering why I was hanging about, so I hurried on into the toilet."

"Were they there for long?"

"Just a couple of minutes. They'd been waiting for your dad and when I came out they were heading for an old blue van. I wrote down the number, BR38- something. Easy to recognise, there's a patch of red lead on the wing."

"I've seen that van at the end of our street. That must be where he goes when he's away from home."

"I thought you'd want to know. I think they'd just come for a beer, staying somewhere else."

"How'd you know that?"

"After the café we went for a paddle, and on the way home here's the van sitting outside some derelict farm buildings."

"Where abouts?"
"You know Biddle?"
"That little village with the church, yeah?"
"Three or four miles north of there."
"I don't suppose you saw a name?"
"I did as a matter of fact, there's a beat-up old sign at the end of a track: Saltfield Mains."

Saltfield Mains, it was the first time I'd heard of it. A name that would stay with me until the end of my life.

"You're sure it was the same van?"
"I told you, there's this patch of red paint."

I was picturing it when there was a knock at the classroom door and Alison Jones came in. She was the star of the drama club, playing Mark Antony, and she was brilliant. Nice, too, I liked her enormously. "Mrs Jamison sent me to find you, she's waiting to do the death scene. Better hurry."

"Yeah, right, coming." I jumped up, caught a desk with my toe and sent the chairs crashing. "How about looking dad up on – on – Sunday?" I said to Teddy. "Go to his lodgings? I can't before then, there's the play. Will you come? Sunday afternoon?"

"Yes, I think—"

"I'll give you a ring." And leaving the chairs where they lay, I ran from the room with Alison.

The awful Miss Bird stood in the corridor, hoping to find something to complain about. "Don't run!" she shouted. Alison and I slowed to a walk, a walk so fast our legs were almost a blur.

Looking back from the corner, I saw her heading for the classroom where the unwelcome 'boy' was straightening the chairs and collecting his schoolbag.

31

Julius Caesar

The play went well as did all Mrs Jamison's productions. The reason was simple, if girls weren't prepared to put in the work, they didn't get to join the Drama Club, and the shows were so highly regarded there was no shortage of applicants. This was my fourth production: I had played the crocodile in Peter Pan, First Schoolgirl in a comedy-thriller called Nightmare Castle, and last year a mountaineer swept away by an avalanche in The Ascent of F6. This year it was Shakespeare, almost every character a man. The settings were terrific: the Roman forum, a square in the city, a walled orchard, and a marching camp with ramparts, flags, tents, weapons, even a horse and two war dogs. Each time the curtain rose the audience broke into applause, and we actors looked similarly splendid in our wigs and beards, togas and armour.

It wasn't possible for the dress rehearsal to finish by four, but half the audience stayed after school and when we took our bows they filled the hall with shouts and applause. Alison got the loudest cheer and she deserved it, she was superb, but I got a cheer too, and several of the others, so it looked like being a success. I was enormously relieved because ever since Mrs Jamison had cast me as the replacement Brutus, I had been terrified I would let everyone down.

You may be interested to know that Alison went directly from sixth form at St Peter's to RADA, and some years later

I saw her play a heart-breaking Juliet at the Old Vic. Even as a schoolgirl she had star quality.

Mrs Jamison had a bulging notebook and all next day and on Thursday morning, we were summoned to the stage to iron out wrinkles, not just the actors but the stage crew, lighting crew, everyone involved.

And then it was first night. Ready in my make-up and toga, so frightened I thought I would be sick, I stood behind the curtain and heard the audience arrive. The cast stood singly or in groups. Some stared into space, muttering lines they knew as well as their own names. The hands of the clock moved round.

"Come on, into the wings those of you needed in the first scenes, the rest into the green room." Mrs Jamison ushered her actors off the stage, girls become men. "Hush! Keep your voices down."

I waited in the wings because after a short opening scene I was to make my entrance amid a crowd of the most important citizens of Rome. You probably know the story, the most famous assassination in history. To remind you of the play: as the curtain rises Julius Caesar has at that moment returned from Egypt after a great victory over Pompey. The two men have quarrelled over the leadership and Rome has descended into a state of civil war. The ecstatic Roman crowd call for Caesar to be proclaimed emperor. He declines repeatedly but is now so powerful that many fear he will change his mind and a group of conspirators plan his downfall. One of the leaders is Cassius, a senator and soldier who is eaten up with jealousy. Another is Brutus, the part I was playing, but Brutus loves Rome and sees an emperor as being fatal to the republic. As the plot develops, the conspirators conclude that Caesar must be killed. On the Ides (fifteenth) of March, a key date in the Roman calendar, they follow him into the Senate and stab him repeatedly with their daggers. It is a violent and bloody assassination.

Every play by Shakespeare has five acts; this is the start of act three. Following the murder, Brutus explains to the crowd that Caesar had become so powerful he was a threat to the state. But Mark Antony, more emotional and passionate, breaks his heart over Caesar's body: *O pardon me, thou bleeding piece of earth / That I am meek and gentle with these butchers*, a wonderful speech by Alison that sent shivers through everyone on stage and I am sure the whole audience. Then Antony has Caesar carried into the market place and shows his wounded body and the blood-sodden holes in his cloak to the Roman crowd. In his famous speech *Friends, Romans, countrymen, lend me your ears*, he rouses them to such anger and mutiny that the conspirators are forced to flee for their lives. They are pursued to Philippi on the plains of Greece by the Roman army led by Mark Antony and Octavian, Caesar's heir, who only appears briefly but in time becomes the great Caesar Augustus. There are battle scenes in the last act at the end of which, knowing that all is lost, Cassius orders a servant to kill him, whilst Brutus, tormented by guilt, commits suicide by running on his sword. The victors, understanding that all Brutus did was for love of Rome, have him carried shoulder-high in honour from the field of battle. It is the final tableau.

Julius Caesar was written around 1600, but although everyday speech and the theatre have changed beyond recognition, it continues to be a great play, the language so powerful, the drama so intense. The Eastport audience loved it, loved seeing the girls of St Peter's perform this Shakespearean classic, and rose to applaud and call out as we took our bows.

"Very well done!" Mrs Jamison joined us on stage as the curtain came down finally. She was delighted and found some detail to congratulate each one of us. I was pleased to be included because although I was acting and speaking verse, I had been caught up in the tragedy more than I anticipated.

As I had bowed in my armour to take the applause, I was so shaken by what had become of poor Brutus that I could could hardly raise a smile.

"Right, on you go," Mrs Jamison told us briskly. "Into the changing room and take off your make-up, every last trace. No leaving a brown face to show everybody you're one of the actors."

It was ten o'clock by the time the play ended and although this was the grammar school, few of the girls had dads with cars. We didn't have to walk home because the buses ran late, but we'd been told to stay in pairs and get a lift if we could. Mr Dixon, the butcher, had offered without my asking and he and his wife were waiting in the lobby.

"My gum, you're a clever girl!" He put an arm round my shoulders. "Author! Actor!"

I had known him most of my life. "Ah, well. It's all this top-class meat you give us. Feeds the brain."

"Aye, that'll be it." He was pleased.

"Couldn't hardly recognise you," his wife said. "I said to Billy, are you sure that's her? Them eyebrows, that brown skin! That's never our Mary."

A wet wind blew the hair across my face. Mr Dixon held the door while I squeezed after his plump wife into the front seat of his butcher's van. Only twenty minutes earlier, watched by five hundred people, I had been a tortured Roman general committing suicide mid-stage. It was down to earth with a bump.

Gran wanted to hear all about it but after an egg-and-tomato sandwich and a cup of Ovaltine, she packed me off to bed:

"Come on, love, your eyes are closing. No, no, leave those. I'll wash up."

It had been an eventful day and as I pulled on my nightie and slid gratefully between the sheets, my mind was a whirl.

It didn't keep me awake; in no more time than it takes to write this I was conquered by sleep and did not stir for nine hours.

*

"Morning, Mary, darling. Wakey-wakey."

"Mm?" The room was brighter than usual. "Morning, Gran. What time is it?"

"Half past eight. I've just—"

"What!" I sprang up in bed. "Why didn't you wake me?"

"Lie down, you don't have to be in till ten."

I'd forgotten. Gratefully I sank back.

"What's that?" gran said.

"What?"

"That mark on the pillow. Are you bleeding?"

I raised my head. A brown mark. Several brown marks. Not blood, make-up. Although I had cleaned myself thoroughly with cold cream and tissues, some corners had been missed.

"It was clean on yesterday, I'll just leave it," gran said. "Likely happen again tonight. No point making work."

I smiled and stretched.

"Fire's on. Come on through and I'll make the toast." She turned away. "Oh, there's a letter for you."

"A letter?"

"No stamp, just pushed through the door."

"Who from?"

"How should I know? It's addressed to you. Probably some boy who saw you on stage and wants to elope."

"With a bearded Roman?"

"Takes all sorts. Come on, I'll make the tea."

I pulled on my dressing gown, pushed the hair from my face and followed her through. A plain white envelope:

Miss Mary Pearson, 17 Wherry Row.
I recognised the handwriting.
So had gran:
Dear Mary,

What a star! Your mam was a great actor, she would have been proud of you. So am I. Lucky I got seats a while ago, it was sold out. Tomas came with me, he's one of the boys. Says I am to tell you he thinks you were terrific. I liked your costume and make-up and things, and the way you acted like a man. And ran on your sword and got carried off at the end. Goodness knows how you remembered all that. I wanted to tell everybody that's my daughter! Well done.

I hope Eva's feeling strong again.
Love to both of you,
Dad

I showed the letter to gran. She was pleased for me: "I'm sure he loves you, sweetheart. I just wish he'd settle down like other men. You know I never speak ill of your dad but he's got a wild streak, there's no denying it."

"But it's nice of him, getting tickets and leaving a note and all."

"Yes, of course it is, good for him. But where's he living? What's he up to? I hope he's not going to get into trouble again. It's bad enough being a deserter with his name up there on the War Memorial."

She was only saying what I thought myself.

"I just don't want you getting involved. You've enough on your plate what with school and helping me here."

Helping her? It was gran who did everything for me. I took her hand, "No need to worry, I won't."

"Well I hope not, you're such a kind-hearted girl, Mary."

I read the letter again and rescued a shred of marmalade

from my dressing-gown. "I wonder who Tomas is."

"How would I know? One of the boys, he says. My brother Billy used to talk about the boys in his platoon, I think it's an army thing. They don't talk like that in the shipyards."

"Mm." She more or less confirmed what I had worked out for myself: the men Teddy had seen, Lucas coming for dad in the middle of the night, the man with a foreign accent who called when gran was there. One-time members of the Paris gang, I was sure of it. They had all been soldiers.

"Anyway," gran said, "you've got other things on your mind today. "You'll be home about half-three so I'll make the tea for four. That'll give you plenty of time to get back for your make-up. Did you say Charlie Williamson's giving you a lift home?"

I nodded.

She rescued more toast from under the grill. "I'm that pleased it went well last night. I can't tell you how much I'm looking forward to tomorrow." Gran was coming with friends on Saturday. They had invited her for tea and would bring us both home after the play. Teddy was coming with Rachel and his parents that night, so were some of my teachers, and the Mayor of Eastport with a few of the bigwigs from town.

But before that there was Friday's performance to get through.

It went well and then it was Saturday, my skin was brown, my hair was black and curly, I was dressed in my white toga with the purple border, and I was peeping through the curtain to see the audience arrive. I knew where gran would be sitting and there she was, her hair permed for the occasion and wearing her best dress with a blue shawl. There, too, were Teddy and his family, and Mrs Surtees and her daughter who had given me the pram, and my class teacher, and Mrs

Frobisher, and the Mayor sitting in the front with his gold chain. The lights dimmed, the curtain rose, the audience applauded the set and swirling crowd of commoners:

"*Hence, home, you idle creatures, get you home,*" cried Jenny Smith in a ringing voice, splendidly robed as one of the tribunes. "*Is this a holiday?*"

The final performance had begun. The crowd dispersed and I made my entry with Caesar and all the leading characters followed by another great crowd. It was a powerful opening but soon, as everyone departed to a ceremonial feast, Rosie Banks and I were left alone on stage to develop the famous scene where Cassius begins to poison the mind of noble Brutus against the all-conquering hero. On Thursday, as I have told you, I had been surprised, in the scenes following the murder, how distressed I became over the guilt and remorse of my character. On Friday I had experienced none of it but this night it started much earlier. As I plotted with the other conspirators to kill my friend, I felt Brutus's reluctance in my belly, and as I plunged my dagger into Caesar and he looked up at me in reproach, *Et tu, Brute*, I could have cried out in horror. I don't think actors should feel like that but I did, not through the whole play but time and again. And after I had committed suicide, as my corpse was being carried from the field of battle and the curtain came down, I felt physically drained. The applause was long and loud, there were some shouts, but as I stood with my fellow actors to take a bow, I had to make an effort to raise a smile.

"Hey, Mary," Alison Jones stood beside me. "I didn't know you could act like that."

"What?" Hardly understanding what she said, I looked her in the face.

"You were great!"

"Oh!" Slowly her kind words filtered through but I was still somewhere else. "Thanks."

"Are you OK?" She was concerned.

"Yeah. Yes. Thanks," I said again and realised who was talking to me. She was our star and as Mark Antony she had been fiery and passionate and wonderful. "I wish I could act like you. Your big speech was—"

"Sshhh!" Mrs Jamison had joined us and nodded to the footlights The Mayor of Eastport, a short fat man, had puffed up the steps to the stage and was preparing to say a few words. We stood back.

"Good evening, ladies and gentlemen:

"Aren't we lucky here in Eastport to have a fine school like St Peter's! All these clever lasses – and the lads next door. I didn't get in, didn't pass the exam. If I had, who knows how far I might have gone." He paused for a polite laugh. "Shakespeare wasn't on the curriculum, the school I went to—"

I stopped listening and slowly, as I stood looking out at the audience, my gran the most important person there, a big lump in my chest dissolved and I started to cry, not sobbing but silently. Tears spilled from my eyes. I lowered my head and backed behind a tall centurion, hoping no one would notice. Why I should have been so upset over the fate of Marcus Brutus, a man who lived two thousand years ago, I cannot explain.

But weep I did, and though I thought about it many times afterwards I never came to a satisfactory conclusion: was it the quality of the writing; relief that I hadn't made a mess of it; my dad not a dead hero but here in Eastport on the run; the sight of my gran out there in the audience? I couldn't say.

It only lasted a minute or two and by the time the Mayor was finished, Mrs Frobisher had said a few words and wished us a happy Potato Week, everyone had been thanked, and Mrs Jamison had been presented with a big bouquet, I was more or less recovered.

Photographs were taken, the curtain came down, and we trooped off stage for the last time. Mrs Jamison spoke to us in one of the classrooms we used for changing: "Very well done – everybody. We took on one of the great Shakespearean tragedies and you have responded even better than I'd hoped. Perhaps even now you don't realise what a mountain you have climbed. Not many schools, let alone girls' schools, could have put on performances like you have the last three nights, and tonight you exceeded yourselves. Good for you! I could not be more pleased."

It was unlike her to be so complimentary and she went through the entire cast, finding something to praise in everyone's performance. When she came to me she said, "Brutus: a big, big part for a fifth-form girl, Mary, and you carried it excellently. I'll talk to you later." I hoped this was not because she had seen my tears, that was over now and I had no wish to discuss it.

Twenty minutes later, my make-up removed and costumes folded on the desk I had been allocated, I joined the crush in the lobby. Girls congratulated me and pointed me out to their parents. Gran was standing with the Cohens and the couple who were giving us a lift. Teddy said, "Hey, that was terrific! I know I read some with you but I thought it would be boring. It wasn't, it was great! You were the best thing in it."

"Not true but thanks anyway."

"You were!"

Everyone was lovely but it was gran with her best handbag and cosy shawl I had most wanted to please. She took my hand. "Mary, love, what a marvellous performance!"

"Thanks, Gran."

"All them weeks we sat going over your lines, and you just brought it to life."

I beamed like an idiot.

"I wish your mam could have been here to see it, she'd have been that proud!" She gave me a tremendous hug, her thin arms pulling me close.

A second time that lump in my chest and tears brimming my eyes. I blinked them away and felt for a hanky.

"Tomorrow." Rachel pulled her mother's sleeve.

"I'm just going to." Mrs Cohen turned to gran. "We're all hoping you and Mary might be free to come to lunch tomorrow. I know it's short notice but David and I have been away and the children keep asking."

Gran looked at me. "That's very kind of you."

"David's brother has given us a couple of nice fat rabbits. I thought I'd make rabbit pie."

"Lovely."

"With apple rugelach for pudding," Rachel said. "And home-made ice-cream."

"Well, I don't know what that is," gran said, "but it sounds delicious."

"It is."

32

Women Friends

We both had bikes, black uprights with three-speed Sturmey-Archer gears: Teddy's had a crossbar, mine didn't. At ten o'clock on Monday morning I met him at the gates of Raintree Park and we cycled out to the King and Country on the edge of town. It was an inn more than a pub, people went there for meals, but dad had made it his watering hole since he couldn't go to the pubs he used to frequent down by the docks. We hoped someone could direct us to Oak Lodge where he had told gran he was staying. I wanted to ask him about the men Teddy had seen at Monkton Parva and what they were all doing.

We had arranged it the previous day when everyone, my gran included, had walked up Strawberry Hill after lunch to fly kites in the sunshine. The grown-ups went down after half an hour but I stayed on with Teddy and Rachel. It was brilliant, the kites dancing high up against the sky, but after a while we lay back in the grass, sheltered from the wind. And it was there, the October sun hot on our faces, that we agreed to cycle out to the King and Country next morning. If we didn't find him there, Teddy had suggested cycling all the way to Saltfield Mains, the abandoned farm buildings where he had seen the van, later in the week. He had found it in his dad's road atlas, fifteen miles north of Eastport, so that would have to be an excursion with sandwiches and flasks of tea.

The King and Country proved to be an imposing white building with black timbers, a sign depicting King Charles II, and a cinder car park. The door was locked, opening time not until eleven. "Come on," I said. We leaned the bikes against the wall and walked round to the back. A gate let us into a yard full of crates, empty beer casks and broken bar-room furniture. A chipped black door stood open.

"Hello?" we called.

The stone floor was wet with mopping. The stink of yesterday's fags mingled with a smell of stale beer. A chesty cough and the clatter of a cleaning bucket came from within. For a popular inn on the smart side of town, it was unappealing on a Monday morning.

"Hello?"

"Eh?" Cough-cough! A skinny old woman in a black dress and apron appeared round a corner. "What you kids want?"

"We're looking for someone—"

"Shouldn't be in 'ere, your age."

"We're looking for someone who can tell us—"

"Go on, get out of it. Cheek, walking in 'ere like you own the place."

Teddy stepped forward. "We're looking for a place round here called Oak Lodge. A lodging house."

"Oh, aye?" She took a drag from her cigarette. "So why have you come to the King?"

"We hoped someone could tell us where it is."

"My dad comes here," I said. "It was someone at the King told him about it."

"Who was that then?"

"I've no idea."

"Well what's your dad's name?"

What was he calling himself? I had to rake my memory. "Mr Wilmot – Charlie Wilmot."

"Charlie Wilmot! And you say you're his daughter?"

"Yes."

"Charlie Wilmot? Cheeky beggar!" She began to laugh, her lungs rattling, and had to remove the fag. "Well, that's the... Hey, Loretta!" She shouted back into the building.

"Yeah?"

"Come 'ere a minute."

"What for?"

"Never mind, just come here."

The woman who appeared could not have been a bigger contrast. She also was a cleaner but thirty years younger and sexy in a dress tied tight to show off her curves. Her hair was peroxide blonde and even at ten-thirty on a Monday morning she wore vivid red lipstick and long eyelashes.

"Yeah, what do you want?" She eyed Teddy and me with contempt. "Who's these two then?"

"You know that fellow Reenie has been going around with? They were in here last night."

" Course. Danny something."

"Charlie," the old woman corrected her. "Charlie Wilmot."

"Yeah, that's right."

"Talking about getting engaged."

"So she says. Good-looker he is too. Commercial traveller, washing machines, isn't it? Doing well, he says."

"Not married nor nothing?

"Not for the want of girls. Waiting for the right one, he says. God knows what he sees in Reenie Carter. What about him?"

"Only got his daughter standing here, haven't we?"

"What, her?" The dark eyes turned on me. "Charlie your dad then?"

"Yes."

"Bloody hell!" She stared then began to laugh. "One in the eye for that stuck-up little tart. Have you heard her: 'Me and Charlie's planning a house up Church Hill. Going to this hotel in Scotland for the honeymoon'." A lock of bright hair fell over her face.

"What you want him for anyroad?" said the woman in black.

"Just got a couple of questions."

"An' you heard he's staying at – where d'you say?"

"Oak Lodge."

She made a face. "New one on me.

"Not round here," said her companion.

"Are you sure?"

"Pretty sure. Working here twenty years, I've never heard of it."

"That's not what Reenie said, anyroad. Didn't she tell Barbara he's lodging with that old woman at Laburnum Villa?"

"I've no idea."

"Is that somewhere round here?"

"Just the next road. But why would he tell you Oak Lodge?"

"There must have been a mix-up."

"An' you live somewhere in town, do you?"

I nodded.

"Why's he not staying with you and your mam, if you don't mind my asking?"

"Well I do, as a matter of fact," I said. "But since you have asked, my mum's dead."

Instantly their mood changed. "Oh, love, I'm sorry."

"And you want to see your dad?"

"That's what I've been telling you. So if you've never heard of Oak Lodge, where's this Laburnum Villa?"

At last it was sorted out and Teddy and I collected our bikes.

*

It wasn't far, a big corner house surrounded by a garden. Once it had been smart but now the shrubs were overgrown and the path needed a brush. I read the faded notice-board:
Laburnum Villa
Superior Residential Accommodation
Apply Within

The woman who answered had permed hair and wore a tweed costume. A string of pearls hung against her neatly-pressed jumper. She spoke with a public-school voice but looked tired and depressed, as if life had been a huge disappointment to her. Her name, I saw from a notice stuck to the stained-glass of the inner door, was Mrs Rattray. Perhaps when she heard the bell she had hoped for something to cheer her day, instead of which she found two fifteen-year-olds on her doorstep.

"Yes?" She eyed us with disfavour.

"Can you tell me, please, is Mr Wilmot staying here?"

"I can't say. People come and go all the time." Although it was only eleven in the morning, I wondered if she had been drinking. "Why do you want to know?"

"He's my dad."

"Your father?" She considered her reply. "Yes, I do have a Mr Wilmot staying as it happens, but he's an unmarried man. A very nice gentleman. Not old enough to have a daughter your age."

"Pardon?"

"I said he's a single man, not old enough to be – er—"

"Well, he just is. Charlie Wilmot, he's my dad."

"Yes, Charles is his name." She didn't like it. Wanted us to go away. Didn't want her day upset. "He gave me to understand he was unmarried."

I wondered what difference it made if a lodger was married, then realised my dad had been using his well-known charm on the landlady as well as 'that stuck-up little tart' Reenie, as Loretta called her. I wondered what age Mrs Rattray was. Older than dad, certainly, but maybe she was well-off.

"My mum's dead," I said for the second time that morning. "She was killed in the war."

"Ah, that explains it," she said. "He never told me. So many people have died, even up here, five miles from the shipyards. There was a house bombed out just two streets away."

"It wasn't a bomb that killed my mum," I said. "Anyway, is dad in?"

"My little cat ran off," she said.

"Pardon?"

"The bombing frightened her – and the shells. We searched everywhere. I pinned notices to the railings."

"Oh, I'm sorry. Did you get her back?"

"Two days later." As if on cue a little tortoiseshell cat appeared and she caught it up in her arms, kissed its head. "An old lady along the road had taken her in."

Teddy rolled his eyes.

"That's good," I said. "I bet you were glad to find her. But I'm looking for my dad. Is he here?"

"No, I'm afraid you've missed him. He went off straight after breakfast. Commercial traveller, but you know that, top salesman. Won't be back till Friday. The company's sent him over into Wales."

"Are you sure?"

"So he told me. Went off with that foreign chap who drives for him. At least I think so, I wasn't down yet."

I had hoped to see dad but she had more or less answered my questions. "Is he away a lot?"

"He's one of my more recent residents, but he had to go off on business the end of last week. Just a couple of nights. It depends where they send him."

"Of course, thank you. I'll come back at the weekend. If

you see him before that will you tell him I called please. My name's Mary."

"Certainly."

"Goodbye." Teddy and I turned away. She didn't reply and as we looked back from the path she opened the inner door and went inside.

"Did you see?" Teddy said.

"What?"

"There's a gin bottle on the hall table."

I hadn't noticed but it made sense. Laburnum Villa was a perfect lodging for my dad; a landlady who liked gin and looked as if she had money, a comfortable pad where he could come and go freely. Although she was stupid, I felt sorry for lonely Mrs Rattray with her tortoiseshell cat.

And what about Reenie, boasting to her friends about the house up Church Hill and her honeymoon in the Highlands?

As for my dad, I felt ashamed.

33

A Long Bike Ride

This is Teddy again. Mary has asked me to write this bit because I speak German and it was important. Incidentally, she should have explained that although it was the Potato Week holiday and friends from St Peter's did go digging potatoes on the farms, neither of us had any plans to do so. If we had, many things would have turned out differently.

I had better get the days right: Saturday, October 16th was the last night of Mary's play; on Sunday she and gran came to our house for lunch; and on Monday we cycled out to the King and Country and called on poor Mrs Rattray at Laburnum Villas. The next morning, Tuesday, we met in town and set off on the long ride north to see if we could catch her dad at Saltfield Mains, the abandoned farm where I had seen the blue van.

It was a day of blue sky and clouds. At eleven o'clock we were cycling up Seaton Cut, or I should say struggling to cycle up Seaton Cut. This is a famously steep hill seven miles north of Eastport, down from the moors to the bridge over the River Seaton and up the far side. On the rare occasions I cycled out that way it was a challenge to ride up the steeper north side without dismounting – and hopefully without my third gear slipping as I stood on the pedals and dumping me down painfully on the crossbar.

That particular morning Mary and I succeeded and stood panting at the top of the hill. A seat had been provided for travellers to rest and admire the view, inland to the moors and distant hills, seaward to the islands and blue horizon.

"I've got to have something to eat," Mary announced. "I know it's not lunchtime but I'm starving."

So we leaned the bikes on the seat and opened our saddlebags. The planks were carved with deep initials, hearts and swear words.

Mary bit into a tomato sandwich. "How much further?"

I checked my milometer: "Eight miles but it's fairly flat from here. Nothing like the cut anyway. Any more thoughts about when we get there?"

"I just want to see dad. I think we've worked out what they're up to, try to talk him out of it."

"If he's still there."

"What's her name, Mrs Rattray, said he'll not be back till Friday. Just have to hope."

"What are the others going to make of it, you turning up?"

"Try to catch him on his own."

"How?"

"I don't know, Teddy!" she said.

"Don't want them to think we're snooping around, they're carrying guns!"

"Maybe keep out of sight," she sucked her fingers. "What do you think?"

"I've no idea."

We talked about it for a while but came to no conclusions and cycled on, a light wind at our backs.

Just north of Biddle, a little village with one shop and a square church tower, the road forked. The main road turned inland; a potholed and much narrower road continued north, hugging the coast. This was the road that ran past Saltfield Mains, our destination, and continued to

Monkton Parva, the busy fishing village where I had seen Mary's dad. There was less traffic now, mostly tractors and farm vehicles.

About midday, the farmhouse and crumbling barns that were Saltfield Mains appeared briefly across the moor then were lost behind rising land. When we saw them again we were quite close. The old blue van was sitting where I had seen it before, so at least some of the crowd were home – or maybe this wasn't home, maybe they only drove down when there was work to be done.

The long-abandoned farmhouse was a stone, two-storey building with dormer windows and a chimney stack at each end. It stood inland from the road, set back a hundred yards at the end of a track. If Mary and I cycled past and anyone was looking from a window – for despite the North Sea gales that must sometimes rage around the house only a single pane appeared to be broken – we would certainly be seen. A short distance from the house, however, a windowless barn hid a stretch of the road from view.

Trusting we had not been spotted already, we dumped our bikes at the roadside and ran to the barn wall. It was a sheltering spot for sheep, nibbled bare and scattered with droppings and tufts of wool. We peeped round a corner.

In all those miles of wilderness the farmhouse was the only dwelling to be seen. It faced east across a quarter-mile of tussocky grass and gorse bushes to the sea, silver that day and patched with cloud shadow. There must have been a cliff but it was hidden from where we were standing. Behind the house lay neglected fields with drystone dykes and a copse of pine trees beyond which the rolling moor rose to a range of far-off hills. It was a remote and lonely location.

There was no sign of life in the house but how, I wondered, could we keep watch without being seen ourselves? Mary pointed. On the far side of the road a grassy hollow was hidden from the house by a bank of gorse. If we could reach that without being seen it would be a perfect spot.

"Come on," she said. "If they see us we can pretend we're having a picnic or looking for flowers."

"What flowers?"

"I don't know, something that grows in the autumn."

"I've heard my mother talk about an autumn crocus."

"That then."

"What does it look like?"

"A crocus, I suppose."

"What colour?"

"Oh, for goodness sake!"

She crept back to the corner. Still the house appeared unoccupied.

"Ready?"

"Yeah."

"Right...Go!"

Was it better to run or to walk? We walked, every moment expecting shouts and a flurry of activity. But there was no one. We collected our bikes and wheeled them down into the hollow.

It might have been unpleasant with thorns, biting flies and more sheep droppings but it wasn't. The grass was dry and springy. What wind there was lost its force in the gorse bushes. Comfortably, once we had assured ourselves that no one was coming, we lay back and enjoyed the warmth of the sun.

If I had been older and Mary were my girlfriend, it would have been a perfect moment to kiss her. It did cross my mind but I thought of Mary as a friend only. So I was surprised when a shadow darkened the sun and as I opened my eyes her lips descended softly upon mine. It was only for a few seconds and only the once, but for those moments it was electric. Then she was gone and as I turned to kiss her in return, she bit into her second sandwich and the moment was past.

"I just fancied doing that, lover-boy," she said, spitting crumbs. "Don't read anything into it."

Some time later I fell asleep. Mary woke me. "Sshhh!"

Four men had emerged from the house. Mary's dad, wearing a waterproof jacket, was among them. So, she told me, was the bearded Lucas, who had called for him one evening. We watched through seeding grasses as they climbed into the van, drove to the road and turned north. Were they heading for the bar in Monkton Parva, where I had seen them drinking? That day there had been five but it was over a week ago. Some might have left, others arrived. How many were at the farmhouse today?

For ten minutes we kept close watch but no more emerged and the windows remained blank. Rooks cawed above the moor and landed on the roof; sparrow-like birds fluttered round the eaves; a scatter of late swallows sat on the wires. Nothing disturbed them. Perhaps everyone had gone.

It seemed a good idea to investigate. We pushed our bikes into the deepest corner of the hollow and returned to the barn.

"Walk up like we're exploring and look through the windows," Mary said.

"Yeah?"

"Better than acting suspicious.

"At least your dad and that other chap aren't there."

"No reason to think we've got anything to do with dad. Come on, they're not going to do us in anyway."

"We can say we told people we were coming."

"Good idea, you're not as dopey as you look."

We left the protection of the barn. Although I tried to look casual, my heart was thudding. Mary looked so confident I couldn't tell if she felt as scared as I was. Her hair tossed in the wind. The four in the van hadn't paused to lock the door but we didn't try it and shaded our eyes to peer through the windows. The room to the right of the front door was an empty bedroom. Wallpaper hung from the walls with damp; in places it had been peeled away revealing the plaster. The floor had been swept. The next window revealed the big farmhouse living room. Three sleeping bags lay against the walls with rucksacks for pillows, an open suitcase and clothes hanging from nails. Some of the men were living there, it appeared, and when we walked round to the back, peering past a deep porcelain sink into the kitchen, we saw a primus stove, billycans, tins of corned beef, eggshells and half a loaf of bread spread on a table. Used dishes were stacked by the sink. Apart from these remnants of a meal the kitchen was tidy like the other rooms in the house: a tea-towel hung from a hook, clean mugs and a couple of plates stood on the shelves. I was surprised then realised there was a good chance these men had been soldiers, accustomed to leaving their kit in apple-pie order.

We passed the rippled glass of a bathroom window and had just reached what may have been a back bedroom when voices stopped us in our tracks. They came from outside the house or seemed to. Instantly I looked for some place to hide but Mary caught my arm. "Sshhh!" She tiptoed back to the corner and looked along the side. No one was to be seen. On she went to the front and peeped round again. The van had not returned, no one had emerged from the house, the path was empty. She looked back at me and shook her head.

I joined her and we listened. After a moment it became apparent that the voices were not coming from outside the house but from upstairs, through the broken window or possibly the window next to it which was part open. We retreated.

"What do you think?"

"No point in advertising we're here," Mary said. "Back to the bikes."

We were just turning away when something in the voices stopped me in my tracks. It was clear there were two men, or at least two, but suddenly I realised they were not speaking English. "Hey!" Softly I called Mary back. "Listen!"

We tiptoed along the front, past the rooms we had looked in previously, and stood beneath the upstairs windows. I strained my ears. Now it was easy to tell they were speaking German. As I have told you, mum taught me my first words of German when I was in my pram and I speak it almost as well as I speak English. It was impossible to make out everything that was being said, only occasional words: "Ich weiss es nicht...ein paar Tage...gut...sehen, was Stefan zu sagen hat."[5]

For a minute there was silence and Mary went to the front door, pressing her ear to the panels. When the men continued their voices sounded different, as if one had gone into another room. Again there was silence. Then one man began singing softly. I could not make out every word but I knew the tune and I had heard the words before:

'Die Fahne hoch!
Die Reihen fest geschlossen!
S.A. marschiert
Mit ruhig festem Schritt...'[6]

My blood froze.

~

---

5   I don't know... a couple of days... all right... see what Stefan has to say.
6   'The flag is high!
    Ranks are tightly closed!
    The S.A. (storm troopers) march
    With a firm, steady tread...'

34

What About My Dad?

Mary rejoined me. "No sound of anyone coming downstairs." She listened. "That's a nice tune."

Then she saw my face. I had slumped against the wall.

The singing stopped. The voices upstairs were raised: "Um Himmels Willen, halte die Klappe! Bist du wahnsinnig?"[7]

Mild laughter from the man who was singing: "Es ist alles in Ordnung. Hier est niemand. Reg dich nicht auf."[8]

"What's wrong?" Mary said.

I could hardly breathe.

"Teddy. Are you OK?"

I pushed myself upright and put a finger to my lips. We retreated to the side of the house.

"What is it?"

"A nice tune?" Although Mary was a hundred times cleverer, sometimes she astonished me. "It's a wicked, evil song! Don't you know what that is?"

"No."

"It's the *Horst Wessel*."

"What's that?"

"Oh, Mary!"

"Well, what is it?"

---

7   For heaven's sake, shut up! Are you mad?
8   It's all right. There's nobody here. Don't get excited.

"Really?"

She shook her head.

"It's the anthem of the Nazi party. They sang it at all the rallies. Hundreds of them. Thousands. Soldiers in jackboots. All giving the Hitler salute."

"I've never heard it before. At least, I don't think so."

"Let's hope you never hear it again. It's been banned."

"Banned? Who by?"

"Everyone: the German government, us, the Americans, everyone. At the end of the War. Like the Nazi salute, the swastika, all the banners.

To be fair, the song was never played in newsreels and Mary had no reason to listen to German radio. We only did occasionally but I'd heard the Horst-Wessel-Lied[9] often enough.

"What does it mean?" she said.

"It was their anthem, a rallying cry, all about the Third Reich: 'Raise the flag, join the great crusade. We are strong! We will triumph!'"

The great crusade! A nation led by one insane man and the whole world torn apart. Millions dead. My cousin Jacob, three years old, whose drawing of a tiger was pinned to my bedroom wall, sent to the ovens. The *Horst Wessel* was a wicked, evil song.

Mary stared at me.

"We've got to get out of here," I said.

There was no problem although suddenly the danger seemed much greater. We circled the house, went behind the barn and in two minutes were slithering into the hollow behind the gorse bushes.

I looked back at the farmhouse. No one emerged from the door, no threatening figure stood watching from a window.

---

[9] Horst Wessel song

"Nazis?" Mary said. "Three years after the war?"

"I don't know but it sounds like it. Nazi criminals are still being hunted down, aren't they?"

It was frightening, Nazis here in England, just a hundred yards from where we were hiding.

"We've got to tell the police," I said.

"Yes."

"The minute we get back."

She didn't reply.

"Mary?"

"Of course," she said and was quiet.

"What's wrong?"

"What about my dad?"

She was right, how could she betray her father? He was in trouble already, this made it ten times worse. Even though the war was over, if the men in the farmhouse were really Nazis, Frank Pearson, a one-time corporal in the British Army, was collaborating with the enemy.

Mary said, "I've got to warn him."

"You mean if we tell the police."

"We've got to, like you said. But not my dad, I can't." She was upset. "He's not a Nazi, we've got to let him get away."

I poked in the grasses. "How?"

"I don't know. Get word to him somehow."

We were back to square one only now it was urgent. I racked my brain but it seemed impossible.

A grasshopper was chirruping. I caught it in my hand, hard and leggy, and showed it to Mary. It sat for a second then clicked and was gone. She wasn't interested.

"What if we wander up and bump into him by accident? Say we've just come for a bike ride."

"And here's your dad? They'd have to be stupid to believe that."

"It could happen."

"A bit of a coincidence."

"Well, have you got any better ideas?"

The sound of waves and cries of seagulls had been in the air since we arrived. "He's not here right now anyway," I said. "They're smuggling, doing something with boats. Shall we go down to the shore?"

There were two routes, both visible from the house: we could cross the moor and see what the cliff looked like, or cycle a short distance up the road and turn down a track. We set off walking, swishing through heather, avoiding the black peat bogs. It wasn't far, half a mile at most. Midway we paused and looked back. My stomach turned over for a man stood watching from an upstairs window. He made no attempt to hide but there was no need for they were staying there openly. We walked on.

In a few minutes we were at the cliff edge. Below lay a rocky inlet, sheltered from the sea by headlands. "Saltfield Bay," I said, remembering dad's road map. A crumbling stone jetty with posts and rusty mooring rings lay on the right. Directly beneath us stood a concrete pillbox, protected from the waves by a boulder beach. It was square with very thick walls, a low doorway in the landward side and as far as we could tell, slit windows for rifle and machine-gun fire facing the bay. There was no sign of a boat although ropes lay coiled on the jetty. In the past this had been used by local fishermen for a scatter of crab pots, broken and strewn with weed, had been flung about by storms and high tides. Where were the fishermen now: had they been drafted as soldiers or sailors to fight in the war? Had they failed to return because they were dead?

But today, on that breezy October afternoon in 1948, was the pillbox occupied? In places the cliff was vertical, in others it seemed possible to scramble down. Clinging to rocks and slithering on grass, we began to descend. It was steeper than it looked. A boulder bounded away and crashed into the concrete wall. Mary stumbled into me. I shouted as my foot skidded and I thought I would fall right to the bottom. Our hands were pierced with thorns. I failed to spot a wet patch and my behind got covered in mud. It was a nightmare.

With relief we stood at the bottom. Since no one had appeared, the pillbox was clearly not occupied. We pulled our clothes straight and ventured inside. Pillboxes on the dunes at Eastport had been used as lavatories, this smelled of seaweed and cigarettes and had been visited recently. An upturned wooden box served as a table and three smaller boxes as seats. A litter of beer bottles and sandwich crusts lay on top. A tin contained cigarette stubs. I carried a newspaper to the light and saw that it was yesterday's Daily Mirror. Someone had been caught by a wave, sodden boots stood to dry and wet over-trousers hung from a nail.

"Teddy!" An open pocket knife lay on a ledge. The blade was smeared with what looked like dry blood. Mary sniffed it. "Fish." There were silver scales on the handle. She put it back.

And that was all, no sheets of paper with German writing, no notebook, nothing to indicate who had been here. Even the cigarette stubs, when I examined them, were Players and Woodbines.

We were glad to leave the claustrophobic pillbox and clambered round rocks to the jetty which lay a hundred or two hundred yards to the right. This, too, was currently in use for the neatly-coiled ropes, stained with rust from the mooring rings, were new. A dark buoy bobbed twenty yards offshore. It was here they came fishing, for a flounder and a couple of coleys lay in a broken fish box. They smelled if not fresh at least not stinking. Seabirds had taken out their eyes and ripped into their flesh with strong beaks. Despite this it was a pleasant spot, at another time I should have liked to go fishing there with dad. Long weed like leather belts streamed in the current.

"Hey, Teddy."

I looked where Mary was pointing. A man stood on top of the cliff. He was watching us and appeared to be shouting.

35

The Man on the Shore

His voice was lost in the noise of the waves, but there was no mistaking his beckoning gestures.

"What do you think?" Teddy said.

"Better go."

The man was silhouetted against the sky. "Pity it's not your dad. It's not, is it?"

"Nope, not Lucas either, they went off in the van."

"Unless it's come back."

"Never saw it. It'll be one of the men in the house."

"Or a farmer."

"Why would a farmer want to speak to us?"

We stumbled back along the shore. The waves surged from the sea, spilling into pretty pools. The soles of my shoes were worn flat, it would have been easy to fall.

The man knew a better way down the cliff and stood waiting by the pillbox.

"Hello!" He was about the same age as my dad with short brown hair and needing a shave. "I am in the house, I see you walk down here to the seaside."

He spoke with a foreign accent, was it German?

"You go exploring, yes?"

"Come up from Biddle on the bikes," Teddy said. "Had a picnic."

"Ah! You not in school today?"

"It's half term."

He didn't understand.

"Potato week," I said helpfully.

Now he was totally confused.

"You go in the building?" He indicated the pillbox.

"There's not much to see."

"You must not go in there."

"Why?"

"We use it for fishing."

Teddy bristled. "Does it belong to you?"

"Men leave their belongings, their fishing rods."

"That's up to them, it doesn't mean we can't go in."

"They might be stolen."

"Do you mean by us?"

"Whoever come. I not know who you are."

"I don't know who you are either. We've got as much right to go in there as you, probably more."

"You have permission?"

"I don't need permission."

"You say?"

"Of course not, it's abandoned, why should we need permission? We're British, it was built to protect us."

I was impressed but the man didn't like it. "You have a lot to say for a boy your age."

"Do you wonder! There's just been a war in case you didn't notice." Teddy became reckless. "Who are you, anyway? You sound German to me. Half my family were killed by the Germans. And you come over here telling M… Margaret and me what to do."

"You think I am German?" He tried to laugh. "No, Polski, I am Polish. The Germans, they take our country, we fight them. Now the war finish we come here and work in your forestry."

"Polish?" I said.

"Tak – ja. We clear the ground, drive the tractors, plant trees. They have build camps. When we not working we come here sometime, fish, stay in the house." He smiled. "The farmer, he know, we pay him."

It was a lie. Teddy had heard them talking, heard their Nazi song, although it was true there were Polish workers in the new forests, it was common knowledge. But these men, the men my father had joined, were German, certainly some of them.

We turned away.

"Polish, yeah, right!" Teddy said.

The man called to our backs. "You see clothes, fishing rods, you not touch, no?"

We trudged down to a pebble beach.

He ducked through the low entrance of the pillbox, perhaps checking in case they had left something incriminating, then stared after us and returned to the clifftop. In five minutes he was gone.

The waves tumbled to our shoes. It was too rough to skim stones so we wandered back and had another look in the pillbox. It revealed no reels or fishing rods, nothing new, and we followed the man's path to the clifftop. It was well-used, better than our own, trampled weeds and earth where stones had been kicked aside. As we returned to our bikes, two men watched from an upstairs window.

We ate the remnants of our sandwiches and filled the flasks at a stream. A while later Teddy nodded. A man, not the man we had spoken to, stared towards us. He went away again. We lay back, inhaling the scent of the gorse and enjoying the late sunshine, hoping for the return of the blue van. Teddy had brought his dad's army binoculars and we watched seabirds sailing above the shore. The house appeared deserted. The sun sank towards the moor.

Teddy looked at his watch: "It's gone five. We really must start back if we want to get home before dark."

He had been saying it for the last half hour. Reluctantly I agreed but just as I was packing my saddle bag the van appeared along the road. We ducked down and watched as it turned onto the farm track and pulled up at the house. Although my dad had been one of the men who drove off, he was not among the crowd that dismounted. I felt no alarm for they were laughing and chatting, a couple carried beer bottles. But where *was* dad? No one was sitting in the front. If they had been to Monkton Parva, he had stayed behind. But why?

"We'll have a think about it," Teddy said, "come back another day. But we have *got* to be heading home now." He was strict about cycling without lights; a school friend had been knocked down and seriously injured.

We set off and soon the farmhouse was hidden behind a fold in the moors. Mostly we rode side by side but at one point Teddy stopped to do what boys do behind a clump of bushes and I drew up to wait for him. As he emerged he called, "Hey, look!" and pointed back the way we had come.

A fishing boat, what appeared to be a small seine-netter with a cabin, had appeared round the north headland and was heading into Saltfield Bay where we had spent the afternoon. Teddy unpacked his binoculars. Even with their aid the name was a tiny white smear on the bow but she appeared to be tidy with a black hull, white cabin, orange mast and quantities of net heaped on deck. A white steaming light shone from the mast and a red light from the port side. She rolled and pitched easily in the following sea and appeared to be in no hurry.

Had it come from Monkton Parva? Was my dad aboard? Would the men we had seen be heading out that night to rendezvous with a ship from the continent? Would it be carrying treasures stolen by the Nazis? Was the little seine-netter carrying them this minute? I longed to go back and watch, hidden among rocks, but with daylight already fading it was impossible. If our families had not been waiting for us, I would have stayed out all night.

Teddy put the binoculars away and we cycled on.

"What are you doing tomorrow?" I said.

Part 3

36

Return to Saltfield Mains

It was a hard ride home for at the end of that perfect day the wind was rising and blew full in our faces. By the time we reached Eastport the sky, which had been so blue, was being eaten up by a bank of storm clouds and it had started to rain. Standing beneath a streetlamp, I scraped the rats' tails of hair from my face and arranged to phone Teddy in the morning. From that point I could freewheel most of the way home but Teddy had to cycle to the far side of town and uphill to his house at the top of Strawberry Bank, a challenge almost as great as Seaton Cut. Later he told me that it was so horrible he quite enjoyed it and by the time he got home he was sodden to the skin. Teddy was tough.

It was a night of storm and heavy rain. For most of that Potato Week we enjoyed beautiful weather, Wednesday was the exception. All day the clouds hung low, gutters ran full, dustbins blew over in the back lane and scattered their contents along the cobbles.

At ten o'clock, when I had arranged to phone Teddy, the rain was simply lashing and made it impossible. An hour later it eased a bit so I put on my mac, school hat and wellies, collected some pennies, and went to the box by the Waterman's Arms. Gran gave me her umbrella, the one with a pattern of pink and blue flowers, but it blew inside out.

"You must be soaked." Teddy stood in his warm hallway.

"Not too bad," I said, dripping on the concrete floor.

"Have you heard the forecast?"

"They reckon it will blow itself out by tonight, tomorrow's supposed to be better."

"Do you still want to go back?"

"I certainly do. If it's not too bad this afternoon I thought I might call and see if that woman at Laburnum Villa has heard anything."

"Mrs Rattray," Teddy remembered. "I can phone if you like."

"Yeah?" I looked on the shelf where there was meant to be a directory but someone had taken it. "OK, I'll ring back this afternoon."

"Why don't you just stay there, I'll do it now. What's your number?"

It was written on the dial. For ten minutes I waited, watching the raindrops on the glass, half-opening the door to let out the stink of fag-ends and dog-muck carried in on somebody's shoe. When the phone rang it made me jump:

"You've just missed him," Teddy told me. "He came back last night, needed to collect some clothes. Said he'd be away till next week. Had another chap with him."

"Bloody man!" I said. "I don't suppose he told her where he was going?"

"No, but whatever he told her it wouldn't be the truth, would it? Anyway, he just stayed the night and left his dirty washing."

"What about the other man?"

"Dark hair, bit of an accent, said he's Polish. She quite liked him."

"What about a car?" I said. "Or were they in the van?"

"She had no idea. Been at the gin from the way she was talking."

"Already?"

"Sounded like it."

I drew a deep breath. "We have to tell the police like you said but I've absolutely got to go back, I can't shop dad."

Teddy thought about it. "Mum's taking Rachel and me to the pictures this afternoon but there's nothing on tomorrow. If it stops raining I could go then."

""Yeah? Thanks, give you a ring first thing."

"I'll meet you in town again, but we'll have to be very careful. Have you worked out yet how you're going to get your dad by himself – that's if he's still there?"

"No."

"Have to see how it goes then. But I've been thinking, there's a good chance they'll see us so I'll take dad's rod, the one he uses for sea fishing. Can you get some stinky fish from those boxes on the quay?"

"Course, but you're not really planning to go fishing?"

"Not unless we have to, but you can't say you are if you haven't got bait. And take your bike lamp in case we're late again."

After a while I asked, "What picture are you going to see?"

"*Treasure of the Sierra Madre*, it's on at the Ritz. Rachel wants to go to *The Red Shoes*. Why, do you want to come?"

"I'd like to see *The Red Shoes*."

"That's the one mum wants to go to, all about ballet. Remind her of her time at the opera house. It's OK by me, *Treasure of the Sierra Madre*'s on next week as well."

I had promised to help gran make bramble and apple jelly. Maybe Mrs Surtees could come over instead. "Won't your mum mind?"

"Course not. It's on at the ABC."

"I'll look like a drowned cat."

He laughed. "See you outside at half-past one."

*

It was as if Wednesday's storm had never been. Next morning the sun shone from a washed blue sky, raindrops hung sparkling from the hawthorns, potato fields stood green and brown and empty, waiting for the earth to dry out a little. Teddy's fishing rod, broken into three sections, was tied along his crossbar and stuck out behind. Our saddle-bags were bursting: tea and sandwiches, waterproof jackets, a primus stove in Teddy's, and in mine a well-wrapped parcel of stinking fish which I had collected from a fishing spot on the South Pier.

Instead of straining on the pedals we walked up Seaton Cut, and in Biddle sat on a bench outside the shop to eat ice-cream. A little further on, the minor coast road, potholed in places, branched off to the right. All went well and shortly before eleven we got a first glimpse of the lonely farmhouse at Saltfield Mains. It was a good way off and soon lost again behind woodland and the rolling crests of the moor.

Even now, at the eleventh hour, I had no plan to contact dad: should we watch the house as we had done before, hoping for an opportunity; leave our bikes where they could be seen and walk down to the inlet to start fishing; or even call at the house to borrow matches for the primus?

As it turned out we did none of these things. The grey North Sea lay on our right and a mile or two offshore, it is hard to judge distance on water, a small fishing boat was heading in from the sea.

Teddy unpacked his binoculars: "It looks like the same one to me," he said. "Yeah, I'm sure it is."

If that little seine-netter, whose name we did not yet know, had sailed into Saltfield Bay at any hour of any other day, we would not have seen her. We would not have stayed to watch. We would not have discovered her cargo. The outcome would have been different,

It was a coincidence, a twist of fate if you like, that was to affect the lives of many people.

37

Human Cargo

"I wonder where they've been." I handed Mary the binoculars, British army issue that belonged to my dad. "Not round the coast this time, she's coming in from the sea."

She studied the boat and looked all round. "Come on, we can get closer than this."

"What for?"

"Why d'you think? My dad might be aboard."

We cycled on. The farmhouse was still out of sight when the road ran past a headland on the south side of Saltfield Bay. It appeared that by walking out a few hundred yards we could have a clear view of the bay and remain unseen ourselves. Winter gales and snow from the east made this a wild coast but farmers had built drystone dykes to protect their fields and there were copses of hardy pine. The road passed close to one of these so we lifted the bikes over a wire fence and hid them among trees, collected a few things from our saddlebags and started out along the headland.

It stood high above the sea with hundred-foot cliffs of sheer rock, unlike the earthy cliff below the farm. We followed sheep tracks, keeping below the skyline. A flock of twenty or so, startled by our arrival, scampered away then stood watching. To get the best view of Saltfield Bay and the jetty, we had to walk half a mile. Following yesterday's downpour the heather was dripping and soon my shoes and trouser legs were sodden.

I had brought a groundsheet to keep us dry but Mary discovered a cleft above the cliffs where we could sit on rocks. It was an ideal spot, protected from the wind and with a view directly across the water. The stones were cold and the sun hidden behind the headland at our backs, so we spread the khaki groundsheet, pulled on hats and turned up our collars. Mary had made a big thermos of tea, we had both made sandwiches and I had brought some cakes baked by Rachel the day before, so we were very comfortable.

It made us careless.

I stood my cup on a rock, propped my elbows on my knees and focussed the binoculars on the boat. As she came closer, pitching and rolling heavily, I could just make out her name, *Seal Maid*. A British boat at least. There was a man on deck, dodging the spray, and a second man in the small wheelhouse. Then I spotted a third, leaning over the side and being seasick, at least that's what it looked like. Good. I passed the binoculars to Mary.

Fifteen minutes after we got settled, the boat entered the calmer waters of the bay, though she still rolled in the aftermath of yesterday's storm. It took another fifteen, for it would have been easy to drift onto the rocks, to take a heaving-line from a man who stood on the jetty. Soon she was tied up, saved from scraping by a row of car tyres slung over the side.

The foredeck was covered by a heap of nets. Two of the crew, or men acting as crew, heaved them aside, revealing a hatch covered by tarpaulins. This led to the hold where the catch would have been stored when *Seal Maid* was a regular fishing boat. The crewmen knocked out wooden chocks, threw back the tarpaulins, grasped the heavy hatch boards by ring bolts and dragged them back.

Europe had been torn apart by war, bombed, ravaged and reduced to chaos. The hold, I assumed, was where these smugglers carried the treasures that had been stolen and hidden away by the forces of the Third Reich. It seemed ridiculous that small items of jewellery, such as brooches or the wrist watches Mary had been offered, should be stored down there, but doubtless most were bigger: pictures, statues, furniture, weapons, gold and silver ornaments, possibly melted down and reduced to ingots. They would be secure in the fish hold, lashed into place, protected from the drench of salt spray.

We waited to see what was being carried, nothing too big on this occasion for there had not been time for *Seal Maid* to cross to the Continent, and transferring heavy cargo from ship to boat in yesterday's storm would have been impossible.

The men stood looking down. I waited for someone to fetch a ladder – then a ladder appeared, thrust up from below. There was already somebody down there. A man held the top steady and a moment later a figure appeared, climbing the ladder with difficulty. Hands helped him to the deck. He straightened and stretched, filled his lungs with the fresh sea air and looked around. People? Were they smuggling people? Who could he be, I wondered, but not for long as a second man appeared, shorter and fatter than the first. He had been seasick, or so it appeared, and had fouled his jacket, for he loosened the buttons and threw it across the deck. One of the crew dipped a bucket over the side for him to scrub his hands and rinse his mouth in the cold salt water. Before he had finished, a third man appeared and then two more. The deck was crowded.

"Who are they?" I said. "More of that gang your dad lived with in Paris?"

"I shouldn't think so," she said. "They hated the Germans, cut their throats."

"I didn't know that."

"I thought I told you, threw their bodies in the river."

Her dad?

"But this lot *are* German," Mary said, "some of them anyway. You heard them talking."

The new arrivals were assisted to the jetty. "So who are these then?"

Mary shrugged but she knew. We both did.

The war had lasted six years. The whole world, from Norway to New Zealand, knew of Hitler's atrocities. The names of the Nazi leaders were familiar even to children, though most weren't sure who had done what: Himmler, Goebbels, Ribbentrop, Goering, Hess, Borman, Heidrich, and for each of these there were many more. Soldiers had made up a rhyme which we sang in the playground. Six months after the war in Europe ended, as many of these despicable, evil men as could be traced had been brought to justice at the Nuremberg War Trials – Nuremberg, the city of Hitler's great parades. For a year the extent of their wickedness was laid bare before a horrified world. Many were executed, some avoided punishment by committing suicide, others were imprisoned for many years. But Martin Borman, Josef Mengele, Adolf Eichmann and hundreds more had evaded capture and were on the run, not just from the army and police but people whose lives and families they had destroyed, none more than a man named Simon Wiesenthal.

Wiesenthal was an Austrian Jew, like my family, who had endured four years of nightmare in Nazi concentration camps, including five death camps. Miraculously and with enormous courage he had survived, and immediately upon being freed from Mauthausen by the U.S. army, he had set up a centre to document atrocities against the Jews and hunt down those responsible. After three years he was already famous and greatly feared by those on the run. I had read articles about him and dad had sent money to support his centre in the city of Linz on the Danube. The men who worked for him were clever and remorseless. Every clue was followed up: Gestapo officers, concentration camp commandants, prison guards (male and female), politicians who condoned murder, officials who organised transportation, brutal soldiers, spies, traitors, informers, all these and more were arrested and brought to trial. But many vanished: some were hidden by supporters, others had amassed fortunes, escape routes were established from country to country. Men who had killed hundreds at the stroke of a pen, made treks over the mountains to avoid capture. Many still lived in Europe where the hunt was most active, so Nazi sympathisers and men who were paid large sums of money provided forged papers. Under these assumed names, berths were organised aboard passenger ships to carry them to distant parts of the world, Canada, Australia, Argentina, where their crimes might be concealed and they could hope to live comfortably on the corrupt proceeds of the Third Reich.

"They're on the run, right?" I said. "I wonder what from."

Mary heard the bitter note in my voice and looked me in the face.

"Well, it's not nicking a car, is it?" I said.

The new arrivals were indistinguishable from other men but when I guessed at their crimes my skin crawled. As far as I could tell they varied in age from about forty to sixty. They wore crumpled suits, their hair was short. Three, who appeared senior in some way, stood apart and held themselves arrogantly erect. One produced a flask and took a mouthful, looked at the others, possibly remembered they had been seasick, and returned the flask to his pocket. When their suitcases were taken ashore, these senior figures made it clear they had no intention of carrying one.

Waves broke on the rocks. In ragged file they started along the shore, looked briefly in the pillbox, and climbed the track to the cliff top. They were unfit, at least some were, clutching at tufts of grass and panting with their hands on their knees.

"I don't see your dad."

"He's not there, maybe in the house." Mary held out the thermos, "Finish the tea while it's still hot?"

"Yeah, why not?" I threw away the dregs and held out my cup. "What do you want to do now?"

There was a noise behind us.

I spun round.

A man stood looking down.

38

We've Got to Get Out of Here

He was dark-eyed, his hair thinning. I hadn't seen him before. The 'Polish forester' we had met two days earlier stood a few paces away.

"What are you doing?" This man's voice was rougher but he had the same accent.

There was only one answer, we were spying on the boat. They had caught us red-handed. I felt my face flame.

"I should have thought it's obvious," Mary was superb. "We're having a picnic, watching the birds."

"Not the *Seal Maid*?"

"*Seal Maid*?" She sounded genuinely puzzled. "Oh, you mean the boat?"

"Yes, the boat."

"Well, yes, we've been watching the boat, of course we have, it's right down there at the jetty."

He clambered down the rocks and stood beside us. I smelled his sweat. "So you just happened to be here?"

"No, we're going fishing . We cycled up this morning."

He looked around. "I don't see any fishing rods."

"We left it with the bikes. Who needs a fishing rod on a hillside? Anyway, what is this? It's none of your business."

The second man stepped closer. "He's the one gave us the idea," I said. "He says you're all forestry workers, come down here to go fishing. We reckoned it must be a good spot."

"We don't like you spying on us."

"We're not spying on you."

"Watching us then. You must pack up your things and go away."

"We haven't finished the picnic," Mary said.

"We want you to pack up and go." It was a threat.

"In a minute." I held out my cup again. "Margaret was just pouring me a cup of tea."

"Now!" The man gripped my arm.

I was overwhelmed by revulsion and wrenched my arm away. "Take your hand off me!"

"Now!" He caught my arm again. The cup fell to the ground. I struggled and accidentally struck him in the face.

"Ach, du kleine Ratte!"[10] He hit me back, a blow that rocked my head on my shoulders. I caught a rock to stop myself falling.

"Ernst, no!" His companion scrambled down beside us. "No!"

But the damage was done. Did they realise he had shouted in German? Mary pretended she had not:

"Stop it!" She sprang forward. "Stop it! Leave him alone."

They stepped back.

"Are you all right?"

"I think so." My head was ringing.

"What the hell do you think you're doing?" Mary was angry. "We're having a picnic and you come storming in here, telling us not to look at your stupid boat, ordering us to go away, pulling Teddy by the arm. Who do you think you are?"

She was terrific, no wonder she had won such praise playing Brutus.

"I've a good mind to report you to the police. Bloody Poles coming over here and ordering us about. Why don't you both

---

10 "Ach, you little rat!"

just go away, push off to the farmhouse, go back to bloody Poland and leave us to finish the picnic in peace?"

"I don't believe you," said the man called Ernst. "You are lying. I want to see your fishing rod."

"Well you'll have to wait. And Teddy's bleeding, look."

It wasn't much, just a scratch, I hadn't even felt it. Mary dabbed the blood with her handkerchief.

The men retreated towards the trees and stood waiting.

"We've got to get out of here," Mary said.

"I thought they were going to grab us."

"They might yet."

"How'd they see us in here?"

"Must have had a lookout." She gazed down at the boat. "D'you still think—"

"Even more now, don't you?"

"War criminals? Like the ones we see in the papers?"

"Any other suggestions?"

It was hard to believe. Here in England, right before our eyes.

The men from the boat were being escorted to the farmhouse. "How did my dad get himself mixed up with that lot? Bloody fool!"

"What do you think we should do?" I said.

"Get out as fast as we can."

"Yeah, but how?"

"Fishing's out."

I thought about it. "They'll see the rod and that. We could let them think we're still going fishing and head off the other way. Stop a car on the road."

"Get to that cottage a mile back. Did you see if there's a telephone line?"

"Don't remember." The two men were waiting. "I didn't expect this."

"You knew they were German."

"Yeah, but it's all changed, scary."

"Bloody terrifying!" She threw out the last of the tea. "I don't suppose you packed a couple of pistols?"

"Left them on the bed."

"Useless as ever." A paper bag gave her an idea. "Have you got a pencil?"

I shook my head.

"Pity. Still—" Shepherds had burned off the heather. "Give us your penknife." She hacked off a blackened stalk. "Stand there so they can't see me."

In smeary letters she scrawled:

NAZIS IN HOUSE

T + M

It took three charcoal twigs.

"Hurry up!" The voice was rough and impatient. "We must go back."

"Just coming." Mary left the paper on a rock and put a stone on top to stop it blowing away.

We clambered from our shelter and led the way across the headland into the trees. The bikes were easy to find. There was my dad's sea rod, three sections in a canvas case. Mary showed them the stinking fish she had brought for bait and chum.

"Satisfied now?" she said.

"All right, you go fishing."

"I told my dad we were coming, "I said, astonished how readily the lies sprang to my lips. "He wanted to know where. I told him you said this was a good spot."

If they grabbed us now and forced us to the road, a car or tractor might come along. If they waited until we were down at the shore there would be no one to see.

"Maybe one of you could show us."

"Maybe," said yesterday's forester.

"There was a silence.

"What do you catch?" I said.

"Pollock mostly."

Still they made no attempt to leave.

"What are you waiting for?" Mary said. "Do you expect us to go down with you?"

"I'm not leaving the bikes," I said.

Ernst was not satisfied. He kicked the ground.

"For goodness sake!" Mary told them. "We'll be there in ten minutes."

Reluctantly they walked off towards the road and were soon hidden by branches. At once Mary threw everything out of her saddle bag: thermos, bait, sandwich box. I did the same: rod, primus, groundsheet, everything to lighten the load and let people know we'd been there.

We began pushing the bikes, weaving a path through the trees. A short distance ahead an engine started up, more like a van than a car. It drew off towards the farm.

A fallen branch raked my shin.

"Ah! Ah!"

There was no time to look. I limped on and felt a little trickle of blood. It reminded me of the time I first met Mary.

An unseen vehicle drove past heading in the opposite direction, back towards Biddle, Traffic on the road gave us hope. We emerged from the trees and hoisted our bikes over the rusty wire fence. A few yards of grass and a peaty ditch led to the tarmac. Without a backwards glance, Mary set off as hard as she could pedal. I followed and by a great effort caught her up. One after the other we sped down the moorland road. Shrubs and heather flashed past. The cottage that might have a telephone was hidden by a distant bend.

A small roadside quarry lay ahead. It raced to meet us. As we drew alongside I saw a vehicle pulled back out of sight. The shock nearly threw me into a ditch. I had seen it before, a blue van with a patch of red lead on the wing.

39

The Men in the Farmhouse

This is me again, Mary.

When I saw the van I got such a fright I ran full-tilt into a pothole. The bike bucked and threw me clear over the handlebars. I might have gone skidding along the road on my knees and face but landed on the heathery verge. It was a thud that knocked the breath from my lungs. I tried to scramble to my feet and run on but it was impossible and I sprawled helplessly, gasping like a fish as two men jumped from the van and stood above me. One was Ernst with his dark eyes and thinning hair. I hadn't seen the other.

Teddy cycled on, already a hundred yards ahead. There were four men in the van, two must have been there all along. I think they had set off for the farmhouse then doubled back in case we tried to trick them. They drove from the quarry and forced me inside then revved hard down the road after Teddy.

In no time, even though he rode like a maniac, we were right on his back wheel, threatening to run him over. Perhaps they would, Nazis had done much worse things than run down a schoolboy, but at the last instant Teddy swung right on to a peaty track. The driver jammed his footbrake to the floor and we skidded on up the road in a shower of grit.

The peat was boggy with yesterday's rain and after fifty yards the track turned into a quagmire. No matter how hard

Teddy trod on the pedals, his wheels stuck fast in the ooze. He fell sideways, picked himself up and and took to his heels across the moor.

The van pulled up at the roadside and two men jumped out. In that remote spot they did not trouble to speak English. One, tall and bony, shouted: "Verdammter Junge! Ich werde ihn abfangen!"[11] At once he started up the hillside.

The second, a stocky, balding man in a black shirt, called back: "Ich werde di Straße hinunterlaufen, für den Fall, dass er umkehrt!"[12]

Teddy looked back and ran on. I couldn't understand a word although the meaning was clear.

The tall German might have been a fell runner. Teddy was fast but not to compare with this man whose long legs carried him across the heather like a greyhound. Stride by stride he came closer. The land rose ahead. There was nowhere to hide, no one to help. A stream ran down the hillside. Like David in the Bible, Teddy snatched up stones and flung them as the man came close. They bounced from his chest. One hit him in the face and made him cry out but he did not fall like Goliath. Teddy was grabbed and flung headlong into the stream. His head was forced into the water. He struggled wildly and thought he was going to drown. His senses reeled. At the last moment, when all his strength had gone, the man pulled him back. Teddy was helpless. Choking and vomiting water, he clung to his pursuer's shirt.

A tractor with a trailer-load of bales chugged towards us. I was pushed to the floor, a rough hand was clamped across my mouth. The stocky German exchanged words with the tractor driver. He laughed and drove on.

As Teddy reached the van he had recovered enough to

---

11 Bloody boy! I'll cut him off!
12 I'll head down the road in case he turns back.

resist and briefly broke free. Finding himself in a bog, he flung handfuls of moss. It did no good and earned a him a beating. Blood ran from his nose. As I've said before, Teddy was a fighter, I was proud of him. At the last moment, as the van doors swung wide and the men forced him inside, he startled them with a flurry of kicks and punches. One shouted aloud then a single, vicious blow to the side of the head knocked him nearly unconscious, and like a sack of potatoes Teddy was flung aboard, cannoning into me. Our bikes were thrown after, followed by the two men. The doors banged shut, the van turned and we set off down the road, back the way we had come.

*

They took us to the farmhouse and dumped us in a corner of the front hall, ankles bound and wrists tied behind with electric flex from a drum they had found in a cupboard. It was tight and dug into my skin. The time, I saw from the watch of the man who was tying me up, was twelve-thirty.

The house was crowded. With the new arrivals I think there were a dozen or more men there. No one knew who we were for at the time my dad was sleeping upstairs and Lucas, who had arrived at Wherry Row one night, was nowhere to be seen; later I discovered that Lucas was a Frenchman who had thrown in his lot with the Germans early in the war. As they came and went through the hall some smiled pleasantly, others scowled and one took the time to give each of us a painful kick.

The man I feared most was an Irishman called Benny, another Nazi sympathiser, who stared at us with savage eyes. He was a powerful man in working clothes with tousled red hair and big bony hands. Among the others he spoke German but to us he said, "Stupid kids! Sticking your noses where they're not wanted. I'd like to cut your bloody throats. Put a bullet in you this minute if it was up to me."

When we were alone Teddy said, "What do you think they'll do?"

"With us? Who knows?"

"They'll have to pack up here, won't they? I mean, we've seen them, we know what they're up to."

We didn't voice the frightening thought that was in both our minds.

"If we're late back people will come looking. I told gran we were heading up this way."

"Yeah, I told dad. Not that they're German, he'd never have let me come, just Polish forestry workers like the man said, and the fishing. He told me to take care anyway."

"Maybe they'll just leave us here and clear off."

But we soon discovered they had very different plans for us. Gunther Krause, as I heard him called, who had arrived that day on the boat, seemed to be the senior figure there, the senior officer if they were using their military ranks. Teddy called him the *gruppenfuhrer*, the group leader. He was a thin man of average height with cropped grey hair, steel-rimmed spectacles and pale blue eyes. On the wedding finger of his left hand he wore a silver death's head ring, a skull and crossbones, symbol of the dreaded Nazi SS. I have said that Benny was the man who frightened me most; I was wrong, it was Gunther Krause.

I had seen him before, or rather, I had seen his photograph. It was prominent among others in an article I had read in the Daily Telegraph about Nazi war criminals who three years after Germany's defeat were still being sought by the police, army intelligence and Simon Wiesenthal's men. During the war Krause had been a senior Gestapo officer, one of those whose job it was to organize the trains carrying Jews, gypsies, handicapped people and other Nazi undesirables from ghettoes to the concentration camps and death camps. Later he became commandant of ----- concentration camp.

I recognised another face also, thick-lipped and curly-haired, a fat little man who had worked in a succession of camps as a surgeon/scientist like Josef Mengele and performed terrible operations. I did not remember his name until I heard one of the others address him as Dr Scholtz.

Not just the Telegraph but other newspapers had carried the photographs and asked readers to study them and keep our eyes open because the net was tightening and it was believed some of these men might attempt to cross to Britain, a staging-post to destinations in far-flung parts of the world. I had done so and to my alarm and horror, here were two holding us prisoner in the farmhouse.

They were surrounded by a small crowd. Among them, I guessed, were other arrivals, not just today but recently, also being pursued for their crimes. Krause looked down and nudged me with his shoe:

"This one's a Jew." He spoke very good English. "Am I right?"

I didn't reply.

He carried a cane and poked me in the throat. "A Jew girl?"

"No," I said.

"I think you are, I can smell you. That's Jew smell."

Again I said nothing and stared up in terror at this skull-faced man who held our fate in his hands.

"God, you're ugly."

"No she's not, what a filthy thing to say!" Teddy had surprised me many times in the months I had known him, never more than now. "She's my girlfriend and she's lovely. And she's not a Jew she's a Catholic, look at her pendant."

I wear a little silver crucifix on a chain. One of the men hooked it from the neck of my dress.

Krause didn't like it, didn't like being contradicted, didn't like being proved wrong, and slashed Teddy across the head and back with his cane.

"Ah!" Teddy couldn't protect himself and looked up with angry, pain-filled eyes.

"Not that it makes any difference," Krause continued, speaking German now. "They know we're here. They've seen us, seen me. They'll have to be got rid of."

Here I'm passing you back to Teddy because among themselves they were speaking German and it is important.

*

Hi, it's me again:

Although the crowd in the farmhouse were all Nazis or Nazi sympathisers, not everyone was like Benny and Krause.

"They'll have to be got rid of," Krause said.

"What!" A man with a pleasant face was shocked.

"They're just kids!" said another.

"Well, what do you suggest?" Krause said.

"I don't know but you can't shoot them."

"Lock them in the barn," said a third man. "We'll be gone in a few hours."

"You're getting soft."

"By the time they're found we'll be a hundred miles away."

"And the police will show them photographs." Doctor Scholtz had a soft, high-pitched voice. "They'll know we've left Holland, close in on the groups here, put an extra watch on the ports."

"By the time you're recognised you'll be out the country."

"No!" Krause said with finality. "If you haven't got the belly for it, ask Benny. He'll do it in a minute."

Benny pulled out his heavy army pistol, one of the big black handguns, Mausers, Walthers and Lugers issued to soldiers of the Wehrmacht in World War 2. Several of the men in the farmhouse carried these weapons and they terrified me.

"It's their own fault," Krause said, "stupid brats, they shouldn't have come poking their noses in. Take them out in the boat, tie a brick to their ankles and drop them over the side."

We stared at the pistol in the Irishman's hands.

"Use your brains," Krause told him, "what's the use shooting them here, you'll have to carry the bodies. Take them down to the boat."

Benny returned his weapon to its holster and fastened the strap. "Wait till it's dark," he said.

Krause nodded. "At last someone's talking sense."

As I followed the conversation, looking from one to the other, I was so scared that I had forgotten I was not supposed to know German. One of the group was watching me: "Du Junge!" he snapped. "Wissen Sie, woven wir sprechen?"[13]

My lips were halfway to saying 'nein' when I checked myself: "Pardon?"

"Do you know German?" the man said in broken English."

"German?"

"You seem very interested in what we are saying."

"Of course he is," Mary covered for me. "Wouldn't you be? We came fishing and got threatened up there on the moor. Teddy got punched on the head. So we ran off. Now we're tied hand and foot and surrounded by a crowd of Germans – Germans not Poles, right? And that man," she nodded at Krause, "hit Teddy with his cane."

A young man with a soft beard was protesting: "Look at them. How old, fourteen? Fifteen? You've got children, haven't you, Commandant Krause? I know Karl has." He looked around the group. "Otto's got boys about the same age. And Andreas, two girls, that right? What if your children

---

13 You, boy! Do you know what we're talking about?

wandered into a group of the English and someone said, 'Just get rid of them, put a bullet in them, drop them over the side?'"

Krause didn't like it, wasn't used to having his orders questioned, but the war was over now, his life was in these men's hands. Or perhaps for one moment he did think of his own children. "All right, we'll think about it, just get them out of my sight! Take them out to the barn, down to that place on the beach. Anywhere, just so long as I don't have to look at them any more." As he turned he stumbled over Mary's leg and gave her a savage kick. She cried out.

At the same moment there were footsteps overhead, shoes on the bare boards, and her dad started down the stairs. Some men looked up. He had been told about the boy and girl caught spying on the boat but Eastport was fifteen miles away, there was no reason to think it might be his daughter. Suddenly there she was, tied hand and foot, her eyes full of pain. "Mary, what on earth – ?" He ran down two or three steps then saw everyone watching and froze.

For several seconds there was silence then Dr Scholtz said in his high voice, "You know this girl?"

40

The Pillbox

They did not like it. Dad was marched back upstairs to one of the bedrooms and left with an armed guard. Someone carried up the roll of electric flex and tied his hands and feet. In vain he protested that he was one of them, was not a spy, had no idea how I knew where he was living. The only link between me and the group were the watches which I had turned down and he had returned. They were wrapped in a French newspaper and he was smoking Gauloises but he had not told me where they came from.

Teddy and I were taken to the big kitchen and questioned: how did we come to be there? We were threatened with a beating. Benny unholstered his revolver and laid it on the table. I told them everything: how we had looked for dad at the King and Country, Teddy's accidental sighting at the bar in Monkton Parva, spotting the van outside the farmhouse, cycling up two days earlier but failing to see him, and returning again today. Did anyone know we were here? Yes, I replied, we had reported meeting the Polish forestry worker as he called himself. I had told gran and Teddy had told his dad that we were coming back today to go fishing.

So while dad was shut away in the upstairs bedroom, tied hand and foot and guarded by a man with a pistol, Teddy and I were escorted from the house to the concrete pillbox down on the seashore. A small crowd accompanied us because the new arrivals wanted to see inside the barn. Anyone exploring the old farm buildings might have wondered why the barn windows were boarded up and it had a sturdy door secured by two strong padlocks on heavy-duty hasps.

As the Nazis went inside, Teddy and I followed. We were terrified, frightened for our lives, but even so I saw enough to realise that the objects strewn in the shadows were very valuable. I don't know how much had been sent on but what remained would have filled a medium-sized removal van. Stacked here and there, like the contents of an untidy antique shop, were pieces of furniture, paintings, statues, tapestries, icons, church furnishings, a magnificent dusty chandelier; and scattered on top of the larger items were ornaments, clocks, antique weapons, objects from museums, tiaras, brooches and boxes of jewellery that flashed fire as the sun emerged and they were struck by light from the doorway. We were only there for a minute but as we were led away I wondered how many galleries, museums, churches and houses had been looted for this collection, how many innocent people had died in the fighting or been sent to the concentration camps like Teddy's family. If there had been time and we were not being herded by violent men with pistols, we might have recognised more, but I am sure I spotted in the gloom a painting of waterlilies that I had seen in a book of great paintings in the art room at school.

It was hard to keep a balance as we descended the earth cliff for our hands were tied behind. Teddy tripped and fell heavily. Having reached the shore, we stumbled across rocks to the pillbox. The entrance, as I have said, was on the landward side. Loopholes for rifles and machine guns faced over the bay and to right and left to allow defenders a wide angle of fire. It had been built well back from the water to prevent flooding. A concrete sill raised the entrance above the surrounding stones after which there was a step down into the interior.

It had changed little in the two days since we were there. The boxes used as seats and a table had been moved, different clothes hung from hooks and nails. A man called Jurgen was detailed to guard us while the others returned to the farm. I had seen Jurgen up at the house, a young man with narrow eyes, cropped dark hair and a wound above his right ear where the hair did not grow. As if to make up for this, his cheeks and jaw were covered by stubble. He wore army trousers and a black leather jacket. Jurgen was a man of few words, not one of the friendly Germans.

He cut lengths of cord. "Sit!" he said to Teddy. "Feet."

Teddy played for time but Jurgen was not in the mood for games. Pointedly he checked the safety-catch on his pistol. "Now."

Teddy did as he was told and Jurgen bound our ankles, doubling the knots until they were rigid. A loose coil of rope hung on the wall. He wove it between our arms and legs and tied the ends to a bracket, leaving us room to move about.

"You have no knife, no?" He patted our pockets and found Teddy's penknife. "Ah!" He transferred it to his own pocket "I go sit outside but I will be watching. If I discover you untie the knots…!" He fired his revolver into the ground. In that enclosed space the bang was deafening. The earth exploded. I spat grit from my lips.

*

At last Teddy and I were alone, free to talk. What were we to do? There seemed no answer and after a while we fell silent, sitting on the boxes. I looked for the fish-gutting knife we had seen previously but it had gone.

The afternoon passed slowly. The loopholes were dazzling.

Patches of sunlight moved across the floor. All was silent save for waves breaking on the rocks and the cry of gulls. We kicked our boxes to the front and looked out on Saltfield Bay. A swell rolled in from the open sea. Seal Maid rocked at her mooring. Jurgen sat rolling a tin of cigarettes.

He came in to check our ropes, pistol hanging from one hand. Satisfied, he grunted and went back outside. We watched through the loopholes. Sitting on the rocks, he took off a boot and examined his toes.

Teddy looked at my watch. "Ten past three."

"Is that all?"

I thought of gran. That afternoon she was going into town with Mrs Surtees. About now they would be sitting in Binns having a cup of tea. I pictured the café, the cherry cake that was her favourite. She was buying me a new shirt and tie for school. It was Mrs Surtees who had given me the pram that cut my leg. I told Teddy and to fill the silence we remembered some of the things that had happened since. We talked about my dad and wondered how he was faring in that upstairs bedroom.

All at once we heard music. Jurgen had produced a mouth organ and was playing lively tunes – very lively, they seemed, given our circumstances. We peered through the loopholes. He sat on a stone halfway to the sea and played very well, cupping his hands and tapping a foot. If we weren't tied hand and foot and Jurgen did not have a terrifying pistol, it would have been the perfect time to make a break for his back was towards us. I looked at his cropped head; how I would have liked to take a stone and knock him senseless.

My eye was caught by a black object bobbing on the water. I had not noticed it before and realised it was the head of a seal attracted by the music for they are inquisitive creatures. It was joined by a second head and then a third. I don't know if Jurgen had intended to attract them but certainly he did and in a few minutes a dozen seals had gathered, looking towards the shore. One swam quite close, maybe only twenty yards from the rocks, rising and sinking in the waves.

In normal circumstances I would have thought it it was lovely but then Jurgen did something that I will never forget. Laying down the mouth organ he sang on, la – la – la, to hold their attention and reached for his pistol. Holding it in both hands, he took carful aim at the seal which had swum so close. There was a terrific bang, the pistol leaped, and in an instant the trusting seals had gone. I'm sure he missed for the water spurted a few inches from the seal's head. I certainly hope so. Jurgen laughed and scanned the bay, hoping for a return, then set his pistol on a rock. He saw us watching and bobbed his head. He was still smiling.

For half an hour Teddy and I sat wretchedly, listening for footsteps, never knowing what they might mean. My dad was in the house; when his pleas were added to those of the kindly Germans, would the senior figures listen?

Our thoughts were interrupted by another pistol shot. Instantly we rushed to the loopholes. A seagull, one wing shattered, struggled across rocks to reach the water. Others flew off in frantic disarray. Jurgen had brought a slab of cake from the farmhouse and seeing some gulls he had thrown scraps. I had done the same myself on the promenade and enjoyed watching them squabble. But unlike me, Jurgen didn't merely want to watch, he had target practice in mind and this time he had scored a hit.

The gull bobbed on the waves in distress, one wing trailing, swimming in circles. Maybe a leg had been broken also. Jurgen threw some crumbs into his mouth and made his way to the water's edge.

The seagull, blindly terrified, tried to fly or paddle away. It made poor progress. Jurgen steadied himself on the stones, raised the pistol in both hands and took careful aim. Another loud gunshot. The water spat viciously a few inches from the injured bird. Jurgen shifted his feet and fired again. Another miss. The third time the seagull leaped into the air and disintegrated. Feathers flew, a broken carcass of blood, bone, feathers and what remained of a head, settled in the water.

Jurgen was well satisfied and after a long look he turned back up the shore. Seeing us at the loophole, his smile broadened and he held up a victorious thumb.

"Bloody murderer," I said to Teddy. Then thinking it could do little further damage, "Murderer!" I shouted down the shore.

Jurgen was enjoying himself and pointed two fingers at us, two fingers with an upturned thumb like a schoolboy. "Bang!" he mouthed. "Bang!" The rocks were slippery with weed. Avoiding pools, he returned to his seat.

Teddy and I returned to our boxes but not for long. Voices called from the top of the bank and men hurried down to the shore. In German, as Teddy translated for me, they shouted to Jurgen: "What's going on? What's all the shooting?"

"Nothing to worry about." Jurgen laughed. "Just taking a few pot-shots at a seagull."

"Pot-shots! Are you out of your mind?"

"Stupid clown! Do you want every policeman within a hundred miles down here?"

"Your job's to keep an eye on these two, not go shooting bloody birds." They looked at the broken remains, rising and sinking in the waves. "Cruel sod."

Jurgen jerked a thumb towards the pillbox. "What about them? Any decision yet?"

"You heard what Major Krause said."

A kinder voice intruded: "It's not just him, there's all the rest of us. The war's over, who wants to go harming kids that age?"

"You've got children, haven't you, Hans?"

"Yes, three.

"Well then."

Someone said, "Put them on the boat and send them over to the people in Norway. Keep them there until we're ready to move on."

"But they've told their families. People will come looking."

"And they've seen us now. Maybe Krause's got a point."

"You'd shoot two schoolkids just 'cause they've seen you? You're as bad as he is."

"And Benny."

"And bloody Jurgen here."

They drifted away. Teddy and I stepped down and he reported what they had been saying. Again we searched for something, anything, to cut ourselves free and use as a weapon. There was nothing and we sank back into silence.

It did not last long.

41

Benny

"Listen!" Teddy said.

I had already heard it, a scrape of feet and a man grunting as he descended the track. He reached the shore and stumbled across stones to the pillbox. A dark shape filled the entrance, the light was dimmed. We stared, who was it? The terrifying figure of Benny, so violent and threatening, stepped down into the chamber. There was a grim set to his mouth, his eyes glittered in the semi-darkness. We waited for him to speak but he was silent, listening, and put a finger to his lips. He felt in his trouser pocket and took out a clasp knife, flipped up the blade and cut the flex that bound Teddy's wrists.

"Not a word," he said in an Irish brogue and laid the open knife on the box that served as a table. "Cut yourselves free. Stay right where you are until I call you. Whatever you do, don't come out, and *don't* look out the loophole. I mean it!"

He was there as long as it took to say the words, then his huge figure blocked the light a second time and he was gone. We didn't need to be told again. The blade was sharp, a few swift cuts and we were free. I kicked back the loose ends.

The knife might come in useful, I dropped it in my pocket.

"Hi, there, Jurgen." Benny spoke German, his voice was cheerful. "I hear you've been shooting seagulls."

"Yeah. Dieter and some others were down. It was just a few pot-shots, what a fuss! You'd have thought the whole

British army was camped out there. Could have been a farmer shooting rabbits."

"Quite right," Benny agreed. "How are you going to keep your eye in if you don't practise? Load of old women."

Teddy heard no more, we were too busy cutting ourselves free, rubbing life back into our hands and feet. For a time there was silence outside then raised voices. I heard a scuffle. A single muffled shot.

What had happened?

Benny shouted, this time in English: "You two in there, get your arses out here. Come on! Quick!"

We scrambled from the entrance. The wind had strengthened, the sunshine stabbed my eyes. A few steps took us to the corner. Saltfield Bay lay before us. Benny stood midway to the water. His pistol hung from his hand. The motionless body of Jürgen lay a few feet away. He was plainly dead. His eyes gazed sightlessly into the bright October sky. Blood ran from his mouth. His clothes were disordered. He had drawn his pistol but not had time to fire.

I was terrified. I had never seen a dead person before. When my mum was killed in the explosion I was not allowed to see her.

"Never mind staring, shift yourselves! Here." Benny prised Jurgen's pistol from his dead fingers and handed it to Teddy. He raked through his jacket pockets and added a handful of bullets.

"The boat, fast as you can."

It rocked at the jetty.

Teddy said, "How does it start?"

"Oh, for God's sake! They leave the key in the ignition. Turn it and press the starter."

"Will it just go?"

"Of course not, there's a throttle, a little lever. Ahead and astern."

"I stared about me: a dead man, pistols, bullets, the boat, big Benny with his wild ginger hair, Benny the Nazi, Benny the Irishman who was helping us to escape.

"Come on, you stupid cow, get a move on! I got to shift this body before somebody comes."

Teddy was already ten yards away. I ran after him.

We were not fast enough. It wasn't anybody's fault, just bad luck. A few men were kicking a ball about near the farmhouse. One preferred to walk to the shore and now stood above the cliff. It was obvious what had happened: a single shot, Teddy and me running towards the boat, Benny heaving Jurgen up the rocks by his jacket.

The man shouted down then back to the others. Teddy and I redoubled our efforts, stumbling on the weedy rocks. Benny dropped Jurgen and stood for a moment then started after us.

We were halfway to the jetty when a crowd arrived on the cliff edge above us. Some had been carrying pistols but discarded them for the football. Now they levelled them at Teddy, Benny and me.

Crack! Crack! Crack-crack! Handguns are not accurate weapons. It's not like the westerns, beyond fifty yards the chance of hitting a moving man is a matter of luck. We were twice that, far below on the seashore, and it was windy. If they had carried a .303 rifle we were dead but the revolver bullets smacked into stones and made the pools leap. It was too far for Teddy also. All the same, he turned to shoot back. The weapon did not fire, the safety catch was still on. He pressed it to *fire*:

Bang!

The men on the cliff ducked. Several, I think five, were on their way down, jumping from stone to stone, crashing through the bushes.

Benny paused to fire back.

Still they came on. Teddy and I were almost at the jetty, Benny fifty yards behind. Then two lucky shots among the fusillade from the Germans: one hit Benny in the side and he fell. The other hit Teddy in his free hand. He cried aloud but ran on. A finger had been smashed, the third finger on his left hand, and hung from broken bone and sinews.

Then we were at the boat. Teddy scrambled aboard. I threw off the mooring ropes.

Benny picked himself up and somehow kept running but he was hurt and held his side. I saw red. Then he too was on the jetty and half-stepped, half-stumbled over the boat's siderail and fell face-down on a pile of fishing net.

Our pursuers were coming up fast. I tugged Benny's pistol from his fingers, took quick aim and pulled the trigger. I don't think I hit anyone but they paused. One ducked behind a rock, the others spread out.

Teddy ran to the cabin, drips of his blood spattering the deck. Before him, in a sort of dashboard, was the key. He turned it. There was a worn button labelled 'start'. He pressed it. The engine choked. He pressed it again and the engine coughed into life. Alongside, as Benny had told him, was the throttle, a lever on a brass plate stamped with the words, AHEAD, NEUTRAL, ASTERN. It was set to 'Neutral'. The bows were heading the wrong way; 'Ahead' would have taken us back the way we had come. Teddy's left hand was agony. With his right he moved the lever to 'Astern'. The engine note changed. The propeller churned, throwing up weed and sand. Slowly, too slowly, Seal Maid moved from her mooring, then came to an abrupt halt. A light rope which I had not noticed held us alongside. I ran to it, ducking beneath the boat's side. I tried to loosen it. The Germans came on.

"Give me the gun." Benny raised a hand. I handed it to him. As one of the Nazis ran onto the jetty, Benny shot him in the chest. The man ran on, carried forward by his own momentum, hit the boat's rail knee-high, and pitched forward into the bow. I stared in horror. He thrashed and gave a single, terrible cough, blood gushed from his mouth, then he lay still.

"The rope!" Benny called. "The rope!"

With the engine running astern it was bar-tight, the knot had jammed.

"Cut it, for God's sake!" Benny called.

His knife was in my pocket. With a single slash the rope parted.

Not realising the problem, Teddy had increased the revs. With a suddenness that threw me on my back, the boat jumped astern. A second Nazi was on the jetty. Benny fired and missed. Teddy shot from the wheelhouse. I don't know where the man was hit but he fell.

A bullet splintered the panelling above my head. Another shattered a window. By this time we were five yards off-shore, the gap widening all the time. Our pursuers might shoot us, they could not catch us. One threw off his jacket, planning to swim across. Another shot from Teddy made him change his mind.

"Keep down!" Benny rolled painfully from his cushion of nets to a safer place beneath the boat's side. I joined him.

Teddy!" I called.

"Yeah, OK." Our lives were in his hands. After what had happened there was no way the Nazis would let us go; the pain was so great I think that was all that kept him going. He crouched on the wheelhouse deck, keeping below window-level. The controls were above his head. He was terrific, he might have been a fisherman's boy not the son of a dentist. Reaching up, he pushed the throttle through 'Neutral' into 'Ahead'. A spoke of the ship's wheel poked him in the ear. Quickly he risked a look. The Germans shouted; a volley of bullets thudded into the panels.

We were thirty yards offshore, out in open water. Teddy spun the wheel and Seal Maid turned slowly. The stubby mast swung across the clouds and the cliffs and hills of Northumberland came into view. The Germans who had been firing alongside were now astern. As soon as the bows pointed down the middle of the bay, he set the wheel amidships and pushed the throttle to 'Full Ahead'. Slowly gathering speed, we left the farmhouse at Saltfield Mains behind us and headed out into the North Sea.

42

Death of a Nazi

What had become of my dad all this time? I found out later:

His situation was not very different from Teddy's and mine in the pillbox, tied hand and foot and guarded by a Nazi soldier armed with a heavy black Luger. Unlike us, however, he had not been threatened with death, his hands were tied more comfortably in front, he was sitting on a chair in a dry upstairs bedroom with a window, and his guard was a friendly young man called Stefan with a broad fresh face and a smile.

After a while, Commandant Krause and the vile Dr Scholtz came up to question him. Until Teddy and I appeared, there had been no cause to doubt him, but he was English and now they were unsure. Moreover, they were tired. It had been a horrible crossing, seasick on the boat that brought them from a Norwegian fjord, and transferred twenty miles off the English coast into the fish hold of Seal Maid which had pitched and rolled until they would almost have welcomed death. Scholtz sat on a chair and yawned. Krause questioned dad closely and was not satisfied:

"He was a corporal in the British army," he told the others contemptuously. Dad did not speak German but he had picked up enough on his travels to get an idea of what was being said. "He is a deserter, a coward, he has told many lies.

This daughter who looks like a Jew and the boy she is with, I do not trust them. Make sure the wire is tight, I will be back to question him again." He stood watching with Dr Scholtz as Stefan refastened dad's wrists and ankles with the electric flex then they returned downstairs.

Apart from this visit the afternoon passed quietly until abruptly the peace was shattered by the discovery that Benny had shot Jurgen and helped Teddy and me to escape. The man who had seemed the most violent and dedicated of the Nazis was a spy. The farmhouse erupted. Everyone, with the exception of Stefan and little Dr Scholtz, who was too fat and unfit, raced to the shore. Dad hopped to the window and saw them cross the moor.

"I am marksman," Stefan told him. "I should be with them."

"You're talking about my daughter," dad said. "You were one of them said they shouldn't be harmed."

"That was before," Stefan replied. "If they escape we are finish here."

The door flew open and Dr Scholtz burst into the room. He was carrying a pistol, not a heavy black Mauser or Luger like the others, but a vicious little weapon with a short barrel and snub nose like gangsters carry in American films.

"Go on, get after them," he ordered Stefan.

"But I'm—"

"I'll take care of this treacherous pig!" Scholtz was wheezing from the run upstairs. He waved at the door. "Go on!"

Stefan eyed the pistol.

"No, I'll not shoot him," Scholtz said in his soft, high voice and smiled with his thick lips. "Not unless he forces me to."

Dad raised his hands in surrender.

"He's been no trouble." Like most of the others, Stefan detested Dr Scholtz, he made their flesh crawl. "He'd better be unharmed when I get back or you'll have me to deal with."

Scholtz sneered.

"I'm telling you!" Stefan turned in the doorway. "If he isn't I'll put a bullet in you myself."

He was gone.

"Sit!" Scholtz gestured to a chair.

The back was broken. There were two spare chairs in the room. Another looked more comfortable Dad tipped off the cardboard drum of flex.

""Yes, all right." Scholtz sat six feet away. Raising the pistol, he pointed it straight into dad's face. "Never mind what Stefan says. You move one finger, I shoot you right there." He touched himself between the eyebrows. "It give me great pleasure."

Dad nodded. He had heard of this sadistic doctor and had no doubt Scholtz was speaking the exact truth.

"No worry about me, Doc. All the same to you, I'll wait for the others."

"You are wise man." Scholtz lit a cigarette and smiled, revealing nicotine-stained teeth. "A stupid man but a wise man."

Dad's lungs were crying out for a cigarette. He recognised the packet, Gauloises. The distinctive smell filled the room. So Dr Scholtz had likely been in France before Norway, not that it mattered.

He leaned forward to see from the window. Stefan had joined the figures clustered above the cliff.

Scholtz raised his pistol.

The house was still, deserted except for the two in the bedroom. Dad sank back and closed his eyes. A trail of flex crossed the floorboards, the electric cable that had been used to tie his hands and feet. As he tipped it from the chair it had rolled and unwound. The spidery trail imprinted itself on his retina. He watched it change colour behind his eyelids, now red, now green, against a background that also changed colour as he squeezed his eyes shut. He looked through closed lashes.

Scholtz sat six or eight feet away, his pistol in his lap. Dad's hands were tied in front. He strained his wrists: the flex slackened a tiny amount and he could move his fingers. Might it be possible to overpower Scholtz? Could he throttle him with the flex? He was among the most notorious and easily-recognised of the Nazi criminals. Prisoners and damaged survivors, men and women treated as guinea pigs, had given accounts of his experiments in the camps. They had been published in newspapers across the world. Scholtz was a cruel and evil man. As was Krause, commandant of --- Concentration Camp, prisoners machine-gunned into mass graves, bodies of skin and bone heaped up like refuse behind the wire. Smuggling artworks was one thing, helping vermin like this to escape was another.

Troublesome thoughts jostled for attention: he was much stronger but tied up like this could he really overpower Scholtz? Was it his best chance of escape? If he failed there was no doubt Scholtz would put a bullet in his brain. What had become of Mary? How long before the others returned? The police must be told but how could he contact them? What would become of him afterwards?

Scholtz was tired and yawned again. Nothing to do but guard a helpless prisoner. His shoulders slumped. The hand holding his pistol fell limp.

Dad breathed deeply, giving the impression of a man who was falling asleep. His knees fell apart. His head sank upon his chest. He watched the man sitting opposite through his eyelashes.

Scholtz was not a soldier, he had never trodden a parade-ground or been sent into battle. He was a doctor, a committed member of Hitler's SS who supported the extermination of the Jews and for this had been awarded the rank of major.

He was accustomed to people doing what he told them. If there was resistance then other people dealt with it. Now, holding a pistol which he would use without a moment's hesitation, and his single prisoner tied hand and foot, he felt in complete control. The situation was little different from the laboratories and operating theatres in which he had spent the last years of the war. It had been an exhausting day, he longed for a bed with a soft pillow and clean white sheets. The house was quiet. His eyes were closing. In the chair opposite, his prisoner had already fallen asleep. Scholtz observed his slow, deep breathing, the relaxed limbs.

But dad had never been more wide awake. He watched Scholtz responding. His eyes closed. His head sank forward. Carefully, precisely, dad judged the distance and everything he must do: how he would hit the sleeping man, how he would snatch up the flex. Minutes passed. There seemed no doubt, Scholtz was sound asleep. Without moving, dad flexed his muscles. If only his hands were free, or his feet, one or the other. His heart hammered. In seconds, if he got it wrong, he would lie lifeless on the bedroom floor.

The moment came. Dad was quite a big man, strong and fit. Without warning, he sprang across the space that separated him from Scholtz and with a single, savage blow from his bound fists, struck the hand that held the pistol. The doctor was taken completely by surprise. The snub-nosed pistol went clattering across the boards. A double-fisted blow sent Scholtz reeling. Dad snatched up the electric flex, flung a length over the doctor's head and pulled it tight against his throat. Scholtz struggled and hit out. Dad fell full-length, landing on his side, and pulled harder. Tangled as cats, they rolled among the chairs. Scholtz tried to scream but no sound would come, just a terrible gurgle. His eyes bulged. The flex dug into his windpipe. An elbow hit dad in the face; a chair cut his cheek; the flex hurt his fingers.

It didn't take long. The doctor's struggles grew weaker. And then he was still. Dad shifted his position, thrust a knee against Scholtz's back and for another half minute continued to heave. There was no need, the man was dead. Then he let go and fell back. The wire fell from Scholtz's neck, leaving a vicious crimson scar. His face was purple.

Although dad was a soldier who had fired his rifle in battle, had been a member of the violent gang in Paris and spent time in jail for burglary, he was a peace-loving man who had never in his life been in a fight or hurt anyone. Now he had murdered, in the most brutal fashion, the man who sprawled beside him. Scholtz was a monster; had he been present at the Nuremberg War Trials he would have been condemned to death. But two or three minutes earlier he had been alive. Now he was dead.

Dad shook from head to foot. It was a nightmare.

43

Major O'Hare

My dad, who all his life had looked after number one, had done a brave thing. Tied hand and foot, he lay on the bare floorboards. His feet were tangled in a chair, Scholtz's awful head lay almost in his lap. Dad looked down at his fingers, the soft skin was bleeding. If things had gone wrong it was he who would be lying there dead.

But there was no time for brooding. Soon, perhaps very soon, the others would return. He looked from the window; a crowd was still clustered above the cliff. What had become of his daughter and her young friend?

There seemed no point attempting to hide the body. Before anything else, he had to cut himself free. It was Stefan who had tied him up but maybe Scholtz carried a knife anyway. He searched the dead man's pockets: cigarettes, lighter, a snot-stained handkerchief, a greasy comb for those curls he was so proud of, but no clasp knife. There were knives in the kitchen, dad had used them to clean the fish. Leaving the body where it lay, he collected Scholtz's automatic from a corner and pushed it into his pocket. Then he hopped heavily to the bedroom door, let himself out onto the landing and pulled the door shut behind him.

The staircase was steep but had a sturdy banister. Halfway down he very nearly fell. It was a dangerous moment, if he twisted a knee he was dead as surely as if he had been shot by the doctor.

The kitchen was familiar. The chef's knife they used for cooking lay in the top drawer. It was awkward and he cut himself in his haste but soon the flex fell free. It left livid red marks. He rubbed life back into his hands and feet. A bucket was used for scraps and rubbish. He threw in the loose ends and hid them beneath old newspapers.

The kitchen was at the back of the house but the living-room windows gave an uninterrupted view to the shore. Still, to his surprise, no one was coming. The knife would be a good weapon but it was too awkward to carry. He returned it to the drawer, checked the pistol in his pocket and let himself from the house.

The back door opened to a wilderness of drystone walls, rusting machinery and discarded furniture through which the weeds grew in profusion. Beyond what had once been a kitchen garden, protected by buildings from the withering east wind, the moor rolled on for ever. The nearby ground was mostly pasture, nibbled short by sheep, but the bracken and heather were creeping closer, a patchwork of green, brown and purple which rose to a range of hills a couple of miles away. A stand of mature pine trees stood a hundred yards to the north. A stream tumbled down through bushes and stony gullies from the crest of the moor. A rusting pipe, half-buried in earth, provided the farm's water supply. Apart from that cluster of buildings, in the whole wide expanse, there was no sign of human habitation.

The owner of the abandoned farm, part of a great shooting estate, was a Major Pickersgill who lived in a lodge on the outskirts of Monkton Parva. There was no way the group could operate there without investigation by keepers or Major Pickersgill himself. To prevent this, he had been approached by members of the group who presented themselves as Polish and German forestry workers who enjoyed sea fishing. They had, they told him, bought an old seine-netter and wished to use the farmhouse as a base for their times off. A small rent was agreed and two of the group took jobs in the vast forestry operations further north lest Major Pickersgill made enquiries. It was an ideal arrangement and a well-chosen spot from which the Nazi cell could operate.

Standing in the overgrown kitchen garden, dad's life was on the line. Which way should he go? If he headed north to the village of Monkton Parva they would easily cut him off. Equally they might expect him to head south. His best chance lay inland.

There was no time to waste. Ducking behind a drystone dyke and crawling through bracken, he made his way to the copse of pine trees. Dad was a strong man as I have said and luckily quite fit. Emerging beyond the trees, he headed for the stream, crouching where the gully was not very deep, always heading for the cover of rocks and bushes. Back at the farmhouse he had worn an off-white seaman's jersey. It was too conspicuous so he had bundled it into a cupboard and pulled on a dull brown jersey belonging to one of the others. His trousers were grey. They provided good camouflage.

Dad made rapid progress and was far up the stream when a barely audible hubbub of voices reached him amid the splash of water. He peeped through rocks and heather. Far beneath him the house looked small and somehow unreal. The body of Dr Scholtz had been discovered and now a crowd of men stood behind the house looking this way and that. Some shaded their eyes and scanned the moor. One pointed north towards Monkton Parva. Beyond them he saw the little seine-net boat, Seal Maid, heading out into the North Sea. What did this mean? Could Mary and her friend have somehow escaped? Might they be dead and their bodies were being disposed of? There was no way of knowing.

Two men detached themselves and headed towards the dark copse of pine trees. If they'd had a dog that could follow his scent, dad was a dead man. As it was, they had no idea where he was or which way he was heading. He did not know himself but at least he had a good lead. Slithering back into the stream, he pressed on as fast as his legs allowed.

*

Aboard Seal Maid, meanwhile, Teddy and I had left the shooting behind and sailed the length of Saltfield Bay. As we emerged from the sheltering headlands, we met the wind and waves of the North Sea. Which way to go? Briefly we wondered about heading to Monkton Parva, a few miles up the coast, but it was only a fishing village. The safer place, the place where we could summon police, was Eastport, so Teddy turned south.

We carried two passengers: Benny had crawled across the deck and lay beneath the port rail where he was protected to some extent from spray blown by the east wind. He had lost a lot of blood and was growing weaker. The Nazi, who sprawled in the bow, had been shot in the chest and was dead.

Teddy was in great pain. The third finger on his left hand was shattered. I searched the lockers for bandages, antiseptic, painkillers, but there was nothing. All I could find that might be of use was a bottle of whisky, two-thirds empty. The alcohol would stop infection. So while Teddy held us on course with his right hand, I wet my handkerchief with the whisky and wiped his hand then poured it over the broken bones and sinew, his fingernail hanging apart. It burned like fire. His face went chalk white, his eyes stared, but he made not a single sound. I have never seen such bravery. Very gently I wrapped his finger in the driest part of my hanky and pulled off a sock to hold it in place.

"Thanks." He clung to the wheel and suddenly I realised he was going to faint. "Here, sit down." There was a skipper's chair by the window.

"No, I'm all right."

"Don't be so bloody stupid. Sit down, I'll take the wheel."

For ten minutes I steered, straddling my legs and gripping the spokes for balance. Seal Maid pitched and rolled in the waves that the fresh wind flung against her side, while the cliffs and headlands to starboard crawled past so slowly we might have been stationary. Teddy sat in the skipper's chair, so close I could have reached out and touched him. His fainting spell had passed and the agony I caused with the whisky had settled down to a throbbing pain.

*

Benny was also in pain, and pain of a more serious kind. Unlike the violent brute who had threatened to shoot us in the farmhouse, he had risked his life to save us. Now he called and raised a hand. I handed the wheel to Teddy and crossed to where he lay. He looked towards the wheelhouse: "Did ye leave a drop?"

I had left more than a drop, there was quarter of a bottle. I fetched it and sat beside him on the pitching boards. A reek of whisky mingled with the salt airs that blew about the foredeck.

"Give the neck a wipe, there's a girl," he said, the Irish strong, his voice softer than the tones he had adopted earlier. "I don't like to think whose mouth it was in last."

I rubbed it with my skirt and he took a long swallow. "Aahh!"

The dead German straggled in the bow. He had tumbled on board when Benny shot him and lay with one arm outstretched. I recognised him as one of those who had sneered when Krause proclaimed me to be a Jew.

"What about him?" I said to Benny.

"Oskar Beck," he said. "I don't like to speak ill of the dead but not a nice man. Too handy with his rifle butt. Put him over the side."

I rose.

"Although no," he plucked me back, "might have some papers on him. Got a wife and kids, not fair on them. He's not in the way."

With difficulty Benny turned to face me. "More important than Oskar."

"Yeah?"

"Your daddy says you're a clever girl. I hope so, for there's things you have to remember." He grimaced in pain. "This telephone number for a start; are you listening? Whitehall 2759."

"Whitehall 2759," I repeated.

"Now it's important! You'll not forget?"

"No," I said, but to be on the safe side I called Teddy above the noise of the sea and the engine.

He came to the wheelhouse door.

"Whitehall 2579, it's a phone number. We've got to remember."

"2759!" Benny said impatiently.

"Sorry! 2759," I called to Teddy.

He raised a hand and returned to the wheel.

"Ask for Colonel Littlejohn," Benny continued. "Like in Robin Hood, you'll not forget that. If he's not there they'll fetch him for you. Tell him Benny O'Hare's bought it; that's Major O'Hare."

"Major O'Hare?"

"That's right. Tell him about the farmhouse. You'll have worked out what they're doing. He knows anyway. But tell him about Gunther Krause, he was a concentration camp commandant, and Doctor Scholtz, Konrad Scholtz. They're the most important ones ones right now, both high on the wanted list. They weren't expected for a day or two. There's an operation planned to pick them up but by that time they'll be on their way again."

He coughed and panted after so much talking. A spatter of sea spray whipped over the rail, salty on my lips.

"Have you got that now?"

"Gunther Krause and Konrad Scholtz," I said. "You should be talking to Teddy, he speaks German the same as he speaks English. He heard everything they were saying."

Benny was astonished. "How's that?"

"His mother's Austrian, they sent her whole family to the camps. He's a Jew."

"The boy?" He looked towards the wheelhouse. "So I guess he's told you."

"Some."

"Then he'd better be there when you talk to Colonel Littlejohn. Did he mention a man called Otto Baumann?"

"Not to me." I called to the wheelhouse: "Teddy!"

He returned to the door.

"Up at the farmhouse, did you hear anything about someone called Otto Baumann?"

"No."

"They weren't talking about him?"

"Not that I heard." He returned to the wheel.

"A bigger fish than Krause and Scholtz," Benny went on. "We had no idea he was coming until they told us this afternoon; high-ranking Gestapo officer, friend of Himmler and some of the top Nazis. A huge catch if we can collar him." He coughed and put a hand to his side. It came away red.

"Can I do anything?" I said.

He smiled. "No, no, sweetheart, it'll be fine. Now listen, they've set up a rendezvous for three o'clock tomorrow morning; ten miles east of Ramsay Point. This lot can't keep it obviously, we've got the boat. They won't hang around so Littlejohn's going to have to work fast. There'll be shooting so tell him to send a couple of gun boats or maybe a destroyer. Baumann won't be alone, Bruno Koch will be with him and possibly Horst Winkler, but they don't matter so much, Baumann's the prize. And there'll be some artworks from the Rijksmuseum: Rembrandt, van Goch, I don't recall the others."

He was growing weak. I repeated what he had told me, as much as I could remember.

"That's right, three o'clock, ten miles east of Ramsay Point. And the phone number?"

I smiled: Whitehall 2759; Colonel Littlejohn. Major O'Hare."

"Clever girl." He patted my hand. "Soon as you can get to a phone. And tell them when they get here to look under a stone the back of the barn. I've written it all down, not what happened today but the rest of it. Now," his eyelids were drooping. "I think I'll have a little shut-eye. Get my strength back."

Red stubble covered his cheeks. His jacket had fallen open. I pulled it across.

"I've got a girl in County Cork about your age. She's lovely. Kind, you know. Bridget."

I rested a hand on his wet hair. He seemed to be asleep, then he gave a deep sigh and looked at me with wide, clear eyes.

And died.

44

On the Run

Hidden on the crest of the moor, dad looked back at his pursuers. Two more had joined the chase and they appeared to be a group of four but were no closer. He had been slowed by keeping out of sight but they also had been delayed by checking for footprints and trampled bracken. A cluster of little summits rose about him and dad wound through them, hoping to confuse his tracks.

The land levelled and he was able to pick up speed, quitting the stream and running as fast as his legs would carry him through heather and long grass. He guessed he had a twenty or thirty-minute lead but in half that time was rewarded by coming upon a moorland road of earth and stones and flooded potholes. It showed the tracks of several vehicles. In that vast expanse of moor there was no sign of habitation but where there were cars and tractors, he told himself, there might be houses. But which way to go, back towards the coast where there would certainly be more people, or deeper into the moors? It was not a difficult choice, the men in their blue van would be seeking him on the coast road, men armed with pistols. Dad headed into the moors.

He moved faster now and after half a mile the track began to descend. Hillsides closed about him; he passed a pine wood. If his pursuers were still on his trail they would not see him until they came close. And then, as he rounded a bend, he was confronted by an abandoned steading, a cluster of stone barns and rotting wooden outhouses. Heather grew right to the walls. It looked deserted but there, on a patch of weeds and lopsided paving stones, stood a battered truck.

Dad was trotting. He broke into a run and soon stood at the door of the nearest barn. All was gloom and sheep dirt. An abandoned harrow stood near a wall. Pigeons clattered from the beams and vanished through window spaces.

Where was the driver of the truck? "Hello?"

There was no response. He wandered round the back and looked in a couple of outhouses. "Hello?"

Still no reply.

Where was the man?

"Hello!"

Ah well, no problem. He needed the truck. It wouldn't be the first time he had hot-wired a vehicle. Car theft was one of the crimes that had sent him to jail. Still calling, he returned to the truck and grasped the handle on the driver's side.

Instantly the cab became a whirlwind of snarling, ferocious dogs, dogs with savage eyes that showed their teeth to the gum and slavered against the glass, dogs eager to tear his throat out. There were two, although it seemed more, a black Alsatian and a bull terrier. Dad sprang back in alarm and as he did so an old man emerged from the doorway of an adjacent barn. He had wild white hair, wore a badly-stained mac with a twisted belt, and carried a shotgun which he thrust aggressively at the stranger.

"Go on! I seen you. After my truck this time were you?" He advanced until they were only a few feet apart.

"No, I shouted but there wasn't an answer. I want to know if—"

"Dirty Jarman! Nosing round here. Get out of it, afore I blow your bloody head off."

"I'm not German, I'm looking for a—"

"Loose the dogs on you, shall I?"

"Will you just listen! I'm trying to tell you—"

But the old man was deaf, deaf and half mad. Somehow the Germans had been round and he'd sent them on their way. Perhaps they'd wanted to use the steading instead of the farmhouse. Perhaps he'd had children killed in the war. He raised the shotgun and fired a barrel over dad's head. Birds whirled from the ruins.

"All right, all right." Dad backed away, both hands in the air.

The old man opened the truck door and the dogs bounded out. Dad fled but the old man called and they stopped halfway, savage and snarling, straining at his invisible leash.

"See you round here again I'll set them to kill!" He fired the second barrel and pulled cartridges from his pocket. "Dump your body in the bog over there."

As he hurried away dad felt the old man's mad eyes upon him, half-waited for the smash of shotgun pellets in his back. After fifty yards he looked back and saw the scarecrow figure still standing, twelve-bore in hand. The dogs stood at his side, even at this distance, it seemed to dad, eager for the word to run him down and tear him to pieces.

*

It was a relief when a fold of the moor hid the steading from sight. In that land of heather and grass a second pine wood lay ahead, half a mile long and a couple of hundred yards wide, not a wood you could get lost in. After a while dad spotted a splash of red and chrome at the roadside, half-hidden by bushes. When he came closer he discovered four motorbikes. The riders and a couple of pillion passengers had stopped for tea and sandwiches. As he arrived they were packing the panniers and preparing to ride off. He wondered if he could persuade one to give him a lift into Eastport.

"Hi!"

They waited as he came up.

"Nice bikes!" They were an assortment, old army Nortons, a heavy Sunbeam, a spanking new BSA Bantam. The older bikes had been lovingly restored, the chrome sparkled.

They waited for him to continue.

"I used to ride in the army," dad lied.

"Yeah? What you on then?"

"Various, mostly a Norton 16H."

It was known as a 16H, no one said Norton. They lost interest.

"Listen," he said, "there's a gang of Nazis hanging out in a farmhouse back there by Monkton Parva. Really! I've got to get into Eastport. Any chance of a lift?"

"Nazis? War's over, dad, haven't you heard?"

"No, I mean it! Smuggling stuff from Europe."

"Yeah? And what's that to you?"

"They're holding my daughter. I managed to get away. They're after me. I've got to get into town and let the police know."

"The cops!" One laughed. "You want us to take you to the police station?"

"Yeah, will you just listen!" Dad caught him by the sleeve.

The man pulled back angrily. "Take your bloody hand—"

They were ex-servicemen, young men who had survived the war. Likely some had been in the fighting, seen their mates killed. "Push off, you stupid old bugger, or I'll land you one."

In a minute they were ready. One wore a helmet, one a maroon beret, a third a khaki battledress blouse. They pulled scarves across their mouths. One after another they heaved their bikes off the stands and kicked them into life. Four-stroke, two-stroke, their revving shattered the silence.

"It's important!" Dad took hold of a handlebar. The rider stared at him in disbelief. His passenger jumped down and pushed dad in the chest, pushed him a second time so hard that he tripped and fell on his back.

"You're bloody mad, that's what you are." He stood above dad as if he might kick him in the ribs. "You need to get yourself seen to." He returned to the bike and settled himself behind his pal.

They swung to the track and roared away, spitting pebbles, picking up speed, growing smaller beyond the towering trunks of pine. When dad could no longer see them the buzz of the engines rose on the silence until it was no louder than bees, and then they were gone.

*

Surely somewhere in this endless expanse of moor, dad thought as he hurried on, there must be a farm or cottage. If not, where did the track lead? And then, half a mile ahead, he saw a car parked at the roadside. No buildings, just a car.

Dad knew about cars. It was a Humber Hawk, Mark 3, newly-released that autumn at the London Motor Show: two-tone, cream with a black roof, very smart. What was it doing parked here, apparently abandoned, on a potholed track in the wilderness? This car would look more at home outside Harrods or the Dorchester.

As he came closer dad realised the car was not abandoned at all for on a lake far below a man was fishing. He wore waders and was well out from shore, casting a fly. What may have been a basket stood on the bank. His dog, a black and white collie, hunted through the heather.

It was like letting a child loose in a toy shop. Despite his pursuers and the horrors of the afternoon, dad smiled. The doors were locked and the windows wound up, not that these presented any great problem; in any case the quarter-lights were open to provide air for an old white poodle that lay on the back seat. It was a bitch for he could see the pink spots on her belly. She had heard him approach and looked up with watery eyes. "Hello, sweetheart," dad said. "Who's a lovely girl?"

She stood, shivering, and looked at him.

Dad pushed the driver's quarter-light wide, reached through and pulled the door handle.

He was in. It was the work of a moment to reach under the dashboard and pull out a tangle of wires. Dad had been hot-wiring cars since he was fourteen, it was child's play. Automatically he checked the gears were in neutral, selected two wires and twisted them together. With a soft, expensive roar, the engine throbbed into life. The fisherman didn't hear but his dog looked up alertly, barked, and streaked back uphill through the heather. The man looked behind him, saw his dog and spotted the movement at his new car.

"Hey! Hey!" He started back to shore, swashing through the water and stumbling on slippery stones.

The doors were shut, the collie could do no harm and it would be a good five minutes before the owner arrived. The poodle was desperate to be friends and clambered over his lap, clawing at his chest, licking wherever she could reach.

"Sshh! Sshh!" He comforted her, holding her fragile chest in his big hand, calming her shivering.

Should he drive on or return the way he had come? It seemed better to head back, pass his pursuers if they had followed him this far, and continue down to the coast road that led in a dozen or fourteen miles to Eastport. Perhaps, driving this smart car, he could adopt some disguise. It was easy to find: a tweed driving cap, spectacles, half a box of cigars.

The collie arrived, barking furiously, clawing at the windows and paintwork. It could do him no harm but dad wound down his window a couple of inches:

"Sshh! Sshh! Who's a good dog?"

The collie redoubled its attack, slavering and clashing its teeth on the glass.

They were excellent cigars. A lighter and cutter lay beside the box. There was no urgency; carefully he cut the head, toasted the foot and lit up, enjoying the fragrant smoke. The cap was too big but he pulled it on and tried the black-framed spectacles. They were reading glasses with thick lenses; instantly the world swam out of focus. He set them aside until such time as he encountered his pursuers. What else? He pulled off his brown jersey. Shirt sleeves would have to be enough.

The gear pattern was similar to a dozen cars he had driven. He clamped the cigar between his teeth, trod on the clutch and pushed the lever into first.

The car was facing the wrong way. He turned on grass and with the owner still two hundred yards away, the collie continuing its brave attack, and the poodle with her paws braced against the passenger window, dad drove back into the moors the way he had come.

His pursuers had been travelling fast; a few more minutes and they would have seen him at the parked car. As the road wound through outcrops, grey with boulders and red with bracken, four men were suddenly before him. The Germans were as startled as he, such a car did not belong in the heathery wilderness. A single stranger, a man in tweed cap and heavy spectacles, was at the wheel. They stepped aside to let him pass. Dad couldn't see, the world was a blur. Luckily at this point the track was well defined. Concentrating hard, he raised a hand, displaying the fat cigar, and drove on. The moment he was past, navigating between rocks and a peaty ditch, he took off the glasses and looked in the rear-view mirror. His pursuers were talking earnestly and looking after him. Had he been recognised? They seemed unsure. But by that time the cream and black car was drawing away, a hundred yards, two hundred yards, and there was nothing they could do about it.

45

Four on a Fishing Boat

As we sailed south, the great North Pier and lighthouse at Eastport stood ever before us, a dozen miles off and never seeming to come any closer. To our left lay the grey North Sea, ten thousand waves capped by white horses. To our right, beyond foam-fringed cliffs, stood the hills and vast empty moors of the north.

A pair of Zeiss binoculars lay in the wheelhouse. I trained them on the shore. There stood Biddle, recognisable by its square church tower and flag of St George, and far off to the north what could only be Monkton Parva although the harbour was hidden by a headland. Lorries crawled along the coast road. My heart quickened for almost directly opposite, a blue van was drawn up at the roadside. It was familiar to me even at that distance, for through the crystal-sharp image of the prisms I spotted a patch of red paint on the wing. The sun, moving into the west, was in my eyes but I was able to see a group of men clustered along the side. Did one have his hands to his face, was he looking back at me through other binoculars? I couldn't tell.

"Is that what I think it is?" Teddy preferred being on the wheel, it took his mind off the pain.

"Looks like it."

"Are they tracking us?"

"They might be."

Now I had seen the van it was clear that they were for it kept pace on the road and waited behind some trees.

"In that case we'd better get ready," Teddy said. "Check the pistols, see how much ammo we've got."

We had three pistols: Jurgen's, Benny's and the weapon belonging to Oskar Beck, the dead Nazi in the bow. Although, as I learned later, in World War 2 the German army was mostly supplied with Mausers and the Walther P38, these were Lugers, still preferred by many. They were identical, black steel with brown wooden handles. Dad had shown me his British Enfield, but that was a double-action revolver that broke in half with cartridges that were loaded into a cylinder. The Luger was quite different, a semi-automatic pistol with no cylinder and a spring-loaded magazine in the handle. I discovered by experiment that they were easy to load; a button by the trigger released a catch and the magazine slid out into your hand. Each held eight cartridges but all three guns had been fired. I ejected the remainder, copper-coated bullets in brass cartridges, bright, deadly and dangerous, and set them on a crumpled flag on deck to stop them rolling around. There were thirteen.

"That the lot?" Teddy said. "See if they've got any more."

"What?"

"Bullets. Cartridge belt or something. Look in their pockets."

"In their pockets?"

"If it comes to shooting again we might need all we can get."

"I'm not going through dead men's pockets."

"Well I can't, not with this hand."

"I can't either."

"Of course you can, unless you'd rather just sit there and let them take pot-shots. Come on, Mary, it's no time to be squeamish."

He was right but I had to force myself. Until an hour ago I'd never even seen a body except in films. Their faces were wet with spray. It gave me nightmares for years.

Benny lay under the port rail, halfway up the deck. I searched him first. He was a big man, red-headed with rough red stubble, his lifeless body heavy to push around. As the boat rolled, he fell against me. He wore a heavy jacket which was trapped beneath him. I had to heave him over to open the buttons. Whatever a cartridge belt might look like, he wasn't wearing one. He carried no ammunition clip either, but in the corner of a pocket, along with a dirty handkerchief, I discovered three loose bullets. I set them with the others. Worse than his jacket were his trouser pockets, pulled tight by the way he was lying. I had to force my wet fingers inside and found them still warm, almost hot. It was too much, I couldn't do it. I didn't like handling my father's trousers on wash day, let alone trousers with a dead man still wearing them. I pulled my hand back and scrubbed it on my skirt then patted his pockets from the outside. There were no bullets, or if there were they would just have to stay there.

The Nazi was much the same although his mouth and chest were red with blood and the pitching in the bow was greater. In his back pocket, which was visible from the way he was lying, he carried a wallet which verified that his name was Oskar Franz Beck. It contained a picture of him in black Nazi uniform with various insignia and a high peaked cap. A nice-looking woman stood at his side with a girl aged about ten and a younger boy whom I took to be his wife and children. The girl would be my age now, maybe a little older. I wondered if Oskar's wife knew that three years after the war ended he was part of a Nazi cell smuggling artworks and war criminals out of the country. As the boat pitched, his head knocked against an iron bracket on the deck. I felt in his jacket and patted the pockets of his one-time uniform trousers but he carried no spare ammunition, only the pistol he had been firing at Teddy and me when Benny shot him dead.

My efforts had produced only three more bullets so we now had a pile of sixteen. There seemed no point in spreading them over three weapons, so I pushed one pistol aside and filled the magazines of the other two. Eight shots each. I checked the safety-catches and set them on the shelf in the wheelhouse.

Benny's eyes were blue. Sightlessly they gazed into the October sky. I closed them the way I had seen in films. Among the Nazis he had seemed hardest of the hard but now he looked very vulnerable. Major O'Hare, to give him his proper name, was a British spy who had given his life to save Teddy and me. Back in County Cork he had a daughter called Bridget, a kind and pretty girl my own age. Now he was dead and I had searched his pockets. I hated it.

There were half a dozen flags in a wheelhouse locker. I had taken one to stop the bullets rolling around. Now I took another, a red ensign, and muffled Benny's face, knotting the corners to stop it blowing away. The dead German, Oskar Beck, had been trying to kill us and was not a nice man according to Benny, but he had children and deserved respect, so I took a third flag and bound his head also. He had bled a lot and I rinsed my fingers in a puddle on deck.

By this time the great North Pier was visibly closer. I had been following the blue van but now, as we approached the outskirts of town, it had disappeared. I searched every road and patch of trees through the binoculars but could see it nowhere.

"We'll have to keep a special lookout," Teddy said. "Maybe they've made a run for it, get as far away as they can before we tell the police."

"What about the stuff in the barn?"

"They'd save themselves first, I would anyway, but maybe

they'll head back and take some." His face was greasy with pain. "I hope they catch them and they hang."

*

Teddy altered course to take us round the lighthouse into Monks Bay, so called, as I said earlier, because in ancient days the monks from St Peter's Priory fished there in their coracles. Now it was sheltered by the great North Pier and much smaller South Pier that curved like a crab's claw round the mouth of the river, protecting the quays and shipyards of Eastport from the storms of winter. As we passed beneath the lighthouse, a tremendous silhouette against the sky, the white horses were left behind and we sailed on into calmer water.

A lopsided red button stood among the controls. A worn inscription read 'siren'. Teddy pressed it; nothing happened. He pressed again; the button wobbled. He pressed a third time, the left side. The siren emitted a loud, crackling parp! He pressed again: parp! parp! parp!

"Hey, that's great! Do you know the Morse code?"

"We did it in Guides."

"What's SOS? Three short…"

"Dit dit dit, dah dah dah, dit dit dit."

"That's it! Are you ready?" He jabbed the button with his right thumb:

Parp-parp-parp PARP PARP PARP parp-parp-parp! The wheezy siren crackled across the water.

Parp-parp-parp PARP PARP PARP parp-parp-parp!

He held the wheel with his injured hand.

I took charge of the button. Parp-parp-parp PARP PARP PARP parp-parp-parp!

Seamen on a ship heading out to sea gathered along a rail to look at us.

I kept pressing. Three times more then:

Parp-parp-parp PARP PARP PA...and nothing. The rusty siren gave up the ghost. I pressed all round the button: two tiny coughs – then silence.

"Bloody thing!" I said and pressed with all the strength in my thumb. Something – a spring, a contact? – went crack and the button flopped to one side.

"Well, that's that!" Teddy smiled. "At least people know we're here. Those pistols, are the safety-catches off?"

I made sure.

"Just in case."

It was a huge bay, the length of the North Pier and as wide. It was nearly low water and silty brown currents flowed past from the emptying river. There was still light in the sky but daylight was fading. The dock lights had been switched on, illuminating the cobbles and rail tracks. Loading was finished for the day, the dock workers had gone home. I scanned the warehouses and surrounding streets for sign of the blue van or anyone acting suspiciously. There was nothing. Giant cranes stood motionless, lorries were parked for the night, rail wagons waited in the sidings. Beyond the railings men returned home in their work clothes. Smoke rose from chimneys. A small group stood chatting by a truck at the gates.

Eastport, as I have told you, stands on the River Brander which flows into the North Sea. There is a broad South Quay on the town side of the river, a much smaller North Quay opposite. As usual, the South Quay was chock-a-block with ocean-going ships. Their heavy mooring lines criss-crossed above the water, taut as they took the strain of the ebbing tide. Deck lights twinkled but few seaman were about for it was meal time, the waiting hour before they headed ashore to the pictures and pubs for the first beer of the evening. I had known the river all my life, especially the South Quay, only half a mile from my home where at that moment gran had my meal ready and was expecting me back from a cycle ride, instead of which Teddy and I were crossing Monks Bay in a stolen seine-netter, pistols primed and two men dead on deck. Like the whole of Eastport, from police intelligence to boys kicking a ball about in the street, she had no idea what had been taking place just a few miles to the north.

We looked for a mooring on the South Quay but there was no space where Seal Maid could be brought alongside apart from a treacherous few yards at the seaward end where the emptying river sucked and swirled. An experienced skipper might have winkled a way between the ships but not Teddy or me with the current at full flow and no one on shore to take a line.

If we had not been so terrified, if Teddy's hand was not on fire with pain, if it was full daylight, we might have spotted North Sea Trader midway among the vessels at the South Quay. If we had done, we would have sailed directly alongside and the outcome would have been different. But we did not and as I have said, the moorings were full.

Across the river at the North Quay, however, two moorings lay empty. Here it would be easy to tie up. I knew it well. Here Barry had his little shack, although by this time on an October evening he was away home. But here were the ring bolts he used for mooring and here were the scrubbed steps up which his passengers climbed to the quay. This was where I crossed the river on a Saturday to look after the deckchairs when Archie went to the match. Occasionally, as I have told you, I even rowed the boat myself.

Ever since the North Quay came into sight, the quay the Nazis must come to first if they were still on our trail, I had scanned it repeatedly with the binoculars: trucks, cranes, rail wagons, warehouses, everywhere. Only a sailor returning for his dinner crossed the cobbles. Apart from my dad, a prisoner in the farmhouse we still believed, Teddy and I were the only ones who knew about Krause, Scholtz, Baumann and the people-smuggling at Saltfield Mains. We had to be silenced. If the Nazis were still pursuing us, it was here they had the best chance.

As Teddy guided us in and the weedy harbour wall came close, I examined every shadow, every crevice, every possible hiding place, for sign of movement. All was still but something felt wrong. My skin crawled; my heart was in my throat. I armed myself with one of the pistols and checked again that the safety catch was off.

"Looks like they've given up." Teddy throttled back until Seal Maid hardly had any way upon her, creeping upstream until we came level with the steps.

Benny had rolled on top of the boathook. I pulled it free and waited for the mooring ring to come within reach.

46

North Quay

Up on the moors, meanwhile, as Teddy and I sailed south, there had been death.

Four deaths as I learned later.

Dad's pursuers had quarrelled: had it been Frankie Pearson at the wheel of that spanking new two-tone car that swept past them? He was a newcomer to the group, little more than a hanger-on, yet somehow, though tied hand and foot, he had garrotted Konrad Scholtz and managed to escape. Could he now be that driver in a flat cap and glasses, a fat cigar in his hand and a little white poodle watching from the window? The question was answered a few minutes later as they encountered a very angry fisherman with a collie at his heels and no sign of a car in all those empty miles of moorland.

They had been tricked and it was serious. This traitor who knew all their secrets would already have reached the coast road, soon he would be in the town. But would he go at once to the police or might he be more interested in saving his own skin? After all, he wasn't exactly an innocent. What should they do? There was only one immediate answer, they needed to get back to the coast and let the others know. As soon as possible. They needed transport.

A few minutes earlier they had passed some dilapidated farm buildings and been confronted by a mad old man with a shotgun. His truck stood nearby with two snarling dogs in the cab. They ran back up the road.

"You don't understand," said the spokesperson for the group whose name was Brandt. "We need the truck and we're taking it."

The old man gestured with his shotgun. "Wanting's not getting. Lay a hand on it and I'll loose the dogs. Nazi scum!"

"We're not playing games," Brandt told him. "We don't want any unpleasantness. Call the dogs off and you'll get your truck back in the morning. And fifty pounds."

"I don't want no unpleasantness neither," the old man said. "And I don't want your dirty money. We just fought a war against you lot, two wars – and knocked you hollow! So push off."

Brandt unbuttoned his pistol.

"Think to scare me, do you?" The old man crossed to his truck and threw open a door. The snarling, barking dogs sprang down. "Not out of here in ten seconds I'll set them on you."

Front paws planted, eyes savage, lips pulled back to the gum, the dogs waited for the word of command.

It was never given. Coldly Brandt raised his pistol and shot first one, then the second. The German shepherd died instantly, the brindled dog with a big head writhed on its side, screaming with pain. Brandt stepped up and finished it with a bullet to the brain.

The old man could not believe it, his constant companions who accompanied him wherever he went, who lay on the rug when he sat by his fire in the evenings. He stared at their bodies bleeding into the dirt of the yard, as he had stared at the bodies of his comrades bleeding into the earth of France in the First War, as his son had bled into a beach in Normandy at the D-Day invasion. Hardly knowing what he saw, he looked up at the man with a pistol, raised his shotgun and pulled both triggers. At such short range the charge of shot kicked Brandt back like a horse and he skidded to the ground several metres away with a hole in his chest the size of a plate.

The Germans stared then one stepped forward, pulled out his pistol and shot the old man in the head. His limbs collapsed like a puppet and he fell to the yard without a sound.

Four men had followed dad into the moor. Now there were three and they gazed in horror at the scene of bloodshed before them. It had taken less than a minute. But there was no time to lose and as soon as they had recovered there was no doubt what needed to be done.

*

My dad had a twenty-minute lead. The long descent from the moors gave him a panoramic view of the coast and he saw the little seine-net boat standing well out to sea beyond the headlands. He had sailed it down from Monkton Parva a couple of days earlier, and as he fled the farmhouse after the death of Scholtz he had seen it heading down Saltfield Bay. There had been people aboard, it looked like three, but who were they, what had happened down there on the rocks? Amid so much shooting it seemed likely someone had been hurt. Now here the boat was again, heading south towards the great pier at Eastport which he could see clearly. Was I aboard, he wondered, or was I still a prisoner back there at Saltfield Mains? Please God not injured, not shot and dropped overboard as Krause had suggested. And my friend, Teddy, what had become of him?

The moorland road joined the coast road about four miles south of Saltfield Mains. Dad turned right towards Eastport. For much of the way, as he drove on, the sea was hidden but at times there it was, blown into white horses by the wind. There too was little Seal Maid, steadily drawing closer to the pier and lighthouse. It was essential he reached Eastport safely and he was so preoccupied avoiding potholes and keeping an eye on the boat that he failed to spot the blue van at the roadside until he was right on top of it. The doors were open and a small group stood looking out to sea. He recognised young Lucas, Helmut and camp commandant Krause who had arrived that morning and questioned him in the bedroom. They were there, they were gone, and took little notice of the smart cream and black car as it sped past.

The obvious place for dad to meet the boat was at the river, probably the North Quay which was nearer and would be quieter. He pulled off his cap and threw the cigar butt from the window.

"Who's a good girl," he said to the old white poodle curled up beside him and rubbed her belly. She blinked up with watery eyes.

Staying carefully within the speed limit, he drove through the emptying streets. The main gates of the North Dock were shut at that hour and fastened with a heavy chain but a small gate stood open for seamen who wanted to go ashore. Dad parked in the road, locked the car door and walked through. Upstream and down the masts and superstructure of ocean-going ships towered against the sky. Two moorings lay empty. The huge stack of coal, floodlit and surrounded by railings, stood close at hand but the guard was not in his box. This was a blow because he had a telephone. Dad had decided that his best plan was to contact the police and tell them everything, or as much as they needed to know, and then disappear. The absent guard was not a major problem for most ships had a telephone at the gangway. He walked to the edge of the quay. It would soon be low water. Twenty-five feet below him the river sped past, brown with silt, emptying into Monks Bay. Dad loved the river, it spoke to him of freedom and escape, and of all emotions, these were closest to his heart.

If he had realised the best spot to intercept the little seine-netter was the North Quay, the gang must know it also, but they were not here yet and it would be a good quarter of an hour before Seal Maid rounded the lighthouse. He looked at the first ship upriver, planning to use their phone. Across the water the South Quay was crowded, enormous vessels moored stem to stern with only enough space between them to avoid jostling. It was always busier, a broader quay, bigger warehouses, right beneath the town. His eyes sharpened: was that...? Could it be? Yes, it was, North Sea Trader! His brother's ship was in port. His problems were solved. For once, he thought, forgetting the countless times he had been in trouble and landed on his feet, God was on his side.

As he drove up into town and across the bridge, still known as the New Bridge although it was eighty years old, the shops were shut for the night. He turned down the cobbled High Street, devastated by bombing. Much had been rebuilt but some was still tumbledown with gaping upstairs bedrooms and naked wallpaper, waste ground red with fireweed. In a mile he came to the sooty walls and high iron fence of the South Quay. A guard sat in a box but the gates were open and he took little notice as dad drove through. A crowd of sailors headed into town:

"Like the car, pal," a cheery AB called as dad parked beneath the legs of a giant crane.

"Thanks."

"This year's model, yeah?"

"That's right."

"Smart."

He lifted down the old poodle. She tottered round the wheels, squatted to relieve herself and lapped from a puddle. A bag of dog treats lay on a shelf. Dad put a handful on the passenger seat and lifted her back.

"Not be long, sweetheart."

He rubbed her ears and locked the door.

The ships were moored upriver as far as the eye could see, but North Sea Trader was only a couple of minutes' walk from the gates. She was heavily laden and this, combined with low tide, made the gangway almost horizontal. A young sailor was reading on gangway watch.

"Hi, there, Sammy."

"Who? Oh, it's you, Frankie. Long time no see."

"Is Dan aboard?"

"Far as I know. He'll just be finishing his dinner. What you been up to?"

"You'll know soon enough." There wasn't time for chat. "OK to go through?"

"Course, he's your brother."

When he'd left Trader some months earlier the crew had been pleased to see him go. He was glad there was no animosity.

Five men sat at tables in the saloon. Clearly there had been officials aboard for they wore uniform although ties were now loosened and jackets hung on chairs. Uncle Dan sat comfortably, his plate pushed back and a glass in his hand.

Magnus, the chief engineer, saw dad first. "Well, well! Look what the cat's brought in."

Dad looked a mess. All his life he'd been a snappy dresser but back at the farmhouse, working half the night to offload the smuggled cargo and carry it up to the barn, there was no hot water for baths and he had only shaved occasionally. Running on the moors he had been sweating, his shoes and trousers were filthy and his shirt was crumpled.

Dan looked round: "My God! It's my brother. What the hell's happened to you?" He hooked a chair out with his foot. "Sit down before you fall down."

Dad felt out of place for Uncle Dan was a decorated war hero, the second engineer had been with him in the lifeboats and all five were Merchant Navy officers. In contrast, he was a jailbird and deserter, ex-member of a violent post-war Paris gang, and until a few hours ago had been part of a gang of one-time Nazis smuggling artworks out of Europe. That day, even worse, they had been helping war criminals, men guilty of torture and mass murder, to escape justice. Added to which his daughter, a favourite of everyone on board, had been taken prisoner and was possibly dead.

Uncle Dan sniffed. "You stink!"

"Very likely."

Dan was surprised for this was not the brother he knew. He poured him a whisky. "Come on, then, what's it about?"

Where to begin? "You know after the war…" The neat spirit made him cough.

"After the war?"

"I told you about that gang I was with in Paris."

"The sons of something."

"Les Fils de la Guerre."

"That's it. You said they broke up."

"So they did and I went off to Italy with Hamish, worked at the fishing."

"Until he got that girl into trouble and you had to make yourself scarce. Ended up here with me."

"I had nowhere else to go."

"Because everyone thought you were dead, you bastard." Uncle Dan said. "What about that other guy, the one you set up?"

"Yeah, yeah. You're right. Don't think I haven't thought about it. But you weren't being shelled, you hadn't just been half buried." He took a big sip. "But that's not why I'm here. After I left you, Greg Thompson, a Geordie guy who'd been in the gang, bumped into one of your crew in a pub in Newcastle and came to look me up. It was that time Eva was in hospital and I was staying in the house. He told me a few of them had got together with some German lads and they were thinking about starting up again; In this country this time."

Uncle Dan shifted uneasily.

"All right," dad said. "I know, I know. Smuggling artworks out of Europe this time and shipping them out to wherever there was a market."

"Stolen artworks?"

"Yes, yes, yes."

"By the Nazis, the people we were fighting?"

"Yes, but—"

"From art galleries, churches, people they sent off to the death camps? Families of people like that boy we took over to Norway with us?"

"Teddy," somebody said.

"That's him, Teddy Cohen, smashing lad."

"I didn't think about that, where they came from, at least not at the start. But there I was, nowhere to go, no one to go to, couldn't get a job, not without papers. And suddenly here's Greg, some people I know, a place to stay, chance to get a few quid in my pocket. So I went." He drew a deep breath. "But all that's not why I'm here. Something's happened. Our Mary and that boy, they turned up out of the blue. Came to see me where we're living and they're in trouble. I don't know what's happened, I was tied up. There's been shooting."

You could have heard a pin drop.

And he told them the whole story, right up to that afternoon, the unexpected arrival of Commandant Krause, Dr Scholtz and the others, the shooting down at the shore, Seal Maid heading out to sea, how he'd killed the doctor and escaped, everything.

Uncle Dan stared at him, his gaze blue and very direct. "And they're heading down this way? Mary and the boy, I mean."

"If they got away."

"To Eastport, to the river?"

"Yeah, they should be at the lighthouse by this time. Like I told you, I reckon that crowd in the van are planning to cut them off."

"Shut them up, more like," said the second engineer. "If they want—"

He was interrupted by a loud knocking and the saloon door burst open. It was Dennis, Sammy's dad, an AB who had sailed with Uncle Dan for years: "Skip, you need to come. I'm out on deck and here's this SOS from a little seine-netter heading down the bay. Packed up after a bit, sounded like the siren conked out. And there's all these men scuttling about the North Quay. Something not right. I think you should come and have a look-see."

Below decks in the saloon they had heard nothing.

Uncle Dan said, "Sounds like them. Could they be in the bay by this time, Frankie?"

"Yeah, I should think so."

"And those men, your lot?"

"Come in a dark van," Dennis said. "Left it by the gate."

"That's them."

"For God's sake!"

Uncle Dan showed the leadership that had saved the lives of his crew during the war:

"Right. Dennis, you know where the keys are, break out the rifles in the chartroom. Fast as you like. Ammunition bottom drawer in my cabin. Tell Sammy to roust out anyone aboard; bridge deck this second. Chief, you look after the engineers. Frankie, you come with me, we've got a phone call to make."

"The police?"

"No, the Tiller Girls! Who d'you think, you stupid sod?"

"Thank God!"

They ran from the saloon.

47

Ebb Tide

The emptying river sped past, parting round our bows, hurrying along the ancient stones of the quay. The dripping wall, tufted with weed, rose high overhead. The steps used by Barry's passengers stood right alongside. Despite his smashed finger, Teddy handled the engine as if he had been born to it, inching forward against the current. I stood in the bow and snatched for a mooring ring with the boathook.

The harbour was at peace, exactly as normal, yet something felt wrong. I fed the painter through the big rusty ring and wound it round a bracket on deck.

"Don't switch off," I told Teddy, "I'll go up and check the coast's clear."

"Right." He pushed the throttle into neutral and Seal Maid slipped back until she was brought up short by the rope. As he released the wheel I saw him nurse his arm, battling with the pain.

The steps were set into the harbour wall. Crossing the river with Barry, I had climbed them a hundred times. Unused steps became fouled with silt but these were scrubbed regularly and sprinkled with grit to keep them safe. Grasping the handrail, I climbed a dozen steps and raised my head above the cobbles.

Two seamen trotted down the gangway of the ship at the next berth, a hundred yards upriver. They were heading ashore for the evening. If they were looking for a cinema or the livelier bars, a twenty-minute walk lay ahead of them, all the way up the north bank and across the bridge to the town centre. As they crossed the quay one called, not to me:

"Hi there, mate. Any idea where we can get a taxi?"

There was no reply.

"Hello?" his pal called. "Hell of a walk into town, we're looking for a taxi."

There was a mumbled reply.

"You OK, mate?" They were heading for the gate but had stopped, looking into the shadow beneath a crane.

There was no one to be seen. I felt a great jolt.

"Teddy!" I scrambled back down the steps. "They're waiting for us! Quick!"

The boat had drifted. I jumped aboard and threw off the painter.

Behind me on the quay there was shouting. Teddy thrust the throttle to full ahead. The propeller thrashed but we were heading into the current and for a few seconds Seal Maid slipped backwards. A man appeared above us on the edge of the quay. He stretched out an arm:

"Stop or I'll shoot."

Teddy beat him to it:

Crack! Crack!

I had a pistol too. *Crack!*

The man gave a cry and dropped from sight.

Seal Maid pulled out from the quay, battling the current. Slowly she began to move ahead.

A second man appeared, a few yards away. *Crack!* A bullet pierced the wheelhouse window. Weakened from the earlier shooting, half the glass fell out.

Crack! Crack! Teddy and I fired together. I don't think the man was hit but he ducked from sight.

There was a third man above us. And a fourth.

I fired and fired again.

Suddenly there was a much louder CRACK, a whipcrack, from somewhere behind us, it sounded like the far side of the river. Simultaneously, one of the men on the quay cried out and was kicked backwards. He vanished.

Teddy and I had no idea that North Sea Trader was in harbour, let alone that Uncle Dan and one of his crew who had been a sniper in the army, stood on the bridge with rifles in their hands.

We crouched beneath the boat's side. A bullet splintered the rail above my head. We kept firing. There was no one on the wheel but it didn't matter where we went, upstream, downstream, anywhere, as long as it was away from the North Quay and the men with pistols.

There was another loud CRACK and a second man spun round, clutching his shoulder.

The North Quay slipped away. The river carried the boat sideways, turning on the current, and then we were heading downstream. Thirty – fifty – a hundred yards, the shooting fell astern. I risked a long look over the rail. The situation had changed:

"Teddy! Teddy!" I pulled his jacket.

Blue lights flashed at the North Quay gates. The police had arrived. How could they be there so soon, I wondered, for the last time we'd seen dad he was being marched upstairs in the farmhouse under armed guard. Even now we had not seen North Sea Trader. The rifle shots were a mystery.

Figures ran about the North Quay. There was shouting. Scuffles. Occasional pistol shots.

"Oh, thank God!" Teddy braced his hand, the hand holding the pistol, against the frame of the wheelhouse door. His head sank, his shoulders shook, his injured hand hung useless. After behaving magnificently, he was weeping.

"You OK?" I put an arm around his shoulders. None of this was of Teddy's making, his dad was a dentist.

He looked round in the half light, his eyes blurred. He wasn't ashamed, he didn't apologise. "Yeah, I'll be fine."

The current had carried us downriver and out into Monks Bay where we drifted aimlessly, turning on the tide.

"Do you want me to take the wheel?"

"What!" He scrubbed his face with a sleeve. "Absolutely not! Delicate piece of machinery like this, it needs an expert." He took his place at the wheel, set the throttle to half-ahead and coaxed the bow back into the flood.

I had always liked Teddy, right from the moment he stood determinedly on his roller skates when I cut my leg on the pram. Over the summer we had done many things together and become the best of friends. I think it was at this moment I realised it was more than that, he had become my boyfriend and I wanted to hug him.

Where should we go now? The police would want to speak to us but there was still occasional shooting. If Gunther Krause, brutal commandant of a concentration camp, were captured he would almost certainly hang so he would never surrender, not while there was a bullet left in his pistol. So would Dr Scholtz, for we had no idea he was dead, and it seemed likely that those who had arrived with them would also be on a wanted list. Maybe the men in the gang too, or some of them, so the shooting might continue for some time. I stared back at the town. We couldn't return to the North Quay and the moorings on the South Quay were crowded, all but the few yards at the seaward end which I have mentioned, where the river emptied into the bay. I had fished there and knew the spot well: there was a flight of steps exactly the same as those I had climbed on the North Quay, only these were abandoned and the ebbing river swirled treacherously as it left the confines of the harbour wall.

"Are you sure?" I said as Teddy set our bow in that direction.

"Are you doubting me, Mr Christian?" he replied, echoing Captain Bligh in Mutiny on the Bounty which we had both seen recently. "We can give it a try anyway. It's not as if we're going to capsize."

Even with one hand, Teddy had an instinctive understanding of how to control the little fishing boat. Expertly he navigated across the current. Before us, the river surged into the bay. As we approached the mooring, hardly a mooring it was so small, I felt the power of the outflowing current beneath our keel. The harbour wall rose high overhead. Then the steps were at our side. I took the boathook, as I had done at the North Quay, and scraped for the mooring ring. Teddy held us steady, inching forward, until I captured it, lumpy with rust and shaggy with seaweed. Black silt ran up my arm. I passed the painter through and secured it to the cleat on deck. Teddy throttled back and let the river carry us a yard or two downstream until we hung on the rope, then he put the control into neutral. In such conditions it was a considerable feat of seamanship.

"Teddy, that was fantastic!" I threw an arm round his shoulders and kissed him on the cheek. It was the opportunity I had been waiting for.

He looked round in surprise then smiled and kissed me on the lips.

48

The Hero

Teddy had brought us to the flight of stone steps. Trying not to tread on Benny, who lay on a tangle of fishing net, I fed a rope through the rusty handrail and pulled it tight to hold us alongside.

Teddy said. "Shall I go first this time?"

"If your hand's OK."

I looked up and was startled to see the silhouette of a man directly above us. Teddy grabbed his pistol.

"It's all right, son," a familiar voice called. "It's only me."

It was my dad! But how had he got here?

Beyond him there was a babble of shouting. Shots were fired, the familiar noise of pistols then the much louder CRACK! of a rifle. A man screamed in pain. More shouting then the slam of a car door and over-revving of an engine as it sped away. Two more rifle shots. Then peace punctuated by voices.

"What's happening?" Teddy called.

"Nothing to be frightened about. Not any longer."

"What do you mean?"

"Some fellows from the gang. I got hold of a car and they followed me down here. Shooting like the bloody war had started up again but they're gone now. Tell you later."

Suddenly he saw the bodies on deck. "Who's that, for God's sake?"

"Benny," I said, "he helped us escape. And another man, you'll know better than us. Benny shot him."

"Benny shot him?"

"That's right."

"Benny helped you escape?"

"Yeah."

"Benny?"

"Major O'Hare. He was…" Again I heard him tell me about Bridget and saw him die. "Like you said, tell you later. Is it safe to come ashore?"

"Dad looked back up the quay. "Yeah, all clear. Looks like one of them's been caught."

"So we can come up?"

"Whenever you're ready."

I looked round at Teddy. After all that had happened he didn't want to leave his pistol behind. Carefully he put on the safety-catch, thrust it beneath his belt and climbed over the side. With his good right hand he grasped the handrail. His shoe squidged in the deep silt on the steps.

"Careful," he called back, "it's very slippy."

I waited until the way was clear then followed.

Unused for many years, or very rarely, the steps were treacherous. The handrail was rusted through in places and fragile. I rested a hand on the opposite wall for balance. Teddy did the same with his elbow and forearm.

In years gone by there had been safety rails at the top, something to hold on to as you reached the quay. They were long gone, nothing remained but stumps. It was a precarious moment. As Teddy climbed the last few steps, he rested his good hand on the cobbles and put out his left arm for balance. Dad stood close by. Eager to help, he caught the outstretched hand and gripped it tight to stop him falling back. It was Teddy's injured hand, his finger hanging off. He gave a scream of shock and pain, lost his footing and tumbled backwards on top of me. My hold on the rail was broken. Mixed up as fighting cats, we fell the length of the steps and crashed back aboard the boat. Teddy hit the deck with a whack that knocked the breath from his lungs and dislocated his shoulder. I banged my head on the side rail and fell into the river.

For what happened then I have to rely on the word of Sammy and Big Lenny, the chef, who came racing along the quay. I was unconscious, although some shred of self-preservation seems to have survived. Instantly the speeding, swirling water carried me away. Dad, not understanding what had happened, looked down in horror. He was not a strong swimmer and many times throughout my life he had let me down but now, seeing me sprawled and helpless in the current, he ran past the boat and leaped into the water. With a great splash he landed almost at my side and somehow – I can't explain it, perhaps desperation gave him strength – he caught me under the arms and struggled to a corner, the very last stones of the quay, where an ancient, weed-covered chain trailed down into the water. Beyond it the river surged out into Monks Bay. I must have felt the chain against me for somehow I grabbed hold of it, twisted my fingers into the links, and there I clung as the cold brown current swirled around me.

Dad got me there, he pushed me, forced my arm, saw me hang on, then grabbed for the chain and my jacket to save himself. But he was deep in the water, the river had him and his grip was not strong enough. He swung his other arm, snatching for whatever he could reach, but there was nothing and the next second the current was carrying him away. He tried to swim, struck out into slack water beyond the quay but it was hopeless. Hampered by his clothes, he was not a strong enough swimmer. Sammy saw him struggling. A red lifebelt hung on a post. He pulled it free and flung it into the water. Twenty yards from dad it floated downstream. Someone threw the boat's lifebelt too but it was a forlorn hope. For a long time they were visible, bobbing on the current, but my dad had disappeared.

He was gone.

And what of me? Teddy was in great pain but he was safe. Any second, it seemed, my hold on the chain would be broken and I would be swept away like dad. Big Lenny, who was a powerful swimmer, scrambled down the steps to the boat, pulled off his jacket and slipped over the side, letting the current carry him downstream until he reached me. With his arm around my waist and his fingers fixed in the chain, I also was safe. Sammy, meanwhile, ran to the end of the quay and climbed down the chain. I was doubly safe.

Other seamen came running. Dennis and a couple more tumbled down the steps to Seal Maid. Slipping the bow rope, they lowered her downstream until she reached the forgotten chain where I clung with my rescuers. In a minute, sleek as rats, we were hauled aboard.

I was coming round. They carried Benny for'ard and laid him beside the dead Nazi, then made a couch for me on the pile of netting. Someone covered me with a warm jacket.

Teddy hugged his left arm, in pain not only from his hand but his dislocated shoulder. Very carefully he unbuttoned his jacket to explore the sickening lump where his arm had jumped from its socket.

Dennis said gently, "Let me have a look, son. It's all right, I'm not going to hurt you." He reached forward.

"No." Teddy turned aside.

"Just to see."

"You should let him." Big Lenny drained on deck. "He's done first aid. Looks after all of us on board."

"No, leave it." Teddy looked away. "Maybe later."

"All right, boy," Dennis said. "I'm not going to force you."

Teddy was always polite. "Thanks, anyway." And just

as he spoke something extraordinary happened. The siren, which had been silent for an hour, suddenly brayed into life. I don't know how because I'd broken the button. Everyone was startled. Teddy looked up and as he did so he lost his balance on the rocking boat, his shoe became tangled in netting and he fell heavily against the wheelhouse. Something in his shoulder went *snap* and he gave a shout of pain. When it had subsided, he discovered that his arm had popped back into the socket. He looked down in disbelief. It was still sore but the agony had gone.

"Aye, it can do that." Dennis smiled.

A voice shouted above the blare of the siren: "For God's sake, will somebody turn that thing off!"

Sammy fiddled with the button and as suddenly as it had started the noise stopped.

The crack of a pistol came from the north shore. It was followed by another.

Heads looked down from the quay above us. Big Lenny called up: "Somebody phone for an ambulance."

"Hurt bad?"

"Bad enough. Mary's had a knock on the head, the boy's got a finger hanging off."

"I'll go," said a sailor in a vest.

"Tell them we'll sail round to the bottom slipway. Might need a stretcher."

"Will do." He ran off.

My head was bursting but I sat up.

"No, no, love. Stay where you are. Nasty crack like that you've got to rest."

I lay back.

"We're going to have a little sail round the bay."

"Now?" My voice was cracked.

"Just have a look-see."

"What for?"

No one answered.

"What for?" I said again.

"Them been doing all the shooting," Sammy said. "See if anyone's trying to escape that way."

"Across the bay?"

"Might take old Archie's boat."

Something wasn't right. I looked round the men on deck. Someone was missing. "Where's my dad?"

*

Daylight was almost gone, black ripples reflected the lights of the town. We searched Monks Bay from end to end and side to side. A few seagulls sat on the water. The harbour lifebelt bobbed by some rocks. Three solitary fishermen, far from the shooting, cast lines from the shore. They had seen nothing. As we returned to harbour the famous lighthouse, darkened for the duration of the war, flashed high overhead.

Of my dad there was no sign.

Epilogue

49

Royal Infirmary

The doctors were kind although when we asked to share a room in the hospital, they said no. In case you get the wrong idea, this wasn't for any boy-girl reason but the company. Teddy and I had been through a lot together and were half in shock. Instead, they gave us single adjoining rooms, which meant moving a patient who'd had his tonsils removed into the big ward. I was grateful.

Not that it made much difference because gran, who was brought to the infirmary in a police car, would have put a stop to it in one minute flat: "Mary Pearson, you are fifteen years old. Teddy's a nice boy but one of you is moving out right now." Also it made little difference because after countless tests and being interviewed by the police, a nurse gave me two blue pills that put me to sleep for twelve solid hours.

Teddy fared much the same . His dad and mum arrived the same time as my gran. Like her, they were horrified by what we had done, the lies we had told – at least what we had not told them – and what this had led to. Teddy, like me, was interviewed by senior police officers but not until his injuries had been examined. His shoulder, which had been so horribly dislocated, was not seriously damaged although he would have to wear a sling for a few days. His shattered finger, which I had cleaned with whisky and covered with my hanky and a sock, was examined by a surgeon and that evening he was taken to the theatre for a long and delicate operation.

*

Gran was sitting by my bed with a cup of tea and a custard cream when I woke the following morning.

"Hello, love." She set her knitting on the bedspread. "Back in the land of the living?"

I yawned.

"My goodness, you've had a long sleep."

"Yeah?"

"How do you feel now?"

I examined myself. The back of my head was sore where I had hit the side of the boat and I had a slight headache. Apart from that I felt all right. "What time is it?"

Gran consulted her watch. "Ten to eleven."

"Ten to eleven!" Eight o'clock was a lie-in at 17 Wherry Row. I sat up in surprise, felt horribly dizzy, and lay back again. "Oooh! How's Teddy?"

"Next door. They operated last night. He's sleeping now."

"What about his finger?" I remembered the mess of sinew and bone.

"They're hoping he won't lose it."

I wanted to see Teddy for myself. Carefully I got out of bed and padded barefoot along the corridor, balancing against the wall. He was sound asleep and looked very peaceful, his sandy head on the pillow. The room was warm and nurses had turned the sheets down. He was wearing the cotton gown they make you put on to go to the operating theatre with short sleeves and tapes at the back of the neck. Both arms lay outside the sheets, his right hand the same as ever, his left hidden in a big white ball of gauze and bandages. As I watched, his features twitched, a little grimace of pain.

Gran had joined me: "It's all right, love, he can't feel it. It's the bones and everything starting to knit together again."

After a couple of minutes we went back to my room. Gran had brought a change of clothes but the nurses wanted me to stay in bed until I'd been seen by a doctor, so after a bath I pulled on my clean nightie, pale blue with five buttons and pretty embroidery, and climbed back between the sheets. It would soon be lunchtime but I was starving so they brought me a cup of tea and biscuits. I was nibbling these when there was a tap at the door and Mrs Cohen appeared round the curtain.

"Hello, Eva." She was lovely, her dark hair windblown. "Hello Mary, how are you feeling now, sweetheart?"

"I'm fine, thanks, Mrs Cohen."

"Well I must say you don't seem too bad after all you've been through, you and Teddy."

"No, I'm all right."

"You certainly look it." She glanced around. "May I sit down?"

"Of course."

She pulled up a chair. "You must think I'm a terrible mother, Teddy lying there with just the nurses looking in. I called earlier but I wanted to go into school and see the headmaster before the rumours start flying around."

"How is he?" gran said. "They won't tell us much, we're not family. I know about his shoulder, what about the finger?"

She confirmed what we had heard: "They've saved it, at least they think so."

"What about his nail?" I remembered it hanging by a shred of skin and felt a bit sick.

"Yes, even that, lucky he didn't lose it. The top surgeon, Mr Holland, came down in the middle of the night. I stayed until Teddy was out of theatre and back in his bed. Mr Holland says he'll need a couple of skin grafts but give it a year or two and it shouldn't look too bad at all. Not so you'd notice if you weren't looking."

"That's excellent news."

"Likely to be a bit stiff, that's all. He did what he could but the end joint was completely smashed." She smiled sadly. "He never did take to the piano anyway, not like Rachel." Before Mrs Cohen was married, when she played for rehearsals at the Vienna State Opera, the piano had been the most important thing in her life."

"He told me he fancied the trumpet," I said.

"Yes, I know, he wants to play in the school band."

"That would be OK."

"If it's what he wants. He reads music so he's part way there. Maybe we can get him some extra lessons, learn to play really well." She straightened. "Anyway, first things first, let's be sure they've saved his finger."

Apart from my gran, who was in a class of her own, there wasn't a nicer woman in the world than Mrs Cohen. I was terrified she would blame me for everything that had happened and she'd have been right. It was my dad who was working with the Nazis, my plan to warn him before we told the police, entirely because of me that Teddy was lying in a hospital bed recovering from an operation. Now he would never be able to play the piano properly, and just as easily, if the bullet had hit him in the chest, he could be lying dead on a seashore. I set down my teacup with both hands, spilling a little, for something inside me broke, and when I looked up and saw her smiling, I began to cry.

"Oh, Mrs Cohen! I'm so sorry!"

"It's all right, love." She took my arm.

"Oh, but Teddy! He might—" My shoulders shook.

"Mary!" she said. "Mary!"

But I couldn't hear, I didn't want to hear. I hadn't wept like that since I was a little girl. My eyes streamed, my nose ran. It wasn't just Teddy and that moment in the hospital, it was everything: Teddy, my dad, the pillbox, the shooting, Benny, the awfulness of the past few days. I sobbed and sobbed,

They were concerned. Gran took my hand and gradually the storm eased. "Oh, I'm so sorry!" I hiccupped.

"I know, sweetheart, I know," Mrs Cohen said. "But listen, it wasn't your fault. I know that's what you're telling yourself but it wasn't. We have no love for the Nazis in our family, you know that, but you wanted to help your dad, Teddy told me last night. You went up there to save him. You're a very brave girl."

"Oh, I'm not!" The tears started again. "I was stupid. And Teddy, he…"

"You don't need to worry about Teddy. He's all right, he's safe now. He wanted to go along, you didn't have to force him." I listened through my tears. "He's brave too, a brave boy. We're very proud of him."

I pressed her hand to my cheek.

"And you needn't worry about his dad and me, either, we don't blame you for anything. The very opposite, we're delighted he's got you for a friend."

"Mm!" Gran would have died for me but she wasn't going to let this pass. "A rather foolish friend on this occasion. Your heart's in the right place, Mary, but what were you thinking of, going up there among all those men without telling anyone? You should have let me know. What would I have done if anything had happened to you? Or Mrs Cohen here?"

"Oh, Gran!"

"Still, I don't suppose there's anything I can say that you don't know yourself."

I shook my head.

"Yes, well!" She relented. "Anyway, the main thing is you're here now. So come on, dry your tears. Teddy's got a bad finger but against all the odds you're both home and safe, let's concentrate on that."

I drew a deep breath and pushed the hair from my face. Gran handed me a hanky, not her pretty going-out one but a plain man's hanky and I had a good blow. A nurse looked in, saw my face all swollen with crying and crossed to the bedside. When she saw I was recovering she turned to gran and Mrs Cohen, making no attempt to hide her displeasure:

"It will soon be lunchtime, I'm afraid I'll have to ask you to leave. We don't normally allow visitors in the morning. Visiting hours are three until four-thirty. You can come back then."

Mrs Cohen raised her eyebrows and I repressed a giggle, but the nurse was kind. After they had gone she brought me a basin of warm water, facecloth and comb, and I did what I could to make myself more presentable.

50

We Talk to the Police

As it turned out, gran and Mrs Cohen were back before three because the police wanted to interview us as soon as possible. Teddy had been woken for lunch and a while later we went to an alcove at the end of the ward where there were chairs and a table. Mrs Cohen had brought Teddy's striped pyjamas and we both wore our dressing gowns.

The senior policeman, Detective Inspector Mitchell, was a fatherly figure with a grey moustache. He wore a crumpled suit with a terrible yellow Pinocchio tie, a present from one of his children, he said, although a warning, it occurred to me, that telling lies to the police was a bad idea. He was accompanied by a much younger sergeant and a pretty WPC who might have come on my account and was there to take notes.

"Gunther Krause, brute of a man. Yes, he tried to do away with himself. When he saw the game was up he kept the last bullet for himself; you know, the way they say. Put the muzzle to his head and pulled the trigger. It never fired. That's right, isn't it, Sergeant?"

Sergeant Evans was a younger man, prematurely balding, with a round, pleasant face. "Yes, I was right there, I saw it." True to his name, Sergeant Evans spoke with a Welsh accent. "Click! Click! Click! three times, then we had him. Fought like a rat."

"No wonder," said the inspector. "He's for the rope and he knows it. Commandant of the concentration camp at ⋯, a place straight out of hell. Those who weren't beaten to death or taken out and shot, died of starvation and disease. But some were still alive when the troops arrived and every last one will be ready to testify. He'll be sentenced to death like those at Nuremberg, no other verdict's possible."

Sergeant Evans said, "Funny thing, though, when the soldier who disarmed him pointed his pistol at the ground and pulled the trigger, it fired straight away. *Bang!* It's as if he was meant to be captured and go on trial."

"Let the world know what he did," said Inspector Mitchell, "him and the others like him."

Teddy was on painkillers but a twinge made him wince. He eased his arm.

"Where is he now?" I asked. "Krause."

"In a cell at the army barracks."

"Until it's decided what to do with him," said Inspector Mitchell. "They checked his teeth for a suicide capsule, and took his clothes in case he had something hidden in the lining. Gave him a shirt and trousers but he wouldn't put them on."

"British army issue," said the sergeant. "Not the quality he's used to. Suit yourself, they told him, sit there and freeze."

"Except they won't let him die," said the inspector, "he's got to go on trial, show his crimes up for what they are. A little bit of justice for his poor victims."

"I looked in on him," said Sergeant Evans, "a horrible sight: hollow chest, pot belly, skinny white legs. They're all the same, these tin pot dictators, our British Tommies are twice the men."

"What about Doctor Scholtz?" I said. "That horrid little man with the glasses and thick lips. He performed operations."

"You haven't heard?"

"No, how would I?"

"Your dad killed him," said the sergeant.

"My dad?"

And Inspector Mitchell, who had got the story from Uncle Dan, told us about the struggle in the bedroom, the chase across the moor and dad's escape in the stolen car. "He's a fighter," the inspector said, "a hero really. We didn't know what was going on up there at Saltfield Mains. Not entirely true, Major O'Hare worked undercover for British Intelligence and we'd heard about the artworks, but no one knew they were smuggling people, certainly not people like Krause, Scholtz and Otto Baumann. The army has a big operation planned but you were the ones brought us news about them."

Teddy said, "Those who were after us, they only had the van. How come they were waiting on both sides of the river?"

"There were two groups," Sergeant Evans reminded him. "Those from the farmhouse were in the blue van, but the ones who followed Mary's dad up into the moors had the old man's truck like the inspector just told you. They drove down to the coast and the two lots met up. There was no telling where you'd land so the van went to the North Quay which was nearer, and the others went to the far side. Luckily your dad got there before you did and gave the captain time to get ready. You escaped from the North Quay but after you crossed the river you'd have been sitting ducks. The crew drove them off before you came ashore."

"And then, of course," said Inspector Mitchell, "your dad saved your life a second time."

Gran, who had little time for my dad although she never ran him down, had told me how he jumped into the river and got me to the chain, dad who could hardly swim a stroke.

"Is there still no sign of him?"

"I'm afraid not." He shook his head regretfully. "They've had teams searching; the coastguard went out last night and again this morning. There were some chaps fishing but they'd seen nothing. I'm sorry."

After a bit Teddy said, "What about the others, the ones in the gang?"

"Three got killed, we captured five. Some got away, him that shot the old man and likely a few at the farmhouse, we're not sure. There's teams out searching."

"They weren't all bad," Teddy said. "Some of those at the farmhouse were nice."

"And some of them kicked us, I've got a big purple bruise." I rubbed my hip. "And shot seagulls for fun. And Krause wanted to take us out to sea and drop us over the side." I took a deep breath, "But you're right, a few were OK."

"I imagine some were just ex-soldiers and hangers-on,"! said the inspector. "Men with no papers, no family, nowhere to go. Saw the chance of a bit of company and making a few bob."

"Like my dad," I said.

"I suppose so but it seems to me your dad's done himself proud: rid the world of a very wicked man, brought us news of a group smuggling war criminals, and given his life to save his daughter.

"As for what happened over there in France – yes, your uncle's told us all about it. Who can say how he'd behave if he'd been ambushed like that, half-buried by a shell, dead men all around him, and the enemy's raking the ground with machine-gun fire? If he'd given himself up and claimed shell-shock, especially after what happened yesterday, I think he might have been kindly listened to. He had a good army record."

"What about the soldier whose place he took?"

"Shouldn't be too difficult to track him down, corporal in the same unit who disappeared the same day. The regiment will have all his records, they know where he's buried."

Inspector Mitchell passed round a bag of peppermints. "Who knows, if your dad hadn't been lost yesterday, he might not be in as much trouble as he thought."

I was caught unawares, this was an angle I hadn't considered. I was happy to hear the inspector say it but whether I believed it was another matter. Dad had never in his life, or rarely, done anything unless it was to his own advantage. All the same, he had jumped into the notorious Brander current to save me, and I was thinking about this when Teddy said:

"What about Benny's diary? We told you last night."

"What memories you two have got," said Sergeant Evans. "Names, telephone numbers…"

"Whitehall 2759." I smiled, "He said it was important."

"And he was right. The man he told you about, Otto Baumann, right up there top of the wanted list. Friend of Himmler: Heinrich Himmler, you know, head of the SS, one of the men who planned the Final Solution."

The words weren't as familiar as they became later. I said, "Does that mean the death camps?"

"That's right," said the inspector. "Places like Auschwitz, Treblinka and the rest, I don't know how many. Hitler's insane plan to exterminate every last Jew in the world, starting with the countries they'd conquered. Himmler was the chief organiser, a man with ice in his veins. He committed suicide at the end of the war, taking all his secrets with him. His wife poisoned their six children. As Himmler's lifelong friend, you can imagine how much everyone wants to get their hands on Baumann."

Teddy was listening intently.

"Teddy's Jewish," I said. "Mrs Cohen grew up in Vienna. Her whole family got taken away."

"Yes, she told me." The inspector rested a hand on Teddy's arm. "I'm sorry to hear about it, son."

Teddy drew his arm away, he didn't want to talk about it. "But what happened last night," he said, "when the boat came across?"

"Thanks to you we had Benny's diary and we set a trap. The Royal Navy sent a gunboat, Coastguard sent a couple of armed launches. Had them standing back, total blackout. Right on time, three in the morning, in comes this trawler from the North Sea, only there's no little seine-netter to meet it this time, you two had sailed it down here to Eastport. The farmhouse crowd had always been there, you know, to offload the paintings or whatever. They didn't know what to do; no place a trawler could come ashore, only Monkton Parva where they'd be seen and they could hardly start producing people from the hold. They had the lifeboats, of course, but it was a rough sea and they only had oars; wouldn't know where to go when they landed anyway. In the end they decided to wait an hour and head back if no one turned up."

"But someone did turn up," Sergeant Evans took up the story, "two Coastguard launches and a Royal Navy gunboat with a loudhailer and searchlights that lit them up like Christmas. They tried to make a run for it but they hadn't a hope in hell, those British boats can do thirty-five knots. Overhauled them inside a mile. They'd armed themselves with a couple of machine guns. Might as well have been popguns, the gunboat could have blown them out the water. The captain wanted to board her but he wouldn't risk his men for creatures like that, so he loosed off a couple of shells to teach them some manners and gave her a little nudge. The timbers must have been rotten because the side caved in and she started to sink. Straightway they began jumping over the side, so our lads threw them a pile of lifebelts and lifejackets and fished them out."

"So did it go down with all the paintings?"

"They thought it would," said the inspector, "but somehow

it stayed afloat, rail under water, bridge shot to matchwood. A few armed sailors went aboard and they managed to tow it into shallow water. I know they rescued a Leonardo and a couple of Rembrandts, not sure what else."

"But what about the men?" Teddy said impatiently. "The one you were talking about, Otto Baumann?"

"Pig of a man, dedicated Nazi. Like Sergeant Evans said, they fished everyone out, or nearly everyone. When it's a choice between drowning and being hauled up into a boat, most people will choose to live, even if it's only for a few days. They certainly got Baumann, not that it will do him much good, he'll hang with Krause and likely one or two others. There were some women along with them, a couple of prison camp guards, Berthe Frohman and Frauke Felder, and Krause's wife Elsa. They'll hang too, cruel beyond imagining. Those two guards beat women to death. Elsa, well, if the stories are true, she was the worst of all. I don't like to think about it."

I stared at him, Teddy and I might have been imprisoned by these monsters. "But they're locked up now?"

"Yes, under heavy guard, we've got the ringleaders. One or two who went in the sea might have made it ashore and we're not sure about the men in the farmhouse. Anyway, we've issued radio bulletins, we're printing posters and we've got teams out with dogs and spotlights. With a bit of luck they'll be picked up. Nothing to worry about anyway."

Teddy said, "Sounds like a big operation."

"You're right, son. Not just here in Britain, there's people flying over from the continent."

Gran said, "I hope Mary and Teddy aren't going to be pestered by reporters, that's the last thing they need."

"I'm afraid they will be." The inspector shrugged apologetically. "The Chronicle's got a reporter and cameraman outside right now. I'm told the nationals have got wind of it."

"Well I simply won't have Teddy involved," said his mother. "He's just a schoolboy, for goodness' sake. They're on holiday for Potato Week, the two of them."

"That's true but it's a big story. The Nazi cell and the escape route, they're the ones brought everything out into the open."

"I can see that but I don't want these wretched reporters hanging round the school gates or coming to the house. And I certainly don't want his picture in the papers. I'm sure you feel the same, don't you, Eva?"

"I most certainly do," gran said. "Come knocking on our door, I'll give them a piece of my mind!"

Mrs Cohen thought a moment. "It's Friday today. I suppose when school starts again I could drive over, pick them up in the quad and give Mary a run home."

Sergeant Evans said, "Why not go away for a few days?"

"Where?"

"Up to you."

"What about school?"

"Their teachers could set them some work so they don't fall behind. That's what they did for my Elspeth when she had measles."

"What a great idea!" Teddy said. "Come on, Mum."

"That would be right up your street, wouldn't it?" said Mrs Cohen. "Don't jump the gun, let's see what happens first."

"No worry about today, anyway," said the inspector. "Assuming they get the all-clear, we'll give them a run home in the police car."

Teddy was all for it. "Can we have the blue lights and the siren?"

"No," said Sergeant Evans.

Then there were questions, the young policewoman filling page after page of her black police notebook: how did Teddy and I become friends; why had we gone to the farm in the first place; why had we gone back; how were we captured; how did we escape; how was Teddy's finger smashed; what did we know about dad and Dr Scholtz; how was Major O'Hare killed; how did we acquire the pistols; how were we so expert at using them; who was the other dead man on the boat; what happened at the North Quay; what happened at the South Quay; how was Teddy's shoulder dislocated; how was I rescued; what could I tell them about dad?

At length they were finished. "Well, quite a story," said Chief Inspector Mitchell. "We'll probably have to speak to you again and you'll need to make statements. For the moment we'll get all this typed up. Thank you very much." They prepared to leave. "Now this evening, assuming these two are given the all-clear. I know you've got the car, Mrs Cohen, but I think it'll be best if we pick up you and Mrs Fawcett and bring you both in. Then we can give you all a run home. If the press are hanging around, we're more used to dealing with them."

"Well, if you think so, Chief Inspector, but it's really no trouble to—"

"It will be our pleasure. Shall we say quarter to seven?"

"Well, how very kind of you."

"Not at all." He smiled. "See you then."

Sergeant Evans squeezed Teddy's shoulder. "Good on you, soldier."

"Aren't we lucky in this country," Mrs Cohen said when they had gone. "Such lovely policemen,"

"Indeed we are." Gran took my hand. "We'll build up the fire, have a glass of ginger wine and a slice of fruit cake. That be all right, love?"

I felt the tears building up again. "That will be perfect."

51

Uncle Dan

After the police had gone we sat talking in Teddy's room then the bell rang for the end of visiting time so gran and Mrs Cohen had to leave. Together we trooped down the corridor. A single policeman sat at the entrance to the ward. I recognised him, it was Constable Brownlee who had broken up the fight with Peg and his pals at the beach. Today he was in uniform, his truncheon at his side, whistle on a lanyard, big dome helmet sitting on a chair.

"Hello," he said.

"Hello. What are you doing here?"

"Just keeping an eye on things."

"What do you mean?"

"Making sure nobody gets past, reporters and that."

Gran was surprised. "Do you know him?"

I reminded her of the fight.

"So you're the young man we have to thank for protecting these two from that gang of hooligans?"

"From what I remember, they didn't need much protecting," he said. "The boy there – Terry, is it?"

"Teddy."

"Teddy, then, he went at that big lad like a tiger. And the girl—"

"Mary," I said.

"She got hold of this big stalk of seaweed. Hadn't stopped her, I think she might have been done for murder."

Gran glanced at us, surprised a second time, and smiled at him warmly.

Mrs Cohen, so dark and beautiful, said, "I'm Teddy's mother. What's your name?"

"Constable Brownlee."

"Well, Constable Brownlee, I must say I didn't realise my son was such a young David, but thank you from me too."

He was pleased. "A pair of warriors," he said.

After we'd waved gran and Mrs Cohen away down the stairs, our policeman friend said, "I thought it must be you. In the wars again?"

"You could say." I hesitated, "You said you're here to keep out reporters. Do you think there's any chance the others might come looking for us? You know, the Nazis, the ones that got away?"

"What would be the point? There's only a handful and they're more interested in saving their own skins." He touched his belt: "They'd have issued me with a pistol if there was any danger. I've had the training."

"Had enough of pistols." Teddy showed the dressing on his hand. A pain shot up his wrist and he winced.

"Aye, I heard. Poor Major O'Hare. Bodies all over the place."

"Not our fault, they were shooting at us."

"Them big Lugers, you done well."

"Thanks."

He was nice. Mrs Cohen was right, we were lucky in our policemen.

We returned to Teddy's room. The painkillers were wearing off. "Sore?"

"Not too bad, I'm due another pill before dinner. It's OK." Teddy didn't like a fuss. Surprisingly he said, "Are you going to be all right?" meaning not just the knock on the head but everything, the after-effects.

"I hope so," I said. "See how it goes. How about you?"

"OK so far." Then he put his head on one side and looked at me with those straight, blue, non-Jewish eyes. "We done a lot this summer. Does that mean you're my girlfriend now?"

"I'm thinking about it."

"Yeah?" He leaned forward and kissed me on the lips. It was soft and lovely.

"Still not sure," I said.

So he kissed me again, longer this time.

"Goodness!" It made me a bit breathless. "Where did you learn to do that?"

"No idea, I've never done it before. Seems to come naturally."

"In that case I think it's a good idea."

"What?"

"That you're my boyfriend."

"Good." And he would have kissed me a third time if I had let him.

"There'll be a nurse along in a minute."

"Come on, I might forget." He was very enthusiastic but somehow our heads clashed.

"Aahh! Aahh!"

And that's how we were, Teddy leaning forward and me pushing him away, when there was a knock at the door and the curtain swished aside. But it wasn't a starchy nurse with Teddy's pills, it was a man, my Uncle Dan in thick working trousers and a seaman's jersey. He hadn't shaved for a day or two, his hair was rumpled and he smelled of the sea.

It was obvious what Teddy and I had been doing. Uncle Dan stopped in his tracks: "Mary Pearson, I am shocked! Finding you like this – and in a hospital bedroom! I wonder what your grandmother will have to say?"

I was embarrassed but all the same: "Oh, shut up, Uncle Dan! It was just a little kiss."

"So you say!"

"It was! Teddy's my boyfriend."

"I don't see that's any excuse. Anyway, who knows what a kiss might lead to?"

"Well, you should know."

"What *do* you mean?"

"What do you think I mean? Half the babies in Eastport look like you."

"Half the – ? Wash your mouth out with soap! What a thing to say to your uncle. Is it my fault the women won't leave me alone? I think we should change the subject."

I laughed. "What are you doing here? How did you get in? Visiting time's over."

"Ah, well, you see. Me and Sister McNeil. She's a friend of mine, so to speak. And she said, seeing as you're my niece…"

"Oh, for goodness sake!"

He winked.

Teddy laughed.

"Don't you start," I scolded, "you're going to end up as bad as he is."

"I hope so," he said cheerfully.

"Good on you, boy." Uncle Dan pulled up a chair and lit a small cigar. "Well, look at the pair of you! A couple of heroes, or so I've been told." The room filled with smoke. "Come on, I want to hear all about it. How'd you hear about this farm?"

He had as many questions as Inspector Mitchell but in the end the story was told.

"Poor Frankie!" he said. "He loved you, you know. He loved all of you. Just, well, I suppose he had a bit of a wild streak."

"If that's what you call it. Runs in the family, it seems."

"Now don't start!"

In case you think I am unfeeling, I did miss my dad, of course I did. What had happened was terrible, he had given his life to save me, and many times in the future I was to brood on it. But at that moment, when Teddy and I were in hospital and might both have been dead because he had thrown in his lot with a crowd of Nazi crooks, I was not in a frame of mind to be told how much he had loved us. What he had been doing was an outrage, one more to add to my ever-present memories of my mother, the disgrace of Durham Jail, deserting gran and me in favour of Brenda, going AWOL, letting us think he was dead for four years, burgling the neighbours, and giving gran such a shock that she was taken into hospital.

"Anyway," Uncle Dan went on, "what a story! I love it." Then he was troubled and looked from me to Teddy and back again. "But you're both all right?"

"As you can see."

"I mean, it's not got to you, you know, flashbacks?"

"Not so far."

"Aye, well, see how it goes. You've had a tough time. After we'd been in the lifeboats, I know a lot of the men—"

Teddy made a face as a needle of pain shot up the nerves in his arm.

"I thought they'd be giving you painkillers," Uncle Dan said.

Teddy moved his hand. "I'll live."

"Good for you. Anyway, Big Lenny and Sammy and all the boys are asking after you. That trip you made, they liked having you aboard. Where was it we went again?"

"Norway."

"That's right, Trondheim, we took a boat up the fjords." He felt for his cigars.

"It was terrific," I said.

"You'll have to come again."

"Does that include me?" Teddy said.

"Of course. Mind, I don't want the pair of you carrying on like you do here and shocking the crew."

"Sailors, yeah!" Teddy laughed. "Where are you off to next?"

"South-about for a change, Tangier and the Med. Get a bit of bronzie before the winter sets in."

He flicked his lighter and the room was filling again with fragrant smoke when the door-curtain was thrown back and a middle-aged nurse appeared. In her hand was a stainless steel kidney dish on which stood two pills in a little container, a glass of water, a thermometer and some other things. She froze and fixed Uncle Dan with a stare that would have sent a more timid man running for cover.

"Who are you?"

"Me?" he smiled pleasantly. "Captain Pearson."

"What are you doing here?"

"I looked in to see my niece, make sure she's being properly looked after."

"She is, I assure you. But it's not visiting hours."

"Trixie McNeil said it would be all right."

"Well it's not! And take that filthy thing out of your mouth, this is a hospital."

"Why are you being so unpleasant? A hospital's meant to be a place of calm. These two have been through hell and back."

"I'm aware of that and the boy's just spent three hours in surgery. He needs total…Trixie McNeil?"

"That's right."

"Do you mean Sister McNeil?"

"Yes."

"Who did you say you are?"

"Captain Pearson."

"Is that Danny Pearson?"

"That's me."

"Oh, well, I'm so sorry." She smiled pleasantly and set down the kidney dish. "It was just so unexpected, seeing you sitting there. How are you?"

"Very well, thanks—" he peered at the name pinned to her uniform, "Staff Nurse Wilson."

"Vanessa," she said.

"I'm very well, thanks, Vanessa."

"Sister McNeil has told us all about you. You're quite the hero."

"Not really. Do you want me to, er," he indicated the cigar.

"No, no, that's quite all right. It's nice to have a man in here." Now she wasn't cross she was quite pretty. I noticed she didn't wear a wedding ring.

Uncle Dan gave her his chair and perched on the bed. "And what about yourself, Vanessa? Have you worked here long?"

I looked at Teddy and raised my eyebrows. He was grinning widely.

*

And that – not the scene with Nurse Vanessa but the conversation with Uncle Dan – is how ten days later I found myself in shorts and a sleeveless top which I had bought in a street market that morning, sitting beneath an awning on the boat deck of North Sea Trader. We were moored in the bustling harbour of Tangier and in an hour would be casting off to begin the long run through the Mediterranean to Naples. A warm wind, carrying scents of fruit, spices and drains, blew from the hot streets of Morocco. My Latin and maths were finished for the day and I was reading a thrilling account of knights in the court of King Arthur. In a deckchair nearby gran sat with her knitting, a glass of fresh orange at her side. Teddy leaned over a card table, colouring in a map of the United States.

It wasn't entirely Uncle Dan's doing, of course, but he was the trigger. I suppose it was to be expected that Teddy and I would be affected by the events at Saltfield Mains and what had happened afterwards, although at the start we thought we were not. We were fifteen years old and although the war had provided a constant backdrop to our lives, it had not prepared us for the horrors of that day, the imprisonment, shooting, deaths and finally injury. At first, fully occupied with Teddy's operation and the constant activity of hospital and police interviews we were untroubled, but when we got home and had time to remember, it all came flooding back. When I tried to read, my book fell in my lap and I was back in the pillbox wondering if I would be shot before I was dropped overboard with weights attached to my ankles. I telephoned Teddy, he was the same. We had bad dreams. And so, when doctors recommended a holiday, two weeks away, a complete change of scene, Uncle Dan's offer seemed the perfect answer. Our head teachers agreed and subject teachers provided schemes of study to keep us from falling behind. Gran came with us and Mrs Cohen was flying to Majorca to join us for the last stage of the voyage to Naples.

Reporters gathered outside the house as Inspector Mitchell had said they would, but I didn't want to talk about it and mostly stayed indoors. When I went to the phone box to call Teddy, a little group followed me and I stopped to answer questions while flash bulbs popped. I didn't dress up but I made myself tidy and put on a bit of lipstick which was just as well because the photos appeared in the papers and it was the nearest I would ever get to being a film star. Teddy told me they were standing at his gate too.

A tug toot-tooted. I saw Sammy throw a heaving line from the bow.

Big Lenny emerged from the galley. He was carrying three Chelsea buns hot from the oven, two in his hand for Teddy and me, one on a plate for gran. "Cup of tea on its way, Eva," he told her.

"Thanks, Big Lenny." She smiled up. "You all spoil me."

"That's what grans are for," he said. "What else would we do, throw you to the sharks?"

"Oh, you!" she said and set her knitting on the deck.

It was Big Lenny who had dived into the river, fully-dressed, to hold me safe at the chain. Happily he went for the tea.

Teddy said, "Just going to help cast off, Gran."

"How's the chemistry coming along?" she said.

"Finished, I'm doing the geography now."

"Good for you, love."

Munching our buns, we crossed the foredeck where the derricks had been lowered and the hatches covered ready for sea. Iron steps led to the fo'csle head. Sammy had been joined by Dennis, who was his dad, and a couple of others. At a signal, the mooring ropes were thrown off bollards on the quay and hauled aboard. The tug, Atlas, took the strain, our propeller kicked us forward, and we moved out into the harbour. A tug at the stern helped us to turn and we headed towards the breakwater. It reminded me of home but the quays and towering lighthouse of Eastport, where so much had recently happened, seemed far away, another life.

Buoys slid past to port and starboard. The tugs cast their lines. Teddy and I coiled them down, Teddy managing as well as he could with his bandaged hand. As we left land the wind freshened from the west, blowing through the Straits of Gibraltar.

"See you later." The crew, who had left harbour a thousand times, went below but Teddy and I stayed on the fo'csle head, leaning on the rail and watching as a smart blue-and-white launch came alongside to take off the pilot.

The end of the breakwater passed to port, the bleached

rocks and shanties and buildings of Tangier fell fell away astern. Teddy looked round, his sandy hair lifted by the wind, his eyes very blue in the African sun.

"Great, isn't it."

And so it was, our bow cleaving the bright water, the bow waves curling to right and left. Soon, as we had seen crossing the Bay of Biscay, we would be joined by dolphins. Ahead lay the sparkling Mediterranean, a million waves tipped with foam, and the long blue run to Naples.

1953

I was sitting in my room in college, making a few last changes to an essay I had to read to my tutor that afternoon: 'George Eliot and the Importance of a Name', not a subject I would have chosen. It seemed OK, not ground-breaking but solid enough with a few ideas of my own. I certainly hoped so because even after two years, reading my essays aloud gave me butterflies.

There was a knock at the door. "Happy birthday to you, Happy birthday to you..." It was Julia, who lived on the same staircase and had collected my mail from the Porter's Lodge along with her own.

"Big plans?"

"Not really."

"Teddy not coming down?"

"He can't. I'm going home at the weekend, see him then."

"Ah, well. Give him a kiss from me. Got to fly."

My birthday, April 22, a day early for Shakespeare and St George, a fact that had always irritated me.

I examined the envelopes. Four cards and a stained, intriguing envelope with Australian stamps, addressed to me at home and forwarded by gran. I turned it this way and that: no return address, no indication what on earth it might contain. I opened the cards first, ripping the envelopes. Two from friends, an affectionate card from gran and a funny one from Teddy. I read them carefully, gave the last two a kiss and stood them on a shelf with some others. Then, using the letter opener Teddy had given me at Christmas, I slit the envelope. Four sheets of paper, neatly written in blue-black ink, better than my own handwriting:

Long Ridge Station,
Quilpie,
Queensland.
Sunday, 12 April, 1953

Dear Mary,

I guess you will be surprised to hear from me. A voice from the dead. Sorry I haven't been in touch sooner but, well –

I didn't go down like everyone thought that afternoon back in forty-eight – you know, meet my maker. Very nearly but the wind and the current washed one of the lifebelts close enough to grab and with a bit of kicking I made it to the shore. There was a guy fishing just where I landed but when I told him the cops were after me he agreed to stay shtum. Then it seemed best to just disappear. Not the first time as you know. A bit uncomfortable the first couple of days but I managed to survive and next thing here's the papers saying I'm some kind of a hero. I could live with that and there seemed no point spoiling it all by running to the police so I took off.

There was a place we'd agreed to meet if anything went wrong – the guys at the farmhouse, you know – but I reckoned it wouldn't be safe, not now. Nowhere to go again so I thought I'd head back to Italy, see how young Hamish was getting along – he got that girl into trouble, you remember, when we worked at the fishing. Poor guy, his life wasn't worth living. She'd had the kid and there was another on the way but he was an outsider, been forced to get married, not much better than a slave. Bloody Italian families! He'd had enough so after a few days the two of us pushed off to the far side of France, right over by the Pyrenees, and took jobs on a farm.

It was good, not much money but enough for a drink and we met some sheilas. Then one day Hamish went exploring in an old ruined house, a big country place shelled to rubble, half hidden in bushes, and he spotted a trapdoor. Pulled some planks back and here was a cellar. Two bodies, years dead, and a hundred cases of champagne, the good stuff. We had a few parties then realised there was money to be made. Three months, we were rich, then the bloody police again, the gendarmes. Like ferrets. Traced us back to the gang in Paris, you remember, Les Fils de la Guerre, I told you about it. Farmer spoke up for us but two years in jail. Again! I thought of writing but didn't like to, not right then.

Anyway, I decided I'd had enough, time for a fresh start. So when we got out, we dug up the money we'd hidden from the champagne and bought a couple of tickets to Australia. Hamish always liked the sea and he got a job with a shipping company trading round the Pacific. I wasn't sure what I wanted so I went walkabout for a couple of months and ended up on this cattle station outside Quilpie, south-west Queensland. Pretty big by British standards, over 4,000 square miles. I love it, travelling round the outback on jeep and horseback. Met a terrific sheila, Josie she's called. Her husband bought it in the war. They had no kids but we have, a boy called Mike. I named him after your grandfather. So you've got a brother, half-brother, anyway, although he's only five months old right now.

I guess I'm settled here. High time, too, forty-one last birthday. So I thought maybe I should get in touch. I wrote to Dan a few weeks back, asked him not to tell you, I thought I should do that myself. When he wrote back he gave me the news. I'd had dribs and drabs, you know, nothing I could rely on, but here's you reading English at Girton College, no less. A daughter at Cambridge, the guys here are very impressed. Me too. Your mother would have been enormously proud. Eva too, I'm sure. And he says you're writing a novel. I remember you won that short story prize a few years back, I bet it's going to be a bestseller.

And that young boyfriend of yours with the sandy hair, Teddy, got his finger shot off. Dan tells me he's done well, studying aircraft engineering at Manchester, going to design jets. Rugby player now, is that right, wing three-quarter in one of the teams? I remember there was that business about his mother's house and some factory. Dan says she's getting them back at last, quite right too. And you're getting engaged in the summer. How will that work out, him a Jew and you a Catholic? I became a Catholic to marry your mum. I guess you've got it worked out.

And that's about it. Oh, I forgot, HAPPY BIRTHDAY !!! Twenty years old ! A week Wednesday. I remember the day you were born, yelling the house down. I see it as clearly as that old windmill over there by the creek. I guess you'll not be able to go home with all the studying. Maybe at the weekend. Will Teddy be coming down?

Only a couple of months until your long vacation. If you cared to come over here I can promise you a good time. I know you got a scholarship, clever girl, but even so you might be a bit hard up so I can send the air fare – for Teddy too if he'd like to come. I know Josie would like to meet you.

Best close now and find an envelope. Denny only

comes past twice a week and I'd like you to get it for your birthday.

I know I haven't been the best of dads but that's not to say I don't often think about you.

A big hello to Eva.

Lots of love,

  Dad

I dropped the pages on the desk. My heart was thudding. Five years. Five whole years!
Bastard!

THE END

Acknowledgements

I wish to thank friends and members of my family for their kindness and support as I wrote this book; in particular my niece, Rebecca Gallagher, my daughter-in-law, Jackie Constable, my good friends Yvonne Bowden, Jerry Slater and Moira Conway, Jean Lawrence for correcting my German, and Hughie Gall for his encouragement and work on the cover.

This book is printed on paper from sustainable sources managed under the Forest Stewardship Council (FSC) scheme.

It has been printed in the UK to reduce transportation miles and their impact upon the environment.

For every new title that Troubador publishes, we plant a tree to offset CO_2, partnering with the More Trees scheme.

MORE TREES
LET'S PLANT A BILLION TREES

For more about how Troubador offsets its environmental impact, see www.troubador.co.uk/sustainability-and-community